NEST OF THE MONARCH

A DARK TALENTS NOVEL

NEST OF THE
MONARCH

KAY KENYON

SAGA PRESS

LONDON · SYDNEY · NEW YORK · TORONTO · NEW DELHI

SAGA PRESS

AN IMPRINT OF SIMON & SCHUSTER, INC.

1230 AVENUE OF THE AMERICAS, NEW YORK, NEW YORK 10020

SAGA PRESS and colophon are trademarks of Simon & Schuster, Inc.

For information about special discounts for bulk purchases, please contact Simon & Schuster Special Sales at 1-866-506-1949 or business@simonandschuster.com.

The Simon & Schuster Speakers Bureau can bring authors to your live event. For more information or to book an event, contact the Simon & Schuster Speakers Bureau at 1-866-248-3049 or visit our website at www.simonspeakers.com.

Interior design by Tom Daly.

The text for this book was set in Bell MT Std.

Manufactured in the United States of America

First Edition

10 9 8 7 6 5 4 3 2 1

Library of Congress Cataloging-in-Publication Data

Names: Kenyon, Kay, 1956– author.

Title: Nest of the monarch / Kay Kenyon.

Description: First edition. | London ; New York : Saga Press, [2019] | Series: A dark talents novel ; book 3

Identifiers: LCCN 2018002294 | ISBN 9781534429734 (hardcover) | ISBN 9781534429758 (eBook)

Subjects: LCSH: Women intelligence officers—Fiction. | GSAFD: Spy stories.

Classification: LCC PS3561.E5544 N47 2019 | DDC 813/.54—dc23 LC record available at https://lccn.loc.gov/2018002294

PART I

AN UNCHRISTIAN WAY TO DIE

1

ASCHRIED, A VILLAGE IN THE
BLACK FOREST, GERMANY

FRIDAY, APRIL 24, 1936. A silver light painted the faces in the cinema's audience. The villagers sat expectant and rapt as the MGM theme song boomed out. Watching from the back of the theater, Hannah Linz counted heads in the audience: Forty-six! And only moments before she had despaired of a decent house for the German-dubbed version of *The Great Ziegfeld*, very dear to rent in Deutschmarks and Nazi disapproval.

She wished her father were here to see the number of people daring to entertain themselves on a Saturday evening. But Mendel Linz had gone to Stuttgart after receiving a summons from the Propaganda Ministry to take delivery—at exorbitant rates—of a few *proper* German films. "Otto is here to help you," her father had told her. Otto, who ran the projection booth. "Three days. I will be back on Sunday, *mein rotes Mädchen.*" My red girl, as he called her, for her flame-red hair, like her mother's.

Just before Hannah closed the velvet drapes leading to the lobby, Frau Grober came through with her daughter Klara, Hannah's closest friend. As Hannah shone the light of her flashlight on the nearest empty seats, Klara whispered to her, "I'm sorry we are not on time!"

"No, don't worry," Hannah said. "Otto began the film late." Everyone there tonight had risked Nazi displeasure to attend a film from the West, and for that, Hannah was grateful. But wasn't it absurd to be moved by such small acts of courage?

With her father, Hannah owned and managed the Oasis, a cinema built for the Black Forest Retreat and Spa that had gone out of business during the Great War, and now, under her family's refurbishment, had ambitions to present a summer cinema festival. It would bring filmmakers, actors, tourists, and their money to Aschried.

But the cinema committee had split on the question of whether to include films showing infidelity, cripples, homosexuals, or women working—all contrary to German ideals. The *new* German ideals. At the screenings, the committee took notes of objectionable scenes. In the end, they compromised: a sprinkling of heavy, Nazi-approved films to placate the officials of the Propaganda Ministry's film division. "Give them a little, and they will be happy," Mendel Linz had said.

But they were not happy. She and her father learned this one day last month from a man with a too-long face.

When she had opened the door of her home to the knock, she had found an SS officer standing before her. He wore a black uniform with a red armband, and beneath the peaked hat, a pallid face bearing a dueling scar that bisected his right cheek from eye to chin.

"Yes?"

Lieutenant Becht would speak with Herr Linz. Since she had no choice, she opened the door and led him into the parlor, feeling his eyes on the back of her neck, as though she had left the door open and a bear had padded in.

Her father, who had been reading the newspaper, stood at the library door holding that day's edition of the *Aufbau*. Removing his spectacles, he took in the unlikely view of an SS officer in their sitting room.

Lieutenant Becht sat on the divan, her father in the best armchair. A silence fell upon them. The curtains were closed against the bright afternoon, leaving the parlor in murk.

Hannah faced them, standing behind a chair, gripping the carved back. "Tea, Papa?"

Becht flicked a hand to dismiss the offer, as though it were his house. The parlor, overwarm, imposed an odd, forbidding drowsiness. As Hannah looked at their visitor, she tried to grasp what sort of man this was. The black uniform and red armband proclaimed his SS status, but this officer had a strange appearance: his pale skin and the pronounced scar, a prominent chin, long and rounded, as well as a very high forehead, revealed when he took off his hat and placed it on the divan.

"You are a widower, Herr Linz? Your wife died during the war?"

"Influenza."

Becht nodded. "And you have lived in Aschried how long?"

"Five years." Her father lifted his gaze to Hannah, then pulled back, as though hoping Becht would not notice her.

"Previously you were employed at a university, were you not?" The officer crossed his legs, getting comfortable.

"Cologne. But I am retired from the position now."

"I think retirement was not your choice, however. It was a profession not suitable for a Jew."

"Some deemed that so."

"A disappointment for you, naturally."

"I do not complain, Lieutenant."

"No? But perhaps you thought that, so far from Cologne, you could protest with impunity. Using the cinema."

"The Oasis, you mean?"

"Certainly. It is the only movie house in town. Therefore it has a certain cultural significance, you see. We have become aware of matters regarding it."

Hannah was preoccupied with the crocheted antimacassar draped along the back of the divan. She must try to pay attention. What had the SS officer said? Something about the cinema. A lethargy had fallen upon her, a feeling that she at first mistook for sleepiness. But how could she feel drowsy with an officer of the SS sitting in their living room?

Her father seemed to be receding into his chair. He was not a large man, and he now became smaller, quieter. Hannah felt a great need to throw open the drapes, open a window.

Becht went on. "Matters such as the showing of degenerate films, decadent movies from the West. Inappropriate for German citizens who should be viewing our own films, celebrating patriotism and the fatherland." He paused, inviting comment, but one could not disagree with the SS, nor really could they bring themselves to agree.

"And then we have the name, the Oasis. And the mural in the foyer, where you have palm trees and pyramids. These are not German scenes." He shook his head. "Camels."

This was too much for her father, who had grown unnaturally still but now seemed to jerk awake. "What would you have us do? The Oasis has been here for thirty years."

Becht drew out a paper from his pocket and unfolded it. "Here is a list of approved films. You will want to conform to higher cultural standards."

Her father sank back into his chair to read the document. At last he looked up. "I do not know these filmmakers. Who are they?"

Becht leaned forward. "You mistake me, Herr Linz. Your approval is not required. Your ownership of the theater is not recognized."

"Not recognized?" He frowned, and in the long pause that followed he seemed to have forgotten what he was saying. "I have papers," he finally whispered.

"I will take those papers. For review, in Stuttgart." Becht made a sweeping motion with his hand. "Get them now. I will wait."

It took some time for her father to absorb this order. At last he stood, looking stooped and far older than his fifty-five years. He shuffled from the room.

Becht stood, turning to Hannah. He was quite thin, his tailored uniform emphasizing a narrow waist. He regarded her with an expressionless stare. *What did he see?* she wondered. Not a person, not even an enemy, but someone utterly dispensable.

"Living with your father, Fräulein Linz, you have no need of a job, is that not correct?"

She struggled to pay attention. He had asked her a question—what was it?—about employment. It was imperative to remain alert, but the whole atmosphere of the room felt heavy with confusion. She struggled to gather her wits. "He . . . he lost his pension," she managed to say. "My father could not take his pension. Under your rules."

He smiled, causing the long scar on his cheek to bend. "You are bitter. Your father will conform, but you—"

"I manage a cinema . . . I do not go to university. I do not live near my friends in Cologne. I have no prospects." Her hands, slick with sweat, curled around the chair's wooden scrollwork. On his collar the curious insignia of a bird with a long, curved neck, and wings swept back like a cloak. It was a vulture.

"So many curtailments," he said. "But even here"—Becht gestured to embrace the house, the village—"even here, we take notice how things are done. Even in the Black Forest! You see, there is no place where you can poison us, where we will not . . . *notice.*"

She shrank back from this attack, a wave of heat rolling over her skin. Time slowed, the room thickened. What should she say?

Her father returned with the bill of sale. They learned that he was to consider himself a temporary manager, not owner.

Did Herr Linz understand? Lieutenant Becht watched her father, a pleasant expression on his face, a demeanor that could quickly change, Hannah knew. Her father nodded, mumbling his understanding, his agreement.

To Hannah's relief, Becht seemed content and gave her a small, flat smile as she accompanied him to the door. The smile was mocking, and she did not return it.

Waiting by the Mercedes, the lieutenant's driver opened the door for him, and he departed, the tires spitting gravel as the car sped off.

In the cool night air, Hannah's lethargy evaporated. Closing the door, she turned to her father. "Papa! We own the cinema. Why did you give him the papers?"

"He asked for them." The words soft, self-explanatory: *Because he asked for them.* He ran his hand through his hair, sighing as if waking from a nap. "I could say nothing."

"But to give them away!"

Looking at the door where Lieutenant Becht had been standing, her father said, "He has the Talent. *Mesmerizing.*"

Ah, now she put it together: how when Becht entered, a fog of unreality had descended on them.

Her father went on. "It was the strongest demonstration I have ever witnessed." Yes, he would know, Talent research having been his specialty at Cologne. "But why does he waste this Talent on the likes of us?" Hannah asked. "He could have taken the papers in any case."

"Because," her father said, "he wanted to enjoy our fear."

Perhaps it was enough for Becht and his superiors in Stuttgart that he had taken the cinema. They would still have a small stipend to live on. Aschried was very far to come just to terrorize two Jews.

That had been a month ago. The disturbing memory lingered, casting its shadow over the happiness of a good reception for *The Great Ziegfeld.* The film was not on the list. They had ordered two propaganda films to satisfy the ministry, but *Ziegfeld* had already been rented.

In the projection booth, Otto made a seamless transition to the second reel. Hannah watched in the back of the house near the drapes screening off the lobby. The whirring of the projector, a faint susurration from the booth. On the screen, William Powell was charming Myrna Loy into joining him, promising her the publicity she had always dreamed of. So handsome, William Powell, the ill-fated promoter, young and self-assured—

The film snapped. A groan went up from the audience. Fortunately Otto was a master at splicing celluloid and would soon have it up and running.

Someone came through the drapes. It was Frau Sievers, who

tried to give Hannah her ticket money. Hannah waved it away, since she had missed much of the film, but Frau Sievers insisted on paying. Finally Hannah accepted a few Deutschmarks and helped her to find a seat in the crowded middle, where Frau Sievers preferred to sit.

A loud thud came from the booth, then a crash. Something had fallen. Hannah slipped from the auditorium. If Otto had dropped the second canister, it would mean a tangle of film and an awkward delay. As she pushed through the drapes into the lobby, she noted a man just leaving through the main door. A black leather coat. A bloodless, long face.

He didn't see her as he strode away. But she recognized him. Becht.

She rushed up the stairs. The projection booth door lay ajar as it should not be during the program. She could hear the film up and running again and whirring on the reel.

Entering the booth, she found Otto on his hands and knees struggling to get up.

Screams erupted from the audience. Leaving Otto sitting upright, she rushed to the aperture to look into the house.

There, on the screen, a scene that was not from the programmed film. A birch woods, with fog drifting, snow remaining in patches on the ground like scabs. And there, some fifteen meters away, a man—what was this?—a man tied against a tree. The movie camera zoomed in closer.

Hannah gasped. It was her father who was bound against the trunk, ropes around his chest and legs. No, no . . . it could not be. But yes, he was roped to a tree, his shirt stripped from him. And oh, the blood gushing from his torn neck . . . It could not be, it could not. "Papa!" came her strangled cry.

A close-up of the knife as a figure walked into the frame. The knife stained red. Held in the hand of the man with the too-long face, the man who had just left the cinema.

Was it her own screams or was it the people in the theater? She could not tell. People jumped from their seats to flee, while others sat rooted in place. She forced herself to watch the screen, willing it to be gone, to be a dream, a nightmare, but no. There was the birch woods, the tree, her father. So much blood, still pumping, the life leaving him. Still the film ran, the camera coming ever closer to his stricken face, until his head dropped down to his chest.

The film flickered off, the end of the spool slapping against the reel again and again.

She staggered from the booth into the corridor outside, her mind black, her breaths harsh and loud. Down the darkened stairway to the foyer. The crowd pushed past, slamming against her in their rush to the exits. She fell to her knees. A moment of stunned immobility overtook her as she stared at the carpet, sandy brown, studded with palm trees and popcorn.

Klara rushed up to her, kneeling at her side. Men were leading Otto down the stairs. He staggered over to Hannah and she held him as he wept. "What is happening," he cried. "What is happening!"

But she knew what was happening. The National Socialists had taken notice of Aschried and its cinema.

She held Otto, comforting him. Thank God she could think of someone else at this moment, because if she thought of her father . . .

He had left for Stuttgart, but it was unlikely that he had been called by the Ministry. She felt certain that he had been lured away and stopped along the road. Her thoughts became stone, as though the world had solidified, never to change after this moment.

Klara helped her outside, away from the theater lights, into the darkness. People were shouting, some clumped into groups, consoling each other. In the cold April night, Hannah's tears turned icy on her face. Then Hannah and Klara were walking along the pavement toward home. Her friend would stay with her. She must have tea, Klara said.

But when they got to her house, she saw the windows shattered, and inside, the furniture upended and ripped.

Klara was aghast, but Hannah looked on the chaos without reacting. How could she care about upholstery and china when her father had died, died alone in the deep woods, tied to a tree?

The SS had come for Hannah and her father and life could never be the same. She must leave here. Tonight. Glass crunched under her feet as she climbed the stairs to her room.

Packing a small suitcase, she dressed in trousers and a sweater and her father's leather jacket with ivory buttons. He had been a small man, and the jacket fit her.

An hour later she left Aschried. Some people had not been afraid to help her. She drove Klara's father's truck, to be picked up tomorrow at the railhead. Driving to the station, she held to one thought: that she would not be solicitous, passive, or silent again. Klara had given her the names of friends in Leipzig. At the station window she bought her ticket, but it was not for Leipzig. That city was not the source of this horror.

It was Berlin. Where they would *notice* Hannah Linz.

SIX MONTHS LATER . . .

WEDNESDAY, OCTOBER 28, 1936. Seated beside Alex Reed on the bench at the railway platform, Kim Tavistock stole a close look at her husband, a man she had only known for eleven days. She had to admit that he was handsome, fair-haired and fit, dapper in his travel coat and tie, hair slicked back, emphasizing his fine profile. He exhaled a long stream of cigarette smoke as he looked down the tracks for the train to Dresden.

Turning his blue-eyed, mischievous gaze on her, he said, "Oh, do sit closer, Elaine," using her cover name.

He pulled her toward him, in a casual, husbandly way. She couldn't protest. They were supposed to be on their honeymoon. Actually, she rather liked pretending to be in love with him. Her last love affair—good Lord, had been back in the States. That long ago.

"Are you going to take the baths while I'm gone?" he asked.

Bad Schandau was known for its homeopathic waters.

"I don't swim."

"*Baths*, darling. No swim cap needed."

"Yes, but they're enormous. How do you bathe with thirty other people?"

"Well, it could have been *two* people if you weren't such a prude."

She smirked. "We were too occupied in the bridal suite to bathe." They had taken to trading suggestive comments. It helped to make them believable as a couple, in case the Gestapo was watching.

Alex dropped his cigarette and ground it out with his shoe. "Tell me, did I enjoy myself?"

"I have no idea. But I enjoyed myself immensely."

He laughed, cinching her closer.

Most of what she knew of the husband the head office had chosen for her came from the dossier she had read and then burned in her fireplace. Alexander Reed was thirty-six, well-heeled, public school, the usual pedigree for the Foreign Service. His appointment as second secretary for trade in Berlin was viewed as a nice promotion after his posting in Lisbon. His father, a provost at Eton; his mother, from the right tribe, active in charities in South Cambridgeshire.

She twisted the heavy ring on her left hand. It was, she knew, a real diamond. Everything else was complete fabrication.

Alex had studied her dossier as well. He understood that his wife was undercover as Elaine Reed, the former Elaine Fraser. But he didn't know much more than that she was on special assignment from the Foreign Office, which he might assume, but not know for certain, meant the Secret Intelligence Service. Doubtless he was curious about her mission, but he didn't need to know.

In case anyone should pry, key details of Elaine Fraser's life were backed up with false documentation in the United States and in Great Britain, most recently at the Chelsea Registry Office, which would document the recent marriage. Alex's parents had been quietly brought into the picture, but since they were the right sort of family, they could hold a secret. They stoically agreed to bear the disappointment of the marriage annulment when it came.

Kim's marriage to a diplomat was how she could credibly be in residence in Berlin, where she could mingle with highly placed Nazi officials. But even as Alex's wife, she would not have diplomatic immunity. If she were caught in possession of product relating to military intelligence, the host country would be free to make a terrific fuss, an outcome that would strain relations with the German government, and cause consternation in the Foreign Office, where they preferred the roles of diplomacy and espionage to be clear and separate. On the surface, anyway.

The train to Dresden approached, huffing and clanking. "I shan't be gone long, just a day," Alex said, picking up his suitcase. "Kiss me, darling." He pulled her close, noticing her stiffness, and whispered, "Oh, let yourself go."

She put a hand up to his chest. "The English don't in public, do they?"

Pressing his hand into the small of her back, he lifted her toward his lips and held the kiss for rather too long.

"I shall miss you desperately!" he said, loud enough to make a few people on the platform smile. And with that, he boarded the train, waving cheerfully and a bit too long. He would make a terrible stage actor.

This was not the way Kim had imagined herself being married. At thirty-three, never engaged, she sometimes dreamed of a conventional life. There might be a time for that someday, when the world righted itself. How strange it was that most people seemed to believe that the world was right enough at present, even though Germany had begun a massive military buildup and had retaken the Rhineland, a clear threat to Europe.

Yet people did nothing. They must not provoke the Germans, a desperate people with a fanatical leader. Everyone had lost someone in the Great War. In a grief that had not faded, she and her father had lost a brother and a son: Robert. People were afraid of another cataclysm, and who could blame them? But fear was not the only reaction to loss. There was also resolve. With SIS, she and her father, Julian, had made a certain choice. It might not change the world. But it wasn't *nothing*.

Since the jitney had left for the spa, Kim decided to go to the village on foot. Her plan was to take lunch somewhere and keep her tourist cover by shopping for gifts. Walking to *der Marktplatz*, she silently named things in German, practicing this very difficult language. Above the red mansard roofs of the town hall and hotels rose the distinctive tower of St. John's Church, its dark turret purple in the October light. On the pavement outside, two policemen narrowed their eyes, scrutinizing her as she passed. It conveyed the distinct impression of suspicion and unhelpfulness, something she had noticed already in Bad Schandau. It was odd that a spa village, so far from Berlin where one heard of increased police surveillance, would not be more welcoming.

There were nights when the thought of being undercover in the heart of Nazi Germany kept sleep at bay. But SIS had intelligence reports on a special German weapon, and His Majesty's Government was keen to know what it was. A new development in rocketry could put London at risk, even if it was six hundred miles from Germany. And then there was the much darker prospect of atomic weapon development. It was years away, unless a highly rated *hypercognition* Talent achieved a breakthrough. England would love to have such a person. Pray God the Nazis did not have one.

So far not even the British mole in the German military intelligence, the *Abwehr*, had uncovered references to a new weapon. Of course Kim would not be the only *spill* artist, *mesmerizer*, or *hyperempathy* Talent trying to penetrate the operation.

For lunch, she decided to join the crowd at a charming beer garden with picnic tables outside overlooking the Elbe River. The tables were nearly full, but as Kim stood, lunch tray in hand, surveying the tables, two women waved her over.

"Please join us," the one in a shawl said in German, smiling and moving over to make room. Kim sat down, thanking them in halting German and nodding at the woman across from her, heavyset, with her blond hair rolled into a helmetlike do.

As Kim unwrapped her bratwurst sandwich, the one in the shawl said in English, "So, I make a guess: American?"

"Ellie!" the blond woman said. "Her German is not so bad."

"No, Sophie, I mean nothing," the other said, tucking into her pastry. They were speaking English now, as a courtesy.

"Well, that was a good guess," Kim said to Ellie. "I was raised in America, but I have been in England the past few years. German is a big challenge to learn!"

"Oh, *ja*, we have many consonants!" Ellie remarked. "But you can catch on."

The river caught the sun as a ferry cut across the water, leaving a swath of molten gold. All was bright and normal, with friendly locals and an excellent sandwich.

"You know," Sophie said, digging for something in her tote,

"it is so much easier to read than to speak." Handing her a folded newspaper, she said, "Here. For practice."

Kim nodded her thanks. It was a local broadsheet. A small heading mentioned local murders. She frowned at the phrases that spoke of violent deaths.

Ellie leaned in, noting the article. "Terrible. They say the two were . . . ripped, do you say? And blaming that it was a bear!" She snorted.

Kim looked askance at her food. Oblivious to the disturbing talk over luncheon, Ellie went on, "To ask me, Jews murdered them. They use the blood in their religious rites, you know."

Kim was chagrined to hear this woman express such an opinion in modern times. Blood libel, the bizarre accusation made against Jews, that they slaughtered Christians for unholy rituals.

"*Nein,*" Sophie said, wiping pie crumbs from her mouth. "They were Jews that were murdered, so no Jew would do it."

"But the blood nearly drained away from them . . . ," Ellie argued.

A mother who shared their table and had been tending to her children's meal frowned at them.

Sophie bent forward over the table, lowering her voice. "My cousin in Wiesbaden, he said the same thing happened there, a Jewish shoemaker. The throat cut open, the blood drained." She nodded with dark solemnity. "It was a *Teufel.*" A word Kim didn't know. "So it does no good to bury them." She flicked a gaze at Kim. "They will come back."

"It says that in the paper?" Kim asked.

Sophie smirked. *"Nein, nein.* It is the bear, you know."

Kim folded the sandwich back in its paper.

"Now look, Sophie!" Ellie said. "You have disturbed our guest."

Kim shook her head. "Oh, not at all. I will save this for later, but I must be going. How kind of you to share your table."

"You may keep the paper!" Sophie said, turning back to her pie.

"Our last night in Bad Schandau." In the spa restaurant, Alex held his champagne flute up.

Kim drank the toast. Tomorrow, Berlin.

"Tell you what, let's celebrate!" He gestured for the waiter. "Another." The waiter nodded, pouring the last of the bottle of Veuve Clicquot.

"Dresden went well, then?" Kim asked. His meeting had been something to do with war bond repayments on which the Nazi Party had been threatening to default.

"It did, rather. I have Herr Eckert's promise to bring a new repayment schedule to Göring. Not full repayment, but I dare say a long way north of half."

The new bottle arrived. Kim covered her glass with her hand and the waiter put it on ice.

"Oh, come now," Alex said as the waiter retreated. "Our last night. Tomorrow is soon enough for business. Whatever your business is." He winked at her, his mood so buoyant, she let him pour. He was being a good sport about not prying into her mission, probably assuming it was garden-variety spying. She had to admit that Alex was a rather good companion, and champagne with a handsome man was never a complete mistake.

"There was an odd thing in the village yesterday," she said, twirling the champagne in its flute. "Some women were talking about local murders."

"People are being murdered in Bad Schandau?" He sat back, waiting to be entertained.

"Yes, and the blood drained from them. It's not just here

but in Wiesbaden, and they can't be buried if a fiend has taken them." *Teufel.* Fiend, the word she had looked up in her German-English dictionary.

He widened his eyes in mock alarm. "Well, we shall certainly double-lock our doors tonight." He tucked into his portion of rack of lamb. "So who was murdered by this fiend?"

"Two, maybe three Jews, at the very least. Don't you think it's strange they're talking of blood being drained from bodies?"

"A village like this is full of superstitions. It'll be different in Berlin."

"They were talking about rising from the dead."

He topped off her glass. "How Bram Stoker of them! Did they actually say 'rising from the dead'?"

"No. They said you can't bury them because they come back."

"I dare say that explains why Germans are never the life of the party." He leaned in, lowering his voice. "Perhaps some of them are dead."

She smiled in appreciation.

After dinner he ordered dessert for her and port for himself. Somehow he knew that she liked apple torte. So *married* of him. It was a good touch and she went along.

But she did not go along with the idea that she should leave the door to the adjoining suites ajar that night.

He stood in the doorway, sleeves rolled up to show very nice forearms, his tie cast aside. "I didn't mean it, anyway," he said when she demurred.

Despite her refusal, she found herself disappointed. At any one moment she couldn't quite tell if his flirting was just an act.

Unless he *spilled* to her. Which was the surest way to end a relationship, when someone thought they had just had words pried out of them. The very reason she had never gotten past brief courtships with men. Not that she and Alex were having a courtship.

He smiled. "Goodnight, Kim."

"Goodnight."

"Fancy a swag of garlic for over the bed?"

She laughed and softly closed the door.

TIERGARTENSTRASSE 44, BERLIN

THURSDAY, OCTOBER 29. Kim slammed shut another drawer. Where would a maid have put her LNER train time-table? Her bedroom was stuffed with dark mahogany dressers, chests, and armoires, all with their drawers and compartments. When she and Alex had arrived that morning, her trunks had already been unpacked, their contents put away by Bibi. The maid had had plenty of time, since the main luggage had arrived five days ago, straight from the steamer at Hamburg.

Now, having been driven from the S-Bahn station down the Wilhelmstrasse past the Nazi government buildings, Kim was in need of her LNER timetable to calm her nerves.

Good God, it had only been German bunting, but the banners were everywhere: the red background, the white circle with the broken black cross, or *Hakenkreuz*, which some called the swastika. It was a powerful symbol, meant to intimidate. Effective too.

She opened the armoire where her clothes hung, checking the high shelf. No timetable. Just as she was about to close it, she saw that one of her dresses had fallen off the hanger. When she picked it up, she noticed that it wasn't hers, but rather a lovely satin gown with seed pearls on the bodice.

Bibi ducked into the room. "Is anything needed, madam?"

Kim smiled at Bibi. She guessed her to be straddling fifty. Her hair, black and curly, framed a pleasantly lined face.

"Come in, Bibi." When the maid stepped in, she went on, "This cocktail dress isn't mine. It must have belonged to the previous tenant."

"Oh," Bibi said. "Those people left things. I will take it, madam, and dispose of it."

"It's such a fine gown. Can you return it?"

A worried look crossed Bibi's face. "It won't be necessary, madam. They were . . . Well, they have left Berlin."

Kim let her take the dress. "Bibi, I would prefer that you not call me madam. Mrs. Reed or ma'am will do. Second, I would like to communicate in German, so I can practice, if you wouldn't mind helping me a bit."

"But Mr. Reed made clear that he wished me to speak English."

"Yes, and do so around Mr. Reed, but between the two of us, German, please. If you wouldn't mind correcting me when I get it wrong?"

"Well." Bibi considered this. "I could try."

"Thank you. I speak poorly, so just make suggestions on the most important lapses, all right?"

"Yes, madam."

Kim let that go. It might take awhile. "And now, I have a question," she said in German. "Where is the little orange book?

I put it with my . . . um, underclothes in the suitcase." She didn't have the word for "trunk," so she held wide her arms to show what she meant.

Bibi nodded. She crossed over to one of the thousand drawers and produced the London and North Eastern Railway booklet. "Here it is," she said slowly in German, as though speaking to a child.

When Bibi left, Kim climbed onto the bed and propped herself up with pillows. She had greeted the three servants, the tall and commanding cook, Mrs. Grunewald, spry Bibi and her formal, quiet husband Albert, who in his midsixties handled duties as Alex's valet and the mover, on occasion, of heavy Weimar Republic mahogany from room to room. Bibi served at table and did light housekeeping; then there was someone named Maria who was to come twice a week for heavier cleaning. Everyone was carefully vetted, with nothing recorded against them, so she had been told.

Tiergartenstrasse 44 was a short walk from the Reichstag and directly across from the Tiergarten, the enormous park at the heart of Berlin. The three-story stone mansion with its decorative wrought-iron fence and a splendid back garden rented at a very reasonable price. Oddly it came furnished not only with the necessary furniture, but personal items such as fine paintings, many old books, brocade runners, and fine porcelain figurines. Alex had been excited to show it to her. "Do you love it, darling?" he had said this morning.

"Well, I haven't quite *seen* it yet." They had stood in the vestibule, its walls sheathed in green silk. He gestured her into the drawing room—enameled black mantel, red damask walls, a gleaming piano—and from there into the rather more cozy library, followed by the dining room to seat eighteen, and the lovely *wintergarten* with a curved wall of glass in front of which sat enormous potted plants obscuring the outdoors. It was all quite Victorian, Kim thought, and could be very much improved by a dog. A well-behaved border collie, say, or perhaps a precocious terrier, to humanize the place.

Upstairs were the imposing master bedrooms, adjoining, and a long hall leading to other bedrooms where doors had been shut to conserve heat. Servant quarters on the third floor accommodated Bibi and Albert.

She found herself wishing Alex had not had to present himself at the consular offices right away; he did seem to brighten up any place where he was. Feeling a bit homesick, she sat on the bed and opened the LNER timetable, allowing the names of the stops—King's Cross Station, Newcastle, Doncaster, Leeds, York—to soothe her.

Tomorrow she would meet her SIS contact, Duncan. With the Berlin station undercover, reporting to her handler would entail meticulous security practices. There would be a dead drop, signals to request meetings, and the need for her to rent a secure flat the location of which no one was to know. The flat would be her bolt-hole in case of pursuit. It brought to mind a vision of her rushing into a dirty hallway of some cheap walk-up with the Gestapo pounding after her, but that was surely a bit over-dramatic. She would start off attending diplomatic functions, meet and mix. Listen for a *spill*.

She raised the timetable again, then let it drift back to her lap. By her Helbros watch, the one her mother had given her before she'd left the States, it was 2:43 PM. A couple hours until Alex got home. She would have time for a bath and an hour of German vocabulary.

But she was too excited to study. The ten-minute ride from

the S-Bahn station to the house had left a deep impression.

When she and Alex had debarked from the train that morning, they had found themselves in the cathedral-like Lehrter Bahnhof Station with its barrel-vaulted ceiling. The embassy had provided a car and driver, and in the limousine, they were whisked onto the Wilhelmstrasse. Soon they passed the immense Reichstagsgebäude, its plaza corners anchored by four soaring columns capped with eagle insignia.

The streets, loud and boulevarded, were crowded with streetcars, motorcars, and double-decker omnibuses packed with people. They crossed the Pariser Platz with the monumental Brandenburg Gate hung with red, white, and black vertical banners, effectively conveying Teutonic grandeur. Alex had pointed out the British embassy, occupying the Palais Strousberg, with its three-stories-high portico and flanking columns. She had noted the British flag, and some distance away, the French on its own embassy.

This was the Germany of the newsreels, the Berlin of Nazi propaganda. And it had been the home ground of Erich von Ritter, a most particular spy whom she had hunted, evaded, and eventually brought down during the Prestwich affair. Von Ritter, appearing at first to be merely a friend of a fascist-leaning Georgi Aberdare, had been *Sicherheitsdienst*, SD, the intelligence arm of the SS. As he lay dying in the ruins of Rievaulx Abbey, von Ritter—she had called him Erich at the last, hadn't she?—knew that the invasion plan had failed. Then, from behind the ancient stone walls, the fateful report of the gun. Rather than be captured, he had killed himself.

After that, and to her delight, the exclusive club of the Secret Intelligence Service had decided to take her in. Kim had not only stymied the invasion plot, she had done so without any assistance whatsoever from His Majesty's Government.

And now here she was.

A knock on the door. Bibi came in with a small stack of cards on a silver salver. No one, Kim had been told, went anywhere without leaving a calling card. Hers read *Mrs. Elaine Reed, Tier-gartenstrasse 44, Berlin*, in flowing script with a gold edge. If one wished to appear more friendly to someone, one would remove a pen from one's bag and cross out the last name.

"Do you approve, ma'am?" Bibi said in German.

"*Ja, danke, Bibi.*" How efficient they were here. In less than a week the entire house had been organized, staffed, calling cards made, and her first social engagements calendared, all without her even being here.

When Bibi left, Kim opened the door, allowing the sounds of the household to float up. She really must study her German for an hour or so, an undertaking very suited to her. Already memorized: 472 words. She added eight words a day—*Mein Gott*, some of them frightfully long—and recorded them in a small notebook that she kept in her handbag. She did so like orderly lists. And if she was to have future postings, languages would be essential. She very much hoped that there *would* be future missions. Sometimes her thoughts drifted to Robert—often in uniform, always spotless—and he would nod to her. Not in admiration, nothing like that, but she imagined a sober approval.

She went to the window and looked down on the sunny back garden. Red-orange leaves studded the manicured lawn, and in the herbaceous beds a few mounds of purple mums still lingered.

Albert, his tonsured white head bent over his task, was crouched among them, dead heading, placing the spent flowers in a wicker basket.

THE STADTSCHLOSSE, BERLIN

SUNDAY, NOVEMBER 1. In the grand vestibule of the Berliner Stadtschlosse the servant carried an enormous silver tray with petit fours ringing a large-domed server. It was a heavy load that the girl must pretend to carry with ease, if she was to look like a waitress at the opening of the anti-Soviet, anti-Semitic art exhibition. Through the open doors of the palace entrance she could see a squad of black uniforms lined up in the plaza awaiting the motorcade. Soon the vestibule would be swarming with SS functionaries, including Reich minister of propaganda, Joseph Goebbels.

She approached the rounded starting step of the staircase behind which she would place the tray. At that moment a Nazi guard turned from his survey of the plaza and spied her. He raised an abrupt hand.

His boots clicked like breaking glass against the floor as he approached. Taking in her black server uniform with starched white apron, he barked, "Why are you here?"

"The reception. . . ," she began, but he stopped her.

Reaching over the tray—her heart almost stopping—he snatched her identity card hanging by a lanyard around her neck. The card was among the Oberman Group's best forgeries. The guard released the card and looked her over for any signs of non-Aryan stupidity.

Her hands sweated so badly she feared she might drop the tray. "Please, I'm sorry, but the reception—"

"Will be in the garden, you idiot!" Annoyed, but eyeing the sweets on the tray.

At least a minute gone. "Have one, why don't you?" she said.

She saw that outside, the doors of a Mercedes were open and peaked hats were ducking out, receiving salutes. She longed for it to be Goebbels, and that he would come straight into the vestibule. So even if the device went off with her still holding the tray, at least that cockroach would be gone. The timing of the detonation had been a source of argument between her and Franz. Three minutes, they had finally decided. If only it could have been four!

The guard looked up at the sharp *Heil Hitler*s coming from outside. Distracted, he waved her off.

With sweat now gripping her neck with a cold fist, she scuttled away. The guard turned to Goebbels' imminent arrival in the hall. Hannah quickly placed the tray out of sight on the floor behind the curve of the stair and walked purposefully away.

Reaching the back hallway, she turned in the direction opposite from the kitchen. Her strides lengthened. Another person walked toward her, then entered a side room. She broke into a run. It was a long way to the square of light that marked the door into the interior courtyard. She charged down the deserted corridor as though in a dream, the exit impossibly far away.

When the explosion came, it was a thunderous bellow accompanied by a tremor in the floor. At her side, a mirror fell from its perch, shattering, hurtling silver shards into her arm. She felt nothing but thornlike pricks and cold air as she ran. A drift of plaster dust escaped like smoke from a carved door. Then all was quiet. Her ears felt plugged with wool. Bursting into the courtyard, she found herself in unearthly quiet. A gardener stood, shears in hand, looking at the door from which she had just come. She whipped off her apron and covered her bloody arm before he could take note of her injuries.

As she walked past him, she nodded. If he thought it odd that she had wrapped an apron over her arm, he gave no indication. The focus of his curiosity appeared to be the muffled noise that had come from the palace interior.

Once on the other side of the courtyard, she slipped into the south wing and from there through stately rooms with pictures the size of houses. She ditched the bloodied apron and, to stanch her cuts, took up a brocaded napkin that lay on a table. At last she spied the exit and walked nonchalantly onto the great plaza.

The Berliner Stadtschlosse was on an island in the Spree, a location once selected by a king to build a keep.

As she emerged outside, she heard shouts and screams from the main entrance far behind her. Looking over her shoulder, she saw smoke billowing from the Stadtschlosse and soldiers spreading out to form a cordon. They were still some two hundred meters away. She meandered toward the bridge.

Franz was waiting there. He held out a coat for her, but noting her injury, he placed it over her shoulders, leading her away. From his pocket Franz took out a scarf and helped her tie it around her head. The woman with the red hair was known to the SS.

Looking straight ahead as they walked, he snarled, "Are you hurt, then?" They had argued about her placing the bomb. It could have been anyone in the Oberman Group, but Hannah had insisted she be the one.

"I am all right. Some glass. Nothing." People on the bridge had stopped to stare at the chaotic scene in front of the palace. She and Franz walked unhurriedly across the bridge as a breeze carried the smell of burning chalk and stone.

"Did we get him?" Hannah whispered.

"No. He stopped outside to talk." With a firm grip on her good arm, he pulled her along faster. "You risked your life for nothing."

Their car was waiting for them on the Unter den Linden.

When they ducked into the back seat, Micha pulled the car into traffic, quickly finding anonymity in the lunchtime press of trams and motorcars.

Franz pulled down the coat to look at her arm. Blood ran in rivulets from several slivers of mirror embedded in her skin. "You'll live." Wry. She was wounded, had accomplished nothing. No doubt he was thinking that next time perhaps she would listen to reason.

Franz lit a cigarette and blew a stream of smoke in irritation. "You are too valuable for this kind of work. You need to get out."

"Out?" Her heart stopped thumping loudly in her chest, and she began to shiver. He replaced the coat around her shoulders.

She went on. "How do I get papers to leave? They're all looking for the red-haired Jewess."

"If you had listened to me from the start. If you didn't love bombs so much."

She sliced a look at him. "You think I do?"

Micha made a half turn toward them. "Shut up, can't you? She's bleeding."

Pulling the coat more firmly around herself, Hannah murmured, "And it wasn't for nothing. Once again, they *notice* us."

Franz snorted. But he patted her knee. They were both hunted Jews. They had to stick together.

THE TIERGARTEN, BERLIN

TUESDAY, NOVEMBER 3. Kim strolled through the Tiergarten. Berlin's enormous central park was a paradise of mature sentinel trees, statuary, and meandering pavements. At 11:30 AM the park was full of people, including a man on horseback on one of the trails.

Across the lawns the morning sun threw long shadows of the almost-bare trees, creating a scene of romantic charm. Through the lacework of tree branches, Kim could just make out the Reichstag's dome, but other than that, she might have been in Paris or London. Benches along the path were meeting places for lovers, housewives, and solitary old men reading newspapers.

Passing a knoll where a young man threw a stick for his Alsatian, she entered a small plaza with a fountain, the place where she was to meet Duncan. The fountain was dry now, skittering with golden brown leaves in the breeze. Two nannies strolled through pushing prams netted against insects. Stopping next to the fountain, Kim took out her tourist map and pretended to study it. At the same time she noted two people approaching her down one of the walkways. Uniforms. By the brown shirts, knee breeches, and gray jackets, they were *Sturmabteilung*, the SA.

She had expected to see Hitler's loyal thugs at some point, but this first sighting sent a knife of anxiety through her. The men's bulk and their ill-fitting uniforms distinguished them from their more fit and stylish SS brethren. Would they give a Nazi salute? She had been told not to return it, as it would not be in character for the wife of a consular representative. Still, sometimes the SA did not hold with diplomatic niceties.

They noted her, and she looked at them, fleetingly, innocently. Her smile wobbled. Should one smile at the SA?

As they passed, they did not give the stiff-armed salute but walked purposively, taking in the park, its activities—and briefly, herself. A red flash of their swastika armbands, and they moved on.

When the men passed out of sight, peace returned to her patch of the Tiergarten. She had need of a deep breath and took it.

Just as she began to wonder if the presence of Hitler's militia would abort her meeting, a man appeared along one of the paths converging on the plaza. He wore a hat and a long coat, open to show a sweater-vest and suit. As he approached, she noted that he wore spectacles and carried a lunch sack. All as expected.

Entering the plaza, he sat on a cement step of the fountain, digging into the sack from which he pulled out a sandwich. He broke off pieces and tossed them to the birds that had begun to converge on him.

She walked up to him, the birds giving way. In English, she asked, "Excuse me, but do you know where the Siegesallee is?"

He looked up. She judged him to be in his midfifties. His round face held the placid expression of a man in the park on his lunch hour.

He gestured. "You'll find it over there." His English, posh. "Ninety-six statues line the street."

The double passcode completed, she thanked him and stepped away a few feet, consulting her travel brochure.

"Welcome to Berlin," he said, as he aimed a crust at a pigeon.

"Thank you." She turned the brochure around as though getting her bearings with a map. "I don't suppose Duncan is your real name?"

"For now. Are you comfortable at number 44?"

"It's fine. But I haven't got my sea legs yet. I don't trust anyone."

"Good. Keep it that way."

"Was that a test? That I'm not comfortable?"

He cut a glance at her. "You're far beyond tests. Flying colors. Don't start by doubting *me*."

"You saw our large friends?" she asked, glancing in the direction the SA men had gone.

"No, I missed them." Heavy irony. "Have you secured the safe flat?"

"Not yet." She had only arrived yesterday. "How do I get away to do so? They almost wouldn't let me take a walk by myself."

He threw another crumb to the pigeon flock. "Become a shopper. Silver, jewelry, gifts."

"What neighborhood?"

"Perhaps Niederwallstrasse or Hausvogteiplatz."

A crow flew into the growing mass of pigeons, taking a choice tidbit.

"Make friends with a local woman. Busy yourself with excursions so that your absences won't attract attention." He stood up, brushing the crumbs from his great coat. "Your drop will be in Wertheim's Department Store, Leipziger Platz, Women's Daily Wear, second-floor WC, fourth stall from the entrance. The toilet water tank. A waterproof pouch is in your bookcase, behind the *Travels in Europe* book."

"You've been in my bedroom?" Who would replenish the bag? Perhaps Albert was in on it. Or Bibi.

"If you need urgent help, place the flower vase in the window. The staff is instructed to always have fresh flowers on the bedroom table."

"And you'll come to the rescue? Someone is always watching my window?"

"We watch. More so if you have some success and the locals take an interest. If you give a signal of distress, a courier will knock at number 44 with a telegram that must be placed in your hands only. He will deal with any unwanted company. It then becomes a bit of a sticky situation. We hope not to see the vase."

"Then why have it?"

"To save your life."

"Or to protect the Office's assets. To make sure I'm not interrogated."

"Naturally, it is both."

"I doubt I'll need it."

"I'd rethink that attitude if I were you." He stared at the lunch sack. It was then that Kim noticed he had two fingers missing on his left hand. "Everyone has their limits." He stood. Their rendezvous was over.

She asked, "How do I get in touch with you?"

"Just come here to the fountain. I'll find you."

She didn't know how he could always be in the park, or near it. Perhaps he was in one of the fine apartment buildings close by and kept the plaza in view.

He tipped his homburg to her, saying in a louder voice, "I hope you enjoy the statues. Frederick the Great is especially fine." And with that, he walked away, throwing the remains of his sandwich into the bin.

A courier will knock with a telegram. Dead drop in Wertheim's, Leipziger Platz, second-floor WC, fourth stall. Make a friend, exploit her for cover. The flower vase in the window. But the last thing she wanted was to be rescued as the result of some misstep. She had a reputation to uphold: the American woman who derailed German plans. She keenly wished there to be an assignment after this one. Although she had been with the Office less than a year, she had found in the service a fierce sense of purpose. A way to give her life, her *spill* Talent, meaning. Women could be assets—often were—but not many were agents. She always felt vulnerable, lacking the club and school connections of her male SIS counterparts.

All in all, the morning had been a success. Evading notice of the SA. Meeting her handler from the Berlin station. Duncan exuded confidence and calm, helpful qualities in case things got "sticky." It all felt completely real for the first time, even if so far all she'd had to do was maintain her cover in the park and show up at the right fountain.

She headed toward the Siegesallee to grab a look at Frederick the Great. It was all going to be smooth sailing. And if it wasn't, there was Duncan and the full force and authority of the Berlin SIS station.

THE AERIE, BAVARIAN ALPS

MONDAY, NOVEMBER 9. Irina Dimitrievna Annakova stood on the chalet terrace high on the mountainside trying to see Mother Russia. It was not such a long way. Merely across Slovakia and Poland, those dismal lands, if one faced northeast as Irina did this raw, blue morning.

In the distance, fathoms of clouds stacked up over the Alps. Always she kept the motherland in her mind, so that even as she looked out on the German valley far below, she sometimes saw Russia instead. Today she imagined her homeland with its forests of aspen, birch, and pine nesting among cold fogs, and beyond, the grassy, immemorial plains.

A door closed behind her, interrupting her reverie. She turned in annoyance, but it was Sir Stefan, a man she could easily forgive.

"Your Majesty." Leaning on his cane, he moved with a

rhythmic dip in his gate to the terrace railing. "It is magnificent, is it not?" He looked out on the carved valley, the white-glazed mountains. Black hair set off his handsome face, as did his finely tailored SS uniform. If only he spoke Russian, he would be perfect. She could have spoken to him in a language of intimacy. Instead French was their shared language, since she spoke only a halting German.

"Yes, beautiful," she said.

He looked at her, his eyes dark and warm. "But today it does not seem as though you love the view."

"I do not love it today, perhaps." She liked that he was sensitive to her moods. He was the sort of man with whom any trace of interested regard was flattering, even to her.

"Someday the clouds will part and you will see your country."

"Yes. As you have promised."

A nod. A stunning smile. "When the *Wehrmacht* clears your path to St. Petersburg."

He would not call it Leningrad. Last summer, an SS officer had used that name in her presence, and his career nearly did not survive the insult. But she didn't respond to Stefan's *Wehrmacht* utterance. She did not like to think of the German army *clearing a path*, even if it was to sweep Russia clean of the Bolsheviks— Lenin's minions who had murdered her uncle Nicholas and all his sweet family; the insatiable fanatics who had pursued her for eight years through the slums of Moscow and then the taiga. Those were the years of isolation, starvation, abuse. The fallen days.

"It is all for Nikolai," she murmured. Her history was not important. She nodded to the northeast. "All that I do, all that I am, it is for my son."

"You have the Führer's word," he murmured. "After you, your son will rule."

Stefan had the bearing of certainty. Unlike Hitler, who shouted his promises, Stefan whispered his pledges, and this was somehow more reassuring. She reached for his hand as it rested on the gray slate of the wall.

His sudden look: a warning.

"Forgive me. You do not wish to be touched."

"Alas, Irinuska. I cannot. You know why."

She withdrew her hand, for a touch from the tsarina meant something: an exaltation. One he did not want.

A thud. The door leading onto the terrace crashed open, hitting the wall.

Sir Stefan turned, then bowed in that Prussian way he had. "Your Imperial Highness," he said to the intruder. "Mind that you don't break the door."

Eleven-year-old Nikolai Ivanovich waved a large sheet of paper. "But, Sir Stefan, *Maman*, I shot a bull's-eye!" he said in French. He rushed up to his mother as old Polina waited for her charge in the doorway.

Irina took the target paper from him, seeing that he had indeed put a bullet through the center. She held it up for Stefan. "Well done, darling."

Stefan nodded with satisfaction. "Your practice pays rewards. Most excellent, Your Highness."

The tsarevich beamed under Sir Stefan's praise, then his brow creased as Irina handed the paper back to him. "*Maman!* Mayn't Sir Stefan call me by my name?"

Irina paused before answering. She hated saying no to him.

"I *could*," Stefan said, as Irina raised an eyebrow. "But then the guards would have to shoot me."

The young prince grinned. "I would shoot back!"

"Enough of guns, Kolya," his mother said. "Polina waits with your French studies."

Nikolai cut a glance at Sir Stefan, but finding no sympathy there, he sighed and made his exit. At the door he turned. "But a bull's-eye!"

"And tomorrow another!" Stefan said.

Polina took Nikolai in hand, and they disappeared into the chalet.

For the past ten minutes Irina had noted a convoy of black cars approaching, appearing around switchbacks in the road far below. Now they rolled up the long approach road past the cordon gates.

She and Stefan watched as the three Mercedes motorcars, black, low, and edged with chrome, came to a stop in front of the 150-meter wall of rock that comprised the unwelcoming face of the Aerie.

"My other children," she said. As they emerged from the cars, she counted seven.

Their black uniforms proclaimed them SS, but the collar vulture insignia would herald them as her special unit. These were the souls she called the *Nachkommenschaft*, her progeny, as she styled them. There were civilian *Nachkommenschaft* as well, and all comprised a growing cadre for whom she felt tender responsibility.

"Are their quarters ready?" she asked.

"Of course. On schedule. We have taken out the airstrip to make room for spacious quarters with views."

In the past, Hitler had occasionally used the Aerie, arriving by aeroplane, but now, having provided the complex to the *Nachkommenschaft* operation, anyone approaching would have to take the road. From the battery next to the chalet, German guns would be trained on them.

As the *Nachkommen* walked out of view, entering the access to the lift, Irina turned to regard her residence, the soaring glass-and-stone-faced chalet. Through the enormous windows, which could be retracted on fine days, she saw that Nikolai and Polina had retreated to the classroom.

Behind the chalet, on the sliced-off top of this mountain, stretched nine acres of grounds with barracks, cabins for senior Nazi officials, a vegetable garden, fire pond, security bunkers, and the great two-story festival hall with military mess and, above, the timbered ballroom for elite gatherings. When her black-uniformed children emerged from the lift, they would be in the handsome plaza. Her domain.

Any visitor would be impressed. It was essential to intimidate and command with architecture. Chancellor Hitler had taught the tsarina a few things about leadership. Intimidate and command was only the beginning. And then control. For this, physical and spiritual terror was needed.

Sir Stefan said, "Shall we greet them?"

Irina demurred. "Let me enjoy the view a few minutes more." Her nostalgic mood having passed, she looked out with satisfaction on the steep valley with its crumpled, forested hills. She could almost envision her *Nachkommen* as they slipped through the moss-clad trees, watching, controlling.

Just because you could not actually see something did not mean it was not there.

THE PALAIS STROUSBERG, BERLIN

SATURDAY, NOVEMBER 14. At night, Berlin came to life, with spotlights trained on plinths and banner-hung frontages, the cafés crowded and, on the Spree, boats with torches flickering on the water. On her way with Alex to the embassy dinner, Kim thought it all bore a frenetic, disturbing beauty.

Their limousine joined the line of cars snaking up to the Palais Strousberg, the seventy-year-old mansion occupied by the British embassy. "Will we see the ambassador tonight?" Kim asked. She hadn't met him when she was shown around the embassy last week, but she had met a number of undersecretaries, subalterns, and junior officials.

Alex tapped his cigarette ash into the silver tray on the back of the forward seat. "Right, Phipps will be there. Can't miss him in that cutaway he's had for thirty years." Alex looked effortlessly handsome in an elegant tuxedo and white tie.

She tried not to be too impressed with him. "Göring will be hard to miss."

"Yes, he'll be twice as wide as anyone." He took her hand. "You aren't nervous, I hope?" The car inched forward.

"Not in the least."

"You look rather nice." He gazed at her, coolly admiring. "The color suits you."

Under her lamb's wool black coat, a slice of pale rose silk peaked out.

"Thank you, my dear." A formal answer, in case he hadn't meant it.

As they approached the next intersection on the Wilhelmstrasse, a commotion broke out on a side street. Kim leaned forward to see.

"Alex, they're beating someone!" Several people were dragging a man out of an alley, landing vicious blows on him. Lighting the scene, torches held by a few accomplices.

Alex leaned past her to see. "The goons." He raised his voice, saying to the driver, "Move on, can't you? Pull out of the line, we'll get out on the street."

As their car broke free of the queue, Kim turned to see what was happening in the plaza. "My God, they're using clubs on him. Why doesn't someone stop it?"

"Because no one interferes with the Gestapo. Most likely this is part of the reprisals for the Stadtschlosse bombing. Three SS were killed; they think it was the Oberman Group." At her questioning expression, he explained. "Jewish agitators."

To her horror, the group began dragging the man off by one ankle, causing his head to bump along the cobblestones. "Will they kill someone in the street?" She kept staring, forcing herself to look.

"They might try him. Make it as public as possible before executing him. As a warning. Some of these dissidents have found a way to strike. Bombs. And nothing the Nazis can do about it, at least beforehand. Afterward . . ." He shrugged. The car had pulled up parallel to the line of cars in front of the embassy. The chauffeur opened the door, and Alex helped Kim out.

She turned back in the direction of the Brandenburg Gate, soaring amid the floodlights, but in the press of debarking passengers, she could see little of the street activity.

"Don't look," Alex murmured, and led her through the mass of cars.

"How do they know who to arrest?"

Alex pulled her along more insistently. "I'm afraid any Jew will do."

The Germans with their appalling anti-Semitism. The rumors of brutality against the Jews were often denied, but what if they were true? Feeling ill, she let herself be led up to the great doors.

"Are you all right?" he asked, pausing for a blessed second.

"Yes." She put on her witless American face, her standard expression when she felt things most deeply. "I'm fine. Let's go."

He squeezed her elbow, giving a rueful smile of encouragement. They entered the portico and ascended the stairs. The doormen recognized Alex, and they were passed through to the vestibule, resounding in excited voices. Suddenly Kim did not want to be here amid the happy guests, finely dressed, talking too loudly, milling and murmuring to one another. The two-story gaslit room with its grand coffered ceiling and two flights of marble stairs felt like a mausoleum hosting an intolerable party, one that mocked the violence outside.

Alex was accosted by Adrian Woodhouse, the third secretary

for culture, and his wife, Something-or-Other, and then by a junior official with a mustache and a bad complexion. He introduced his guest for the evening, Rachel Flynn, a robust woman with her dark hair in a chignon. A large smile and something about being a correspondent for the *Chicago Daily News*, which *was* interesting. Alex murmured to Kim that over there, a trim man in wire-rim glasses was William Dodd, the US ambassador—looking very much the history professor—with his wife and daughter. Then they were all moving into the reception hall, another enormous room. As Alex disappeared into the crowd, she found a seat in a grouping of sofas and gradually got her bearings, taking stock of the party guests.

Alex's quick recovery from having witnessed the beating disappointed her. But he was a political man; this was an important embassy dinner, and he could not be seen to criticize the actions of the German security police, at least not tonight.

The woman who worked for the *Chicago Daily News* had sunk onto a chair nearby. Rachel Flynn. Bending over the woman was a man in a German naval uniform, smiling and laughing. By the bank of windows showing onto the Wilhelmstrasse were a group of men in SS black with red armbands. They were fair-skinned and fit, at ease, holding their drinks, one hand behind their backs.

Momentarily left alone, Rachel turned a frank gaze on Kim. "You have an American accent, am I right?"

"Well, I've been living in England, but I spent my childhood in America. How nice to see an American in Berlin."

"Everyone likes the Americans. Well, except the German officials don't much care for Dodd." She held up her empty champagne glass to a passing waiter, who supplied a new one.

"Oh, why ever not?"

"The American ambassador isn't a fan of the Nazis. And has the poor taste to say so." Her eyes sparkled. "Now, over there," she went on, nodding at the canapé table, "that's his daughter, Martha."

Kim noted a young woman with dark blond hair in a dress with a plunging neckline, obviously enjoying the attention she was getting. "She looks completely at home amid all this."

Rachel cocked an eyebrow. "And you're not? Well, of course you're not, you just arrived. It takes some getting used to, Berlin does." She didn't wait for an answer. "See the man dipping into the caviar? That's Armand Berard, a French diplomat who Martha's carrying on with. Lots of bodies in her wake."

"Her father doesn't mind that she's . . . carrying on?"

Rachel laughed. "Oh, he minds all right." She glanced at the man just lighting up a cigarette by an enormous Chinese vase. "And then, when she's not with Armand, she's with *him*."

"Quite a handsome man."

"A Soviet press attaché." She smirked. "So he claims."

Kim looked him over. Did she mean he was a spy? And everyone knew it? "Anything goes in Berlin, I guess," Kim said, warming to her role as the innocent. "You're with the *Chicago Daily News*? What story are you working on?

"Boring stuff. The Four-Year Plan, the Anti-Comintern Pact with Japan." She rolled her eyes.

"It seems like a plum assignment in Berlin if you get to come to all the diplomatic parties. I dabble in journalism. Women's magazines." They spent some time talking shop, with Kim avoiding mentioning her stint at the *Philadelphia Inquirer*. There was a chance that, given Kim's acquaintance with the SD agent Erich von Ritter, her name would be known by German intelligence services. Their chat was occasionally interrupted by people coming by to greet Rachel.

At last Kim stood, aware she'd spent too long as a wallflower. "Alex is eager for me to meet his associates," she said, "but I do hope to see you again." She drew a card from her bag and used a small pen to strike out her last name. She handed the card to Rachel.

Rachel supplied her own card, also striking out her last name, and suddenly they were on a first-name basis. Perhaps Kim had found her shopping companion.

Before she could depart, an SS officer came up to greet Rachel. She introduced him as SS Captain Rikard Nagel. Kim declared her pleasure to meet him, all the while taking in his odd appearance. Tall—indeed, most of the SS officers had the ideal Aryan physique—but Rikard Nagel was very lean indeed and long-faced as well, his receding hairline adding to his gaunt appearance.

"Frau Reed," he said in heavily accented English. "A very great pleasure." He bowed in a quick, ducking motion. "I have met your husband." He had a distinct insignia on his collar, but before she could take a closer look they were distracted by a murmur in the room. Everyone turned toward the entrance. A large man in a white uniform studded with medals had entered. He beamed in high pleasure at the fawning crowd. It could be none other than Hermann Göring.

When she turned back to Rikard Nagel, he was staring at her with a disconcerting intensity and—how completely bizarre— his nostrils flared as though he were smelling her.

Then he turned his gaze away, appearing to have already forgotten her, and moved into the crowded center of the room toward Göring. Kim was rather relieved to escape the officer's peculiar stare.

When he was gone, Rachel said, "Where do they find such people? Too fat, too thin, it's as though they collect all the strange ones."

"Perhaps only the strange ones can applaud what goes on." The image was still vivid of the man being dragged by one heel in the plaza.

Rachel smirked, and Kim felt she knew the woman's opinion of Germany's current government.

"And here comes Sonja Nagel, Rikard's wife." Rachel glanced in the direction of a woman approaching.

Bright blue eyes, with a delicate beauty, Sonja took a place in an armchair across from them. "I hope Rikard was not rude," she said to Rachel, whom she apparently knew. There was nothing one could say to that, so Rachel made the introductions. Since Kim was already standing, she felt she could move on, and she left Rachel and Sonja Nagel to their conversation.

Making her way through the throng, she reentered the vestibule and found the women's lavatory tucked under the marble stairs.

The cold of the large tiled room settled soothingly over her flushed face. A few women chatted at the sinks, reapplying their powder. When she emerged from her stall, only one person was at the mirror, a young woman dressed in sequined brown, with shoes that did not entirely match the dress.

The woman, whose red hair looked striking with her bronze dress, smiled at Kim, then applied a bright red shade to her lips. As Kim finished washing her hands, the woman said, "You are the wife of Alexander Reed?"

Kim turned to the woman. "Yes, I'm Elaine Reed. Do you know my husband?"

"No, I do not. I have, actually, a request to make. I hope you do not mind talking to a stranger?" She looked around the powder room as though to say, *We have not been introduced, but women will chat in the WC, won't they?*

"Of course."

The woman glanced at the door. "No one at the embassy will see me, so I have sought you out." Her English was stilted, but otherwise excellent.

"Would you like to walk into the foyer, where we are certain to have a moment to ourselves?"

"Yes, please. Thank you."

In the hall, the young woman—she looked to be in her very early twenties—led her up a short staircase into the atrium with its glass ceiling, dark now, as the night deepened.

"Mrs. Reed," she began. "I am a Jew, and they are searching for me." Her gaze, frank, almost challenging. "I may be killed if I cannot find asylum in your country. Of course the embassy would not bring me out of Germany just for myself. But I have . . . things to report. If there is someone at the embassy who can help me—perhaps your husband?—I will return this favor with information your country may greatly need."

"Why would no one at the embassy see you?"

"Because they do not wish to rescue German citizens from their own country. It makes it appear that Germany is bad, and you see here all the members of the National Socialist Party who will be sitting down at table with you."

"Why have you come to me specifically?" Kim asked. "My husband works in trade issues."

"You are not the first embassy wife I have approached."

"I should like to know who I am speaking to."

"I am Hannah Linz. A name to be careful with, Mrs. Reed."

They were not alone in the vestibule, but nearly so, and were not attracting attention. "Why are they looking for you, Fräulein Linz?" Kim asked.

"I am, in their eyes, a criminal. Some things I have done to protest the rounding up of Jews, the confiscation of property, the new rules against Jews. Murders as well."

Linz's words called forth in Kim the distressing scene from the plaza.

The woman went on. "A few months ago my father was murdered by the SS. They filmed it to make us fear them."

Filmed it? This surpassed anything that she had thought even Nazis were capable of.

Alex came out of the reception hall, scanning the vestibule and, seeing Kim, began to walk toward her.

Hannah Linz noted this too. "Tell your husband that I know of a Nazi scheme that is called Monarch. All I ask is ten minutes of his time. I am sure I can offer something the British government will want very much. If he will see me, he should leave his card in the only mailbox without a name on it. At this address." She handed Kim a card. With that she crossed the atrium, leaving through a door that led into the banquet room.

Tucking the card in her bag, Kim produced a pleasant face for Alex as he came up to her.

He glanced in the direction Hannah Linz had gone. "Who was that?"

"Oh, I've met so many people." She rummaged in her bag, as though trying to find the card again. Giving up, she said, "We'll sort everyone out when we get home. I saw Göring arrive, did you?"

He led her through the back way into the banquet room. "The dinner gong. Didn't you hear it?"

People were taking their places at a table that looked like it could seat a hundred. The woman with the red hair was nowhere to be seen. The woman who knew about a Nazi scheme called Monarch.

Curiosity coiled inside Kim, awakening her instincts. Soirees like this were rife with gossip and traded secrets; some had import for the intelligence service and some did not. Often people had motives of money or favors, but that might not negate the significance of what was offered. Nor did it prove value, of course.

Alex pulled out a chair for her in the center portion of the table, just above where the junior diplomats took their seats. China gleamed, and cut glass stemware reflected the light from crystal chandeliers. Outside, a different world of alley beatings and murder. Hannah Linz's world, where murders were filmed for maximum terror.

To her chagrin, Rikard Nagel was about to take a seat next to her. But his wife, seeing Kim, protested. "No, Rikard, I'll sit there." Nagel drew out the chair for Sonja, and the two women smiled at each other. Alex leaned across Kim, greeting Sonja and offering to make introductions, but finding none needed, he turned to the person on his other side. Across from Kim sat a man who might be a banker or industrialist of some kind, and on either side of him junior secretaries from the consulate. Kim nodded to a few of them.

She felt quite distracted, distanced from the chatter in the hall, as though she were a shadow in a room of more solid beings. Waiters were already pouring wine, and protocols be damned, Kim took a surreptitious gulp of hers.

Near the head of the table, Göring commanded a position of prominence, listening to Captain Nagel, who bent down to converse with him.

Sonja observed this too.

"Your husband," Kim said, "appears on close terms with the aviation minister."

Sonja glanced at her with some irony. "The *Reichsluftfhart-*

minister knows everyone, of course." She watched the two men confer. "But Rikard is on close terms with no one."

Kim allowed her brow to wrinkle.

"Oh yes, Rikard goes his own way. As do I. But he has sold his soul to them."

"The Party, you mean?"

Sonja shrugged. "It is how one advances these days. You climb and climb to the glittering heights." She put her napkin in her lap, looking lost. "And then, of course, you fall."

Göring raised his glass and turned toward Sonja, appearing to toast her. Blushing as several people took note and glanced at her, she did not pick up her glass.

Rikard Nagel looked across at her and then, incongruously on such a face, smiled.

8

TIERGARTENSTRASSE 44, BERLIN

THAT EVENING. In her dressing gown, Kim made her way downstairs to the library. She found Alex at the escritoire opening his mail. He looked up in surprise. By the carved wooden clock on the wall it was 11:41 PM.

"Something the matter?" He still held his letter, so she had caught him at something he wished to read.

"Yes. But maybe you can help."

He put the letter down and swiveled in his chair, inviting her to sit on the overstuffed couch. She did so, using a smile to cover her discomfort at having to ask her simulated husband for a favor. They weren't married and they didn't entirely share agendas, even if they were both under the Foreign Office.

"Still upset by what you saw in the Pariser Platz?"

"Alarmed and disgusted, rather. But no, it's something else."

He waited, looking attentive. In the shadowed library he and his desk occupied a pool of lamplight, an emblem, she suddenly thought, of the power he held.

"It's about a woman who is in danger of her life. She—"

"In danger? One of ours, do you mean, or a German?"

"German."

He frowned. "Who is it?"

"A woman approached me at the function tonight. She's been turned away by embassy staff, and she asked me to intercede with you. She hopes for an interview regarding extraction. I thought you could talk to someone in the Passport Control Office." His eyes narrowed; not a good sign. "Her father was murdered by the Nazis and she's become a protestor against anti-Jewish regulations. The authorities are looking for her and will probably send her to jail or worse."

"So she's Jewish? Was this the woman I saw you with in the foyer tonight?"

"Yes. In exchange for your help she's offering what she says is important information, including a project called Monarch."

"She hasn't made your cover, has she?"

"I doubt it. She's been asking embassy wives to intercede. So far no one has been willing to help."

Alex shook his head. "I'm surprised that you fell for her story."

"It might not be a *story*."

"But she thought you'd be a sympathetic ally. And here we are, talking about a person who may be a criminal, a Communist. Anything."

"Even a criminal may have important information."

"Elaine." They avoided her real name, even when alone.

"This is the reason our embassies shy away from recruiting sources. It's unsavory and jeopardizes the trust the host nation has in our consular activities."

"Oh, please. It happens all the time."

"If you're so keen on her, why don't your people get her out?"

Lots of reasons: because Kim had little clout. Because she was on her first Continental posting. Because it likely had nothing to do with her present mission.

Alex went on, "I remember that a woman came unannounced to the embassy last week. She was without a passport and couldn't supply any background. Naturally, we refused to see her. And now that I know what she was after, I certainly won't see her, either." He held up a hand as Kim started to speak. "The embassy can't be involved in internal German affairs."

"You don't have anything to lose just by listening to what she has to say. I'd get her to tell *me* what she's offering, but it would jeopardize my cover to be curious."

"And what is she offering? Something called Monarch, did you say?" He stood and made his way to the sideboard. As he poured whisky, he said, "I have no idea what that is."

"Well, it's odd that you aren't even curious."

"You're right, I'm not. Things are a damned mess in Berlin right now. By interfering we risk losing the confidence of the party officials, so that we'd be further hamstrung in moderating whatever excesses her family is suffering."

He brought the drinks over and handed her one. "For all you know, this woman is involved with that Jewish resistance group. Bunch of saboteurs. They're trying to take the law into their own hands."

She put her drink on the coffee table. "*Law?* What law? Hitler suspends rights, persecutes people in the streets without so much as a trial . . ."

Sighing, he went on. "Look. I'm not unsympathetic to the misconduct surrounding the Jews."

"Misconduct? Is that what you call the beating we witnessed?" How sanguine he was about it.

He sighed. "I know it's bloody hard to watch these thugs carry on in the streets. But we aren't in control. This isn't England."

He sipped his whisky. "Did you get her name, her contact information, by the way?"

"No, we were too rushed." He didn't need to know. Just as he didn't need to know that she had taken a flat near the Alexanderplatz in the center of the city. Nor that she had the *spill*. He didn't know her any more than she knew him.

"If the woman didn't give you a card, how was she going to find out whether I would see her?"

"She said she'd find me."

He glanced at the lace-clad windows. "Splendid. She might be watching the house right now, waiting to join us for a whisky."

But she's a Jew, so that certainly won't happen. She was surprised that she had rushed to that conclusion. But she was liking Alex less tonight and wouldn't put such prejudice past him.

"Elaine. Your idea of following up—it's needlessly provocative. We do have the bond repayments to finalize, and it's touch and go right now. We can't have anything get in the way."

Nor in the way of his likely promotion to first secretary for trade if he could nail the deal. The current first secretary was in London for cancer treatments.

He raised his drink to her. "Let's have our night cap, shall we?"

She gave him an *I give up* smile. Alex had gone to some

inconvenience to provide her a cover in Berlin, so she really must get along with him.

He leaned back on the sofa, putting his arm along the back, still in his dinner jacket but the tie missing, always a good look. "How was the evening, other than this cloakroom appeal?"

Everything he said grated, but he needed to be sure he'd won, and she must let him. "Well, I met a woman I quite like."

"Sonja Nagel?"

"I mean the reporter, Rachel Flynn. I might ring her up for an excursion."

"Right. The American. The Germans admire the Americans." He clinked his glass with hers, looking into her eyes. "So do I."

"Such a flirt. Scandalous in Berlin."

"Is it?"

"Yes, in a city like Berlin, you flirt with *other* people's wives." She sipped her whisky.

A bit more small talk, and she bid him goodnight. In the dark foyer with its green silk walls, the glass next to the front doors flashed with the passing lights of motorcars on the Tiergartenstrasse.

The chat with Alex, a bust. True, she couldn't save every dissident in Berlin. But Hannah had offered quid pro quo. It took a stubborn disinterest not to be at least curious. Monarch, Linz had said. *Something your government may greatly need.* But it appeared that Alex's ambition went as far as making nice with repulsive officials and smoothing over murders in the street.

And she had rather liked him for a while.

Making her way upstairs, she paused at one of the paintings on the wall, one of a couple holding an infant. In the background, on a side table, a branched candleholder, a menorah. The woman wore the satin gown that had been left in the armoire. Seeing the dress on this dark-eyed, contented young mother roused an unpleasant idea. All the lovely things left behind, perhaps in haste . . .

She put her hand on the railing, letting the thought settle in: this house had belonged to Jews. A family that had not had time or permission to pack up all their possessions when they were rousted out. She wondered how it had gone, their last moments in this house. In her imagination: raised voices, a crying baby, the smash of a vase. She shuddered.

Alex had come into the foyer. "Everything all right?" He came up to stand beside her, looking at the painting.

"They lived here once," Kim murmured. "Maybe the recent owners. They left so many things behind when they were kicked out, their possessions confiscated." She turned to look at him. "Jews, persecuted for what they believe."

"Oh please. You don't know that."

"I found a dress on the floor of my wardrobe. It's the one in this portrait. Why would the family have left this painting behind?"

"You're really cooking up a story there, don't you think?"

My job, dear husband, is to put two and two together. She let her gaze linger on him, waiting for him to see her point. He didn't. "You should have the embassy look into it. Don't you think?"

She turned abruptly to climb the stairs. Behind her he said, "It's been a long night. Get some sleep."

In other words, be quiet. She went up to bed, now not the least bit sleepy.

BADEN-BADEN, GERMANY

THURSDAY, NOVEMBER 19. In the large meeting hall of the Steigenberger Hotel the stooped, white-haired guest of honor crossed the stage and, reaching the lectern, fumbled with his notes. In the audience, fewer than fifty people had turned out to hear the renowned theologian, Hanns von Lerchenfeld.

The low turnout pleased Juergen Becht, sitting in the audience, observing his target. He fingered the pin on his SS collar, tracing the small *Nachkommenschaft* insignia, the vulture that established him as a *Nachkomme*.

At the lectern, von Lerchenfeld shuffled his notes as people waited for him to settle himself, perhaps wondering if the old man was quite up to a lecture. At eighty-one, he had lived to see the Catholic faith much diminished in influence. Of course he believed that the church had been persecuted and subverted by the National Socialists. He still did not understand that in the Third Reich religion must take second place to German patriotism.

Von Lerchenfeld began to speak, his voice surprisingly steady and deep.

"What are we to say for our beloved church in these times? This is perhaps the very question that you, gathered here, have asked yourselves. We have seen things that even five years ago were unthinkable. Thousands of priests, nuns, and laypeople have been arrested on spurious charges. The leader of Catholic Action was, as we have seen, murdered. Catholic publications are suppressed and even—even!—the sanctity of the confessional violated by the Gestapo. Yet the party program guarantees liberty for all religious denominations. This, of course, is a bald lie. What, then, are we to do?"

Von Lerchenfeld looked over the top of his spectacles at his audience, which had noticeably quieted at this direct attack on the government. He swept his gaze through the auditorium, stopping for a moment when he saw an SS uniform among them. Then he went on.

And on. He inveighed against anti-Catholic propaganda, incitements, and outright threats against the church, enumerating them.

Becht felt the heat of these insults, felt the old fool's gaze on him, as he increasingly addressed his rants to the only uniformed man in the room. Even now, after the Nazi Party had established its dominance, people still clung to the old ways. Like so many that Juergen Becht had had to reeducate: the professors at universities, inferior doctors who thought they would always have standing in society, Jews running subversive cinema programs, thinking that, deep in the forested countryside, they were safe from discovery.

Twenty minutes later, the speaker began urging an awakening of the moral feelings of the German race as articulated by the church. Becht judged it the right moment to cast his *mesmerizing* power over the group, to numb their minds, to allow him to have his way.

As von Lerchenfeld concluded, a few people clapped, but given the profound stupor he had willed upon the gathering, most did not. People shuffled in their seats, perhaps wishing to leave, but feeling a lethargy that forbade it.

In the surreal quiet, Becht strode to the stage and walked up the stairs, crossing to the podium. A woman with a flushed plump face was shaking von Lerchenfeld's hand but dropped it as Becht approached.

"Herr von Lerchenfeld." Becht looked into the man's gray eyes, seeing no recognition of what was to come. "We have an appointment."

The old man frowned in confusion.

"You do remember? We were to have an important meeting after your address."

"Oh," the woman said, looking relieved that she could be excused. "I won't keep you then, Herr von Lerchenfeld." She seemed to take note of Becht's dueling scar, a facial mark that he was well aware added to his aura of intimidation.

"My coat," von Lerchenfeld said. "My coat . . ."

Becht fixed a look at the woman. "You will bring Herr von Lerchenfeld's coat." He could smell her, with her ample flesh, her powder. The blood flushing her cheeks.

"What?" she asked, surprised to be addressed. Then seeing Becht's expectant stare, she wandered off in search of the wrap.

Von Lerchenfeld had taken off his spectacles and was stab-

bing them at his breast pocket, trying to put them away. "A meeting, you say?"

"Yes. Of the utmost importance." He led von Lerchenfeld to
the stairs. They were met by the woman carrying the old man's
wool coat. She helped him into it, then watched in perplexity as
Becht led him down the steps.

He had cast the *mesmerizing* throughout the room, but it could
not hold for long over so large an assemblage. Best to depart
while the plump frau and the crowd of religious enthusiasts were
still unaware of what was happening. Surely the evening's hosts
had planned a repast at a fine restaurant. When the air cleared,
they would wonder where the guest of honor had gone off to.

Out in the chill night air of the plaza, the old man blinked
in the light from the gas lamps. Becht led von Lerchenfeld down
the cobbled street toward the neighborhood where he lived.

"This meeting," von Lerchenfeld said. "Who was it with?
Was it the parish priest, but no—we met yesterday. I am forget-
ful, you will say."

"Not the priest, no."

Another block and the old man said, "I am not used to walking so far. Is it much farther? This meeting?"

"No, it is close now."

As they walked through the ever-darker streets, Becht's
anger fell away. Now he simply walked with a frail old man who
believed that the church should hold sway over the state. A mistake. He must be made an example of.

But though Becht had killed many men, he had begun to feel
a reluctance to kill this one. He was himself a Catholic. Years
past, he had been, before he became a believer in Adolf Hitler
and the salvation that Nazism brought to Germany. Could not
one be a Christian and a Nazi? Surely. But here in this wooded

yard leading to von Lerchenfeld's house, he would end a fellow Catholic's life.

The old man looked up in perplexity. "But this is my home." They stopped short of the rectangle of light thrown from the front window on the yard and pavement.

"This is the meeting," Becht said. "The one between you and me." And, because he had been ordered to do so, he led von Lerchenfeld into the completely dark lawn and made an example of him: a blow to render him unconscious, the puncture wound at his neck, and blood welling. The smell, coppery and thick. Intoxicating. He knelt and feasted.

When they found von Lerchenfeld, they would know the work of the *Nachkommenschaft*.

Becht removed the plain black coat he wore to protect his uniform and left it at the scene. Withdrawing a handkerchief from his pocket, he carefully wiped his face and hands. Yes, finding von Lerchenfeld thus, people would know terror, physical and spiritual. It was in service of the Führer's aims; and yet the old man's words churned through him. The fellowship of Christians. The sacred church.

Ah, what was he becoming? In the quiet of the garden, his appetite slaked, he felt a strange and unwelcome pang of guilt. He had slain an old man, a Christian. And then this unholy drinking of blood that, in his new role, he had craved. He had trusted that horror was needed in the polluted world to make it clean again. Over the months, the years, he had receded further and further from the man he had been. Did not everyone change on the path of life? But it was not just that he was unrecognizable to his old self. No, it was worse than that. He was damned. For truly there was no going back. No forgiveness, not even in Christ.

Having acknowledged this brutal truth, Becht took a deep breath of the icy November air. Hovering about him, from stray drops jeweling his trousers, his boots—the cloying, sweet smell of von Lerchenfeld's vintage blood.

WERTHEIM'S DEPARTMENT STORE, LEIPZIGER PLATZ, BERLIN

THURSDAY, NOVEMBER 19. Kim combed her chin-length dark hair behind her ears, then changed her mind and combed it straight. As she stood in front of the mirrors in Wertheim's second-floor lavatory, the person in the fourth stall seemed to take forever.

Kim had left Rachel Flynn in the ladies' shoe department downstairs and couldn't reasonably spend too long in the powder room.

At last the toilet flushed, and a woman in a stylish suit emerged, straightening her fitted jacket.

Kim entered the stall and sat on the toilet seat, removing from her handbag the pouch that she had retrieved from her bedroom bookcase.

The paper inside described her meeting with Hannah Linz and suggested that the woman might be of value as an information source. She requested approval to pursue the contact, to pin down specifics about her claim of an operation that would be of interest to the British government. If the information had value, SIS might want to consider an extraction.

Kim acknowledged that the information she'd gleaned so far had not been the product of a *spill*. The woman had sought her out specifically because of her supposed influence with Alex Reed.

Await instructions.

Stepping out of her shoes, she balanced on the toilet seat and reached up to partially lift the cover of the water tank. Slipping the waterproof packet inside, she held on to a short chain that was attached to it. She affixed a small hook to the side of the tank where it could not be seen from the front.

Kim maneuvered herself down from her perch and slipped back into her shoes. Her decision to file the report felt right. After only two weeks in Berlin, she had already acquired a possible productive source worthy of debriefing—though perhaps by a different agent than herself. The service might even choose to extract Linz. Since the woman was already underground, it was not likely to come to the authorities' attention or create an incident.

She flushed the toilet to make sure the chain from the pouch did not clink against the porcelain. Washing up, she used the mirror to memorize the faces of the other women in the lavatory and took the escalator back to Ladies Shoes.

Rachel waved from across the expanse of the showroom, beneath the glass-roofed atrium and elaborate chandeliers.

"I thought you'd gotten lost," Rachel said, holding her Wertheim's shopping bag.

"So many escalators!" Kim said. "I shouldn't wonder if I had."

But of course, if she could lose her way in a department store, even the world's largest, she would deserve to be drummed out of the service.

SATURDAY, NOVEMBER 21. Water dripped from somewhere, pinging onto old floors, releasing the earthy smell of mold and ancient bricks turning to powder. From the shadowed corner of the room Hannah watched as Franz interrogated their guest, tied to a chair.

Next to Hannah, Micha muttered, "We'll get nothing more. End it."

Their captive was Gaèton Paquet, a French citizen, a railway worker. He deserved to die, but he had not yet caused damage. In the Volkspark Friedrichshain, her fellow partisans had intercepted him before his Berlin handler could contact him.

The building was abandoned, one of a series of bolt-holes the Oberman Group used in their rotation from place to place. This one was unheated, and Hannah pulled her father's leather jacket more snugly around herself, fingering the ivory buttons.

In France, Gaèton's recruiter had only given him a meeting place and a passcode, so he had not recognized the personnel substitution when it happened. Armed with forewarning from Tannhäuser, their excellent mole, Micha and Leib were waiting in the park for Gaèton. They had met him with the passcode and the Frenchman had willingly left with them. He believed he was on his way to transform his life from railway worker without prospects to a valued Nazi asset. But instead of being welcomed into the new brotherhood, he had found his worst nightmare: Jews with weapons.

Franz turned to look at Hannah, signaling that he was done. With his better command of French, he had conducted the interrogation, but he was letting her decide if there were more depths to plumb. Although Franz was the group's leader, he often deferred to her, and after some initial hesitation her compatriots did also. After Miriam had been captured last summer, Hannah was now the only woman in their small group of partisans.

She stepped forward. This one's Talent—very strong, rated at 7.2—was *site view*. By virtue of that Talent, he was probably terrified since he might well have experienced visions of the basement interrogations that had gone before.

She looked at the stocky Frenchman with his puffy face distorted by Franz's beating. If he thought he was suffering now, he had not seen much of the world. Gaèton Paquet was a virulent anti-Semite, and the world would be better off without him, but she believed that he knew nothing more about the Nazi agents in the Alsace where he had been recruited.

"Take him to the French embassy," she said. They would handcuff him to the wrought-iron fence with his false passport stuck in his pocket, along with an accusation that he had offered his Talent to the Nazi government. It would be another demonstration of the Oberman Group's powers, one that would not be lost on the French *or* the Germans.

"And if he comes back?" Franz looked at the prisoner with weary contempt.

"If he returns, then we kill him." Hope began to seep into Gaèton's face.

Hannah turned to the man. "You will not use your gift for Nazi ends." She spoke in English, which the man could understand, if barely. "You comprehend?"

He nodded with great conviction.

"You swear?"

Pleading with his eyes, he said, "*Oui, oui,* I do. I swear."

She and Franz walked out together, leaving Micha to arrange the car and the dead-of-night delivery to the embassy.

The heavy door was sprung on its hinges. Franz scraped it shut, and they made their way upstairs. Here the water from the roof fell in a stream down the wall, the afternoon sun having melted the early snowfall that had earlier frosted the neighborhood. Even amid the pockmarked bricks, the dirt and mold, and wearing a tattered coat, Franz managed to look patrician. The way he carried himself, his hair—always clean and combed. He had given up much to join the resistance. Not that he'd had a choice.

He lit one of the Frenchman's Gauloises, blowing an irritated stream of smoke. He would rather have killed him. "Nothing from the wife of the British diplomat?"

"No. I think Alexander Reed was not receptive. If she even spoke to him." There was no reason why the wife of a British trade secretary would try to get a stranger an appointment with her husband. But the woman had had a look in her eyes, one that had encouraged Hannah; it felt like she had actually listened, since she hadn't just brushed her off. But how foolish to think that a socialite like her would upset protocols! Mostly people did what was expected of them.

"There are other embassies," Franz said. "Try the American next."

All their conversations were about this subject. Her escape from Germany. He wanted her gone. She should be of use to the Western powers, but Hannah was not convinced that Britain or France would mobilize if Hitler made moves against his neighbors. So if she left, she would likely be out of the fight. She and Franz had argued many times about this, and eventually she capitulated. But when nothing came of the British embassy appeal, she was secretly relieved.

Franz went on, like the dripping of the water onto the bricks in the next room. "William Dodd may listen. The American ambassador. Or his daughter."

Hannah removed her knit cap and massaged her sweating scalp.

"And get rid of the red hair," he said. "It's like a sign: *I am a Jewish criminal.*"

"They need to know it is the Rotes Mädchen. The Red Girl. I want them to know."

"You are proud, Hannah. That may kill you."

She remembered how she and her father had allowed the pallid, scarred SS lieutenant to intimidate them in their own parlor. Becht, his name was. But in her mind, she called him *the vulture.* She remembered how she had fallen to her knees on the carpet at the cinema, weeping and helpless.

So now she was proud? Not the word she would have used. *Disobedient* was one she liked. Well. Franz always looked for more from her. He wanted evidence that under the soldier lay a person. How tiring it was. There was nothing underneath.

He snorted, annoyed by her silence. "They know your name. The Gestapo has your description. You are on borrowed time, and all because of your love of bombs."

After the bomb destroyed the Nazi staff car last summer, she had been seen fleeing. Her description was later put together with the former cinema operator, and it was not hard to imagine who had made the connection. The explosion had badly injured an SS colonel. How dearly she wished it had been the vulture.

"Do you know why I love bombs? Do you?" He didn't bother to answer. "Because all we do otherwise is take out recruits here and there, the ones our mole knows of. But it does not stop the Russian Witch."

"We do what we can."

"And it is not enough!"

"You are too ambitious, Hannah."

"I will die young, so I am in a hurry."

"We die when our time comes."

She shrugged. Life was full of uncertainties, but she could not imagine herself living long.

"You are ungrateful," Franz said. "If it were not for Tann-häuser—"

"Oh yes, your great friend from the old days. Who stood silently by when the Nazis denied you permission to play Chopin in public. Your loyal friend."

He ignored the old provocation, going back doggedly to his embassy plans. "So you will go to the Americans?"

She sighed. "I need better shoes."

"Shoes?"

"A woman is judged by her shoes. If I am not going to look

like a revolutionary at the embassy, I need good shoes. Expensive ones."

Franz nodded. He would probably steal them himself.

She gave him a brief smile. Franz needed some emotion. Then, pulling her knit hat firmly over her head, she slipped out of the building onto the wet streets, steaming in the wan sun.

A TAXI, BERLIN

TUESDAY, NOVEMBER 24. Even midweek and at 10:00 PM, Berlin's endless party carried on. In the taxi, on her way to drinks with her new friend Rachel, Kim watched people still arriving for dinner. They walked arm in arm, smartly dressed. She let the crowds on the Kurfürstendamm distract her for a few moments.

Then the message from the Office came back to mind. They had rebuffed her. Duncan had sent on to London her request to exploit the Hannah Linz lead. In a swift turnaround came the answer. No.

Duncan had relayed the message to her in the Tiergarten, including the galling phrase, *Don't let your heart lead you.* His Majesty's Government, he had explained, was not eager to cause friction in Berlin or meddle with police actions.

In Stahnsdorfer Street, in the Steglitz–Zehlendorf area, Kim entered a cozy, cigarette-charged restaurant, Die Toskana, with mirrors surrounding banquets and every table filled. She made out Rachel's crowded table in the corner, the scene of a nightly gathering of correspondents that went on into the early hours of the morning. Rachel had said Kim would be welcome anytime, and tonight she felt the need for a distraction.

The introductions included a large, florid man in an ill-fitting suit, Chuck MacIntyre of the *United Press*. Fiftyish and dapper Peter Grann of the Berlin bureau of the London *Times*, and the bearded and barrel-chested Ernst Rauschning, foreign press chief of the *Arbeiter-Zeitung*. Peter Grann had a date, Annie. Next to Rauschning, a man was introduced as Theodor, his pomaded hair parted on one side.

Rachel introduced Kim as a member of the tribe, citing her freelance magazine work.

"Breezy stuff," Kim said. "Recipes and fashion."

"Well, women's fashion beats dispatches on Germany's Four-Year Plan," Chuck MacIntyre said, raising his whisky in a weary salute.

Rachel smirked. "Don't say that too loudly." She slid a meaningful glance at a table across the room.

As Kim got settled, she followed Rachel's glance to a table with several men in uniform. She was startled to see that one of them was Hermann Göring, and Rikard Nagel as well, who was accompanied by his wife. Sonja caught Kim's eye and nodded.

Ernst Rauschning glowered at the table of Nazis and muttered, "Standards in this place are slipping." He waved his empty glass at a waiter.

MacIntyre settled his large frame against the back of the banquet. "You're American, then? Sounds like."

Kim trotted out her cover story of having been raised in

America and meeting her husband in Lisbon when she'd been on holiday. A new round of drinks arrived, whiskies on ice for Kim and MacIntyre, and without ice for the others.

"Göring is quite attentive to Sonja Nagel," Kim observed to Rachel. The air minister had the woman deep in conversation, leaning in close.

"Yes, he likes those wraithlike Scandinavian women." Rachel blew smoke out the side of her mouth like a man. "And she *is* his mistress."

That was news. "Does Rikard know, do you think?" On Kim's other side, she noted that Rauschning had placed his hand on Theodor's knee. Lovers, then.

Rachel watched Göring's table. "He must know, but what can he do?"

Kim could think of several things he might do, but perhaps there were career advantages where Göring was concerned.

Talk turned to Peter Grann's coming posting to Istanbul, which the table considered a promotion. Annie complained of his leaving. Kim tried and failed to listen.

Don't let your heart lead you. As though she had simply made an emotional judgment about Linz. Ambassador Phipps, Duncan had said, did not like the arrangement of her supposed marriage to one of his consular staff and had taken issue with the Foreign Office's decision to embroil—as he had put it—the embassy in espionage, at least with something so brazen as the sham marriage.

Rauschning left for the men's room, leaving her next to Theodor, who had said barely a word so far. The man caught a waiter's attention, pointing at himself and Kim. His eyes glittered, reflecting the restaurant lamps, the mirrors, too much whisky. "One has to keep ordering," he said, his words slurring. "You must have noticed—it's how you survive."

"Is Berlin so bad?"

"Bad?" He stared into his empty glass. "It's splendid. Frightfully splendid, depending on who you are." He switched to German, speaking more to himself than to her. "We are all celebrating. Eating, making love, reporting enemies, having champagne, staying up so we do not have to lie down and close our eyes. A splendid time. Even the fiends think so."

Teufel. That word again. "The Nazis?"

He chuckled. "If you need to ask, you aren't drunk enough."

She did not care for his tone, not in her present mood. At the table in the corner, Göring stood up and helped Sonja into her wrap. They left together, with Rikard sitting there, accepting it, or acting like he did.

Rauschning returned to claim his spot, as Peter from the *Times* began a story of the parties that were *de rigueur* in Istanbul, as proof of which someone named George Bennet had had to be carted home from a party in a wheelbarrow.

By midnight Kim was making her excuses and bidding the table goodnight. She thanked Rachel for including her. Offers of rides sprang up, but she had begun to relish a quiet taxi back to Tiergartenstrasse 44.

At the curb, the words came around again in orbit. *Don't let your heart lead you.* It could have been advice straight from Julian, the type of thing a father would say to a daughter, and not what the head office would say to a male agent. In any case, whether Julian had been brought in to account for her or not, she had miscalculated. Still, she felt that Hannah should at least be interviewed.

Kim's mistake had been to suggest asylum; that had been rash, perhaps. London's rebuke about her supposed emotionality suggested that she had not yet proven her operational judgment to them. It was her first foreign posting; she'd have to watch her step.

But a thought nagged. Linz had said the authorities hunted her because she had protested the treatment of her family and other Jews. She wondered if that was the part the Office didn't like, that she was Jewish. Otherwise why had the idea of extraction been so summarily dismissed? It might suggest a prejudice in the ranks of SIS against Jews. She could not believe it of her father, but the higher-ups?

She had been standing at curbside for ten minutes without seeing a taxi. Just when she decided to return to the table to accept a ride, Captain Nagel emerged and looked down the street, nodding at a line of parked cars. Distracted. Well, his wife had left with another man.

A low-slung black car with an arrow hood ornament pulled up to the curb. The driver hopped out, opening the door for the captain.

Nagel turned to Kim. "Here, Frau Reed. You will get in."

Kim looked at the open car door. "I'm sure it's not on your way."

Still, the door open, Nagel waiting. She approached, looking at the restaurant for a last-minute reprieve.

He waited, expressionless. The gold-threaded insignia on his collar glinted. A bird with a bald head, a long neck. A vulture.

Nothing left but to join him. "*Danke*, Captain Nagel. Very good of you."

Once they were settled in the car he murmured to the driver, "*Tiergartenstrasse vierundvierzig.*" Tiergartenstrasse number 44. They pulled away from the curb. So he knew her address.

The car sped out of the little neighborhood with its smart shops and eateries. In two turns they entered a cramped residential street, darker despite the occasional gaslight standard.

Nagel sat in shadow, black uniform against the black glass, the dark upholstery.

"I hope I won't put you too far out of your way."

Silence. No response to the niceties, then. "How do you know where I live?" She didn't turn to look at him. In the dark there would be no point.

"I do not forget details." In heavily accented English. The car sped down a side street, the neighborhood shabbier now, with old five-story apartment buildings. On the front stairs, boxes and sacks, possibly garbage. "I notice your husband does not come with you so late at night. This despite that you have been on honeymoon after your marriage twenty-seven days ago."

How very specific. She had been noticed here after all. "I am used to my independence, though." *As is your wife, Captain.*

"A city that is new to you, a new husband. All very convenient. Perhaps rushed?"

High alert kicked in. It was one thing if the Gestapo checked on foreign diplomats, but quite another if the SS took an interest. *Schutzstaffel.* Fanatically ideological, brutal. "It does feel rather exciting. I have always wanted to see Berlin."

As a light rain fell, sequins of light glittered and streaked on the side windows. They crossed a bridge into a neighborhood of stucco homes with ornamental balconies.

"I notice," Nagel suddenly said, "that you have an interest in my wife."

"I don't think so. We have just met."

"At the embassy you are sitting with her in the salon. Then at table as well." His voice lacked inflection. Perhaps he did not care; this was his way of making conversation.

She wanted to say that Sonja had chosen to sit with her both times, but he must already know this.

He went on. "And again, tonight, *ja?*"

With some effort, she kept her voice chatty and casual. "Not really. I didn't know she was at the restaurant."

Her fingers were clutching her bag rather hard, and she relaxed them. The man was exceedingly peculiar.

"You are not English like your husband, but American," he murmured.

"Yes. I was vacationing in Portugal when I met him."

The car passed under the S-Bahn as a train clattered overhead. "I know this."

"You do not forget details." The light riposte fell dead.

They were on a major street—the Hohenzollern? She tried to remember if she had taken it getting to the restaurant. She began to wish for some landmarks. Where, in fact, were they headed?

"Or perhaps it is Air Minister Göring?"

"I beg your pardon?"

"Air Minister Hermann Göring."

"I did hear you, but I don't know why you think I am *interested* in him." Did he think that she was spying on Göring through his mistress?

If so, they might well not be heading to the Tiergartenstrasse.

"My husband has meetings with party officials. I, of course, do not." She keenly felt how tenuous was the protection of the consulate when she was in an unmarked car with a Nazi who might have peculiar ideas of his authority.

She didn't recognize the smaller street they had just turned onto. "Are you saying, Captain, that I should not speak to your wife? I would like to be clear."

"Sonja!" he growled. And with that utterance, he slammed his fist down on the seat in front of him. It shuddered under the crushing blow and sagged, remaining crooked. A sprinkling of dust settled to the floor. The driver did not react. Venomously, Nagel said again, "Sonja. . ." and looked like he might ram his fist through the window.

Kim held her breath. They rode in silence for a few minutes as she tried to calm herself. Now she was desperate to identify the buildings they were passing, or the streets. Overhead, the S-Bahn passed in and out of view, over and over.

At last Nagel's surprisingly modulated voice came to her. "You admire your American leader, Herr Roosevelt?"

It was a shock to find his demeanor had snapped back to modulated. Kim found her voice. "Well. I live in England now."

"I know this. But you have esteem for him."

She feared another outburst and tried to soothe it over. "One respects the leaders of government, or one tries, Captain."

He snorted. "Despite that he is a crippled man. His body, failing him."

At last she recognized where they were, on the boulevard Kurfürstendamm, full of people, normal people, on the sidewalks, in motorcars. They passed the Kaiser Wilhelm Memorial Church with its steep spires. The path home, surely.

"So?" he persisted.

"I do admire him. Many people do not. I take it you do not."

"Admire?" Now, in the light from the headlights of the many vehicles, she saw that he was smiling, his mouth wide. It was a gaping grin that she had never before seen on a person's face. Strange was not the word for him. Mad?

"My life . . . ," he began, pausing so long she did have to look over at him. He was not smiling, so that his face relaxed into a more normal aspect, his hair slicked back from his high forehead, a few strands curling at his neck.

"My life," he went on, "it is in service of the monarch."

She paused. "The Führer, do you mean?"

The car pulled in front of the familiar wrought-iron fence. Number 44. "I said."

But you didn't say Führer, she thought. The driver came to open her door, leaving the car running.

"Thank you so much for the lift, Captain Nagel." She was pleased to hear her voice steady and smooth.

He nodded to her, and they made eye contact for the first time that evening. His gaze was even and blank, as though for him this had all been quite routine.

"A very great pleasure," he said without intonation. Someone must have taught him phrases he could use so as not to utterly offend and appall.

When she stepped out of the car, the driver shut the door and returned to his place behind the wheel.

Standing on the pavement in front of the house, she took in a long, deep breath. The air, silken and pure from the rain. As the car sped away, she clicked open the gate and entered the portico, shaken.

And also deep in thought. Monarch, that word again. *My life in service to the monarch.* In a spike of excitement, she considered that it might be a word he very much wished to hide. A *spill.*

Albert opened the door as though he had been waiting.

THE AERIE, BAVARIAN ALPS

FRIDAY, NOVEMBER 27. The blankets held Irina in a suffocating embrace. "Devils! Devils!" she cried, but as her face was covered with dusty brocade, it came out only as a wooly scream. Finally waking, she gasped for breath, fighting with the covers that held her arms pinned to her sides. "Damn you forever!"

"Your Majesty . . ."

A broad, flushed face stooped over her, trying to push her back into the sea of covers. Irina thrashed in protest.

"Your Majesty, you dream. It is nothing but a dream."

With one final heave, Irina pushed the coverlet from her sweating body. Cool air flowed over her hands and feet. She could breathe again. Light pierced the room from the bedside lamp where Polina hovered.

It was the Aerie, her refuge.

"Your Majesty, shall I—"

"Be silent." The terrors of the dream. Always the filthy pillow over her face, the shouts, the smell of gunpowder, the soldiers tearing at her underclothes.

The nightgown stuck to her hot skin. She began peeling out of it, with Polina *tsk-tsk*ing, but helping. "Get me a dress and cloak."

"The middle of the night, Majesty . . ."

"Do it, you old fool." The emotions of the dream clung to her. Only one thing helped on nights like this. Evgeny Feodorovich. He would help her banish the dream, the power of the stinking soldiers, what they did, over and over.

She was halfway out the back door of the chalet before Polina had found her own cloak and rushed up, preparing to accompany her. Irina turned to Polina. "No. I go alone."

"But Majesty, the—"

"—the middle of the night. Yes, yes, so you have said. Stay with Kolya." Polina had been the chambermaid to her aunt, the Grand Duchess Tatiana Nazarova, and for Aunt Tanya's sake— she who had starved to death in a Bolshevik prison—Irina had taken on Polina. Another link to the times before. Some days she wished that the nagging creature had never found her way to Germany.

She emerged into the garden, cold and smelling of wet earth. By the sallow light of the quarter moon she padded her way past the frost-blackened vegetable garden with its small storage shed, the bird feeder on its pole, crusted with snow. Thirty meters farther on, the gun emplacements with machine guns aimed at the road. In the plaza, a sentry recognized her, coming to attention. The guards had seen her take this path before, of a night, the path to the cabins.

The cold swirled around her, under her gown and cloak,

down her neck, but she relished it. Holy Mother of Christ, how she abhorred confinement and the deathly, gagging heat.

Up the rise of the little path she saw smoke drifting from Evgeny's chimney.

He waited for her under the deeply sloping eaves of his front door. Her heart lifted to see, once again, how he *foresaw* things; that she was approaching at this dark hour. She joined him at the little porch.

"You knew."

"As always, Irinuska." Evgeny's gnarled hand pushed open the door, and they entered. A fire groaned and spit in the fireplace. It was a stark and simple cabin by her standards, but they had lived in filth and hovel and muddy field. This was like a palace to him.

Throwing off her cloak, she sat in the chair he reserved for her.

He brought tea laced with vodka and placed the steaming cup in her hand. Taking nothing himself, he sat in the wingback chair, facing her. He wore the formal dress of the old days, with waistcoat, a jacket with broad lapels, and a cravat. "No one sleeps tonight," he said.

"What, no one?" She smiled, warming to his presence, to the beloved sound of Russian words.

He looked up to the rafters, squinting. His voice was very soft. "Owls and mice. Can you hear them flapping? Skittering?"

She hoped he was not going to have one of his spells, where he saw impossible things, or spoke of true things, but in riddles. "Is this what you hear, Evgeny Feodorovich? Do you hear owls?"

"*Da*, Irinuska. The owl. He sweeps down, his shadow falling across the prey below. On the staircase."

What staircase? What owl? She let it pass. If it was important, he would speak of owls again.

He sat back, gazing at her, scratching his white beard. The firelight made deep shadows of his face, but she did not need to see his features, so familiar they were to her.

Evgeny Feodorovich had been her protector through the fallen days, the fallen years. He had foreseen when the soldiers would come, and so they had slipped away just ahead of them. He had safely led her from one hovel to the next, one sunken, stinking village to the next, one starved farmyard to the next, and on through nine winters of Russia. Except once. His vision was not perfect.

Still, in those days he had protected her with his forward vision. Now she no longer needed protection from the Reds, but merely—oh, merely!—a glimpse of a happy future. Or if her future could not be happy, then Kolya's future. So that she could sleep.

"Tell me something, Evgeny. Something of comfort." Something that would expunge memory that had clung to her over the years: the sight of ugly faces rocking over her, rocking . . . "If you do not, I cannot sleep. I think of the fallen days. And the . . ."

"Yes. The pillow."

She held his gaze. He knew how it was with her.

"On Saturday, you said . . ."

He stood, suddenly agitated. "I say what I see! And then it is gone." He paced the room, throwing open the curtains and peering out. "I cannot remember what I say, and I cannot repeat for you like a schoolmaster."

"But you do remember some things you have seen. You do."

He darted a look into the shadowy corners, his brow furrowing deeply. "They scratch and scramble. The mice. Dirty, scrambling things."

Ah, Evgeny, my friend. It was sad to see his mind in this

condition. The doctors said it was a dotage of the very old, senility. True, he was eighty-six years old, but it was terrible to see his sharp mind so enfeebled. Every time they had a good conversation, she hoped it meant he had regained his faculties, but he faded in and out. She sighed. "And that is all you have to say, about mice and owls?"

"It is everything. The owl looking down from his perch, he will stoop and kill. But the tsarevich—"

"Kolya?" She leaned forward. She must know if he saw Kolya's future. "Yes, Evgeny. The tsarevich?"

A knock at the door.

"My son . . . ," she pleaded. "What do you see?"

Evgeny's eyes rolled far up, his eyelids fluttering with the effort of foretelling. "He is there. He takes his prey."

What did he mean? "Kolya is victorious?"

The knock again.

Evgeny snarled, "Open the door. Maybe it is the old tsar, come to take away your crown."

Oh, that he would say such a thing to her. But it was not Evgeny at his best. "Enter!" Irina called.

The door opened; Stefan stood on the threshold. "Forgive me if I intrude, Your Majesty."

"Stefan," Irina said, relieved to see her adjutant, now that Evgeny had turned cruel. She rose.

Evgeny muttered, "Stefan is not his name. A man should have his own name."

She gathered her cloak and Stefan came forward to put it around her shoulders. "Evgeny Feodorovich is tired," she said. "We shall leave him."

Stefan nodded a bow and led her from the room. At the little stoop, the cold wrapped her in a numbing embrace and she drew up the hood of her cloak. As they walked down the path with its cabins and stunted fir trees, Evgeny threw open his door and shouted after them. "The owl!"

Yes, I hear you, my friend. The owl.

She and Stefan walked in silence toward the plaza. His cane thunked on the icy pavement with every step, reminding her that she should not have been the cause of this long walk to the cabins. Even after seven months, his leg was still healing.

"Evgeny Feodorovich does not like your name," Irina said.

"It only matters that you prefer it."

She looked up at his remarkable profile. "I like *Stefan*. It is more Russian."

"It is good that one of the names my parents gave me pleases you."

He pleased her on many levels. On all levels, except one. For his service, she had bestowed on him an honorary knighthood, the Order of Stanislaw, which Hitler allowed. Some in Hitler's service did not like the trappings of nobility. It mattered only to be loyal to the Führer. But blood did matter. It was why she was the successor to the Russian throne, and after her, Nikolai. She did not know the name of her son's father, one of the Cossack brigands who had forced her, but she had named Nikolai for the old tsar. Her blood made him royal.

"I did not think you were here, Stefan. You had gone to Berlin."

"I arrived late and could not pay my respects."

"You did not find her?"

"No."

The street-fighter woman who had booby-trapped his motor vehicle. And oh, his terrible injury. Worse, it was not even in service, in battle, but at the hands of a Jew. It could not go unavenged.

In the gaslit plaza, they walked past the booth that formed the entrance to the lift in its five-hundred-foot shaft. Guards at this post saluted them.

They made their way through the frost-silvered garden. At the door to the chalet, she turned to bid him goodnight. She wanted to talk longer with Stefan, but it was very late to invite him inside.

Still, she lingered. In the moonlight his skin was alabaster. In the magical light, the quiet midnight, she let herself ask, "Have you ever been in love?"

"No, Your Majesty."

"Speak to your Irinuska. You can tell me your heart."

He was still as a statue. So formal, her Stefan.

"Perhaps once."

She made herself smile, but her heart flared with envy. He had once loved someone. Why, why, had she asked? She could not have him, could not touch him, so he should be free to love another.

But there it was. Once he had loved someone. The knowledge curled in on itself, settling in her heart like a small, dark stone.

13

THE NOLLENDORFPLATZ, BERLIN

SATURDAY, NOVEMBER 28. Kim stepped off the electric tramway. A heavy fog rolled through the plaza, smearing the light from the gas lamps into tufted halos. It had been no problem to find her way to the Nollendorfplatz, for she did love transit timetables, even German ones.

It was nine on a night when Alex had left for a function, and she was hunting down a woman who might be a criminal, one who offered information in return for asylum. That was the opening gambit, and Kim wanted to play out the hand. The next step, Hannah Linz had said, was to place a calling card in a mailbox, signifying *Yes, we can talk.*

The coat she wore, gray wool with a mink collar, was one she had found in a household armoire. It was made for a larger woman, the one in the painting, she suspected, but it looked fine if she let it swing open. At one level it didn't seem right to be wearing it, but in the service of Nazi resistance, she felt it would be approved. The blue velvet beret finished her disguise, not that it would throw off the SS if they were interested in her. Her hunch was that Captain Nagel had been no more suspicious of her than he was of everyone. He had offered her a ride to shake loose any motivation she might have for befriending his wife.

Nonetheless, she watched for a tail, possibly Gestapo agents in plain clothes. The Gestapo, the SS—all under Heinrich Himmler—each feeding the objectives of the other like the family of outlaws they were. She reminded herself that despite their growing reputation, the Gestapo was not the omnipotent secret force some believed. Underfunded, spread thin, they could not be everywhere. They targeted their brutality, relying on private citizens to provide denunciations. Surely there was no one in Berlin who could denounce *her*.

Nevertheless, a look in a shop window to check out the reflections from the street, to memorize clothing, faces.

Leaving the plaza, she headed for a side street lined with imposing apartment blocks. When she got to the address on Hannah Linz's card she found herself in front of a cabaret. A short flight of stairs led to a shallow apron of cement. The address stenciled on the grimy window: Café Unten, or Café Below. Music pulsed from the club, an easy jazz mixed with laughter from within.

Couples lounged on the steps and leaned against the wrought-iron fence along the pavement, sipping cocktails brought from inside, their coats open to a chill breeze. A few steps away from the nightclub, complete darkness; there, a couple embraced.

While reconnoitering, she used a compact to apply her lipstick and pretended to watch for a car. After a few moments she descended the stairs, pushing through the crowd and into Café

Unten. The mailboxes would be inside the door, if she even had the right place.

The entryway gave directly onto a deep room with a bar along one side. Beyond were tables and a dance floor, with the band just out of view. She stopped at the door, taking stock of the place, noting dapper men with rolled-up sleeves, women in casual dresses waving cigarettes in holders as they talked—a busy bar flanked by a long mirror. But no mailboxes. When she turned to leave, she bumped against someone.

"Oh, sorry!" she said.

A barrel-chested young man with slicked-back hair smiled cheerfully. "If he's stood you up, would you like to dance?" English with a German accent. "I noticed you waiting outside, and now here you are."

Entirely too much interest. "No thanks, I'm meeting someone." She smiled and turned to the door.

Out front on the below-grade cement entryway, she noticed for the first time that there were two sides of the building, a feature she had missed from the crowded street level. She walked toward the darker part of the frontage where she found another door, perhaps leading to apartments. The door opened to her push. She was in a tight hallway with a staircase leading up, and though the entryway was illuminated merely by a distant wall lamp, she made out a line of mailboxes. Running her hand along the row, she found that they had labels pasted on, impossible to read in the semidark. She patted them and found a smooth one without a label.

She dropped her card in the slot. It was not the card her contact was hoping for—Alex's—but it might be the one she needed. Of course, the head office had warned her off Hannah Linz. But they didn't know about Captain Nagel's *spill*, so she reasoned she must reevaluate her instructions.

On the fog-shrouded street once more, she headed back toward the Nollendorfplatz, at this distance a mere blur, as though it were a fathom under water.

Someone hailed her from behind. "You are leaving?"

She turned. The man who had spoken to her in the cabaret caught up with her. "We have both been jilted, I think," he said in English. He cocked his head. "We might commiserate."

"In there, how did you know I spoke English?"

"Ah. You said 'sorry' when you stepped on my foot, not *'Entschuldigung.'"*

The sound of accelerating cars. She looked up to find several motorcars converging on the club from different directions.

"Herrgott noch mal, die Gestapo," her companion said, throwing his cigarette down and watching as the doors flew open and men in leather overcoats charged out, brandishing guns and shouting for people to assemble.

Here, at the edge of the proceedings, in the masking fog, she quickly ran through her options. Stay, reveal her identity, have the Gestapo contact the embassy to say that they regretted picking her up. It would scream amateur to Duncan and the station. And if they were looking for Hannah Linz . . . that was a connection she did not wish to establish, no matter how tenuous.

Several of the agents had run down the steps toward the cabaret; others remained on the street. The music halted and loud voices could be heard from within. She began backing off.

"Not a good idea," the young man said. "There will be trouble if you leave."

An imposing figure emerged from one of the motorcars and scanned the crowd. An SS uniform.

"That one might be an *empath,*" her companion murmured.

"They bring them along sometimes, to see who is lying. It will not be us, so do not worry."

That rather settled it.

The Gestapo herded people onto the pavement from the café and lined them up against the fence. In the ensuing confusion and with dozens of people milling about, Kim turned and walked away.

No orders to stop. She crossed the street, daring a look back.

People stood along the iron fence as the man in an SS uniform stopped at each person. If he had *hyperempathy* she did not want to fall under his gaze. He couldn't read her mind, but he would certainly pick up on her acute nervousness.

From behind came a shout, *"Anhalten!"* Halt.

She ran. In an instant, she was committed. Her hope: to reach the corner where she would turn out of view . . .

"Anhalten!" A gunshot rang out, sending shards of concrete off the building next to her.

God, they were shooting at her. Her nerves screaming alarm, she rounded the corner. A darkened street, the fog black and dense. Only seconds to find a hiding place. Stairs led to apartment stoops, but no good; the doors might be locked. Seeing a walkway between two buildings, she charged down it. More shouting from around the corner.

She was in a fenced backyard. Oh, for her safe flat in the Alexanderplatz! Thin light from the apartment block windows revealed a few outbuildings. She raced past them, her high heels stabbing into the wet ground, catching. A gate loomed before her. She fumbled with the latch and slipped into a lane. The night was coal black, the lane barely visible, but she ran, breath straining, seeking cover with blind determination. Coming to an unfenced wooded area, she charged into it, throwing herself into the bracken.

A nearby sound brought a spike of terror to her chest. Her hands found a wire fence. Clucking. A chicken coop. As she listened for pursuit, she rested her head against the fence, breathing in the harsh smell of slime, mud, and droppings.

Quiet enveloped her, punctuated by low clucking. She removed her hat, shoving it into the cold, wet grass.

In mud, in dismay, she crouched, quietly stunned that she had run from the Gestapo. At last she leaned back from the wire mesh. Wiping the sweat from her face, she found round divots imprinted on her forehead.

The soft crunch of gravel beneath a boot. From the alley. She crouched lower. A shadow walked the lane, someone in a long coat. He stopped. Had he heard something? The beam of a flashlight fell in her direction, lighting up, three feet away from her, a startled chicken with a red comb and black glassy eyes. Her heart thrummed, taking over her chest, driving out breath.

Then the cone of light shifted away, probing the empty lot. It moved on down the lane. She listened for others to come. How many had followed her? Her leg began to cramp; she endured it. Nerves flared down her shoulders, around her belly, lighting up her senses so that she jerked at every sound: a dog barking far away. The hens cooing softly.

After some minutes, she could bear the cramp in her leg no longer and carefully stretched out her foot in front of her. At times she heard voices on a nearby street, but whether they were partiers or police, she could not tell.

The night grew long, and at last the cold drove away her abject fear; she debated trying to leave. By dawn she would be exposed anyway. Why had the secret police come to the nightclub? They could not have known she would be there; bad luck, that was all.

Time to leave. If they found her, she would surrender, invoke diplomatic status. It would be all right. On her hands and knees, she buried the beret behind the cage. Then, creeping to the lane, she sat on a cement block and scraped mud from her shoes with fallen leaves.

She hailed a cab. Given the cloak of fog, she thought she looked almost respectable.

But she could not enter Number 44 so filthy. Outside the entrance she removed her shoes, hoping that no one was awake, or if they were, that they would think she had removed her shoes to be quiet.

Inside, no one stirred. She made her way to the kitchen waste bin, where she removed a layer of garbage and placed her shoes inside, covering them with food scraps. She stood a long time at the sink washing her muddy hands. A dark stream trailed into the basin. She savored the warm water, thinking of the gunshot. They had fired at her. The sound of exploding stone.

Once in bed—with neither Alex nor Bibi roused—she ran the scene of Café Unten over in her mind several times before plunging into sleep.

In the morning she called Rachel.

"Would you mind terribly telling my husband, if he asks, that we were together last night? I know how this sounds. Please say no if you'd rather not."

"Oh my. This does sound interesting. Where shall I say we were?"

"How about the Marktcafe on the Spree? Drinks. From 9:00 to 11:00 or so." She would use Rachel as an alibi with Alex if he knew she'd been out very late. But not with the Gestapo, if they came. She wouldn't endanger Rachel.

"Will Alex call me?"

"Probably not. But if he does."

"I hope you had a good time."

She felt a wild laugh welling up and suppressed it. "I'll tell you sometime."

"No, don't." A pause. "Take care, Elaine. Berlin makes us all a little mad."

That afternoon, while she was reading in her bedroom, Alex came in, failing to knock. Carrying a sack.

He closed the door behind him. "We found your shoes in the garbage."

"Well, you're welcome to them, they're quite spoiled. And who is 'we'?"

"Kim. What's going on?"

She put a finger to her lips. He had used the wrong name.

His annoyance showed. "The shoes aren't spoiled. They're destroyed." He dumped the sack at her feet and sat down on the chaise longue opposite her.

"Rachel and I were at a bar on the river having drinks last night. I thought the ground was more solid along the bank. Damned foggy."

"I see." He looked at the vase of flowers. Today, chrysanthemums. "There was an incident last night down on the Nollendorfplatz. The police are looking for an American woman in a fur-trimmed coat."

Damn. That young man had blabbed, describing her.

"I didn't know you were so close to the German police."

"Gestapo, actually."

"Same question. And if you think the woman was me, I don't have a fur-trimmed coat. Honestly, Alex, what is the problem?"

"It was in the paper this afternoon, a raid on a nightclub

known to have connections to Jews. Shots were fired. You came home at 3:00 AM."

She slammed her book down. "You don't—"

"And I found the coat."

All right, then. She stood up, adopting the arch attitude that was the only way to deal with a man like this. "I don't report to you, and I'm not married to you."

He stood up, facing off with her. "Whatever you're up to, I don't need to know. But you're making a hash of it. If it's about this Linz person, you should know that she's a member of the Oberman Group, the one that's been assassinating Nazi officials for the past year. You cannot drag me or the embassy into this."

"You're a bit cozy with the Nazis, Alex. Just how important is this bond repayment deal you've got in the works? How nice do we all have to be?"

"It's my job to be cozy with them." He drew a stem out of the vase, popped the bloom off the top, and stuck it in his jacket buttonhole.

Looking at him, nattily dressed, a perfect shave, steady composure, she struggled to contain her aversion. But he had the ear of the embassy, which was under the Foreign Office, the same as SIS. He could do damage if he spoke against her. His boss already didn't like the clandestine arrangement of them living together as man and wife.

She softened her tone. "I suppose it is your job. But you must let me do mine—as long as I don't harm our standing in Berlin."

A beat while he gazed at her. "They *shot* at you."

"But they didn't catch me." She tried out a small smile. "*You* caught me. And now I think someone in the household is reporting on me." She let her face show some amusement. "I'm surrounded by spies." In fact, who had dug out her shoes and given them to Alex, or had he gone rummaging on his own?

He made a silent laugh. Picking up the sack of shoes he said, "Shall I toss these for you?"

"Please." He headed to the door. "And Alex?" He turned back to her. "I do understand your position. Let's try to get on, shall we?"

A mollified smile. "For better or worse," he said with easy irony.

14

TUESDAY, DECEMBER 1. The steward placed two whiskies on the side table and retreated, leaving Julian and the chief of SIS alone in the billiard room. The rain had turned to sleet, so the fire in the fireplace was cheery. If it hadn't been for the damned letter.

They occupied facing chairs, close to the small blaze in the fireplace. Julian finished reading the letter, not bothering to disguise his annoyance. He handed it back to E.

"So, Kim has come to the attention of the Foreign Office."

"I'm afraid she has."

To Julian's chagrin, Sir Eric Phipps had written to the permanent under secretary of the Foreign Office, Robert Vansittart, complaining about an episode involving the purported wife of the second secretary for trade assigned to Berlin. If Phipps was going to meddle, he should have spoken with E. True enough, Kim's escapade was a bit of a blunder, but since she hadn't been caught, it did not exactly constitute a diplomatic incident.

E tapped his finger on the leather chair arm, keeping his counsel. The spacious room was seldom used for billiards. It had become his private drawing room when messengers arrived from Broadway. He was never joined by other club members at this spot in front of the fireplace. In the whole history of SIS, though several staff members at White's knew E's clandestine role, there had never been a hint of gossip about him.

"Alex Reed's fingerprints are on this one," Julian said. "He was in a position to know she'd been out that night. Phipps's mention of the situation jeopardizing the bond repayment talks rather clinches it. That's Reed's main assignment. They're interfering in our operations. Damned awkward."

"That's one issue," E said, "and I'll deal with it. But she almost blew her cover." He sipped his whisky as pellets of sleet hit the windows fronting St. James's Street. "In the first month of her posting."

And almost got herself killed, Julian mused. Which *would* have been an incident—and broken his heart. "I've asked for a report on this from the station. Right now it's all secondhand." It had better not be true that at a routine Gestapo roundup, Kim had bolted and refused to stop at shouted orders. He could only hope that she hadn't panicked like that.

E folded the letter and slipped it into the folder on the table containing the day's correspondence. "Whatever the circumstances, going forward she must use discretion. I believe she was to be our *spill* Talent at diplomatic functions. Now she's had a run-in with the secret police and wanted to yank that bombing suspect out of Berlin."

Julian had to grant the point. "She does get the bit between her teeth."

In the ensuing silence, the subject ripened.

Perhaps the SIS chief, like Julian, was thinking of services rendered by Kim in the not-too-distant past. How she had foiled the notorious Dutchman on a murder spree that had panicked the country. And the Storm Way operation that could have brought war—and defeat—to British soil, had it not been for his daughter following her exquisite instincts.

But now that Vansittart was involved, there was the political aspect to consider.

E fixed him with a let's wrap it up stare. "What do you recommend?"

"Urge her to tread carefully, but let her follow through. It's rather hard to direct things from London." She reported to him through the Berlin station, and it was best to keep it that way. "I suspect she's got intel that she didn't have time to share."

"So she used her initiative." The way E said it, it was not a compliment.

"It cuts both ways, chief." Initiative did. His Majesty's Government had never approved of initiative, but in the secret service, with communications suppressed for the sake of covert operations, one sometimes had to use best judgment.

"You don't suppose she's letting the Jewish problem influence her, do you?"

"No reason to think so. She's got ahold of this Monarch code word and believes it's worth pursuing."

"Are we hearing Monarch from any of our people?"

"No." Julian had to admit they had not, but he was still waiting for answers to the questionnaire he'd sent to their agents in the field. "Still, it might be our target military op. It's her job to listen for such things."

"And not go chasing after Jewish refugees."

Julian wished he had not brought up what people too easily called "the Jewish problem." The comment smacked of anti-Semitism. He'd heard worse among his class, of course, but it was unworthy of his boss.

That aside, it would indeed be like Kim to step in for the underdog. He had urged her not to be led by her heart. Logic and instinct, but not sentiment. He supposed she had rather resented the advice, but there it was, and she had better conform.

With a soft thunk, a log shifted in the fireplace.

"All right," E said, "she goes forward." He reached for his folder, signaling the meeting was over. "I trust the FO undersecretary will be hearing no more of Sparrow."

Vansittart knew her as "Sparrow," her code name in the files, in the reports. He was already more than aware of her; the service had polished the reports until she shone. But the fact was, Sparrow could be impulsive.

Whitehall hated that. Except when it worked.

WERTHEIM'S DEPARTMENT STORE, BERLIN

TUESDAY, DECEMBER 1. In the women's lavatory on the fourth floor, Kim checked her watch: 10:21 AM. She paced the empty room, wondering how Berlin station had managed to close the women's restroom on this floor of Germany's biggest department store. A uniformed janitor—doubtless working for Berlin station—manned a mop and pail just outside the closed door. When she'd arrived, he'd nodded at her, letting her pass. He'd make sure the public didn't come in.

She reapplied her lipstick. Checked her Helbros watch again. 10:24.

The door opened and Duncan entered. The same dark wool coat and the homburg in his hand. He gazed at her for a moment. "No worse for the wear? Your little run-in at Café Unten?"

A surprise that he knew. "I was going to tell you about it, but I see someone has saved me the trouble."

"Phipps put a report in the diplomatic bag."

God. Straight to the Foreign Office. So this was Alex's idea of getting along. The conniving bastard. "Well, he wasn't there, so I can't imagine what sort of report it was."

"Let's see. A nightclub owned by Menachem Garran, a Jew. The Gestapo showed up as they sometimes do, and you were outside the club. Instead of identifying yourself as the wife of a diplomat, you ran. Drew fire. Hid near the Nollendorfplatz for a couple hours and shook them off."

She was going to explain the redeeming details—surely there were some—when he said, "I'm glad you got yourself clear on that one."

A pause while she adjusted her attitude. Not the lecture she had expected. "Yes. Thank you." She went on. "There's another development. I had an interview of sorts with the SS Tuesday night."

He raised an eyebrow.

"Captain Rikard Nagel."

The door of the lavatory rattled. A murmured conversation, retreating steps.

Without taking note of the interruption, Duncan said, "Nagel is one of Göring's bodyguards."

"Is he? Well, my friend Rachel Flynn of the *Chicago Daily News* and I were at the Die Toskana in the Steglitz-Zehlendorf district when I left without her and ended up having to accept Nagel's offer of a ride home." She went on to explain his strange fixation on her supposed relationship with his wife and his attempt to rattle her.

Duncan mulled this over. "Why is he sniffing around you?"

"Trying to shake something loose?"

"Elaine. The head office wants you to use the utmost discretion." That would be Julian and whoever he reported to. "You do understand."

"I do." She paused. "Without sacrificing opportunities."

The statement simmered between them for a few moments. He saw that she meant to push against constraints. Push against *him*, if need be. Poor fellow. He not only had a new agent to break in, but it was a woman. She was sure it galled him.

"Everyone has their limits," he said, repeating something he had said before.

"I suppose. But I've always found most people quit too soon." And wasn't it true? Hadn't Owen Cherwell backed away from the breach? Hadn't the *Philadelphia Inquirer* lost courage when her investigative journalism crossed the wrong people? And hadn't the brass at the head of SIS let a peer of the realm lengthen his killing spree last summer when they feared the king's displeasure?

He moved on. "What happened with Nagel, then?"

She explained how she felt he had *spilled* the word *monarch* to her, the same word that Hannah Linz had offered intelligence on. *His life in service to the monarch.* How Nagel denied using the term, perhaps very strongly chagrined that he had.

"Well, watch out for that one. We've suspected for some time that he's a *hypercognition* Talent."

That was interesting. A man who did not forget details. Who could draw conclusions based on seemingly unrelated facts. It did fit with some of the things he had said that night. Kim had to wonder if it had driven him mad, to always question if his version of things had any connection to reality. Because she did think him mentally unbalanced.

"So," Duncan summarized, "you want to drop your cover and debrief Linz."

"Yes."

"You can't offer her asylum."

"If she's able to convince us she has worthwhile intel, perhaps something *can* be on offer."

"You're moving fast." He looked pasty in the fluorescent lighting, as though he spent most of his time at a desk without natural light. His bright eyes, the only lively aspect of him, watching her, evaluating. His two-fingered left hand grasping his homburg.

"I want to follow up. There's no point in waiting."

He nodded. "All right."

A beat. That was it, then. Alex hadn't been able to sandbag her after all.

Duncan asked, "How will they contact you?"

"I was at Café Unten to put my card at a drop, a signal to proceed."

He paused a moment, considering. "If you get caught, you've got a plausible story. The Linz woman went to the embassy, and having been turned down for extraction, she went to the wife. You took pity and agreed to hear her tale. Poor judgment, husband will be furious, that sort of thing." He shrugged. "If she blows your cover under interrogation, the embassy has deniability. You were meddling, etcetera. Deny everything, of course."

She thought Rikard Nagel would easily see through such an act, but she smiled at Duncan, going along with it.

"One thing, Duncan. Who got the house on the Tiergarten-strasse for us?"

"The embassy handles placements."

"It belonged to a Jewish family who were driven out."

"That's not our problem, is it?"

Kim shook her head in exasperation. "What is going on in this country?"

"They're going to extremes. It'll settle down. Anyway. Going forward, I want you to be careful. Remember: flowers in the window if you need it."

He went to the lavatory door, then turned. "You're certainly keen on your job. Why?"

It was an obvious question. Wasn't he keen on his? Was it worth doing or wasn't it? He gazed steadily at her, waiting.

"Because it matters."

Still the appraising stare.

"Because I hear things." Oh yes. Little pings from the deeper world, the world we didn't know much about. That inner world that people hid, but that followed them everywhere like a shadow following a skater under the ice. "I hear things," she repeated.

A rueful smile, as though he pitied her. "I suppose you do." Duncan wasn't used to an agent with the *spill*, an agent who had to rely on intuition when dealing with *spills*. He was a bit at sea with handling her, that was obvious.

He slipped out the door.

She reapplied her lipstick—God, what would a female spy do without lipstick?—and waited ten minutes until a woman entered with a pram and a toddler in tow.

Kim smiled at the family and went shopping.

PART II

A TASTE FOR BLOOD

15

A SILVER SMITH ON THE KURFÜRSTENDAMM

SUNDAY, DECEMBER 6. On the boulevard Kurfürsten-damm, Kim entered the small shop specializing in silver and bronze. It was 11:15 AM. She spent a few minutes examining engraved tureens and antique tea trays. At 11:20, as instructed, she went out the back door. Here, a quiet side street with ornate villas. Skeletons of street trees poked through the fog.

A car approached, stopped. Someone leaned over from the inside and pushed open the door.

"Mrs. Reed. Hannah sent me."

She entered, settling herself next to a man—really little more than a boy—with a patchy goatee. His suit, a size too large for his thin frame. As she closed the door behind her, the driver slipped into the stream of traffic.

"If you would sit on the floor?"

She did. Next to her, now at eye level on the seat, was a brimmed hat and dusty-smelling scarf.

They drove in silence for ten or fifteen minutes, at last entering a cramped neighborhood of tenement buildings, visible from her perspective from the car floor. A stew of noises reached her: children shouting, peddlers calling out wares, goats bleating.

"Put on the hat and scarf. Then sit up, please."

They came to a stop, and she was ushered out of the car and across the pavement. She had time to see food markets, an outdoor café with bicycles stacked against ancient brick walls, a wooden wagon pulled by draft horses, delivery men unloading barrels from it. They passed through a narrow, arched entryway into a courtyard surrounded by leaning five-story tenements. The square yard, though stuffed with a wintry fog, was crowded with children, women hanging wash, old men smoking, and the sound of pigs groveling and snorting for food. It was a Berlin she hadn't seen before—more like a Pittsburgh slum than the shining rival to Vienna and Paris or, in Berlin, the Mitte district, or the Kurfürstendamm. She doubted the sun ever hit the paving stones here, even when there *was* sun.

The young man with the goatee led her to a blistered door. They entered. Inside, the smell of pipe tobacco and boiled onions. Somewhere, a baby wailed.

They passed doors behind which she heard the sounds of a sewing machine, loud voices, pots clattering. At the end of the corridor, a door led to another hall, giving the impression that one could travel around the courtyard through the various buildings without having to go outside, a warren where one could escape in case of denunciation or dragnet.

At one of the doors, her escort knocked once and twice more, then gestured her through. She found herself in a darkened room, smelling of floor wax and machine oil. A man sat behind a small table as though ready to conduct an employment interview. Her guide took up a position by the door.

The man she faced gestured her to a chair. "I am Franz," he said in English. Dark curly hair, a homespun sweater. "And I call you?"

"Elaine." She removed her hat and scarf, setting them aside.

"So, on first-name terms already." His sarcasm barely under control.

He tapped out a cigarette, offering her one. She declined and he struck a match, lighting his own. Blowing out a stream of smoke, he leaned over to pick up a babushka-size scarf from the table. He tossed it to her. "Wear this over your head when you leave."

"Am I leaving?"

"Eventually."

She settled the scarf in her lap. "I was told I would be meeting Hannah Linz."

"And I was told I would be meeting Mr. Reed."

"My husband isn't interested. So you're left with me."

He watched her for a few moments. "Why should we wish to speak to Mr. Reed's wife?"

She looked toward the door. "Could your associate leave us for a moment?"

Franz smirked, perhaps at her use of the word *associate*. He nodded the boy out of the room.

When he had gone she said, "You will want to speak to me because I work for Britain's intelligence service."

Franz snorted. "They are all spies at the embassy." He was not a man to easily admit there were things he didn't already know.

"Actually, the embassy prefers to keep its hands clean."

"And you are offering asylum? Without that, the meeting

is over." He leaned back in his chair with a measure of grace, an almost aristocratic air.

"To get Hannah out, I need something to convince my superiors that this operation that Hannah mentioned, Monarch, is of interest. What it is. Why it might be important to my country."

"So you have given up your cover for something that may have no value?"

Exactly her gamble. She plunged on. "I've heard the word *monarch* again from an SS officer whom my husband and I know socially." She took a moment to be sure she had his complete attention. "I have the Talent of the *spill.*"

He sat back as though afraid he would himself be the victim of her Talent. "Do you now? What is your rating?"

"6."

"Exactly 6?"

"It's the British scale. We leave the finer calibrations to you Germans."

A long pause as he digested this. "You seem to know a bit about Talents."

"Well, I would, wouldn't I? But if we're done sparring, kindly tell me whether you are going to trust me or not. I've risked my cover, so I'd like to know."

A long drag on his cigarette as he regarded her. Then he went to the door. She heard: *"Bringen Sie Hannah hier runter."*

So she had passed muster. She had not expected a gatekeeper and wondered at how much they protected Hannah.

Outside, the clang of a trolley car. In the distance, an organ grinder. She had no idea where she was. Perhaps Prenzlauer Berg. But she did not feel uneasy. Franz looked more like a university student than a revolutionary, one who had been chased and harried, maybe jailed. The existence of the Oberman Group was reassuring. Someone was organizing against the Nazis. The Office had not briefed her on the group or mentioned the possibility that there were partisan organizations, nor that one of them was run by Jews. Perhaps they were Communists as well—something that Alex had hinted at—an aspect that was likely to cause the service to dismiss them. HMG was far more alarmed by the Soviets than the Nazis.

At a sound, she turned to find Hannah Linz standing at the door.

"For the past year we've been intercepting foreign Talents who come into Germany." Hannah sat backward on the chair, leaning on the high back. She looked much younger without lipstick and the shiny dress. In fact, Kim guessed her to be not far past twenty. Her hair lay matted against her head, a fiery cap.

"These Talents," Hannah went on, "they are recruits for the Nazis."

Kim was disappointed. "We are all recruiting." In Britain's case, haphazardly, it was true.

"But you are not recruiting like the Nazis. We have a friend inside. In the SS. He knows who is coming through Berlin to join this operation, which I have told you is called Monarch. They are highly rated Talents. *Suggestion, attraction, trauma view, precognition, hyperempathy, darkening,* and so on. All rated at least 7."

Kim remained silent, hoping there was more.

Hannah flicked a look at Franz. He nodded. So he was the one in charge.

"What I was going to tell your husband is that the cadre of Talents is just the first stage. Every country has Talents, yes. But every country does not have Irina."

"Irina?"

"Irina Dimitrievna Annakova," Franz interjected. "She has a major gift that will change everything." He had been leaning against the table, and now he went to the room's only window, parting the curtains just enough. He turned back to her. "She can optimize people."

Kim didn't like where this was going, not at all. "Go on."

Hannah lowered her voice. "She is one who can remove barriers to reinforce a Talent. The Nazi doctors, they think that all Talents lie within a range of dormancy, buried at different levels in individuals. All have potential to be great. This is what Irina Annakova proves when she enables purification. As they call it."

A deeper quiet fell upon the room. Kim tried to absorb this unwelcome news. "Your man in the SS is risking everything to work with you. Who is he?"

Franz and Hannah exchanged looks. She answered, "We call him Tannhäuser."

"How highly placed is he?"

"High enough. High enough to know—"

Franz interrupted, "—that her *purification* works fiendishly well." He turned back to Hannah. *Hurry up.*

"So then," Hannah said, "this is Monarch. A person who can augment the Talent of any person she embraces. The *catalysis* Talent."

A new Talent. Kim tried to work it out. "People she embraces . . ."

"Anyone she makes contact with for long enough. It is not a Talent one can turn on or off. It is always in her touch."

Kim tried to imagine what it would be like to live with a Talent like this. The ability was not volitional; it must be a harsh sentence to live under. But surely such an ability would be well documented by now. "If there is such a Talent, we would have heard of it, or guessed at it. Over time, high ratings wouldn't be rare."

Franz snapped, "Let her finish." A noise from the courtyard, a shout. He checked again. They were like hares in the woods, ears primed, distrustful, always moving.

Hannah went on. "It isn't known because *catalysis* Talents die young. It is the most damning ability in the list. You give your strength to others, and over time it takes your own. As well, the uplift is temporary. One must be augmented again for it to last. So if such a Talent dies young, and the effect on other Talents is temporary . . ." She shrugged. "No one takes note. Or if they do, they do not ascribe it to the right reason."

"How do you come to have all these details about *catalysis* if the Talents die off so fast?"

Hannah lit a cigarette and blew a stream of smoke out the side of her mouth. "I have told you. Tannhäuser. He has been part of Monarch from the start."

Kim chewed on this. "But can the Nazis be certain they die young? They have only this one person . . . and she is still alive."

"Look," Hannah said as though Kim were not quite getting it. "Ever since Annakova came to them, they have been combing for information: old records, medical references that might point to case studies of *catalysts*. They found a rare few, maybe not always confirmed, but suggesting patterns in the progression of a potential *catalyst*'s condition. Even my father, who was a Talent researcher at the University of Cologne, tracked down at least one other case. He heard a rumor of the ability and followed up with a colleague. Knowledge exists here and there, but the Nazis know the most about the Progeny."

"Progeny?"

"*Nachkommenschaft.* The official name. For those *Nachkommen* in the military, you will see the insignia. The vulture on the collar."

She had indeed seen it. On Rikard Nagel, he of the *hypercognition* Talent. So, if he was purified to a high-enough level . . . perhaps he *did* know, *did* intuit, that she was a spy. It could mean she was under surveillance. Nerves flared on her skin.

"Monarch's purpose," Hannah said, "is to send the *Nachkommenschaft* into Europe. To infiltrate, control. Terrorize. Individual *Nachkomme* who can *mesmerize* leaders, cabinets; who can *attract* and *compel* newspaper editors, religious leaders. Receive *spills* from military general staff. Where persuasion fails, they slay and torture. And *Nachkommin*, women, as well."

The infiltration of Europe, Kim thought with dismay. Oh yes, London would be interested.

"Already in Germany," Hannah went on, "there is a reign of physical and spiritual terror, beyond the Gestapo and the usual tyranny."

"Spiritual terror?"

Hannah leaned forward, flicking the ash of her cigarette on the floor. "You have read *Mein Kampf*? If people are steeped in fear, they will not act. As you see all around you. Hitler knows this very well. So the *Nachkommenschaft* enforce loyalty and obedience among the people by torture and murder.

Kim's mind was racing. "So then, after the *Nachkommenschaft* are all in place . . ."

"The *Wehrmacht* has information, collaborators, correct propaganda. The Party has control of political leaders and to some extent, the people themselves."

Monarch. It was about the control of Europe. Monarch, she thought with amazement, was the operation that she had been sent to uncover.

"Where is this operation based?"

"That's what we have to trade." Franz shot Hannah an angry look. "You have told her enough."

Hannah frowned at him. "Just a little more."

"No, Hannah. She has promised nothing."

Kim jumped in. "You wanted to interest me in Monarch. All right, I'm interested." But a number of objections began to arise. "If you're kidnapping people that the SS expects to meet, they must know there's a security lapse. A mole."

"They do not suspect. They have contempt for non-Germans, however useful. They believe the recruits have lost courage. So our man next to Annakova says."

"He could be luring you into a trap."

Franz rolled his eyes. "If he was, we would have been dead months ago. Besides. I know the man. He will not betray us."

"This Irina Annakova," Kim said. "What is her Talent rating? Is it strong enough for Monarch's purpose?"

"The Nazis must think so. But there is no rating system established for *catalysts*. No one has seen enough cases to determine a sequence."

Kim thought about the Russian woman, and her ability that might be profound indeed. Perhaps enough for a head start on the master race that Hitler dreamed of.

"One thing to know," Hannah resumed, "is that the optimized ones deteriorate. Very noticeably."

"Madness?" Kim guessed.

"Each embrace comes at a price. More side effects for the one touched if the augmentations happen more often than every three months. But no matter what, eventually, after repeated uplifts, there is a taste for blood. Then the drinking of it."

"They go mad."

"Of course. But in this particular way. So the loved ones find their father, or daughter, drained of blood. The slayer with blood on his lips."

The women at the picnic table in Bad Schandau. This is what they had been talking about.

"You see what they fear?"

The old myth, Kim guessed. "That they will not stay buried."

"So death is not the end of the terror. You fear your lovely dead child will never find peace. It is the worst dread, worse than death."

"Why," Kim asked, "is their madness associated with a taste for blood?"

Hannah shrugged. "Little mix-ups in the brain's wiring. Who knows?"

Kim could imagine Duncan's reaction to this part of the story. "So the Nazis encourage the blood-drinking idea."

"They do. And in fact, with previous *catalysts*, it is how the vampire myth began."

"Hannah. You don't know this!" Franz snapped.

She stabbed a look at him. "Think about it. Hundreds of years ago, a few people were raised up, augmented. Some of them repeatedly. They began to indulge their appetites on the local population. They faded in time, but the damage was done, the stories were told and told." She ground out her cigarette under her shoe.

Kim weighed the story, its cohesion. It could be.

"Also they become unnaturally strong."

Kim thought of how Captain Nagel had smashed and broken the seat in the car.

"This strength also feeds the story. Especially for Christians. For you people, death is all mixed up."

The door opened. Their young watchman. *"Zeit zu gehen. Schnell!"* Time to go, quickly.

Hannah sprang from her chair, grabbing her jacket.

Franz hissed at Kim. *"Der Schal!"* She grabbed the scarf as he took her by the arm and urged her toward the door.

As they rushed down the hall, Kim tied the scarf under her chin. They came to a staircase leading up to the next level and ran down another hall, dimly lit by a window at the far end. Someone waited for them at the window. Franz peeled off from the group and, now with Hannah and the new man, Kim exited onto a wooden fire escape.

"You will go into the street." Hannah pointed. "Turn right and walk away slowly. The car will come for you. His name will be Alvin." She paused, watchful, but took a moment. "So. Is it enough?"

"It's a beginning." She wanted to know where the *catalyst* was. Where Monarch was. To get Duncan to listen.

Hannah sliced a look at her. "I need your side of it now. You promise?"

She couldn't, not yet. "I've seen things in Germany that square with what you're saying about these *Nachkommenschaft.* But the claims are still extraordinary. I need something more."

Hannah and her companion scanned the backside of the tenement. Dogs rummaged in bins of refuse. A wooden cart lay collapsed in the mud, slumped to one side. Farther back, masked by fog, a plump woman pulled tubers from a garden black with rot.

Hannah looked keenly into Kim's eyes. "Are you brave, Frau Reed, or just playing the game?"

"I'm afraid all the time. I do it anyway."

"Then, if that is true, I will take you to a place. The fourth floor."

Her companion groaned. She cut a glance at him. "Mind your own business, Micha." Turning back to Kim, she said, "Will you come with me?"

"What place is it?" Kim asked.

"Where the SS *Nachkommen* end their days. You will see what they become."

"Their infirmity? Their madness?"

"Yes. But to *see* these things. It is something more, as you say." Kim hesitated.

Hannah snapped, "If you need proof, then it will not be enough. I am sure, though, what you will see will corroborate everything I have said. The SS guard this place; it is a place they wish no one to discover. But if you have no interest . . ."

"I am interested, yes. But I can't risk capture."

"You will accomplish nothing without risk. My people have been to the fourth floor. We have penetrated it, and I will show you how." She waited as Micha watched the area, nervous, watching for pursuit.

"Elaine Reed. Are you coming or not?" Hannah had a way of challenging that seemed to ask one to do their best. Kim liked her, or at least sensed her integrity. She would make no snap judgments, but you did learn to take people's measure in this business.

Kim had to earn the Oberman Group's trust. They were the only source on Monarch. "Yes," she finally said.

"Good. Then at least you will know that the Germans are creating monsters." Hannah locked a gaze on her. "We will go on Tuesday."

In two days. Kim nodded.

She memorized her instructions. Then, as Hannah and Micha raced up the stairs, perhaps to the roof, she hurried down to the overgrown lot and made her way to the street alone, except for the riot of her thoughts.

16

GÖRING'S HUNTING LODGE,
SCHORFHEIDE FOREST

MONDAY, DECEMBER 7. Outside the library, Sonja Nagel, full of confusion and alarm, heart thudding in her chest, backed into the hall table. A rattle and clink as the Etruscan statuary swayed but remained upright. *God in heaven, if she had broken it.*

A reprieve.

But then Hermann Göring's bulk filled the doorway to the library. Panic flared across Sonja's chest. She had no good reason to be in this part of the lodge. And what she had heard at the library door, she should not have.

"My darling." Göring's eyes squinted in confusion. "I thought you had gone."

"Yes. But you see, the car is late. The snowstorm . . ." She cast about for an excuse to be here, outside the room where he had been meeting with SS Colonel von Gottberg. She had not meant to overhear, but she had been curious and, fatefully, had stepped closer to the door.

Göring's eyes still held her. "Did you speak to Major Scheel about the car?"

"Oh, I did, of course. He says the roads have become treacherous." She looked at the row of priceless statuary. "I was very clumsy."

He opened his hands and smiled. *No harm done. I cannot be angry with you.* "Well. What will you do? Stay until the storm passes?"

An idea sorted itself out. "I was going to ask if perhaps Colonel von Gottberg might consider giving me a lift." Yes, this was something she might have done, a perfect excuse. She tried to summon a calm aspect but, to her chagrin, she felt a twitch at her mouth. "Unless he is staying?"

"No, as it happens he is not staying. But I am not sure he returns to Berlin."

Major Scheel entered the hall. He gave a Nazi salute. "*Reichsluftfhartminister.* Madam's car has arrived."

Göring spread wide his hands again. "So then." He nodded at Major Scheel, then turned back to her. "Are you nervous to try the roads?"

"Oh, I'm sure it will be fine. It is just snow, after all."

The air minister took her hand and bowed his head, pressing her hand in his great ones. "Goodbye then, Sonja. We shall see you soon if you are not tired of me."

She called up a smile at this gallantry. He knew that her husband could not be a man to her and he thought that she savored his vitality. He believed this, a man who could afford to believe all manner of grotesque things.

"I could never tire of your company, Hermann."

Major Scheel led her down the hall, more a gallery than a corridor, with paintings clinging to their perches above and below one another, covering the five-and-a-half-meter-high walls. Her bags awaited her in the atrium. As a guard held open the door, the smell of snow and motorcar exhaust met her. Though the snow had stopped, the landscape bore a caustic white drape.

As she crossed the broad porch to the waiting car, she saw Göring watching her from a window of his stone mansion, a baron in his keep, no matter how he called it a hunting lodge. And she, his concubine, no matter how he styled her his darling.

They drove off into the snow-laden forest.

She stared out the window, dismayed by the conversation she had overheard. The *Nachkommenschaft* were, as she had suspected, being experimented upon to heighten their Talents to serve as feared enforcers of Hitler's programs. But for these men, the treatments ended in madness and restraint in an asylum, an outcome she had just heard Göring call an "inconvenience."

Things were clear to her now, blindingly clear. They had a plan for Rikard and his cohorts. Of course they did. Her adopted countrymen did nothing spontaneously, but followed their plans, the Führer's demented dreams. How simple she had been to worry about Rikard and what would become of their marriage! Their lives belonged to the Reich. And if the experiments they conducted upon him made him into something she could not care for, nor even understand, it was all according to plan.

She shivered in the back seat, drawing her fur coat more tightly around her throat.

Her marriage. How strange that she had thought she still had one.

Rikard could not love her anymore, could not share her life. He had become a creature who lived for the night. Insomnia, he called it, but she saw how he shied from the light, how he could eat nothing, his body wasting away. And his mind. His extraordinary mind, now decayed into an engine of calculation. It grew worse. Or he would say, better, for he recognized no limits to what he could know, the value he could be to his wretched master, her absurd lover. A lover whom Rikard allowed. Or rather, required.

The memory came of the *Nachkommenschaft* creatures at the lodge, standing in a circle—this she had once seen from one end of the Great Hall as she entered—Rikard and his cohorts raising their crystal glasses for a toast, the flames from the roaring fireplace setting the red wine aglow.

If it was wine.

Oh, Rikard. You have given up your very soul.

Was it not his soul? Or was this science, the planned future of the race, and it had nothing to do with God?

An elk bounded across the road, just missing the car, his rack of antlers a heavy crown he carried with ease. He disappeared into the bleak landscape, a glimpse of normal, exquisite life. They drove on.

THE LAKE DISTRICT, NORTH OF BERLIN

TUESDAY, DECEMBER 8. Kim and Hannah were on a deeply rutted road an hour north of Berlin, Hannah at the wheel. Every time the tires hit a dip, the sound of glass clinked at them from the back seat.

Kim turned around to look. "What's in the box?"

"Radiophosphorous. Eight vials. Special delivery to Treptow Sanatorium."

A TB facility, with three stories of treatment rooms and dormitories, and on the fourth floor, a secret critical care unit. For *Nachkommen*. SS in the final stages of their lives. Not proof of Monarch's purpose. But something more than a story from the Oberman Group. Something that Kim could say she had seen with her own eyes.

"Radiophosphorous," Kim repeated. "Radioactive?"

"Of course. An experimental TB therapy."

Kim hadn't been told about that part. "The vials have enough packing?"

"Don't worry. They are in a wooden rack. Nothing will spill."

They would gain access to the sanatorium by delivering the drugs and using the name of a doctor who was gone this week. For the fourth floor, however, they would need stealth and diversion. A middle-of-the-night delivery would put the staff off guard. And besides, Hannah had said, *All you need to say is "radioactive" and you have them under your thumb.*

Catalyst: the unnerving new Talent that the Oberman Group claimed existed. If meta-abilities could be augmented, it would alter the balance of psi gifts in the world. Could it be true that, deep within, each person of Talent held a full measure of power, a ten on the scale? And that a touch from a *catalyst* could remove the dross to bring it out in full? The reason we do not know of such a power: it is temporary. The *catalyst* dies young. Those uplifted die as madmen.

It might be true. If so, it was a stunning claim. She put Hannah's story together with what she had already seen in Germany: the rumors of fiends; the symptoms displayed by Rikard Nagel; his fervent declaration about being in the service of the *monarch*. Kim couldn't know with certainty, couldn't solve the calculus of lies, if that's what they were. But she knew she couldn't walk away from discovering more.

They passed through a woodland with skirts of white on the north side of boulders, snow left over from an early-winter storm. They sped on, meeting few other cars, crossing into a region of meadows cradling small lakes.

As they drove, Kim filled in more of the missing pieces. "How did the Nazis get this Annakova, the *catalyst?*"

"They call her the tsarina. She will rule Russia when the Soviets fall. They link arms, the Third Reich and the pretender to the throne. Two devils."

An alliance between Germany and Russia. It was not the one everyone feared, the one between Hitler and Stalin, but the one between Hitler and Tsar Nicholas's successor.

If tonight's operation failed, the fallout went beyond her drawing the attention of the SS. London could lose confidence in her, especially after warning her to use discretion. Once she no longer had their trust, they could recall her. Her career might not survive.

In that case she would spend her life, her gift, listening to the dark longings of villagers and the sins of friends. So the fourth floor both called to her and warned her.

"Getting into the sanatorium. Who are we supposed to be?"

Hannah shrugged. "That depends on Fivel. From his cleaning service, two uniforms will go missing. So it depends on which hospital they are from."

"You've got an impressive network."

"Network." Hannah snorted. "Franz has an uncle who lives in Lindow, who knows the wife of the butcher, and Fivel is her nephew who works at the laundry that serves the regional hospitals. If that is a network, then I guess we have one."

The Oberman Group was not strong. A few daring feats of sabotage and kidnapping. But it appeared they had few members, were hunted relentlessly by the Gestapo, and had quite limited resources. And yet, radiophosphorous. That could not be easy to acquire.

They turned onto a side road skirting a lake. The car shuddered as it hit a rut. From the back seat came the clinking of glass tubes.

Kim glanced behind, noting that the box was very small. "You're sure the vials aren't going to break? We'd be exposed."

Hannah threw a droll look at Kim. "To beet juice."

Slowing the car, Hannah turned them down a narrow lane.

They sat at the kitchen table eating corned beef sandwiches Charlotte had prepared. The stone-flagged kitchen was hung with a chandelier that looked to be a small wagon wheel, candles rimming it. Unlit for now. It was early afternoon.

Charlotte, rotund and red-faced, watched them eat, now and then looking up at her husband, Eli, who could be seen in the next room hunched over a treadle sewing machine. Fixing one of the uniforms. A tailor, Eli didn't need Kim to try it on but measured her with a practiced eye and had gone to work.

"This is not a good idea," Charlotte said again. "We know what is in Treptow. Why see it again?" She worked as a cleaning woman at the sanatorium.

Hannah paused, as though considering whether to answer. "We need more information."

Charlotte frowned in Kim's direction, saying in German, "This one doesn't speak German. As soon as she opens her mouth, they'll know." Kim caught the gist of it. Charlotte was right.

"She will not open her mouth." Fixing Charlotte with an iron stare, Hannah said, "Tell us about the doctor. In English."

A sigh through pursed lips. "Doctor Amstutz, he is gone until Monday. A symposium in Magdelburg. He is assistant director, someone who can order medicines. But the treatments, they are heliotherapy, fresh air, why would there be medicine?"

"Radioisotopes," Hannah said. "They are used in research. I think it is something that the duty nurse will not want to criticize. She will wait for Doctor Amstutz to explain." Hannah brought their plates to the sink. "Don't worry so much."

The whirring of the sewing machine stopped. Eli, lanky and bearded, appeared in the doorway holding a nurse's uniform and apron over his arms. He nodded to Kim. She rose from the table to take the outfit. The blue wool cape would suit as it was, and she had worn sturdy shoes that might pass for nurse duty.

"*Danke*," Kim said to him.

Charlotte sighed. "As soon as she opens her mouth."

17

TREPTOW SANATORIUM,
THE LAKE DISTRICT

11:20 PM. In the car park Hannah killed the engine. "Ready?"

"As ready as I'll ever be." Kim got out of the car and retrieved the little box from the back seat.

The sanatorium loomed out of the woods with a fairy-tale glow. Its elaborate brickwork and mansard roof with dormer windows gave it an aesthetic, humane aspect. Beauty was important to recovery. Stained-glass windows flashed shards of color from dim lights within.

The starched uniform collar pulled at Kim's neck. But the outfits with their white bib aprons, starched white hats, and capes helped put her into the role.

"Be careful," Hannah said, glancing at the little box.

A joke. Kim's smile felt like ripping stitches. She had come here to see the *Nachkommen*, their bodies pale yet unusually strong, their minds slipped free of moorings. She would know they were the Progeny by how similar their faces and hands were and by the powerful straps of their restraints. Rikard Nagel was bad. Apparently, it got worse.

Ascending the steps of a portico, Hannah pushed through the double doors into the entryway, holding the door for Kim, who carried the box with elaborate care.

A woman at the night desk was rising to meet them, probably having heard their car. She said something to a man in an SS uniform. Kim and Hannah approached the desk. The guard's uniform bore the stylized lightning bolt insignia on the collar, not the vulture.

Hannah rolled out their story. Kim picked up enough to know it followed the script of Dr. Amstutz's requisition of radiophosphorous—here a keen look at the little box from the night desk nurse—and apologies for their late arrival caused by a puncture on the road, and the need above all to bring Dr. Amstutz's material to a safe location. She had also hurt her ankle while changing the tire, so she would like to be about her assignment as quickly as possible.

The nurse was clearly unhappy about this development and, as the SS guard appeared out of his depth, she took charge.

"Doctor Amstutz has said nothing about such an order. It is most irregular. We have no ability to hold something like this."

Hannah agreed it was unusual. Perhaps nurse would like to wake her superior? Or perhaps the material might sit under lock and key until morning, when Dr. Amstutz might be reached by telephone for his instructions.

Soon the nursing director was roused, and the conversation was repeated. Nurse Bernauer, thin and brisk, was a calmer individual than the night desk nurse.

"We will bring the package to the dispensary where it can be stored. Then we will discuss how this came to happen without my knowledge." Her low, assured voice conveyed an unflappable German attention to procedure. First this, then this. Then we shoot you.

She walked with the two of them down the corridor, Hannah limping slightly, and the SS officer, referred to as lieutenant, bringing up the rear. A building this size could never be warm in winter, nor was it, but with the wool cape Kim felt hot and flushed.

At the door to the dispensary, Hannah said, "We will need a larger box to store this in. One with padding."

The nurse frowned. "But you have come all this way without padding."

"It is not strictly necessary, but it contributes to safety. Dr. Amstutz did not want any accidents when the medicines came into his keeping. Perhaps the lieutenant?"

Nurse Bernauer paused in irritation, then sent the officer in search of a box and insulating material.

Hannah made eye contact with Kim, then nodded at the box. Kim placed it in Hannah's hands as though it were a prize Ming vase.

Having unlocked the dispensary door, the nurse let them inside. Kim, last in, left the door open.

Spotless white cabinets lined the walls, along with several refrigerators and, in the center, a stainless steel table. Turning toward it, Hannah stumbled as though her ankle had buckled under her. The box slammed into the table edge. Nurse Bernauer charged forward, but too late, as Hannah lost her balance and dropped the box onto the floor, creating a sickening crunch of glass.

"Mein Gott!" Hannah rasped.

Kim's cue to disappear.

She backed into the corridor, leaving behind the chaotic scene in the dispensary, and hurried to the first intersection of the hallway, where she turned the corner. Ahead was a curved stairway leading up, with its decorative handrail of turned ironwork, and at the landing, tall leaded-glass windows.

With Charlotte's description of the hospital's layout firmly in mind, she ascended. Behind her, the shouts from the dispensary had ceased, leaving the building in eerie silence.

She rushed up to the second floor, taking care to make no sound.

A corridor lay before her, a fey light warming the walls. Down the hall, a nurses' station attended by someone hunched over a book. She pulled her dark cloak around her uniform and moved as slow as a sloth up the next flight of stairs, clasping the keys in her pocket, ready to say, *A delivery of radioisotopes. A box is needed.*

No one stopped her. Coming to the top, she found a broad hall with wheelchairs and chaise longues lined up for use on the sun deck, accessed by a line of French doors.

She crossed the room to the double doors that closed off what Charlotte had called the east wing. Here, a metal pipe was secured through the rounded door pulls. It rested at both ends on hardware screwed into the paneling. As Kim slid the heavy pipe free, it clanked against the door, sending alarms along her nerves. She set the pipe on the floor. Then from her pocket she removed the two keys secured on a lanyard, the keys that Charlotte had provided. Using the larger one, she shoved it in the lock and turned it.

With a resounding click, the lock released, and she was

through. It seemed her journey to this point had taken many minutes. She had to hurry. Turning up the narrow staircase just inside the doors, she reached a stairwell lit only by ambient light from the wall sconces below. She climbed to a door at the top. The fourth floor.

If you turned a lock very slowly the tumblers might slide into place without a click. But despite a brief prayer, this was not the case. The lock clattered like a shoebox of marbles. Kim hesitated at the noise, but Charlotte had said that fourth-floor patients were not only heavily sedated at night but were restrained in their beds.

Entering, Kim stood unmoving, surveying the room. She was in a large dormitory with beds along both walls. By the light of a lamp on the desk by the door, she saw the headboards on one side pushed up against windows that were sealed with shutters and crossbeams. About half the beds were occupied. None of the forms moved.

Drawing out a subminiature Minox camera from her pocket, she approached the first bed. A man lay sleeping on his back, his head sunk into a pillow that bulged around his face. Her first impression was that he was a cancer patient, so emaciated he looked. The covers hid his body, but by their drape, he was very thin. A high-domed forehead and long jaw made his head unnaturally long. Only wisps of hair remained on his skull. His lips, full and smooth, his skin with no hint of lines or sagging. She could easily imagine that this was what Rikard Nagel would become, a cadaverous, almost inhuman creature. She clicked off a picture.

Two beds farther on, a woman lay. She thought it was a woman, by the long strands of hair, the slightly smaller features. Her blanket had slipped to the floor, allowing Kim to see her elongated body. The fleshy part of the hands was stretched long, and the remarkable fingers spanned joints to create what must be a formidable grasp. Crisscrossing the woman's chest and limbs were heavily woven cloth belts. These connected by buckles to restraints on the side of the bed. The shutter of the Minox, a whisper as Kim snapped the pictures.

She continued around the room, working more quickly now, but each skeletal body was indeed of a type: muscular and gaunt, unnaturally long hands and feet, and faces disturbingly lengthened, most noticeably at the forehead and chin.

A motion on the far side of the room. Kim snapped around to look.

"Nurse," came the voice. Speaking German.

She froze.

"Nurse." More insistently.

So as not to cause him to call her more loudly, she approached.

When she reached the foot of the bed, she found a *Nachkomme* gazing at her as he lay strapped in the bed. He was completely bald, adding to the elongated impression of his face. A sign hung from the end of the bed, displaying a word she couldn't translate, and below that a clipboard on a chain.

"I know I should sleep," he said, with a modulated, deep voice. "But I cannot."

She felt a pang of sympathy for him, knowing that his condition was fatal, and imagining the misery of ending it in this place.

His voice was wistful. "Do you ever try to sleep and fail?"

She hesitated to answer him. It would be best to leave now, but something about him gave her pause.

"I'm sure you know what I mean. But for us"—he looked around the room—"we prefer to sleep at different hours than others." She caught most of what he was saying and filled in the blanks.

He moved his body a few inches under the covers. "The straps hurt. I have sores. You could check if you don't believe me."

"I believe you," she said in German. She didn't want to pick up his blanket. Why had she spoken? A trickle of sweat sped down the side of her rib cage.

"You are new."

"Yes. I am just learning."

"You aren't like the others. I knew that when you first came in and started to take pictures."

Time to leave. No one would hear him if he cried an alarm.

"Just loosen the strap around my hips one notch. The bruises, they hurt me so."

She glanced down at the end of a leather strap dangling below the covers.

His eyes flickered with pain. Well, just a notch, then. She bent down and unbuckled the strap, slipping it into holes farther down.

"What does the sign say?" She gestured to the end of his bed.

"Ah," he said, nodding. "It is my condition. You know it, *ja*? You are a nurse."

"No," she said, sweat now pouring from her face. She folded the cape away from her shoulders.

"The sign says *compulsion*." A long, flat smile carved across his face. "But we don't need to worry about that. This is a hospital."

"We don't need to worry," she agreed.

"And perhaps the other straps? I know it is a great deal of trouble." His voice was soft and even, like snow falling on a river and disappearing.

She fumbled with the buckles on his ankles. The straps were very tight and hard to unfasten, but she finally managed.

"Why not just take them all off? Now that we've started, that's what we should do."

He was right. Kim had finished with the right side of the bed and now went around to the other side. As she worked, she asked, "What will you do when you escape?" She was very curious about this. What his plans were. As though in a dream, she knew his answer would be vitally important, but she wasn't sure why.

"I think I'll have supper."

She didn't like hearing that, but could think of nothing to say. She left one strap buckled. *They keep them restrained, because they are mad.*

He erupted from the bed. Bellowing, he slammed his feet onto the floor on the opposite side of the bed from her. Slowly he bent down, then like a whale breaching, he threw his arms into the air, and the strap ripped free. All the straps were still attached to him, and he swung them around like whips, howling with glee.

Kim stumbled backward into the empty bed behind her. Between her and the *Nachkomme* there was only the bed he had lain in. She scrambled over the next bed, terror turning her movements clumsy, while he pranced into the middle of the room, slashing the straps back and forth around him.

Crashing backward, Kim fell against the next bed, sprawling against the patient, who groaned. She sprang up and ran for the door as other patients began to wake. Some shouted in German. Some begged the free patient to release them.

He dove onto the bed of one such, straddling the patient secured there. He leaned down and used one of the buckles barbing the end of a strap to rip open his throat. He bent over the gash and, while holding the victim down, thrust his face into the neck.

Kim reached the door as the room filled with screams. She yanked it open.

The key. She slammed the door behind her and dug for the key, her hands shaking so hard she barely controlled them. Finding the keys, she drew them out, but dropped them. They skittered across the landing as she heard a crash from the other side of the door.

She fled down the stairs just as the door slammed open, and the *Nachkomme* stood in the opening, covered in blood and with the straps drooping at his side like strips of flayed skin.

All she could think of was the metal pipe. She pounded down the stairs and jammed toward the double doors. He was right behind her, but with a crazy, shambling gate. He was slowed by the straps that whipped against his ankles.

Yanking the double doors open, she slammed them shut and grabbed the metal pipe. Sliding the pipe through the door handles, she turned and charged across the room, hurdling over the line of chaise longues toward the French doors. *Get out, get out.*

The doors were locked.

Behind her, the door with the pipe crashed and swayed. She raced for the stairs. "Help!" she shouted. "Help!" Now she hoped for guards, for nurses, for everyone to hear her.

At the landing she heard a great smashing noise from above. The doors breaking.

She skittered around to the next flight of stairs. From below, two nurses came running down the corridor toward her, along with several guards.

Kim pointed behind her. "He's killing patients!" she screamed, remembering to do so in German.

They met at the foot of the stairs. One of the nurses grabbed her. "Who are . . ."

A guard had pulled his gun and loosed a volley of bullets at something coming down the stairs. They might not know what it was, but Kim did.

The nurse screamed. Kim exploited the moment to rush down the hallway, her lungs almost bursting. Behind her, an animal howl and the eruption of shattered glass. Perhaps the *Nachkomme* had smashed the windows or thrown a soldier through them, she didn't know. More soldiers raced past her toward the chaos.

When she got to the dispensary, the door was closed. Heavy tape sealed off the room. The atrium, empty.

She rushed outside where the car waited, engine running. Kim opened the door behind Hannah and threw herself in. Hannah gunned the engine and they screeched away, the back door swinging open on its hinges. Heart thudding, lying sprawled in the back seat, Kim fumbled at her uniform pocket, patting it. Empty. The Minox, missing.

They flew around the bend in the driveway as the windows in Treptow Sanatorium newly flared with light, casting a phantom pall on the front line of the woods, and then receding like a bad dream as their car barreled down the road and into the black woods.

18

THE ROAD FROM
TREPTOW SANATORIUM

MIDNIGHT. Nerves primed, Kim kept an eye on the rearview mirror, watching for headlights. They had changed into their civilian clothes, having buried the uniforms in the woods. "What if we hit control points?"

Hannah drove fast on the country road, trying to put as much distance as possible between themselves and any SS pursuit. But there was a good chance that the soldiers had not figured out yet that the middle-of-the-night delivery was a sham.

"They will not have them up so fast."

Kim thought they might. A few telephone calls is all it would take. "I could pretend to be pregnant." She reached into the back seat for a scarf and began shoving it under her dress. Her hands were shaking, still. "An emergency, and you're taking me to the hospital."

"All right."

Kim put her hand on her belly, as pregnant women did. She was sure her pallor and sweat-lined face were already on display.

They slowed as they entered a village, shuttered and quiet. Then back out onto the open road, faster. Kim would take the train to Berlin from Wittenberge—she could not be on the train soon enough—while Hannah took her own route back.

Emerging from heavy woodlands, they sped along a river valley illumined by a half moon, flashing now and then from the river Elbe.

Seared into memory, the fourth floor. The beds with their occupants lying on their backs, all drugged. One not enough.

"How many of them are there?" She imagined a cadre of them, advancing into Europe; a fifth column, ahead of conquest.

"We are not sure. Many." Hannah shrugged. "Enough."

"You said the effect fades. How long before it does?"

"Our man close to Irina Annakova says the augmentation lasts ninety-one days."

Ninety-one days. The Germans and their specificity.

Hannah went on. "They used to call them the ninety-one. But the Nazis enjoy their dramatic names, and Annakova likes them to be hers, so they call them *Nachkommenschaft*."

The Progeny. "Who is this Russian woman?" Kim asked. "Where did she come from? A relative of Tsar Nicholas?"

"A White Russian. We do not know how she justifies her claim." She rounded a curve too fast.

"For God's sake, slow down."

Hannah ignored the advice. "The Nazis do not need justification of her claim. They despise the Communists. Annakova would like her country back and Hitler will give it to her."

A German invasion of Russia was a breathtaking idea;

surely Hitler would never be strong enough. But Westminster and Whitehall shared Hitler's Soviet aversion. They would certainly listen to this. And yet, would they believe Hannah's group was a credible source? Would they believe Kim herself and her tenuous collection of clues?

Pictures of the *Nachkomme* in the final stages would have been at least something tangible. Even if it didn't prove Monarch's European mission. But she had lost the Minox in the tumult of the fourth-floor debacle.

"Why didn't you tell me they had a *compulsion* Talent? He could have killed me."

"It was something we did not know! Do you think everything must be perfect?"

"You might have told me there *was* such a Talent."

Hannah shook her head. Irritated, snappish. "I did not know about it either. Oberman Group did not know. We are two dozen fighters without funds, without support, without the trust of people who could help us."

Kim took a deep breath. None of this would be solved right now. "How do they ever keep a *compulsion Nachkomme* restrained?" She shook her head, remembering the one whose straps she had unbuckled.

"Earplugs," Hannah answered easily. "That is what I would use."

A car approached, its headlamps glaring through the night. It passed, and Kim resumed breathing.

In the light from the passing car, Kim saw that Hannah was smiling. "Imagine the doctor's fury when they tell him that his name was used as having ordered radioactive medicine for TB patients!"

Kim was having trouble savoring that image. Her thoughts

had turned to Duncan and how to make her report. She imagined telling him that she'd seen a disfigured man drinking blood. She imagined Duncan's summation of Kim Tavistock: *Poor old thing, went off the deep end. Hated the Nazis and fell for a Jewish story of a blood cult.*

"I am one of them."

"What?" She came out of her reverie. "One of them?"

"I have a Talent."

Another thing Hannah had withheld. Kim's annoyance flared. "Well?"

"I will trust you with this. The reason Franz protects me, the reason I must leave Germany."

"And you didn't trust me before?"

"Trust is a matter of degree. So. My Talent. My father, I have told you, studied meta-abilities at Cologne. This was 1929, 1930. He was a researcher, a psychology professor."

"He tested you."

"*Ja.*" She cut a glance at Kim. "I want you to know I am revealing this on purpose. It is not something I am *spilling* to you."

"All right, you're not *spilling.*"

"I have the ability. *Catalysis.*"

Kim sat in shocked silence.

A *catalyst.* Kim found herself reeling. Hannah, a *catalyst.* It changed everything. She put her hands to her pounding temples, trying to settle her thoughts. The vampires, the blood, the radio-isotopes, a fugitive beside her in the car, one who could change the nature of the coming war.

"When you touch people . . ."

"Yes. The augmentation. Any Talent I am with, if I touch them, they come away stronger."

Kim turned to look at Hannah. A *catalyst*. The dashboard lights gave her face an eerie glow.

Hannah went on. "My father had never seen anyone with this Talent, but even before testing me, he had heard rumors there was such an ability. It was not openly discussed because it had clear military implications and also because there was a stigma attached. No one would want to be in your presence for fear of a touch. It is a hard thing to bear." She glanced at Kim. "And do not worry, you will recall that I have never touched you."

Kim thought back and could not remember even a handshake. Hannah had been careful.

"So you see why Franz insists I go to the West."

"You'd be a weapon against the Nazis."

"But I am already a weapon," Hannah said. "Here in Germany."

Kim didn't bother to hide a flare of bitterness. "If I'd known this, you could have saved me the trouble of breaking into Treptow." She wouldn't have needed to go. Being a *catalyst* would have earned Hannah extraction all by itself. "Damn it to hell. You could have told me earlier."

"Would you have believed me?"

There was that. Treptow was a turning point in her receptivity to the Oberman claims. Before, it had merely been intriguing. Now . . . now she had seen the ward of monsters.

"You cannot blame me for being careful," Hannah said. "Our group survives by trusting no one but our own members. I was not sure I wanted to tell you, but now—you risked your life. You are one of us."

The car jolted from a pothole, and Hannah gripped the steering wheel harder. "I think it is time we trusted each other. For wherever we go from here."

So they would go somewhere from here. Kim noted that with some hope. "Have you ever . . . augmented a Talent? Outside your father's research center?"

Hannah didn't answer for a long moment. Then she murmured, "I try not to touch people who may have a Talent."

A farmhouse came into view, all the windows dark. Hannah parked and turned off the headlights. "This is where we change cars."

"Hannah." Kim made no move to get out of the car. "Is there anything else you're withholding? I'm about to put my career on the line, so I need to know." Hannah had said that Kim was now one of them. Trial by ordeal. But Kim wasn't the only one that needed to prove herself. "Have you ever killed anyone?"

Hannah's voice, edged with bitterness: "Is this my interview for extraction?"

"Yes."

"Killed. Maimed. It is war." Her face was set in a scowl. "I could ask you the same thing."

Kim thought of Sulcliffe Castle and the man she had killed. Yes, it was war.

"Or," Hannah went on, "is it a standard that pertains only to Jews?"

And was it? Bloody hell, yes; and Kim was the interrogator, obligated to report on the potential asset who was also a saboteur. "We have to be prepared for how London thinks." She fixed Hannah with a look. "You and I."

In the last hours it had indeed become her and Hannah. When you went through things with someone—dangerous, terrifying things—it formed a tie. Kim knew this was true for men in wartime. And now, it formed this connection with Hannah, though they had only known each other a few days.

As they got out of the car, several dogs came charging around the house toward them. "Easy! Stay down!" Kim hissed at them. At her tone, they paused in their assault, but continued barking.

Light from a candle flared in the window, and Hannah strode to the door.

WITTENBERGE STATION

2:15 AM. Hannah left her at the station on the outskirts of town. They would meet in Berlin. But when they did, in order to learn where the Monarch operation was, Kim would have to offer extraction.

The Wittenberge Station was a sprawling and busy place, even at this hour. Kim was not in proper travel attire, lacking a hat or gloves or even a town dress. Her trousers and sweater had been selected for the appearance of being on an outing with Hannah. Hannah, the *catalyst*. Who, for this reason as well as having maimed or assassinated Nazi officials, had to escape Germany. It was a different game now. Hannah was valuable not only for what she knew, but for what she was.

Kim bought her ticket at the window. Her hand shook even though it was clear sailing from here. The clerk, with a pencil mustache and a frown, paused when he heard her accent, saw her nerves. It was 2:20 AM, and she was traveling alone. But so were others at the busiest train station between Hamburg and Berlin.

She stared him down. There was a time to be ingratiating and a time for the air of privilege. She raised her chin. He issued the ticket.

Almost home. After all she'd been through, and she could

still out-intimidate a German clerk. She wasn't green anymore after Treptow.

A half hour wait, no more, Hannah had assured her. The Flying Hamburger or another train would be along. In her handbag, from the farmhouse, the remains of a hunk of cheese and piece of bread, wrapped in paper.

In the station lavatory she washed her hands and face. Ran her hands through her hair. Stiff strands here and there. Dried blood. She yanked the spigot on full blast. *Get it out*, her only thought. She stooped over and heaped cold water into her hair, hands pulling it through. Oh God, blood, the room, the screams. She was saying *Oh God* out loud.

She grabbed a piece of paper towel and lashed it through her hair, rubbing hard.

In the mirror, a wraith looked back at her. Tendrils of dark hair plastered to her forehead. A bright, stunned look in the gas-lights. *Get ahold of yourself.*

The comb in her purse. She found it, used it. Chills now, in the cold lavatory. Her coat sleeves wet. A deep breath, ragged as hell. *Just get home.* Pinning her hair back so it wouldn't look bedraggled, she judged herself ready for the train.

Outside on the platform, men in civilian clothes. Checking papers. Gestapo. Looking for her?

She sat down on the nearest bench to collect herself. In the escape from Treptow she hadn't considered the story she would need in Wittenberge if confronted. All the while, she had imag-ined control points as being along roads. But of course they would also be at train stations. *My story. My story.* Exhaustion dulled her thinking as she tried to rouse her best lie.

A train was coming in on the western-approach tracks. As she stood, one of the checkpoint men saw her and walked toward her.

"This is your train?" he said in German. The leather coat and fedora. Bland face with alert blue eyes.

"*Ja, ist er.*"

"*Englisch?*"

"*Ja.*" The passengers debarked from the train. Her train.

"The papers," he said, switching to English. Her hand shook as she handed him her identity card. Scrutinizing it, he said, "It is very late for travel, Madame Reed." He had seen the consular stamp.

"I have cut short my visit. An illness in the family."

"But in Berlin?"

"No. In London. I'm returning to Berlin to arrange my affairs for a lengthy absence."

He gazed at her for a moment. "Who has become ill?"

"My niece."

The locomotive sighed. A conductor waited at trackside, checking his watch. She glanced at him.

The agent noted this. "Another train comes after this one."

"Well. But it is very late."

He nodded, handing her identity card back to her. "I expect you enjoy German trains. They are the best in the world."

No, those would be British, she fiercely thought.

And then she was boarding the train, heart hammering, remembering that she should have had a suitcase. He hadn't asked her about one. Why not?

She found her first-class compartment. Through the window, she kept watch on the Gestapo agents on the platform.

Had the Treptow incident rippled as far as Wittenberge, or was the Gestapo presence about something else? Couplings clanked as the train got underway, slowly, slowly, as though the iron conveyance had doubts about leaving. Had the *Staatspolizei*

questioned her because she looked like the disguised nurse at
Treptow or because Rikard Nagel wanted her watched?

If the Gestapo was interested in her, they knew where she
lived. She leaned her head back on the cushioned seat and closed
her eyes. Despite an almost painful alertness, she needed to
sleep. The wheels of the train squealed and grabbed the tracks
as they picked up speed.

Flower vase in the window, came the thought.

The White Russian. She would like her country back.

Just loosen the strap. The bruises, they hurt me so.

19

THURSDAY, DECEMBER 10. "Too many soldiers, Stefan," Irina said. Beneath the Nazi and Imperial Russian banners hanging from timbered beams, SS guards lined the reception hall. "It is not suitable for my birthday dinner."

"Your Majesty," Stefan said, "we have been alerted to a threat. Minor, but we take no chances with your welfare."

"A threat?"

"Someone has been taking pictures where they should not."

"Not here, surely."

"No, no. Not here." He led her to the table where Heinrich Himmler waited.

Having resigned herself to an evening in the *Reichsführer's* company, Irina summoned a regal demeanor and put her gloved hand on Stefan's arm.

Fat vases stuffed with flowers were brought to the Aerie at

great expense. Beyond the bunting and flowers, the tall windows looked out onto the plaza below, nestled under an ermine cloak of new snow.

Himmler met her as she approached, bowing before her, pushing his ratlike face into her hand.

At table this night were four SS officers. Stefan, of course, and two who had accompanied Himmler from Berlin, as well as Colonel Bassman, the taciturn and bespectacled commandant of the Aerie. Evgeny Feodorovich was here too, in his much-laundered suit with a new cravat. The SS officers were all darkly powerful in their dress uniforms, but Evgeny had his own power. Perhaps even now his forward vision told him how Heinrich Himmler would die. Or Stefan. Or herself.

Irina wore a white evening gown with a pearl-studded bodice, tailored from one of Aunt Tanya's gowns salvaged by Polina at the end when everything had been in chaos. Accented by the low-cut gown, her neck, not as smooth as it once was. At thirty-seven, her skin had gone as slack as a fifty-year-old's. She fed the Progeny with her vigor and did not begrudge them.

Stefan took a seat at her side to translate while Himmler sat opposite. She tried to pay attention as Himmler droned on about the Führer this, the Führer that, while acutely aware of her adjutant. At court, Irina had known many handsome men. Ah, but Stefan, the bittersweet knight. How could he bear to be so beautiful and not use it as a weapon to seduce and control? Perhaps he did. She had never seen him around other women.

Himmler was saying something. "Will I have the honor of meeting his Imperial Highness tonight, Your Majesty?"

Annoyingly, he spoke German, his only option. Stefan repeated the question in French for Irina.

"He sees to his prayers," she said. "And then sleep. Tomorrow."

"I trust I will have the pleasure."

Down the table, Evgeny blurted out in Russian, "My soup is cold." He pushed the bowl away, slopping it on the table.

Himmler glanced at him coldly.

Let Himmler stare. It was her table, and she would decide who was welcome at it.

The *Reichsführer* went on. "Russia is a land of the orthodox church. Will His Imperial Highness foster the church?"

Hearing Stefan's translation, she frowned. Himmler spoke as though she were dead already. It was always about Kolya. It both gratified and grated her. She would rule for a few years, surely.

Stefan interjected. "He is a dutiful son. In due time, he would likely continue the wishes of the tsarina." A fleeting glance at her, rewarded with her smile.

"It is my belief," Himmler went on, "that Christianity gives rise to agitators, those whose loyalties are to God and not the true sovereign. We must not allow the people to hope for approval except from Your Royal Majesty and the Führer. Obedience is undermined by false loyalties."

A shadow passed over her heart. What did Heinrich Himmler the chicken farmer know about the Motherland and its traditions?

"Surely," she murmured, "when the Reich destroys the Soviet oppressors, it will clearly establish my authority."

Hearing the translation, Himmler's mouth twitched beneath his slash of a mustache. "Armies can take, Your Majesty, but they cannot keep. The people must be broken."

Stefan avoided eye contact with her when he translated. The remark could not stand, even if Himmler was the second-most powerful man in Germany. She allowed a frosty pause. "The Russian people will never be broken."

All talk at the table hushed.

Himmler declined to challenge this, but his silence in itself was an affront.

Stefan said, first in German, and then in French for Irina's benefit, "We will deal with any who would dare oppose you. Communists will soon see the error of their ways, and they will be of no consequence."

Himmler flashed a look at Stefan, perhaps annoyed that he had answered for his superior. "We must teach them to fear us. The *Nachkommenschaft* will do for the job. Soon." Himmler raised his champagne glass. "May I propose a toast. To our enterprise, Your Majesty."

She raised her glass and nodded. The *Nachkommenschaft* would undermine Stalin and his henchmen, not the entirety of the Russian people.

Evgeny was not at his best tonight. He was glaring steadily at Himmler, as many at the table had begun to notice. Irina nodded to an attendant who approached Evgeny, whispering in his ear. Perhaps he promised him a special treat, because Evgeny rose and allowed himself to be led away. Irina smiled, catching his eye. *We must befriend the Nazis, my dear, but only until we are home again. Then we will live in the old palace, in the old ways.*

Himmler watched as Evgeny left the room. "Perhaps he would do well with special care at a convalescent home, Your Majesty."

And perhaps you would do well to know your place, Herr Chicken Farmer. Evgeny did need care, she did not need to be reminded. It would mean his retirement with the best nursing, of course. She had been delaying that day. But it would come soon. Sir Stefan had suggested a renowned place in Switzerland. She would miss Evgeny Feodorovich desperately.

† † †

Though it was bitterly cold on the veranda, Irina stole a moment alone there with Stefan. The moon had not yet risen, leaving the heavens black but dappled by a slow descent of snow, glittering past the plaza torches.

"We could be in St. Petersburg," she murmured. "The palace in winter."

"Let us pretend it is so, Irinuska."

"Then, if this is my palace, you must tell me anything I wish to know."

Playing along, he said, "Command me."

"You fell in love once, so you said. Who was it?"

He turned back to watch the snow, pausing before he answered. "I had duties in England. It was there."

"She was English."

He did not wish to speak of it, she could tell. But they would play their game.

"She felt that she was English. Born there, but looking hard to belong."

"Strange that she did not . . . belong."

He shrugged, letting that part of the story pass by. "She lived in Yorkshire."

"A countess?" It could be no commoner.

"A spy." He looked at her, smiling, to show it was no longer of any consequence. "Her name was Kim."

"You loved a traitor." She wished she had not said it after he had confided in her.

"I hoped for her to turn, of course."

"But she did not turn."

"No."

"You had to kill her."

His gaze held hers. *Don't ask me.*

Irina looked out onto the lamplit plaza, murmuring, "It is a bitter thing to know that you loved someone else."

His hand folded over hers on the railing. Her gloved hand.

So now he knew her feelings for him. She felt stripped before him, no royal pride left. "Was this a truth you brought forth from me . . . with your gift of the *spill?*"

"Irinuska." He gazed at her. "I do not know. I never know if I have taken or it is given to me. You must forgive me, whichever it is."

He held out his arm for her to take and rejoin the group. She rested her hand on his arm, grasping it for a moment through his jacket sleeve, reaching through the layers that separated them from each other. He had loved an Englishwoman. Her name, Kim, a name that sounded like a boy, or a pet. Kim. How difficult it was to hear the name!

After the cold of the terrace, Stefan's limp deepened. He should use his cane, but for the occasion he had left it behind. They entered the candlelit hall.

Himmler turned from the small circle he had been speaking to. "Ah, Colonel von Ritter, join us, please." He frowned, noting Irina's bare shoulders. "On such a night Her Majesty should have a wrap!"

Indeed, the cold from the porch had followed her inside. She had thought that jealousy was a slow fire. But now she knew it was not. It was glacial ice, creeping through the valleys of her heart.

THE TIERGARTEN, BERLIN

THURSDAY, DECEMBER 10. Kim faced off with Duncan. They stood in a short tunnel in the park under an arched overpass. Just as well that she couldn't see his face clearly in the shadows. The incredulity that must have been there. The pity.

"The risk you took," Duncan said. "Breathtaking, I must say."

She had toned it down a bit for her report, leaving out the detail of blood flying off the straps of the straitjacket as the patient spun—but there was no way to pretty it up without losing the point.

"London already had questions about your operational judgment when you bolted from the Gestapo. Now this." He shook his head slowly. "Why, Elaine? Why didn't you run this by me?"

Because London thinks I'm letting my heart lead me, she might have said. But instead: "I thought you'd need one more piece of the puzzle before you could support my investigations."

"Well, I have that piece now, and I'm not convinced. There are other interpretations of what you saw. Linz brought you to a madhouse. Tucked away since our Nazi brethren don't like to admit that the super race has mental failings."

"They all had a similar and distorted body type." She described the physical symptoms to him, but he did not seem impressed.

"All right. Then it's a German experiment with Talents gone wrong. You have no proof the patients were SS; it could have been Poles, mental defectives, whatnot."

Kim tried taking a calming breath. It didn't help. "Treptow had SS guards. Why would the SS be involved?" It didn't matter what she said. He wasn't going to support her.

"Not to mention you lost the camera." His voice expressionless, making it even worse. "So now they know they've been penetrated."

"That was unfortunate. But as it happens, going through with the break-in has earned me the trust of this group. They have a mole in the operation, so now we have direct intelligence about Monarch."

"If—and it's a very big if—Monarch is this major military strategy that Linz and her people describe."

"Right. We don't know that yet. But we have access to an intelligence source that could confirm it, as I keep saying. Tannhäuser, the mole at the operational base."

He paced away, trying to shed his agitation, then walked back. "All right, Tannhäuser. But how likely is it that an outfit like Oberman could recruit someone in the SS?"

"There are people who are starting to doubt Hitler. We know this. And the mole, the SS officer, had been friends with the leader of the partisans."

From above, the shouts of children racing over the bridge, sounding far away, another world.

She went on. "And because I was willing to do something dangerous at Treptow—"

"Some kind of club initiation?" Said with contempt.

"Because I was willing to go to Treptow," she doggedly went on, "we have a potential *catalyst* willing to come over to our side. The Oberman Group needs to trust us. Their lives are at stake, and they already know we don't care about one Jew's fate." He rolled his eyes. The Jews were an internal problem. "You can call it an initiation. But you know how important it is to gain the trust of assets. It's crucial, or no one would ever risk sharing intelligence with us."

That struck home, or so she thought, by his silence.

"So, because of Treptow, I earned an extraordinary piece of intel."

"About *catalysis*," he said. "If true."

"Yes, and *if* it's true, it's a Talent that could give Nazi military capabilities—and ours—a major boost." Or was the service so blinkered in trying to manage the Nazi government that they would consider this Talent just another in the list? Another Talent for Owen Cherwell's *Bloom Book*, to join *trauma view, conceptor, mesmerizing, disguise, hypercognition, object reading,* and others; that index of meta-abilities that was always out of date.

"If the Linz woman has this ability," Duncan finally said, "that could be very big. I do see why you're so charged up about it." He nodded to himself. "The thing is, though, they could be cooking the whole thing up to get her out of Germany. Suppose she and Franz are lovers, and with the Gestapo closing in, he wants to protect her."

Her face flushed hot. "Why do we have agents in the field if you can just sit in your office and *cook up* your own intel?"

"Elaine. I'm trying to help you. In this business, it's not just what you're able to pull off; it's how you do it. Building confidence from the higher-ups. Showing you're on the team."

And was she on the team? Maybe over tea, listening, waiting. But what about the real team of agents, those who could pursue leads?

Duncan watched her with a worried expression. "If you push wild ideas, if you risk incidents because of it, your career is over."

The words seemed to echo in the tunnel. *Over, over.* Career over. Exactly what had kept her sleepless last night.

He pulled out the report he'd just read. "Modify this. The madman drinking blood, chasing you . . . They won't stand for it."

She let her anger show. "I guess it proves you can't control me."

"And can we?" When she didn't answer, he went on, handing back her report. "Fix this. Say it was a hospital, visiting hours, some such. You can describe the patients' physical changes and the woman's claims, but deliver a reasoned analysis. Show them you aren't jumping to conclusions. No vampires, for God's sake."

She took the paper and stuffed it into her shirt, anger filling her throat so full she couldn't speak. Vampires. Only the legends of them. She had known it would be a disagreeable notion, but it was a real part of the story.

He buttoned up his coat. "And no more contact with her unless directed."

"Duncan." She was going to regret saying this, but it seemed so right other than that. "How long have you been on the Berlin station?"

His expression made clear he wasn't going to answer.

"So long that you're beginning to hope for Paris? Istanbul?

Afraid a copy of my report will go in *your* file?" Silence. A dark pause. "So long that the Third Reich is starting to look normal to you?"

She turned and stalked out of the tunnel into the dour but marginally brighter landscape of the Tiergarten. Striding down the paths of the Tiergarten, she tried to discharge her anger.

Duncan disliked her methods, and in his view they undermined her conclusions. Damn it, her intel should at least arouse concern about a number of alarming scenarios. The Germans might have a frightening asset: Irina Annakova. She wanted her country back, she would be the tsarina. In return, she would raise up Nazi Talents, whether they were German or fascist supporters, or criminals hoping to rise to power. Talents, formerly minor, would become major: 4s would become 8s, 7s would—could they?—become 10s. She imagined a Talent for *disguise*, for *compulsion*, for *precognition* . . . raised so high. The *Nachkommenschaft*, with their great meta-powers. Add to that, formidable physical strength and a penchant for madness. With all this, Nazi control of Europe became ever more possible. It would begin with infiltration. Then control.

In a final advantage, the fiends had a taste for blood. Thus inducing what Hitler called *spiritual terror* to keep the people bound.

And all Duncan could see was a conspiracy to deceive.

Her anger simmered as Hannah's words came back to her: *People who can* mesmerize *leaders*; attract *and* compel *newspaper editors, religious leaders. Receive* spills *from military general staff. Where persuasion fails, they slay and torture.*

So, amend her report? Make it nicer, more palatable?

She had to plan her next move, and quickly, before the Gestapo captured Hannah and silenced the only information source for Monarch.

The setting sun was sinking fast, giving up on the day before it got worse.

Not far from the empty fountain, sitting on a bench, was her husband.

She approached him warily. This wasn't good, Alex following her into the park.

He put down his paper and gave her a cocky smile. She sat beside him, gazing for a moment past the sentinel bare-limbed trees, the acres of yellowing grass. "Never follow me into the Tiergarten."

"I wanted to talk to you."

"Did you hear me? Never."

"Calm down. I'm sitting on a bench. If you're meeting your sources, I don't know a thing."

She scowled at his condescension.

"I wanted to invite you on an excursion," he said.

"I'm busy."

"To Bonn. I'll give a talk at the Institute for Economic Studies and thought we could take a couple days, see the sights." He drew out a cigarette, lit it, and offered it to her. Accepting, she inhaled as deep as she could. He went on. "Ours should look more like a marriage. You go haring off on outings, trips, whatnot. People will notice."

"Requirements of the job." She knew she sounded a scold, but he had caught her at the worst possible time. She blew an angry cloud of smoke, feeling like she didn't really need the cigarette to do it.

"Right-o, I know that, darling. But we must keep up appearances, get along a bit, as newlyweds do. And you haven't seen much more of Germany than the capital and Bad Schandau." He threw up his hands playfully, fending her off. "Or maybe you have, I don't keep tabs. But you'd like Bonn. On Sunday, if you're interested. Think about it, anyway. " He snugged his wool scarf closer around his neck. "Shall we go in?"

She produced a smile that she hoped wasn't positively serpentine. "Right."

He took her hand as they made their way home. "Your fingers are freezing. A whisky will help."

She needed a lot more help than that. As they crossed the Tiergartenstrasse, an idea occurred to her: there was one person who might corroborate the claims about the *Nachkommenschaft*. Someone married to one.

Sonja.

THE BELGIAN EMBASSY, BERLIN

FRIDAY, DECEMBER 11. "I told you the violet gown would suit." In the drawing room, Rachel Flynn smiled knowingly as several members of the diplomatic corps stole glances at Kim.

As the Soviet consul general passed, Kim nodded in greeting, since they had met previously on the circuit. These receptions felt less like parties than chess games. A game with a dozen players, some without portfolio. For now, she was the piece in violet, and she was hunting a pawn married to a *Nachkomme*.

An enormous Christmas tree in the receiving hall tried mightily to impose a yuletide spirit, aided by vast quantities of champagne. Protocol dictated that minor countries should not claim Christmas party dates after December 12, so the Belgians had pounced on December 11. Next weekend the French and the Italians. Unfortunately, the Belgians had chosen the very date that King Edward VIII happened to have abdicated his throne, dampening the enthusiasm of the British legation. Sir Eric Phipps and several other consular officials deemed it unbecoming to attend, but Alex was the exception, as European trade must soldier on despite the fall of kings.

Nazi officials threaded through the crowd, some in white tie and tails and others in the uniforms of Hitler's sworn forces, the SA, Gestapo, and SS.

"Your mystery man isn't German, is he?" Rachel claimed she didn't want to know, but couldn't help herself. "A Nazi official?"

"French," Kim murmured.

Rachel's eyes instinctively raked the crowd for the French legation.

"If we see Sonja Nagel, can you get her husband away? I have a small favor to ask her when he's not around."

Rachel narrowed her eyes while blowing smoke, making her look rather fierce. "Does Alex suspect you're seeing someone? Or doesn't care?"

"It's a flexible marriage."

"I'm shocked," Rachel said with an insouciance that lent the opposite meaning. "I'll keep my eyes peeled. But why don't you just strike up a conversation with her?"

"Captain Nagel doesn't seem to like me. He can't throw me in jail, can he?"

Rachel raised her chin and smiled as the minister from Uruguay passed by. "I doubt it. Unless you're caught with snaps of the Baltic fleet." When Kim failed to laugh, Rachel added, "Oh dear. I really do not want to know."

Nor shall you. Unless Rachel had the *spill.* That was the problem in Berlin; one distrusted everyone, and with excellent reason. Even if you weren't an agent of a government, you might be a Gestapo informant, on or off the payroll, sometimes just to ingratiate yourself with an official, sometimes under blackmail. Rachel, however, was a kidder, she felt sure. Nothing more than that.

But Kim must have a moment with Sonja. Captain Nagel was a *Nachkomme*, as proven by his vulture insignia and patent madness. Sonja was married to a monster, a man who had *become* a monster, perhaps slowly, but unmistakably. Kim thought it likely that Sonja was unhappy. A *spill* about the *Nachkommen- schaft* might be ripe for the taking, as it would be a secret the woman would surely be determined to keep.

Just over there, Alex. Mixing, like the raconteur he was, with the German state secretary von Bülow, the French ambassador Francois-Poncet, and a woman who must be an actress by her flamboyant gown with a feathery fringe edging the neckline and the revealing back that plunged to her waist.

Rachel chatted on, but Kim heard little more. Berlin had become vastly more complicated than she had expected. She had stumbled with her enthusiasm for extracting Hannah; too soon, too soon. If she had only waited, when she had more compelling clues regarding Monarch. Now her information might be received as crying wolf.

Last night, in high annoyance, she had revised her report on the sanatorium. She had to placate the head office as well as the Berlin station, but it was a challenge to convey all the crucial information without mentioning in detail the gruesome behavior of the escaped patient. She had convinced herself that revising the report wasn't cowardice, just a bit of judicious subterfuge. The important thing was to get the *catalyst* discovery out in the open. The Office couldn't ignore that piece, even the rumor of which should set off alarms from London to Prague.

While the head office chewed on the cleaned-up report, Kim

would push just a little further. Lunch with Sonja; harmless and perhaps crucial. Her chief hope was for Hannah's escape from Germany. Before she was recruited away by other governments.

Through an opening in the crowd, she saw Sonja on her husband's arm.

Rachel saw her too. "Tell you what. I'll drag Rikard off to meet Madame Regendanz, the one in the backless dress. He won't like it, but he'll go along. For about three minutes."

She pulled Kim through the crowd, photographers circulating, taking pictures and causing people to form threes and fours and raise champagne flutes as the flashes went off. In these situations, when stuck in any group, Kim always made sure to be moving at the moment the pictures were taken, a little waggle she executed with precision.

As soon as her friend claimed Rikard, Kim approached her target. "Sonja. So nice to see you." They exchanged air kisses.

"I, too." She looked even thinner than before, the shadows under her eyes matching the powder on her lids.

"I've been so busy since we arrived in Berlin," Kim said. "I haven't had time to be sociable. Would you fancy lunch sometime?"

The woman looked like it was the furthest thing from her mind, to have lunch, to be sociable. She glanced over at Rikard, who stood at German attention beside the actress in fur, the two looking like different species. As perhaps they were.

"I don't think . . ." Then a pause as Sonja set her mouth. "Perhaps a cocktail some evening? If you can get away."

I'm not locked in, Sonja. Are you? "Perfect. Call me." She opened her handbag to find her calling card, passing one to Sonja. "Oops, Alex is looking for me. Thank you!" She skated away, hoping that Nagel had not seen her—but reluctant to look.

† † †

Alex noted Kim making her way toward him. He gestured Gestapo Captain Lessing toward the bank of doors leading to the terrace. "Shall we step out for a moment?"

Captain Lessing snatched a pork-stuffed prune from the hors d'oeuvre tray proffered by a server and accompanied Alex to the porch.

A wooly fog, the same one that had swathed the city for a week, drifted through the remains of the garden. Alex snapped open his cigarette case, and as the two men smoked, they gazed into the distance where, along the Wilhelmstrasse, Christmas lights saturated the fog with a red and green aurora.

"Berlin is going all out for the holidays," Alex said.

"It is good for business. The same in London, *ja*?"

"Yes. And the fog. I feel right at home."

"That is excellent." Lessing allowed a few moments to pass before he broached an uncomfortable subject. "On Tuesday, she was in Wittenberge in the early morning hours. At 2:30 AM she took the train to Berlin."

Alex hadn't a clue what Kim would be doing in Wittenberge, but he bit his lip as though this confirmed his worst fears. "Alone?"

"And without a suitcase. Her hair, quite wet. She claimed that she had been on holiday and cut short her stay due to an illness of her niece in England."

"Wittenberge." Alex chewed it over. "No one seeing her off?"

"*Nein*. She was alone on the platform."

"Thank you, Captain. Very good of you to let me know." Wittenberge at 2:30 AM. No doubt lying that her niece had taken ill, since she hadn't mentioned it to him.

"These things are always difficult," Captain Lessing said. "If you wish us to detain her next time?"

"Oh, I shouldn't think that would help." A wry smile. "You'd scare her."

"Perhaps useful?"

"No, I'll deal with her. I'd just like to know who he is." The pretense that he thought she had a lover. He did need to preserve her cover so that he couldn't be faulted for anything. But he also needed to get enough information on her mistakes to have her recalled. She was a loose cannon and could easily ruin his reputation with the German authorities.

"Of course," Lessing said. "It is your right to know. We will watch, and if there is anything new . . ."

"Thank you." Alex glanced toward the party, the blaring lights of the drawing room, the muffled laughter. He thought he spotted Kim in her lavender dress, or whatever color it was, across the room. "I am indebted to you, Captain—and appreciate your discretion. Please give my regards to Major Müller. The Gestapo is being most helpful."

A click of heels, a curt bow. Not all Gestapo were brutes.

But neither were they the brightest lights of Hitler's crew.

Lessing rejoined the soiree, leaving Alex to wonder what Kim had been doing in Wittenberge, and where she might have been before that, since she'd been gone all day and most of the night. Just one more gaffe and the FO was sure to recall her. It was time to dissolve the marriage. The agreement had been that she would be on his arm for the diplomatic circuit. Instead, she was involved with Jews, rabble-rousers, dive bars, and God knew what else. If she got in trouble, it must be clear to the German government that he had no part of her schemes.

It was hardly surprising that she had refused to join him in Bonn, but really, the charade couldn't go on. It was an unsuitable arrangement all the way around. And Wittenberge in the wee hours. If she was on to something unpleasant, the sooner she was gone the better, and they could all get back to the live-and-let-live world of the Foreign Service.

Through the French doors he saw Kim approaching. She joined him at the balustrade. "Are you tired of the party already?"

"Just taking a breather," he said.

She came closer and put her arm around him. Acting the part. "Who were you talking too?"

"Out here? Viktor Lessing. With the German Automotive Association." He threw his cigarette into the garden. "Let's go in. Maybe we can leave early."

Kim smiled. "Let's have a night cap at home, then."

She *was* being nice. The thought occurred that, before she was summoned home, he might yet get her into bed. Once would be enough, he was rather sure.

THE AERIE

SATURDAY, DECEMBER 12. Positioning his miniature soldiers in battle formation, Kolya sprawled on the floor at Irina's feet, leaning on his elbows. By his side the schnauzer puppy, Lev, that one of the German officers had given him.

Polina, sewing in a chair by the window, said in Russian, "You remember your manners with our important guest, Your Highness."

Kolya, without lifting his eyes from the ranks of soldiers, said, "I stand next to mother, and when I am told his name, which I already know is *Reichsführer* Heinrich Himmler, he will greet me and bow. Then I must incline my head this much"—he dipped his head at the carpet—"and say, 'I am pleased to meet you, *Reichsführer*,' but I must not crease my waist, because he is a commoner."

Polina frowned. "Ssst. We do not use such words. In private you may say he is not royal."

"Oh, leave off, Polina." Irina was enjoying watching Kolya play, the chateau great room cozy in the quiet morning, with the crackling fire staving off the winter gloom.

"Should I show him my silver box?" Kolya jumped to his feet and fetched it from the table. Opening it for his mother, he recited, "A book of stories by my favorite author, Edgar Allan Poe, the topaz I got for my birthday, Uncle Arcady's ring, and the bear claw from Siberia." He put the box in her lap and lifted out the gun. "My revolver that I shot a bull's-eye with."

Irina raised her eyebrows. "Not loaded, Kolya!"

"No, it isn't. And it has a pearl handle and engraving on the barrel." He looked up at her happily. "Small and deadly."

"I'm sure it is. But who is this Mr. Poe?"

By her tone of voice, he paused, unsure if she would be angry. She pursed her lips. "Not English, I hope."

"No, *Maman*, American!"

Polina rolled her eyes. "And it should be Chekhov."

Noises at the front door. "Take the puppy away," Irina told Polina. "Our guests are here."

At that, a servant announced their visitor. Kolya took the box from Irina's lap and laid it on the end table, conscious that his mother should not be holding something when guests arrived. He stood at her side.

Himmler entered, followed by Stefan. The SS chief bowed to her, not deep enough. He pretended not to know royal protocols, yet at the same time he considered himself smooth. A charmer.

Sir Stefan made the introduction to Kolya in French. "Your Highness, may I present *SS-Reichsführer* Heinrich Himmler." Turning to Himmler, he said, "His Imperial Highness, the tsarevich Nikolai Ivanovich."

Another bow from Himmler. "Your Highness," he said in German.

Kolya stood at relaxed attention, as he had been taught. He inclined his head, just so much. "A pleasure to meet you, *Reichsführer*," in German, the one phrase Irina had allowed him to memorize.

There was the issue of the toy soldiers now strewn on the carpet before Irina. It was out of the question for Kolya to pick them up, but the tsarina was fenced in by them.

Stefan saw the difficulty and stooped down. "Your Highness." He picked up a cavalryman on horseback and smiled at Kolya. "I had such a set of soldiers when I was a child. It is good to see the tradition continues." He looked up for permission, and Kolya, catching on, ducked his head in permission. Stefan picked up enough of the metal figures to make a path for Irina.

As Irina stepped forward, Himmler said, "Your Majesty, thank you for inviting me to your home. For the demonstration we could have used the Festival Hall. We do not wish to disturb your family." Stefan translated.

How guttural and unattractive the German language was. Yes, Himmler wanted a demonstration, and she would give him one, but on her terms. "It is no trouble. Did you bring my *Nachkomme?*"

Himmler turned to the corridor leading to the front door, and from the shadows a man in uniform stepped forward, bowing deeply. It was Lieutenant Juergen Becht, one of her favorites.

Irina extended her hand, something she never did except when wearing gloves. "Lieutenant, welcome. It is good of you to come early, since *Reichsführer* Himmler will not be able to join us for the Christmas celebration." The lieutenant spoke excellent English, and she used it with him. Stefan murmured translations for Himmler, who boorishly had no foreign languages.

"It is my pleasure and honor, Your Majesty." A stiff, very correct bow. She had not seen Juergen Becht for two months. In that time he had taken on the predestined look, drawn, pale, and iron-strong. The dueling scar on his right cheek was now a deep valley carved in a face pale as bone. She thrilled to his power, which she could sense in his presence, behind his eyes. He had come to her as a high 7 and now 9 was within reach, she hoped.

Juergen Becht was a particular favorite of Stefan's, and hers, since he was the one who had helped to identify the so-called Red Girl criminal.

"I am happy to see you looking so well, Lieutenant."

He bowed, clicking his heels.

Even though Himmler had never seen a purification, she was sorry it was to be Juergen Becht who would assist. It was worrisome to *catalyze* a month early. Some of the effects seemed to worsen if purifications were too frequent. But she would indulge the SS chief, since Hitler had asked it of her.

Stefan caught her eye and slid a glance at Kolya.

"Colonel von Ritter"—she called him by his formal name since his superior officer was present—"perhaps the tsarevich would enjoy a visit to the pond. They said it is beginning to freeze over."

Stefan took his cue and left, Kolya in tow.

The maid brought in a tea service, and the two men joined Irina near the fireplace, where she deliberately took the divan, the two SS officers in chairs.

"Yesterday," Irina said, "King Edward gave up the British throne." She asked Juergen Becht to translate, which he did. It would be interesting to see how Himmler would handle this delicate subject.

He was not diplomatic. "To our sorrow, Your Majesty. He understood our nation." Becht translated.

"But he would make a divorced woman Queen of England."

"The Führer would have welcomed it. They drove him to abdication, hounded him out. A disgrace."

"Perhaps, when events demand it, a country must find the most worthy monarch."

Becht paused before translating, understanding the insult that hovered amid them.

Himmler pushed on. "The Duke of York succeeds him, but he has not the keen intelligence, the discernment of King Edward." He smiled ingratiatingly. "The Führer is greatly disappointed."

Since Irina had dismissed the maid, Juergen Becht poured tea. She noted that his hand shook. Perhaps he was agitated that Himmler had not realized—or did not care—that Irina Dimitrievna Annakova approved of the change of English kings, a transition of monarchs. Since the Imperial Romanovs had been slaughtered and someone must be raised to her homeland's throne.

A sound like pellets from a shotgun hit the window. Himmler jerked a look at the soaring glass of the great room, but it was only bullets of ice driven by the wind.

"Lieutenant Becht," Irina said, removing her gloves, "sit with me."

He looked up at her, his face softening, his voice low. "Your Majesty."

She glanced at the space on the divan next to her.

Himmler put down his china cup and became attentive, his eyes unblinking in their effort to miss nothing. The demonstration he had asked for.

When Juergen Becht took a seat beside her, she turned to gaze at him, taking his hand. His fingers, all steely and long, instruments of obedience. "Juergen Becht," she said. "Do not fear me."

"No, Your Majesty, I shall not."

"I remember," she murmured to him, "that you are a man of the church. This pleases me." She glanced at Himmler. "It is not forbidden." The Third Reich allowed the church, within reason.

Becht's reserve began to fall away. She felt his hand relax into hers. Then the intertwining of their fingers, his own hot against her cooler skin. They sat thus as the wind cracked against the chalet and the fire snapped. "Turn to me, Juergen."

He did so, with a face that was haunted and soft, though no one could call it lovely. She murmured to him, "My command is that you use your gift to *mesmerize* the room and that you accompany *Reichsführer* Himmler . . ." Here she whispered into his ear. Then she pulled back, saying, "You understand?"

He glanced at Himmler, who nodded he was to comply. "Yes, Your Majesty."

She leaned into him. Cupping his head in one hand, she brought him close to her, his cheek against hers. Then she placed the flat of her hand against the side of his scarred face. He burned as though fevered. Now that her power was aroused by this embrace, they matched heat. She held him.

Wind and ice. The fire in the hearth. She heard Himmler's breath loud, the thud of soldier's boots on patrol, Juergen's heart beating strong, the blood coursing in her veins. She listened to these things. The creaking of the timbers as the bones of the earth shifted miles below, her thoughts falling away like silt in still water.

When next she looked up, they were gone. The *mesmerizing*. It was always like this: the dreamlike peace, the acute hearing, the stupefaction.

Vaguely, she could recall them walking away, Becht saying something to Himmler, but she had not listened, had not cared.

The *mesmerizing* had dissipated now. Becht had left, crossing the plaza as instructed and descending in the lift, down through the stone foundation of the Aerie to the base.

She stood up, reaching for the fur cape that lay over a chair. She draped it around her shoulders as she went to the veranda door.

Outside the wind carried gusts of icy rain, while below, far below, gray fog roiled in the valley. Leaning on the railing and looking down at profound drop to the front of her fortress, she saw Himmler and Becht.

Himmler was surrounded by his officers, who had noted his emergence from the shaft. Becht had released him, and now Himmler saw that he had traveled rather far under a profound *mesmerizing* from which even such a personage as he was not immune. The hail had turned to rain.

Irina raised a hand in greeting. One of the officers noted her appearance, above, and soon Himmler was gazing up at her. His face and uniform, drenched. She might have arranged a different proof of *mesmerizing* power, one that allowed Himmler more dignity, but this one pleased her more.

Himmler saluted her. He must be pleased. They were his *Nachkommenschaft* too.

SATURDAY, DECEMBER 12. Bibi served the lamb. She had lit candles at the table, as though the master and mistress of the house might benefit from mood lighting.

Kim took a portion of the dish. Even after six weeks in Berlin, she and Alex had seldom eaten dinner together. The press of duties, the demanding schedule at the embassy, their growing animosity.

"How are discussions with the German finance people going?" Kim asked. The dinner had been her idea. She must make a better effort to be nice. Charming might also be useful if she could muster the effort. Their marriage should at least appear convivial.

Alex helped himself to the lamb. "On and off." He shrugged. "We have no leverage, and Herr Hitler knows it. I'm hoping that further down the hierarchy, clearer heads will prevail."

"Will you meet with the chancellor?"

"I shouldn't think so. But you may be sure the marching orders come straight from him." Outside the bay window, fog clung as though pressing close to listen.

"You'll bring me along, if you get the chance, though?"

He gave her an amused, knowing look, equal parts of *I know you despise him* and *I'll just bet you'd love an introduction.* "Of course."

They were starting to communicate without words, just like real marrieds. Sometimes Alex almost treated her as wife, one in need of curbing, and she predictably pushed back against direction. And there had been times when he had acted as though sharing a bed might easily be a part of the charade. In fact, she had entertained the idea several weeks ago, even if only after a half bottle of wine.

But their arrangement had seriously wobbled. Alex had complained about her to Whitehall, and now the head office was watching her closely for signs of—what?—provocation, indiscretion, or it seemed, any damned initiative whatsoever. With the sanatorium, she had taken initiative rather far. She felt exposed. Duncan, Whitehall, Alex, all watching for a stumble.

"Still sure you don't want to join me in Bonn on Tuesday?" His interest in her coming along surprised her. Perhaps he realized that she could undermine him if she tried. Robert Vansittart in the Foreign Office was his ultimate boss as well as hers. So she wasn't the only one who must make nice.

She shook her head. "I've planned to see an art exhibition with Rachel."

"Oh? Which one?"

"I forget. French impressionists or something."

Alex raised an eyebrow. "I didn't think the Nazis went in for impressionism."

"Oh? I'm not sure what Nazis go in for." They exchanged

married smiles. A little dig, softened by a smile.

He sliced the lamb in the British fashion, loading his fork. Bibi returned to offer more creamed potatoes.

When she left, Alex said, "What does your family make of your prolonged absence? Are they in on our little play?"

Inwardly, Kim frowned. They should not be talking about her family, her real identity. "Well, no one is keeping track of me."

He persisted. "Not your parents? Siblings?" He sat back in his chair, savoring his wine. "That niece in London?"

Kim paused, trying not to look startled. "You know how spread out my family is. None of us are close." Her niece . . . how in the world did he know about her niece? She had made up the relation under Gestapo questioning in Wittenberge. No such relative existed in the cover dossier Alex had memorized.

"Your father is in England?"

"Yes, but . . ."

He leaned forward, refilling her glass. "Sorry. Not a subject for us, is it?"

She kept her face neutral.

"Sometimes," he went on, "it seems as though we *are* married." He made a self-deprecating smile. "I'm not accustomed to dissembling, so I get off course."

She lifted her glass. "To our little pretense. We're better actors than we knew."

Not accustomed to dissembling? *Oh, Alex, you are very good at it. But I believe you have just* spilled *to me.*

There was no niece in London or anywhere else.

Later, as Alex went over his correspondence in the library downstairs, Kim entered his bedroom. Without a flashlight she had to risk turning on the light.

She made a swift assessment of the room: end tables, desk, highboy. Where would a man like Alex keep his acquired business cards? Crossing to the desk, she rifled through it, finding a rather large stack of them, some larger than customary. Just what she was hoping for: his Nazi contacts with their penchant for bigger cards.

Here was Rikard Nagel's card. But of course Alex did know Sonja's husband. And now, Hermann Göring's. Nothing unusual there. Who else was he hobnobbing with?

She continued shuffling through the cards, then stopped at one, puzzling over the name. Vaguely familiar.

Viktor Lessing. The name of the man whom Alex had spoken with on the terrace at the Christmas party.

But this was not an individual with the automobile association. *Captain Viktor Lessing, Geheime Staatspolizei.* The Gestapo.

The Gestapo was in a position to believe that she had a niece. It was a lie she'd made up on the spot at the Wittenberge train station. So the secret police were feeding information about her to Alex. How very cozy.

How very disturbing.

THE VICTORIA AND ALBERT
MUSEUM, LONDON

SUNDAY, DECEMBER 13. Julian had the unsettled feeling that Kim was in a great deal of trouble with the authorities. But whether the trouble was with the German government or the British, he was not sure.

He made his way across the lobby and up to the second floor of the Victoria and Albert to rendezvous with E. The chief had now read Kim's report. Julian hoped Kim would have E's backing.

She was hard on the trail of a possible conspiracy. One having to do with a new Talent weapon. She apparently trusted her source, the Linz woman; trusted her intel on Monarch—not to mention her startling claim to be a *catalyst* herself. But her Berlin handler disliked the risks she'd taken, perhaps resenting that she'd taken them without consulting him, and now he was recommending that she be recalled. A bad situation; but he was fairly confident Kim would win this one. Still, he could not lobby too hard on her behalf since, as her father, his objectivity could be suspect.

It helped that she had uncovered the potential *catalyst* Talent. It helped immeasurably, elevating the importance of her mission. Such an ability, if true, would topple the theory that an individual's Talent rating was immutable. And then Hannah Linz claimed that the Germans had such an individual working for them. If so, they would certainly exploit the advantage in Europe.

He had sent out a questionnaire to their German agents to report on Treptow Sanatorium, hoping that a confirmation of its secret purpose would corroborate her findings.

Julian spied E in the gallery just ahead, and he made his way to their frequent meeting spot, the bust of Queen Victoria on a pedestal.

E gazed up at the regal sculpture, alabaster on a black marble plinth, set high enough that one must stand rather far back to get a good view. E murmured, "Why do you suppose they didn't put the sculpture down where people could examine it properly?"

Julian said, "Perhaps she did not want to be examined properly."

E grunted and circled around to view the bust from another angle. Julian followed. "Well, your girl has got her way. She's to bring Vesta out. Immediately." Vesta, Hannah Linz's code name.

Julian was surprised. All he'd hoped for was that she be allowed to pursue Hannah Linz as a source. Now, extraction. It was a relief to see things beginning to tilt in Kim's favor. "The FO—Vansittart—made the decision? Or did it go to the Joint Intelligence Committee?"

"Van made the call. He wants one of these Talents. If the Nazis have the White Russian, then he wants the Jew." He shrugged. "You can't pick your bedfellows."

Julian forced himself to ignore E's distasteful remark. "It's also our chance to debrief the woman on the project she claims is underway." It was difficult to hide his delight with Vansittart's decision. Having Hannah *walk in*, as the spy trade called it, was the kind of break that the Office lived for, and now they'd take advantage of it.

The chief went on. "We don't know how much augmentation a *catalyst* might actually be able to exert. But if the claim is exaggerated, at least we'll be sure. Monkton Hall needs to test this new ability. We can't be caught flat-footed on the matter." He contemplated the old queen's visage as though probing for signs of doubt. Victoria, however, did not appear to put much stock in doubt.

"She's to lose no time. Can't tell who's on Vesta's tail, nor when she'll grow impatient and offer her services to someone else."

"I'm not sure she's offering her services to *us*."

"Of course she is. It's what she has to trade. Or damn well better."

"I'll get in touch with the station directly." Berlin station would be displeased, of course, but they'd toe the line.

Julian stayed behind to admire the sculpture as E left the gallery.

24

SUNDAY, DECEMBER 13. Winter was a strange season in Berlin. As her cab sped toward her outing at the Hotel Esplanade, Sonja reflected how grim, how wrong, it was so near Christmas to endure icy fogs and bitter rains. She longed for the clean, bright snows of Stockholm and had begun to hate everything German, even her husband.

But tonight, meeting a friend.

Someone Rikard would not approve of, but what did he approve of anymore? If she was not to befriend the English, the French, or the Russians, nor indeed any of the diplomatic wives, it left her more than ever alone. If Rikard had been jealous . . . if he had wanted her to be with him . . . But he did not.

Nor, it now seemed, did Hermann. When they were together—but not since last week at his lodge—she felt doted upon. But she also feared him. Increasingly, over the last few days, since he had not called. Did he harbor doubts about her? Did he suspect she had been eavesdropping the last time she saw him?

The taxi slowed to a stop. A rally in the street just ahead.

Motorcars stacked up on all sides. "A patriotic march down the Wilhelmstrasse," the driver said.

She could hear the distant cadence of many voices raised in song. Nearby, trams jammed up, ringing their bells. People hopped off them, lining up on the street to watch.

This close to the Potsdamer Platz on the Leipziger Strasse, it would be faster to walk. She paid the fare and stepped out to cross the street, safe because nothing was moving. Once on the pavement, she found it slow going with people juggling for position to see the procession. When she got to the Wilhelmstrasse, in the distance she could see the banners hoisted, the fog carrying halos from the torches.

Elaine Reed would be arriving now at the hotel bar, unless she, too, was delayed by the demonstration. The parade approached, the *Sturmabteilung* marchers taking over the great street, threading among the cars, their boots thudding rhythmically. It was while seeing the river of Nazi banners approach that she felt she was being watched.

Every time she stopped, attempting to see her way across the street, someone paused behind her. She could not make him out clearly in the fog, but his peaked hat marked him among the throng. He could not be following her; she was the wife of an SS officer. She moved quickly up the pavement to prove this was so. But as the blaring SA marched by, her pursuer still shadowed her.

A spike of anxiety rose in her breast. Was Göring having her followed? Did he know she had heard things that she shouldn't outside the library? She had, but it had been an accident. The door ajar, the voices. Hermann's affairs so mysterious . . . How she wished she could take back that moment! Göring had looked at her so strangely. He could be tender, and she knew she pleased him. But on this dark December night, with the braying marchers and their torches, she felt alone and in peril.

She spied a gap in the march and plunged into the street to cross it, wishing only for the safety of the hotel.

One of the marchers shouted at her, waving her out of the way, and she dashed for the curb, fear mounting in a wave of emotion.

Sonja was late. Kim waited outside the Hotel Esplanade. Home to the busiest intersection in Germany, the plaza was breathtaking at night, anchored by the Anhalter Bahnhof, several major hotels, and the Haus Vaterland, its fabulous dome lit by thousands of strung lights.

She had almost canceled her date with Sonja. Since the Office had given her instructions for Hannah's extraction, it appeared her work here might be coming to an end. It would take a couple of days to put in place a plan to get Hannah out, including backup paperwork for the visa. But Hannah would soon be in safety and working with British intelligence. When Duncan had delivered the instructions, he seemed rather sour about it, but Kim was beyond worrying about what Duncan thought. The Office had finally come through for her and, despite the delay in their response, she savored her success.

At the mailbox at Café Unten near the *Nollendorfplatz*, she had left a message for Hannah to meet her on the *Schiffbauerdamm* on Tuesday. She didn't want Hannah to call her at her home telephone, since there was Alex to worry about now. She had not quite decided what to do about Alex. He was still useful as cover for the duration of her assignment—just a few days longer.

She heard the sounds of a march or demonstration a few blocks away, probably the cause of the stalled traffic beginning to clog in the square. Trams fired off blue sparks from the over-head cables, as though impatient with the delay.

Deciding to use the lavatory, she entered the hotel lobby.

A doorman held open the glass door of the hotel for Sonja.

She rushed into the palatial lobby, her stomach twisting, a hot sweat breaking out on her skin. Throwing open her coat, she made her way past the massive reception desk, the divans, the carved tables with lavish lamps.

Inside the lounge, lights sparkled among a display of liquors. The maître d' offered to seat her. She chose a table in the corner. Finally able to catch her breath, she realized she had panicked over nothing. She was falling apart, seeing threats everywhere.

A waiter came to take her order.

Behind him, Rikard appeared in the arched doorway. His expression was hard and dark. God, he was the one who had been following her. He turned in her direction, but she leaned in toward the waiter to block his view.

The thought stabbed at her: Rikard would kill her. Göring had sent her own husband to dispose of her, and in the heart of Berlin.

A loud party entered the bar from the lobby. Under this cover, she bolted from her chair and fled along a row of tables, away from Rikard, finding to her relief a corridor leading away from the bar. She could not think or plan. Where could she go if her own husband stalked her?

Now in the lobby, she rushed to the main doors. Not giving

the attendants time to open them for her, she pushed through onto the street.

Kim saw Sonja just as she was leaving the hotel. She called her name, but Sonja didn't seem to hear, slipping out the hotel doors. Once on the street, Kim lost sight of her.

Traffic was moving again. She spied Sonja, running across the lanes of traffic, dodging a car. A screech of tires, a soft thud. The awful realization: Sonja had been struck.

Dashing into the street, Kim wove and danced through the cars, now slowing for the accident. She ran to where Sonja lay.

A man was already beside her. "She's breathing," he said.

Kim knelt at Sonja's side. She turned to the man, possibly the driver who had struck her. "Call for an ambulance!"

Turning her attention to Sonja, she murmured, "It's Elaine, Sonja." Blood pooled beneath her head. Sonja's eyes fluttered open, closed again. Alarm rose in Kim's chest; this was bad, perhaps very bad. God, the blood. The blood pooled thick. The sickening thought came: Sonja was fatally injured. But it could not be, should not be. Pebbles on the street knifed into Kim's knees as she shifted her weight. She bent low over Sonja. "I'm here with you. We will get you help." She looked up, hoping to see an ambulance. No sign of one. People were gathering around her.

The terrible image came, of Sonja's mad rush into the street . . . why, why had she plunged into the heavy traffic?

Sonja's eyes flickered again. Was there still hope? But in truth, she thought that these were Sonja's last moments. Kim stooped very close to her, repeating her name so that she would know she was not alone. Then the awful thought sprang free: she must ask her questions. Now, before she died.

She took Sonja's hand. "I know what Rikard is. He's unnatural. Help me to stop this." Someone in the crowd draped a coat over Sonja.

"*Nachkomme*," Sonja whispered.

Kim glimpsed someone rushing toward them through the stopped traffic. It was Rikard.

Sonja struggled to speak as a rasp issued from her lungs. "Fiends! All of them."

"I know, I know. Where do they gather? Where is Monarch?"

"Tolz . . . ," Sonja whispered, as bubbles of blood frothed at her mouth. "Tolzried. The . . . Aerie."

"We'll stop them," Kim whispered. "We will. I promise." *I promise.* It was all she could do for Sonja now.

She saw boots. Rikard loomed over them. "Leave her."

When she ignored him, he yanked her to her feet, holding her with an effortless and adamantine grip. Panic rose in her chest as she considered what he might have heard.

Sonja bled at their feet. "Go to her," Kim said, pleading with this most unnatural of husbands. "For God's sake, Captain."

"She is dead."

They stared down at Sonja's unmoving form. Rikard would know about such things, would have a finely honed concept of the moment of death. Kim began to tremble from the shock. *Oh, Sonja.* The death had been swift, brutal.

Kim looked down at her bloody hands, sticky and bitterly cold. Rikard's nostrils flared. He did not care that his wife was dead. The world seemed pitiless and evil.

"I will take you home," he said. The clang of an ambulance close by.

Her mind finally kicked into gear. He was offering to drive her somewhere. She did not want to get into a car with Rikard Nagel. Looking into his pale eyes, she feared him. "My husband . . . ," she began, trying to think of something. "He is joining me at the Esplanade. I will go with him." He looked fixedly into her face. Did he wonder why she had been with Sonja, what she had heard? Perhaps he would not allow her to go. But then he released her arm as the ambulance workers arrived.

Using his indecision as a window of escape, Kim turned into the crowd, making her way across the lanes of traffic to the pavement.

At any moment Rikard might change his mind. Still, he could not have heard what Sonja said to her. Or could he?

Guests streamed out of the hotel to look at the accident scene. Kim pushed past them, entering the lobby, thrusting her bloody hands into her pockets. Sonja was dead, came the unreal thought. And Rikard had seen her bending over his wife, murmuring to her. Anxiety made its way to the front of her consciousness. He had *hypercognition*: enhanced speed of deduction, a profound, accurate intuition.

She stopped an attendant. "Is there another entrance to the hotel?"

There was. She found it and charged into the street to find a taxi.

Tiergartenstrasse 44 was only a few blocks away. In moments they had pulled up in front of the mansion. Rushing up to the door, she managed to form a plan: she would decamp to her safe flat before Rikard Nagel thought better of allowing her to leave. She'd keep her meeting with Hannah in a couple days, and do so from her safe flat. She ducked into the downstairs lavatory to wash the blood from her hands. Her coat! A large, shockingly red stain fringed the hem. She yanked it off, quickly rubbing the stain under running water.

That finished, and charging into the hallway, she heard someone coming down the hall from the solarium. Folding the wet coat in her arms, she rushed up the stairs to her room. There she packed a small suitcase. Grabbed the waterproof pouch from behind *Travels in Europe.*

On the table, the daily flowers: lilies. She stared hard at them. They must go in the windowsill. Someone will come to help. But she paused. Duncan had been obviously unhappy that London had given the go-ahead to extract Hannah; he was convinced Kim was a loose cannon, not under station control. First, she had run from the Gestapo; then her break-in at Treptow. Now Sonja Nagel had died in her arms—something she could not reasonably be blamed for, but Duncan might well fault her for drawing the attention of a Nazi with *hypercognition.* Now, if Nagel tried to arrest her, there would be another black mark against her. She didn't need Duncan's help, not yet. At the very least she needed time to think. She turned away from the flowers.

Bibi appeared at the door.

"Bibi, I am joining my husband in Bonn after all."

"I can help you pack, ma'am," she said in German, reminding Kim that she had wanted to practice her German.

"Oh, not necessary, thank you," she said, switching to German. "Is Albert free to take me to the station?" She needed to leave quickly. Nagel might well come after her. She was the wife of a consular official, so he wouldn't dare hurt her—or, in his state of mental imbalance, would he? What would the Nazis dare if they thought Sonja knew about Monarch and had told Kim with her dying breath?

Bibi looked at her, her glance traveling down to her legs. "Is anything amiss, ma'am?"

"No, not at all. If you could find Albert, please, Bibi."

When she was gone, Kim examined her legs. A wide streak of blood soiled the silk stocking on her left leg.

In the lavatory she washed her leg, rinsing the blood from the basin. Snatching her suitcase, she went downstairs.

Bibi met her at the bottom. "Albert will be just a moment."

"A moment? My train, Bibi."

"He was not dressed to properly drive you. But he is bringing the car to the side door. I would be happy to help, ma'am. Albert and I know that you have special duties that may require assistance."

What? They knew? Her mind flooded with questions. And suspicion. Why had Duncan not told her this? "Nothing needed, but thank you, Bibi." Turning on her heel, she took her suitcase down the hall to the back door to hurry Albert along. She found him in the garage, dusting off his chauffeur hat.

"Never mind that, Albert. I wish to leave immediately."

"I will put your suitcase on the other side," he said. *Gott im Himmel*, he was moving slowly.

Actually, delaying her.

She stooped down and picked up the suitcase before he could take it. Hefting it into the back seat, she said, "There and done." She slid in beside it. "Ready then, Albert?"

They got underway, driving under the port cochere on the north side of the house and onto the Tiergartenstrasse. As they pulled into the street, Kim saw the flowers in the upstairs window.

They hadn't trusted her to signal for help. Bibi and Albert had taken matters into their own hands, trying to alert Berlin station that there was trouble. It had been one of Bibi and Albert's assignments, she thought with increasing distress. Paranoia washed over her. Somehow Bibi and perhaps Albert were under the impression that she needed extra caring for. How strange, if they knew she was an undercover agent. And if they did, that they believed she didn't have the wits to place the flower vase herself.

What had caused Bibi to panic? Kim thought she had handled the story of her trip to Bonn rather well. Perhaps her cool facade had not gone off well. Instead of the prospect of a spur-of-the-moment holiday, Bibi might have seen in Kim a wild-eyed alarm.

The blood on her leg might have clinched it.

To his credit, Albert actually followed her instruction and dropped her off at Lehrter Bahnhof Station. After watching until the car had disappeared, Kim hailed a taxi to the zoological gardens on the Kurfürstendamm. Then two trams to the Alexanderplatz.

Arriving at the great square, she checked her watch. 10:21 PM.

She climbed the stairs to her apartment, the one no one knew about, not even the Berlin station. With shaking hands she let herself into her safe flat and leaned against the door in her wet, stained coat. The neighborhood settled around her. Her ears rang with sounds, any of which could mean pursuit.

Turning, she locked the door.

THE AERIE

SUNDAY, DECEMBER 13. Irina had been hearing gunfire in her dream, but when Polina came into the bedroom, the light from the hallway stabbing into her chamber, she knew the shots were real.

"Your Majesty," her attendant said. "There is trouble outside."

Irina threw off the covers and swung her feet to the floor. The windows dark, her maid in shadow. "What—what is it?"

"Evgeny Feodorovich Borisov is shooting on the hill. Among the cabins."

"Shooting?" Irina shook off sticky tendrils of sleep. "Evgeny, shooting?"

"Yes, so the officer has told me."

"Send him to me."

"Majesty, you must dress. I will bring a robe."

Irina pushed the woman toward the door. "Bring him, I say!"

Polina fled into the hallway. Voices, one a man's. Lieutenant Strasser entered. He bowed.

"Your Majesty, Evgeny Feodorovich has a pistol and is shooting at trees. He is raving."

"No one is to harm him!"

"We have not fired on him, but he is threatening also to kill himself."

"My cape, Polina!"

"You must have shoes, Majesty, you must . . ."

"Bring them! Hurry!"

Buttoning her shoes, she threw a cape over her nightgown and led the way down the stairs of the chalet and through the main entrance. A blast of icy air engulfed her.

A thick frost furred the paving stones as she left with Lieutenant Strasser. They rushed across the plaza toward the trees that crowned the residence hill. "Did you try to give him his injection, his sedative?"

"We can't get near him, Your Majesty."

"How long has he been out there?"

"Twenty minutes. We waited for him to run out of ammunition, but he has one shot left."

They ascended the hill. Through the trees, Irina could see guards spread out. Foremost, Stefan, who was speaking to Evgeny Feodorovich at a distance of fifteen meters.

Stefan turned to Irina. "Your Majesty, please stay back for your safety."

When Evgeny saw her, he began howling. In the harsh moonlight she could see that he aimed a pistol at his head.

"Evgeny! It is your Irinuska. All will be well, my dear."

"No! You will kill me!" he shouted. He looked around at the guards, some with their guns drawn.

"Put away your weapons," Irina called out to the soldiers. The men looked to Stefan, who nodded permission.

"Oh," Evgeny moaned. "Not yet, then! But soon! By your order . . ."

"Never, Evgeny Feodorovich. Never."

"I have seen it." He moaned piteously. "Put down like a useless thing, like a horse, an animal!"

As she began to approach him, Stefan put out an arm, barring her.

"Leave me be!" Irina hissed.

"Your Majesty, please. Do not go closer, he is deranged."

Glaring at him, she said, "Stand aside." He gave way. She moved closer to Evgeny, looking for her old friend in his wild eyes, the man who had once been all courage and strength, now standing with a gun barrel resting against his temple.

"I am your Irinuska," she whispered to him. "Always your Irinuska. You had a false dream, nothing more."

He cocked the gun.

Stefan ran forward, and Evgeny swung the pistol around to him.

Then from behind, an officer rushed in and threw Evgeny to the ground. As two more held his thrashing body down, one of them administered a shot. He fell limp.

Irina knelt beside him, shaking now in the cold, in the dark of the trees. What did his vision mean, that she would kill him? That he could believe it of her . . .

She looked around at the German soldiers. The soldiers that were sworn to protect her, but only for what she could offer Adolf Hitler: Russia. Even Stefan was not a true friend. Only Evgeny Feodorovich, only him. She put a hand on his ravaged face, wrinkled and stony cold, as though he were in fact dead . . .

Soon he would have his well-deserved rest. Stefan had arranged that after Christmas he would go to a convalescent facility, one of the most renowned in Switzerland. They had always been together; she could hardly think what it would be like to lose him.

Stefan helped her to her feet. "Come, Your Majesty."

They made their way out of the copse of trees onto the path winding among the cabins, as two guards carried Evgeny to his cabin.

"The doctor will stay with him." Irina said, and Stefan snapped an order to see it done.

In Stefan's quarters on the second floor of the Festival Hall, he turned on a lamp and settled Irina on a small couch facing the fireplace. His room was simple and spare: the couch, a desk, a small bed, a chest of drawers. She looked for some sign of Erich Stefan von Ritter the man, but he displayed no photographs or decorations of any kind. Everything in military order.

He brought two whiskies in water glasses, nodding at her that she must drink. "Evgeny will be fine. In the morning he will have forgotten."

Irina began to relax, taking a sip of the harsh whisky. "What will become of us?" she whispered.

"You will reclaim the throne, and Kolya beside you."

But tonight she doubted herself, and Hitler, too. "Stalin is strong. Russia is strong. You have no idea how strong."

"He does not have *Panzers*," Stefan said. "He does not have the *Wehrmacht*."

He meant to reassure her, but his words only raised new alarms. "I send your soldiers against my own dear people."

"The Russian army, without a worthy leader, is undisciplined,

Irinuska. I am sorry to say so, but this is the fact. If they fight, we must defeat them, but they will have a new reign of plenty once you are in the palace."

It was too much to contemplate. They cradled their drinks, staring at the dark fireplace as though conjuring a light that was not there.

The divan they sat on was not wide. Stefan's hand rested on his thigh, holding his drink, turning the glass. Warmth rose into her chest and throat in a flush of wonder that he was so close.

He put his drink on the floor beside his boots. Then he took hers from her hands. That, too, put aside.

The moment stretched long. She would not touch him, no, not unless he decided to take her in his arms. His choice.

He turned to her. Then he cupped her face in his hands and kissed her. The taste of him, the pressure of his lips—exquisite, as she had so often imagined. Oh, but he played with fire, did he not? Then, almost immediately, he pulled back. So he did not wish to become one of hers.

He drew his hand down the side of her face, gently, touching her again. But one more time he pulled away. His voice, very low and deep in his throat. "I do not wish to be . . . more than I am."

"Does not every man wish for something more, more than he has ever had?"

"Some do." *But not me,* he left unsaid. "I would be as much as I can be. But not beyond my . . . limits."

Behind her hungry longing, resentment built. He could afford to think so, but he had not *the touch,* had not lived with its blessing. Which she knew came from God. If God had given her this gift, did he not wish for her to use it, and for souls to accept it? She could not think otherwise, lest she despise the world and God with it. She looked into Stefan's dark eyes. Had he, even for just a moment, considered coming to her, to grow in power? Perhaps, for a moment. A split second between yes and no. Bitterness dragged at her heart.

A knock at the door.

Slowly, Stefan got to his feet to answer it. At the door stood Lieutenant Juergen Becht. A conversation in harsh German, and then Stefan was back.

"Forgive me, Irina, I must leave. For Berlin."

"The middle of the night?"

"They have cornered one of the Oberman Group. A terrorist."

She stood, laying the blanket aside. "Is it the red Jew?"

"We have learned where she is. Lieutenant Becht will go with me, since he can identify her, having dealt with her once before." He pulled on his greatcoat. Perhaps he had already forgotten their intimacy. "I will walk with you to the chalet."

"No. You must hurry. Send one of the guards to escort me." She put her hand on his arm, cushioned by the wool of his jacket. "Take your revenge. You have waited long enough."

He nodded, searching her face. If he looked for signs of heartbreak, she was sure he found some.

26

MONDAY, DECEMBER 14. Hannah and Leib shared hard tack and sardines at the kitchen table. No plates, and the table so dirty they ate from their hands. Not that they could see much of the table in the dark house in the middle of the night.

Franz watched them eat, smoking and leaning against the sink. Micha kept vigil out the window, scratching at his neck. It had been weeks since any of them had had a bath.

"We have a new target," Franz said. "Belgian. Set to meet his SS handler on Friday."

Hannah licked her fingers clean. Her father would have cringed to see her do this. "I am tired of these miserable creatures."

"And what will we do with that American from Alba Cookie? There is such a city?"

Hannah shrugged. "I don't know. Albuquerque, so her passport says."

Franz shrugged. "We could let her go." Sarcastic. Prodding her.

"Where is Zev? He was supposed to bring the nitroglycerin." They would assemble the dynamite at the dining room table. They depended on Zev, who had a cousin in a chemical supply company.

No one responded to her question. They weren't looking forward to the assembly of the shock-prone explosive.

Hannah pushed the package of hard tack closer to Leib. He was so thin, no trousers could be found that were not twice his girth. He used a rope to hold up his pants. "We intercept them, but more come in their place. Like standing outside a cockroach hole with a hammer."

Leib cut a glance at her. "Please." Delicate sensibilities, that one, when he wasn't stuffing Gestapo exhaust pipes with flammables.

Hannah went on. "We should strike so they feel the pain."

"You and your bombs," Franz wheezed through a stream of smoke. "It is too dangerous to bomb vehicles. Now they inspect the undercarriage."

They were all tired, discouraged. Sometimes, when Hannah felt despair waiting at the edges, she thought of the Nazi officer, Becht, who had executed her father. The one with the scar down the middle of his cheek. The skin puckered around it, his white skin pink along that line. A face chiseled in memory. She hoped to see Lieutenant Becht again. She dreamed of it.

Franz threw his cigarette in the sink. "We are small." He spread his hands. "Look at us. The whole group, merely fourteen people, and some are afraid to do more. Once you are out, we have thirteen."

"Fourteen people can take out an SS staff car."

Franz ignored this as Micha crossed the room to check out

the other windows. "The British aren't going to get you out of Germany. You know that."

Hannah shrugged. "An open question. Maybe."

"Have you tried the French embassy yet?"

The same conversations over and over. "Not yet."

He shook his head. "You can't still believe that the British will help you. You must go to the French."

"Hear that?" Micha hissed. The sound of people running. The steps, the porch.

Franz pulled his gun from his waistband as Hannah knocked back her chair, drawing her own.

A crash against the door, splintering it. Franz grabbed her by the arm and hauled her into the living room. The kitchen door collapsed. Gunfire like the end of the world.

Through the kitchen door, for a split second Hannah saw Leib fall against the counter, bullets riddling him, blood spraying on the windows.

Micha was still firing, but there was no way he could make it to the escape door. In the living room, Franz pulled Hannah after him through the door to the basement and closed it. They rushed down the stairs. Muffled shouts and cries from above. Running to the tarp, they crawled under it to the tunnel hole. Once through, they pushed the steel drum over the gap. It would hold for a few minutes.

Pausing just long enough to secure their guns so that they could crawl, the two of them scrambled along the rough dirt tunnel, an escape route dug over months, leading to the brewery next door.

"Leib and Micha." Hannah groaned.

"Don't think of them. You must escape. We all agreed you must be saved."

"They must have picked up Zev." She had a black moment to imagine what he would have gone through before finally giving up their location.

They came to the iron grate in the floor of the factory. Franz pushed it up and clambered out. Around them loomed distillation tanks and a tangle of pipes. Franz drew his pistol and they stood unmoving, listening. The sweet, cloying smell of hops. From clerestory windows high above, a dusty light shone through from the street. The Gestapo were certain to search the brewery. They had to get out.

A door creaked from somewhere. They held still, barely breathing.

After a few moments, they heard footfalls nearby. Franz pressed Hannah against a vat, cold on her sweating skin.

A man in an SS uniform stopped within an arm's reach of them, looking. His profile was just visible, his dark hair under his peaked cap.

Ah, Hannah knew this one. The handsome one, the SS colonel who had opened the vehicle door last summer. The one they had sabotaged. His men had dragged him away after the bomb fragments settled. So, he had lived. This was her chance to fix that. Hannah raised her gun.

Franz cupped his hand around the muzzle. The report of the gun would bring them all.

The colonel moved away, hardly making a noise, in the way of *Sicherheitsdienst*, the spies of the SS. He disappeared in the gloom. After a few beats, Franz moved into the corridor between the vats, gun raised. He would kill this SS man if he had to. No matter what came next. But the colonel was out of sight.

They crept through the brewery to the alley door and stepped out into the night. Faintly, the sound of voices shouting.

With the arrival of the SS, the street had gone vacant. Franz and Hannah would be visible if they walked on the pavement, but they risked it. Hugging the side of the tenement buildings, they slunk along, avoiding shafts of light from windows here and there. All was quiet. A slice of moon, just visible through the tattered fog, looked down on them with indifference.

They had known it would come to this someday. The sudden crash, the doors flying open. The carnage. Leib had died the way he wanted to. Quickly. Hannah hoped Micha would be as lucky. Hoped it for herself. Someday. Perhaps tonight.

Then someone came around the corner a hundred meters away. Saw them. Gun raised, the man shouted for them to stop.

Hannah and Franz ducked into a dark alley. At the end, a tall fence blocking the passage, barring escape.

"Go!" Franz hissed. "Go!"

"The fence. No use!"

"Climb it, goddamn it. Go!"

Then, to her horror, he walked out into the street, hands raised.

He was giving her time to run, but how far could she get? Franz, you fool, we could have killed him, we could have . . .

Franz said something to the Gestapo agent, the one just out of Hannah's view. She began backing up. She turned and ran down the alley. The fence, very high, three meters or more. No handholds, none she could even jump to. She saw that the buildings here were built of stone, uneven and rough-hewn. Pushing her feet against the building and her hands against the fence, she began edging her way up the corner.

In the street, Franz still stood with his hands in the air. Someone was shouting at him. Oh, Franz . . .

Then he turned the gun inward, at his face. The sound of the gunshot.

At the top of the fence, she let herself topple over. Hitting the ground with terrible force, her knees buckled, pain stabbed her feet, a hundred nails. The view of Franz in the street, gun rising to point not at the SS officer, but himself.

As she hobbled and limped away, tears welled, slid down her face. Was it for Franz? Or was it just the cold wicking water from her eyes?

All so dark, the moon useless, the tenements saving electricity and lamp oil. She ran blindly down alleys and pathways and through courtyards where dogs erupted in snarls and down stone steps smelling of piss and slime. Then, the danger past, she slowed. Normal steps, a plain woman, a regular night.

It was bitterly cold. She remembered that she had left her jacket with the ivory buttons on the chair in the kitchen. Something welled up inside her at this loss, but then she recalled that she had no emotions.

She wiped her eyes on her sleeve. So, then, it was the cold.

PART III

A TOUCH OF MADNESS

27

A TERRACE ON THE
SCHIFFBAUERDAMM

TUESDAY, DECEMBER 15. Just when Kim wanted it the least, the sun came out. Gone was the cloaking fog of the last weeks, now when she feared having been followed. If not by Alex's Gestapo friends, then by the SS. And if so, she would be leading them right to Hannah Linz. The Spree glared in the sunshine where the early-morning rays slanted between the cafés and posh apartment buildings.

Her disguise was simple: a long gray coat, wool hat, and glasses—all stored against necessity at her safe flat. But she found herself alone on the pavement, as she logically would be this early, with the cafés not yet open.

It was 8:47 AM. She had fallen into bed the night before, exhausted, fleeing the shocking events of the day. At 8:10 AM she had jolted awake, knowing immediately that she should find a telephone and call Duncan's secure line. But she had previously told Hannah to come to a meeting place at nine in the morning and then, if she could not, nine at night.

She watched the approaches. On foot, by boat, the S-Bahn—there were many paths through Berlin, defying the Nazi preference for control. Just one of many circumstances that helped to foil their purposes.

While she tried mightily to stay on mission, her thoughts staggered back to last night: the Esplanade, the traffic converging on the intersection, Sonja lying in the street, blood thickening in her hair. Rikard Nagel watching it all impassively. That agile mind—perhaps even at this stage festering, demented—trying to discern what place Elaine Reed had in relation to his wife, in relation to Monarch.

But he had let her go. She played her diplomatic card, *my husband is meeting me*, and it had given him pause as she wound her way back through traffic to the Esplanade and Tiergartenstrasse 44.

And now here Hannah was, her hair covered by a tam, wearing a raincoat belted tightly and carrying a prim little handbag that probably contained a Luger.

"The Neues Theater, back door," she said as she walked past.

It was a place Kim didn't know. She followed Hannah at a distance and saw her enter a side door of a baroque building with a distinctive tall roof.

Kim entered, finding herself in an unlit hallway.

"This way," Hannah said, appearing for a moment on a flight of stairs, and then leading her backstage, behind the proscenium arch, a cramped space smelling of dust, glue, and sweat.

Hannah faced her, waiting.

"We're going to get you out," Kim said.

Hannah snorted. "Are you. Finally you decide?"

A lone lightbulb showed swags of curtains and high above, a catwalk with spheroid lights perching like owls. "We need to move quickly. I may be followed."

Hannah walked out of the wings onto the stage. It did not seem the right move, but Kim joined her. The auditorium was a cavern, washed with a gray light from the open doors leading into the lobby.

"Franz is dead." Hannah stood with her hands in her coat pockets, her shoulders slumped.

"Oh no, Hannah. How?"

"They captured one of ours. An interrogation, you understand? Then the raid. *Geheime Staatspolizei* and *Schutzstaffel.*"

The Nazis were closing in on Oberman. "You need to come in today. We can get you to safety."

Hannah stared into the auditorium. "I'm not coming."

Kim tried to absorb the words. Not coming? After all this?

"Franz was always the one in charge. He wished to keep me out of German hands. He wished me to help the British create better Talents. To get ready for war." She turned to smirk at Kim. "A safe little job. Laying hands on your *darkening* Talents and *hyperempaths.*"

She wasn't going to come over. The conviction was clear in her face. But now what? Kim found herself on a stage without knowing the play.

Hannah murmured, "Now it is up to us to stop Monarch."

"Us?" Outside, a boat horn blared. Kim was conscious of the life of Berlin swirling around this theater, the conflicting desires, ideologies, plotlines. And here she was, engulfed in Hannah's *raison d'etre.* To strike at the Nazis. By whatever means.

"We will kill Irina Dimitrievna Annakova."

Kim looked at her in mute incredulity.

"I have the way in. To the nest. But it must be now, when they are preparing for their operation—"

"The operation? They are launching an operation now, with the *Nachkommenschaft*?"

"Yes. The day after Christmas. And because of this, many people are arriving to have purification from Annakova. You will not be noticed among so many."

Her? She wanted *her* to go in? No, she was so wrong. Deluded.

"Hannah," she said, hoping to reach her with logic. A logic that might have no effect on someone with her frightening focus. "We're all at risk if one of your group goes under questioning. Did they know about your mole at the Aerie? Did they know about me, who I am? It will all come out."

"No, no. Zev was a supplier. He knew nothing except where we were last night." She maintained her gaze, waiting for Kim to step up. Become one of them.

That was not going to happen. Going into the Aerie was outrageous; it was surely fortified, heavily guarded, impossible. Even if such a thing could be done, it could not be her. It would require a trained assassin.

"Come in first, Hannah. Before we go so far."

Hannah rounded on her. "Franz is dead. Germany is dying by degrees. I will not run to England. I never wanted to, and now that Franz is gone, I do not report to him. And I am going to stop Monarch."

"If you fail, you'll expose your informant among them. After that, they will be much harder to penetrate. You're rushing into this. It won't work."

Hannah was unmoved. "You can get in. I have arranged it."

The woman was infuriating. "My people won't allow it. I'm not an assassin. I don't have enough German. I'm a *spill,* that's all."

"You are perfect. I need a woman who does not speak German." She paused. "Besides, I will not work with anyone else."

Kim doubled down, trying to salvage this. "You need to work with us. We already know that the operation, the Aerie you described, is near a place called Tolzried. Give us a chance to form a plan."

Hannah narrowed her eyes. "Tolzried? What makes you think so?"

"I knew Sonja Nagel, wife of a *Nachkomme* named Rikard Nagel. I met him at a diplomatic function. She was afraid of him, I think. And died in a traffic accident Wednesday."

"Murdered, then."

"Maybe. But she wanted me to know where the Aerie was." She thought of Sonja lying in the street, dying, and her husband watching her, providing no comfort. "I think Rikard Nagel may suspect me of spying."

Hannah's chin jerked up. "Why would he suspect you?"

"Because, when his wife lay dying, she unburdened herself of things she knew. I was alone with her for a few minutes. And when he came to Sonja's side, I thought he knew that she had told me things. He disliked that Sonja and I were friendly. But we were in the middle of a busy street, and I told him my husband was on the sidewalk. I left before he could decide to arrest me. I'm at a safe house no one knows about."

"Your people leave you to fend for yourself?"

"I'm to come in and let someone else deal with you."

"Ah. I am to be dealt with. Forgive me, but I do not think so. I have had enough of *obedience* and of your people here in Berlin and your chiefs in London. They have been saying no for weeks. Now *I* am saying no."

They stared at each other. Kim's curiosity got the best of her. "How can the nest be infiltrated?"

"I will tell you. Later."

Kim smirked. "A better plan than the sanatorium?"

"Oh, yes, much better. You will approve it." Hannah's gaze went up to the balcony as though looking for something.

"I once had a theater," she said. "In the old days it was a stage, but in my time, a cinema. Years before, my father and I assumed I would go into the law. Not a profession for women, but I wanted it. He had a friend at university, and they had a program where the chair allowed women. It was all arranged. After the National Socialists grew strong . . . it was all over. We took on the cinema. For a while. But now there is nothing left, not even the Oberman Group." She looked at Kim, her face all of a sudden very young, lost in memories of things she could not change, things that required her to be hard. "Life is different now. But there are still things I can do."

"Hannah . . . I need to think."

"All right. One day." She wrapped her trench coat belt more tightly around her waist. "And do not betray me, Elaine Reed."

Was she talking about betrayal to the Germans? Or the British? Kim badly needed to sort things out.

"I may be followed by the Gestapo," Kim said. "I'm staying in a safe flat, so don't call me at home. How can we meet?"

"Come to Prenzlauer Berg." She gave an address. "Take the little path on the side next to the brick shed. At 4:10 tomorrow afternoon. I will find you in the back. If you are followed, go to the used bookstore at the end of the block and buy books by Friedrich Hegel, their specialty, and turn the spine of *The*

Philosophy of Right to face the back. Then I will know to find you instead back here at 11:00 PM."

They walked into the deeper shadows of the stage wings.

Hannah said, "You are not going to do it, are you." Despite these words, her face uncharacteristically held hope and vulnerability.

"I have no bloody idea what I'm going to do."

Unfortunately, it was the truth.

THE ALEXANDERPLATZ

AN HOUR LATER. "Let me speak to Duncan."

The person who had answered the telephone said, "Give me your number, and we will call you."

Ten minutes later the telephone in the phone box rang. She picked up the earpiece. Duncan identified himself; it was his voice.

"I'm using my safe flat," she told him. "Things have happened."

"Yes, all right. What's happened?"

"Well, you already know some of it. Because you've had Bibi and Albert watching me."

"Watching your back."

Making sure she toed the line. Maybe that was normal procedure. Or was it? Duncan might be playing for the wrong side. Why wouldn't he have told her at the start that she could rely on Bibi in a pinch?

"I'm being watched. Gestapo."

"We'll come for you. Where are you?"

She watched the street, the pavement. She was like Franz

and his group in their hideout, expecting a chase at any moment.

"Last night Sonja Nagel was struck by a car and killed. I was with her. She was lying in the street. She told me her husband is a *Nachkomme*, called him a fiend. This is the operation I was sent here to uncover."

She couldn't prolong this call, but she did want to put Alex on the watch list. "I don't trust Alex Reed. He might have put them onto me."

"Don't be absurd."

Absurd. There she went again, jumping to conclusions.

Then his voice, more conciliatory. "What makes you think so?"

In the crowds of the plaza, two men in fedoras, long coats. She kept them in view. She had things to report and must do so quickly.

The silence stretched out. "Elaine, let us come for you. Where are you?"

In a phone box in the Alexanderplatz, she didn't say. Surprising herself. Instead: "I'm in contact again with Hannah."

"If you're being followed you'll lead them right to her. Listen. Someone else will handle the extraction. Come in."

Kim scanned the busy square, watching for men pretending to look in shop windows. She should have waited for the cover of night. But it was all happening so fast.

"I don't think I *can* come in."

A long silence.

"Hannah says they're going to let the *Nachkommenschaft* loose right after Christmas. And she won't work with anyone else."

"What does she want to do?"

"Kill the *catalyst*." She was using all the forbidden words, forgetting the code terms. Demonstrating incompetence. And there was worse to come.

"This is too big for you," Duncan said.

"I know. But if I leave her now, she cuts us off."

"She needs us, though. Offer her money. Fifty thousand would not be too much. If it's not money, then anything she wants."

"That's the trouble. She wants me."

"Christ. And she won't work with people experienced at this sort of thing?"

How to convey to him the sort of person Hannah Linz was. A woman who only trusted those whom she had tested. A woman whose family and friends had been brutalized, murdered, and their just cause ignored by British interests. But no was her simple answer.

A pause. She could imagine him calculating, trying to handle her. "What are you going to do?"

"I don't know."

"Where are you, for Christ's sake?"

Kim took a deep breath. It felt like falling on a knife. Things that you said couldn't be taken back. Things that you did. "Why do you want to know?"

"Elaine. Once you start distrusting the Office . . . you'll fall. You'll fall a very long way."

She stared at the earpiece for a few beats. Then she carefully placed it in the cradle.

28

A SAFE FLAT, THE
ALEXANDERPLATZ

LATER THAT AFTERNOON. Kim sat on the narrow bed,
feet pulled up, head resting on her knees. The confining box of
her flat: ancient wallpaper with vertical maroon stripes. A gas
ring with cracked enamel teapot. The wooden table and chair.

Amid the world spinning out of control, she did approve
of the orderliness of the wallpaper, yet she missed her timetable for the London and North Eastern Railway. It was her
talisman, had gotten her out of a jam in Wales when she desperately needed a map of England. She was not superstitious,
but not having the LNER timetable nudged up in her list of
worries.

Such as: the call with Duncan. She had refused to come
in, refused to tell him where she was. Something she would

not have thought possible just a few weeks ago: she had gone rogue.

She no longer trusted Duncan, not after Bibi had decided to put flowers in the window and after Albert had tried to slow down her departure from the house. It might all have an innocent explanation. It might be standard procedure not to tell an agent that house staff were on the station payroll. And the housekeepers might have genuinely feared for her safety, thought that she had panicked and was incapable of making her own decisions. Maybe, maybe. But if it wasn't standard procedure to withhold knowledge of such backup, it raised questions about Duncan's reliability. Had he been suborned by the Nazis? It was not unusual for spies to infiltrate intelligence organizations, or to be bribed or blackmailed into cooperating with the enemy.

Bibi and Albert. Would they phone Alex and reveal that she claimed to be meeting him in Bonn? Because if they did, Alex's Gestapo friends might try to round her up.

She hugged her knees. What was this Aerie in Tolzried? Where, even, was Tolzried? Sonja confirmed that the *Nachkommenschaft* existed. It was corroboration of the Monarch operation, or good enough. The great secret she had been sent to Berlin to find. With this last piece they might well be convinced about the *Nachkommenschaft* operation. But now she had no time to get word to London. Even if she could, there was a big problem. Hannah would only work with her.

She followed the faded maroon stripes, the watermarks angling down from the ceiling.

Her thoughts, now beginning to line up.

† † †

DOROTHEENSTÄDTISCHER
FRIEDHOF, BERLIN

DUSK. A bouquet of flowers in hand, Hannah waited by the mausoleum until Captain Nagel left his Mercedes and his chauffeur and threaded his way among the graves.

She wore a threadbare black wool coat, dressed up with a scarf. It would not do to look shabby in such a nice cemetery, but the Oberman Group's stockpile of clothes was distributed in flats no longer safe, now that Zev was held by the Gestapo.

Some two hundred meters distant, on the far side of this portion of the cemetery, Nagel's chauffeur was having a cigarette while taking a piss, offering her an opportunity to enter the vicinity of Sonja's grave without attracting his notice.

How convenient that the *Nachkommenschaft* avoided the daylight hours. As dusk came on, no one else was within sight in the Dorotheenstädtischer Friedhof.

Sonja Nagel had been buried yesterday. Hannah's source at the funeral home had told her that no ceremony had occurred, nor was one planned, a situation that greatly disappointed her. These Nazis could make such a fuss about the death of their own, but perhaps they did not consider Sonja one of theirs. But if they had gone through with a graveside ceremony, what a lovely opportunity it would have been to take care of a pack of vultures all at once!

Hannah trailed among the graves, glancing at the headstones as though looking for the right one. The cemetery was a landscape of artwork, with elaborate memorials and bronze statues. She wondered if Sonja had been accorded a distinguished resting place, or if she had died in disgrace. At least she had been buried. Not all dead had that honor.

Nagel had now noted her approach, but ignored her. A

diminutive woman with flowers. What could be more natural, less concerning, in a cemetery? The SS *Nachkomme* officer stood alone in a tree-shrouded plot.

She had guessed that Nagel might come here by himself. Such a one would have complex social anxieties. Not for him a crowd around a hole in the ground with people shedding tears and expressing condolences. Nagel would have no idea how to respond to such people and might have just enough humanity left to know that he was not fit for occasions like funerals. No, Rikard Nagel, like all *Nachkommenschaft*, preferred to be alone.

She drifted closer. Now she had his complete attention.

"Excuse me," she said as she approached. "I am looking for the grave of someone. Sonja Nagel." She glanced at the new headstone. A simple one. "Is this she?"

"Who are you?" he snapped.

She came closer. "I am Carla. Did she ever mention me?"

"There is no Carla. I would remember. Go away."

Hannah allowed herself the beginning of a smile. "Well, if there is no Carla, then who would I be?"

On alert, he unsnapped the holster on his belt.

"I am a friend," Hannah said, feigning alarm. In that moment he hesitated. Fatally.

She dropped the flowers and pointed the pistol at his chest. "*Das Rotes Mädchen*, actually," she murmured. And fired.

He did not fall. She fired again, this time aiming more carefully for his heart.

Nagel went to his knees, then collapsed. Ghoulishly, he began crawling. Not toward her, but toward the grave with its newly turned earth.

She followed him a few steps, hearing him hoarsely whisper, "Sonja."

It surprised her. Perhaps he had some feeling for his wife after all.

He bled very hard onto the grave, but he did not move or speak again.

She noted that the chauffeur, who had dashed toward them after the first shot, was almost through the trees. Hannah picked up the bouquet again. When he burst into full view, she shouted, "Help!"

Stalking onto the gravesite, he took in Nagel lying on the ground, a woman in mourning.

"The man . . ." She pointed behind her. He crept closer, both hands on his gun, sweeping. He motioned her aside.

As she passed him, she took him out with one shot.

Before she left, she placed the flowers on Sonja's grave, saving one for her buttonhole.

29

PRENZLAUER BERG, BERLIN

WEDNESDAY, DECEMBER 16. At 4:10 PM the city was already in heavy dusk. In the sleeting rain, people carried paper-wrapped parcels close to their chests, mufflers around their faces. Kim had guessed wrong again about what to wear. No one used galoshes over their shoes; her coat was too fine. The scarf was good, though, the one Franz had given her.

Hannah met her behind an abandoned house. A small patch of weeds corralled by the neighbors' fences, each a different kind, leaning inward.

Kim followed her to a place where she opened horizontal doors leading underground. They descended the stairs. Hannah's flashlight clicked on as she lowered the doors. At the bottom, they were in a room smelling of mold and coal dust. Hannah led her into a room with boarded-up windows near ground level. The air was the heavy cold of basements, where frigid air sank

and stayed. Tidy, though. Shelves with candles, a stack of clothing and tins of food. A chair and a barrel to sit on.

Hannah waved her to the chair. "I keep thinking I will never
see you again." She took out a pack of cigarettes and offered one
to Kim.

"I think the same."

They smoked and let nerves settle.

No one would call Hannah beautiful. Dark slashes of eyebrows,
deep-set eyes, a face some might describe as pixie-like. Unruly short
hair, carnelian in the light, mahogany in the fog. Wisps sprang free
from her wool cap. But a strong face. Interesting.

Hannah broke the silence. "So you have come to persuade me
to go to England."

"No."

Hannah smirked. "Everyone wants something."

"I want to hear the plan."

A raised eyebrow. Hannah savored her cigarette, watching
Kim, maybe gauging what she was made of. How much a patriot,
a good subject of His Majesty's Government, how much the
rebel.

"The nest of Monarch," Hannah began, "is in the Bavarian
Alps. Near Tolzried, as you know. This is one of Hitler's retreats,
which he gives to the *Nachkommenschaft*."

A scraping sound from behind a door she hadn't noticed
before. At her startled look, Hannah shook her head. *Don't worry.*

Hannah removed a ragged pair of gloves and flexed her
fingers to keep them warm. "You would go to the Aerie as a
recruited volunteer. I have cover materials for you. From the
state, is it Arizona? Albuquerque?"

Strange to hear these words in a slum in Berlin. "New
Mexico."

"Yes. We have the credentials. Many Talents have been arriving; some are not Germans. The non-Germans are lesser recruits. But they will all—Germans, foreigners, civilians, SS—become Annakova's *Nachkommenschaft*."

She went on. "You go in. You kill Irina Annakova. Afterward, there is a secret way out, our man knows this, so you escape."

"Why doesn't your man—Tannhäuser—kill her?"

"He will not go so far; he helps, a little." She shrugged. "Once they lose the mother of the beasts, gradually her monsters fade. Many lives saved, Russia is delivered from a bad queen, the revolution is secure. And when Hitler goes to war with Europe, he must do so without the *Nachkommenschaft*."

"There is one problem with this plan," Kim said.

"Yes, what?"

"I am not going to kill this woman. I don't do that."

"Well, I thought you would say this." She ground out the cigarette into a chipped coffee saucer. "And, in truth, I wouldn't want to turn you into a killer. To become like me. But there is another way."

Another way. Kim's heart sank. It was going to be hard now, she felt sure.

"You can deliver a disabling drug, one that will destroy her Talent."

"Not poison."

"No."

"How can you have such a thing?"

"I have it. Do you trust me?"

"Hannah. I need to know, I need to know everything."

The woman sighed. "All right." She got up and paced to the boarded-up window, peering out through the slats.

"I told you that my father tested me. His laboratory in

Cologne. But it was because of something that happened. In those days I would sometimes go to my father's office and bring him his lunch.

"There was a young man in the lab; we became lovers. He had a Talent, *object reading*. He began to notice a heightened ability and unpleasant symptoms as well. The symptoms came on quickly because of our frequent . . . touching; obviously not at three-month intervals. He had been tested in support of the research, and when my father retested him, he had a much higher rating. He suspected that I had the rumored Talent, which is *catalysis*, but which at that time had no official term. He broke things off with me and left his position at the university.

"But I had lost the man I loved; I faced a difficult life, trying to avoid touching people, wondering if they were Talents. My father reached out to his contacts. One man, a doctor in Norway, had a drug. One that would disable the *catalysis* ability, which he believed was a diseased state of the body, unlike other Talents. A few years previously, this researcher had been approached by a couple. The wife had a *trauma view* ability. Her Talent was increasing, and the madness came upon her, rapidly worsening. The doctor finally diagnosed the husband as a *catalyst*. It spurred him to develop a treatment and the husband underwent it, enduring some side effects. Weight loss, fatigue, insomnia. My father secured the tincture for me. But I never wanted to risk it."

"How do you take the drug? The *catalyst* swallows it?"

"No. Stomach acid destroys it. Through the skin is the best way. We would transfer the tincture by making contact with a very sensitive part of her skin. The palms of her hands." Hannah saw the understanding come into Kim's face. "Yes. During the purification ceremony."

It was intriguing; deliver a treatment that would neutralize this bizarre ability. What if they could actually pull this off? A long shot. But intriguing: "It's permanent?"

"My father thought yes, from what the doctor told him."

A thunk from the next room.

"Who's in there?"

Hannah got up and beckoned Kim to follow. She pulled aside a door that was off one of its hinges. In the next room, darker, with pools of water on the floor, sat a person tied to chair. Blindfolded and gagged.

"Here is an American we found. Nora Copeland. On her way there from Albuquerque." Hannah approached the woman, who turned her head to follow the sound of the voice. "She was very much looking forward to joining Hitler's team." She turned to the bound woman. "Weren't you."

The woman furiously shook her head.

"If you are going to lie, you keep the blindfold on for a week."

Kim started to feel sick. She turned from the room and walked back into the other one.

"Let her go," Kim said when they were alone again.

"What do you think, I am going to shoot her?"

"Yes, if necessary. War, you said."

"Anyway, it is not necessary. I hold her for two weeks, maybe three. When you are safely out, I release her." She tore off her heavy coat and threw it on the barrel. "You have all these objections. So cautious."

"Anyone ever tell you you're rash?"

"Yes. But he was one who when he had a pistol and an SS man standing before him, he killed himself rather than one of Hitler's butchers."

The blindfolded woman was one of those intercepted by the Oberman Group. Hannah said she would release the woman;

Kim wanted to trust this promise. She did, in fact, trust it. Hannah had a ruthless streak; her father's death had made her hard, but she was not cruel.

"You said there's a secret way out of the Aerie. If we got outside the compound, the German guards would still be close by."

"Not close by. A tunnel extends under the Aerie and the exit is half a kilometer away, in the woods. You can then make your way to a place where one of your planes can land."

"An airfield?"

"No. A place they will never suspect a plane would go. A lake—"

"A water landing? Hannah, no."

"Remember, this is in the mountains. It is frozen."

Kim thought about whether the Office would want a plane sent. Maybe they would. London wanted Hannah; they might want her very much. But the extraction they were now talking about involved more danger. "Can a plane land if there's deep snow?"

"There is not much snow in that valley yet. It has been a dry winter so far, and the elevation is not high."

Kim continued down her mental list of objections. "They may know my description. Rikard Nagel might have alerted them I'm a possible spy. I'd never pass their security."

"Nagel will not tell them." She picked at her gloves. "He was silenced. Yesterday."

"You killed him."

Hannah rolled her eyes. When Kim stared hard at her, she threw out, "You are shocked? Shocked that people die, cut down without a trial, that saboteurs blow up cars, shoot people in a cemetery?" Her eyes flashed. Ready for combat.

"In the cemetery?" At Sonja's funeral? The air left her lungs.

The sheer audacity of it, the foolhardiness. "You could have been killed."

"He was alone." She went to a small brazier in the corner. "You would like tea?"

Kim nodded, and Hannah nestled a few lumps of coal in the metal cradle. A little oil on the coal fed a quick fire. Then a samovar and a tin of tea leaves. Hannah looked up at Kim. "You are thinking how to get this information, this helpful drug, to the secret service. You are thinking they will do something."

Yes, she was, even while knowing they wouldn't risk it. They wouldn't even believe it.

Hannah spit out a bit of loose tobacco. "But they don't trust you. You are cozy with Jews in Berlin. Bad girl."

Kim tried to focus on what was being asked of her. To be rash. Or perhaps merely bold. How had she gotten to this point, hiding in a Berlin slum with a fugitive and newly minted as a fugitive herself. And now this scheme. Hannah's scheme, Hitler's schemes. Where did it end, this contest for the world? And for her, where had it even begun? With her brother's sacrifice in the Great War, that ever-present loss. But also with the creep of hatred into her adopted country, when Rose had been deemed a mental incompetent who must be locked away.

And now came a time for action, action more perilous than ever before.

They were not at war. Not yet. But now was the best time to act, when evil was still crawling out of its hole, not yet fully fledged.

Hannah brought two mugs.

Kim accepted the tea, fragrant, calming. "You said the operation only accepts 7 or above. What if Annakova can tell I'm not that high? Or what if they test incoming volunteers?"

"You are right; they do test."

"I told you I am a 6."

Hannah had taken off her gloves, cradling her cup, letting it warm her hands. Kim looked at her pale hands, her fingernails with coal soot under them.

Kim set aside her tea. "Oh, God."

Hannah nodded. "You have figured out the plan."

"Christ." Now it was Kim's turn to be angry. "Your plan is to turn me into one of *them*?"

"Now you know it all. You know everything."

"Nothing more? Would you like me to sidle up to Hitler? Hermann Göring? Do you run me like one of their ghouls? Where does this end?"

"End? I don't know where it ends for you. When you stop, I suppose. When you get a posting in Buenos Aires. When you vacation in the Cotswolds."

Kim winced, and the anger trickled away, leaving her deflated. Ready to know the things she'd been pushing away for weeks, maybe years. What you really had to do when you went against them.

Hannah murmured, "For me, it ends when they catch me."

It was so cold in the basement. Kim had begun to shiver. "The woman in there," she whispered. "Nora." She looked at the door tilted off its top hinge. "What is her Talent?"

"*Precognition*, a 7. But listen: yes, they will test you, and you are not *precognition*. But they have contempt for the American tests. You say, 'No, excuse me please, I am a *spill*.' They will test you, and you will say, 'Yes you are right, my people got it wrong.'" Hannah pushed on, ignoring the expression of skepticism on Kim's face. "In Albuquerque, Copeland's recruiter reported her as *precognition*. But whoever recruited her, he will not be at the Aerie. And of course, we make you a passport saying you are Nora Copeland."

"And I would be a 7."

Hannah looked away. "You will be something. I can get you to a 7, even if you are low 6."

"We don't have test equipment. How do we know the optimization would go far enough?"

"We don't. But a *catalyst* senses when an augmentation is strong or weak."

"Your mole at the Aerie told you?" Kim asked.

"No. It is what I remember. Sometimes, it felt like a kind of . . . serenity. When stronger, almost a rapture. I thought that with my boyfriend, it was the sex. Then I learned it was a symptom of the augmentation. And there were other things. It's hard to explain. Senses, especially hearing, are more acute. So if I feel a strong effect, I will know I brought you up a good amount. A big amount."

"And if you suspect there is a weak effect?"

Hannah shrugged. "Then I do it again."

"Again! You said that short intervals make the symptoms worse."

"Yes, but it would only be two times—three times when Annakova touches you—but it is not dozens, as when I had a lover. You see?"

Kim paused, allowing all this to settle. She could still back out; meanwhile she wanted to hear the plan details. "How would we get the medicine inside? They would search everything."

"Inside your women's sanitary towels. They will wave those through."

Kim rose and paced to the window where, through the nailed-up boards, frozen rain squeezed through. She must decide, and it was very hard. Gone were the comfortable soirees where she had imagined getting lovely *spills* and afterward going home to a cozy mansion. She had been playing at resistance.

Here was the real thing.

She saw the choice Hannah offered: to switch places with another American, infiltrate a Nazi hideout, meet the *catalyst*, and put her down before the December 26 launch. It was the ultimate gamble, the final test.

Of what? Of herself, maybe. Even while she had these thoughts, she knew the choice was already made. Sometime in the last minutes, it slid into place, like something she had always known.

She would do it. When your lieutenant is shot from his horse, and you are the only one left to ride forward to do the job, you do it. All the dead at Ypres had made such a decision. And all the living who were left behind asked themselves, would they have done the same? Certainly, many thanked God that they would never be so tested. But now came *her* test. It was necessary for some to die. Even if it was herself.

Erich von Ritter had known her. He understood her, or seemed to, that day at Rievaulx. Those left behind can never understand why they are alive. And so one thinks of one's own death and it's not as bad, not nearly as bad, as people say.

She turned back to Hannah, and her face must have revealed her heart, because Hannah came to her where she stood under the boarded-up window. Her dark eyes now with a new look; maybe respect. Or maybe it was compassion.

"How does it work, this transfer? How long does it take?"

"It is a touch. More than a brush against the skin, more than a fingertip." Her face softened in encouragement, and Kim was grateful for it.

"I will do as they tell me Annakova does. Place my hands on your face. Then the augmentation happens within a minute or two. You may not notice much."

Kim realized she was postponing. But still: "What if the contact is too long? Is it a stronger effect? I only need to get to 7."

"You are nervous for a spy." She put her hand on Kim's arm. Even though Kim wore a jacket, she jumped.

Hannah gripped her arm reassuringly, and went on. "A *catalyst* cannot control the strength of the augmentation. No matter how intimate and no matter how long the touch—this is what Tannhäuser told me. He has been watching Irina's optimizations for more than a year."

"And it must be skin to skin, you said."

"Yes. What I will do now is what Annakova does every time she purifies her *Nachkommenschaft*. I will touch your face, and you must hold still." She drew closer to Kim. "You are ready, then?"

Kim nodded, unable to speak, suddenly terrified.

"No, say it."

"I'm ready," Kim whispered.

Hannah's palms cupped her face, pressing into her temples and cheeks. Though Kim couldn't tell if she was receiving power, she had the strange sense that she was being annointed, annointed by one who knew true courage.

Hannah kept her gaze steady, and after a few moments Kim began to feel—unless it was her imagination—that the two of them were connected at some fundamental level of trust, obligation, and sisterhood. Tears leaped into her eyes.

And then the touch ended. Hannah leaned against the wall, looking up at the ceiling. Perhaps it had been a powerful experience for her, or it had taken something from her.

"It was strong," Hannah whispered. "It was very strong. I believe, at least a 7."

So it's over, Kim thought. This part was over. She still had all her options open, she could still back out.

But she wasn't going to. Leading Hannah to a chair, she reheated the tea and poured her a cup, steaming in the heavy cold of the basement.

30

AN APARTMENT, BERLIN

THURSDAY, DECEMBER 17. "Do not smile." Joel lined up his camera shot. "For the passport, they do not like a smile."

Kim tried to comply, but gazing into the camera lens, the smile hovered. She finally knew her place, the thing she was to do. And she was around people who supported her, were willing to work for the cause. Hannah, the mastermind. Joel doggedly doing his part. Gone, now, was the strain of pretending, fearing, struggling with everyone in her sphere. And, worst of all, fighting with herself. She suppressed the smile, but she felt it below the surface.

The camera flash popped. The after-image in blue, gliding across her eyes. Joel disappeared into the darkroom to develop the pictures.

In his apartment, Joel had drawn heavy drapes over the windows, leaving a grayish morning light to squeeze out the sides. The apartment smelled of wood polish and books. Posh, for Prenzlauer Berg.

On the sideboard, her letters requesting the airplane that would get them out of Germany.

Earlier, they had considered the issues and, together, fine-tuned the plan.

"You will have to meet me at the lake, Hannah. My people want you; me, I'm less sure about."

"I will be at the lake, I promise."

"Have you been there? How will you get to the lake?"

"A service road. I'll have a truck, which will also be our backup transportation if your friends don't show up."

"Can you really get so close to the Aerie? A half mile . . . They must have patrols."

"They focus on the road from the village to the Aerie, feeling impregnable otherwise."

Hannah had arranged sliced beef and dark bread on the dining room table. "Eat something," she said. A topographical map of the Aerie's locale lay where they had been studying it.

She wasn't hungry, picking at the slices of beef. At times, she had the urge to laugh for no reason.

"Is it starting?" She looked at Hannah, who had taken a seat next to her, hovering a bit, as though her maternal instincts had been triggered. "The meat looks very good. Is it all I'll want?"

"Do not think about it too much," Hannah said, sitting beside her. "Who knows how it will go?"

They had talked through the possible side effects, including the danger that she would have to endure another *catalysis* from Irina Annakova in order to deliver the powder. The only way to make physical contact with Annakova and transfer the tincture was when the woman would initiate the close contact of *catalysis* during a purification ceremony. Depending on where Kim was in the line to see Annakova, more or fewer of the *Nachkommenschaft* would receive new power, but after she touched Kim, her powers would unravel. In the line behind Kim would be faded monsters living out their last weeks of power.

It did mean that Kim would undergo two *catalysis* sessions, not just one. But the effects would weaken and evaporate with time, Hannah had reminded her. So whatever the initial shock to the system, she would not deteriorate, or at least not much, or at least not for long.

Hannah brought the map closer. She pointed to the topographical lines that indicated ridges and valleys. "Here is the main ridge that follows along the road leading to the Aerie. It is lower than the others and close to a higher ridge that extends all the way to the lake."

"We've already been over this," Kim said.

"Yes, and now again." Hannah pointed to the small lake. "The valley fingers right here all lead to the lake, so when you get out of the tunnel, head downhill at an angle following the ridgeline and you will find it. On the south side is a shack used as a warming house for ice fishing. I will be waiting for you there. If your friends do not send a plane—"

Kim interrupted. "I think they will if the weather allows. Remember, they want you with your Talent."

"All right. But it's a good backup. I will have a truck parked on the service road here." Kim noted a dotted line leading down to a larger road, presumably paved.

Hannah repeated what she had told Kim before: "The airplane can find its landing place when there is enough light. That will be no sooner than seven thirty this time of year. In any case, we shouldn't wait past eight o'clock. Your absence will be noticed at some point. It isn't likely they will immediately think you have gone into the secret tunnel. They will search. That gives us some time; not much. If the plane does not arrive by eight, we take the truck."

"We have discussed this, Hannah."

"When you may be running from the SS, people tend to forget things. But these are the details you must not forget."

Kim cut up a few mouthfuls of beef, conscious of needing her strength for what was to come. "And you'll come to England."

"I said I would."

"But when the plane comes for us you won't change your mind."

"I have said yes."

Of utmost importance, Kim would have to make contact with Tannhäuser. His name was SS Captain Dietrich Adler. He spoke English. Irina Annakova had a German handler, Sir Stefan, who stayed very close to her. He was SD, secret intelligence. Annakova preferred to speak French but had some English. Evgeny Feodorovich Borisov was Annakova's Russian friend from the old days, badly deteriorated.

The Aerie was one of Hitler's summer retreats, given over to the Monarch preparations. It perched nearly five hundred feet above the nearest approach and backed up against sheer mountain cliffs. Not only was it protected by heavy security on the sole road leading to it, but a gun emplacement atop the cliff covered the road and the surrounding woods. The retreat was accessed by a lift that led to the middle of a small plaza. Captain Adler knew another way out, a secret way.

Behind the plaza, the ground sloped up into alpine trees under which were the officers' billets and a distance away, barracks for the *Nachkommenschaft*. Between them, a pond served as a source of water in case of fire. There was a gun range beyond the barracks. Facing the plaza, a large hall for gatherings and across from it, a chalet housing Annakova and her eleven-year-old son, Nikolai.

Hannah finished by saying, "I expect that the intake center at the Aerie will want you no matter what your Talent. But you must be at least a 7. It is unlikely to be a problem, but if I did not manage to augment you so far, they will not take you into service. Tannhäuser said that sometimes they send people away as unsuited for one reason or another. In that case at least we will have tried."

Kim nodded, finding it a little hard to concentrate. She felt a little wild, too alert. Was that how it began?

"You will not have time to sleep today," Hannah said. "Nora Copeland is already late for her rendezvous with her German handler, Luther. So today, we go forward." On Hannah's wrist, Kim's Helbros. To prevent the Nazis from confiscating it at the Aerie. She liked the fact that Hannah wore it, a sweet gesture, unless Hannah just had nowhere else to put it.

She and Hannah had a story ready about why Kim was five days late meeting her handler. "I've had a bug," she recited, "and couldn't leave my hotel room."

"Perhaps it was food poisoning from the ship," Hannah said, helping her practice her story.

The *Queen Mary*, they had decided, by the transatlantic schedule Hannah had found. "Yes, it might have been the shellfish on that last day. I should have known better." She felt mirth bubble up and barely restrained it.

Hannah frowned. "The SS will not tolerate amusement."

When Kim acknowledged this with compressed lips, fending off the smile, Hannah went on. "Where did you undergo your Talent rating test?"

"In San Diego, at the Rawlings Institute. It's new, a slapdash setup, but awfully nice people."

"They rated you a 7 for *precognition*."

"What? *Precognition?* No, it was the *spill*. Didn't Ken Meyers tell you?" Nora's recruiter in Albuquerque.

"The *spill* is no use to us. It is only good for spying. We have plenty of those."

"But I've come all this way! To serve. You can't believe all the nonsense in the US right now. The smears and lies about the Führer. The inferiors who are coming into positions of responsibility, even in government! It's disgusting. So you will allow me to contribute, I hope?"

"Good. You didn't say he *must* do something, or they *have to* do anything. The SS expects deference. Some do not like women as Talents at all."

Kim pushed the plate of food away as Joel joined them in the parlor. He laid the passport before her.

She opened it. Her face, looking back at her. Hair cropped short, with bangs. A calm on her face that some might mistake for innocence. Five feet nine, 130 pounds. Birthplace: Tucson, Arizona. Paging through, a stamp for Mexico, 1921, a splurge after high school. Scuff marks on the cover, a wine stain on the back two pages.

"Beautiful, Joel."

"I was an art student at Heidelberg." Wistful. What he might have done besides forgeries. "I did my first passport for a girlfriend. As a thank-you, she went off with another man."

Hannah paged through it, frowning. "It smells new."

He nodded and took the passport back into the other room to fix it.

Kim stared after him. "A *spill*. The girlfriend. He didn't want to tell me that."

"You think so? Maybe. But do not talk yourself into something."

"No, it was a *spill*. He could hardly wait to leave the room after he said it." She was certain of it, in a way that she had never felt positive about *spills* before. Overconfidence? Or heightened powers? She pushed the plate of food away. "Is this what a 7 can do?"

"If my father were still alive, he could tell us. But we are lucky, Elaine. You are doing so well."

Kim stood, crossing to the little suitcase they had prepared for her. She opened it, checking that all was familiar to her. The clothes, a couple of books.

It was almost time to go.

She turned back to Hannah. "That's not my name. It's not Elaine. You knew that?"

Hannah held her gaze. Maybe she didn't want to know her real name. What use for real names?

"What is your name, then?" Hannah said, softening.

Kim clicked the latches closed on the suitcase and lifted it off the chair. "It's Kim Tavistock."

"Ah, Kim, is it? That suits you." She nodded and the two women regarded each other for a long moment. Then Hannah rose as Joel came back with the passport. "From now on I will call you Nora, though. Until we are done."

Done. It was a lovely thought. To be done. But, at the same time, she wanted to enter the Aerie and go through with it all.

Fivel was assigned to load the dead drop with her report. If Duncan was having the dead drops watched, he would be picking up Fivel, not Kim. In any case, the Berlin station would get her message. Fivel was to wait three days, dropping the message off on Monday at a secondary drop at a brick wall in a cemetery called the Invalidenfriedhof.

Duncan:

I'm pursuing the operation. Yes, against orders. Our contact has devised a method to remove the problem. It's a risky plan. You wouldn't like it. But the contact has decided it is impossible to work with us—unless it's me. This may be our only chance to eliminate the threat.

Below are the coordinates of a pickup point if you want to extract our contact, as you've said you do. Once this operation is complete, the person has agreed to work for us and she'll be with me at the pickup point. I'm afraid it's a risky landing for an airplane. On a frozen lake. It's only a mile from our target, but that area is not guarded. Be there on Christmas Day as close to first light as you can. The signal by flashlight will be "Robert."

I've sent the gist of this on to London. I feel better setting the record straight in case I never get the chance to tell what happened.

A loose end: the cover I was given in Berlin is almost certainly compromised. Alex told me a piece of information that he got from a routine stop at a railway station where I was subjected to a few questions from a Gestapo agent. Clearly, they reported on me to him. If it's important to you; maybe you already knew.

So. *All laid out now. I don't trust your
handling of this mission. I suppose that means, as
you said, that I've fallen a very long way. It's war,
or nearly. I just wanted to say that as I see it, I am
loyal to our country and doing the right thing.*

*If the plane doesn't show up, I'll try to get to
Berlin and will contact you. I guess I can't leave
flowers in the window, can I? And on that subject,
I still think it was rotten to rent that mansion on
Tiergartenstrasse when it belonged to a family
who were hounded out of their home because of
their religion. I hope you investigate and write up
a report. We may not be able to stop the Nazis from
their persecutions, but we don't have to help them,
either.*

—*Elaine*

31

LATER THAT DAY. Clutching her small suitcase, Kim stood in the great Potsdamer train station. All of Berlin's train stations held a grandeur that Germans lavished on transport: a celebration of industry, timeliness, outsize beauty.

Luther would find her here, next to the ladies' powder room. She must stand holding her hat, not wearing it. She had not been given any clues as to his appearance, except that he would ask if she was Nora Copeland.

Trapped between the distant ceiling and the tile floor, the unearthly rumble of a thousand voices echoed in the booking hall. By the great clock it was 3:19 PM. The meeting time, 3:30. If the meeting time had been just an hour later, she could have slept for an hour. If she could just lie down on a bench, even the roar of the depot would not disturb her.

Through the boarding gates she saw the locomotives huffing

and venting. In this temporary anonymity, Kim felt a momentary urge to flee. Maybe to Paris. This mission was exceedingly dangerous. And what if Hannah knew there was no emergency back way out of the Aerie? Did she consider Kim expendable? She could not really believe it, and yet Paris beckoned. *One way, please. When is the next train?* Until three thirty she would be unknown to anyone in the station. She could still escape this. But then she thought about the Nazi asset Irina Annakova and, like a bubble popping, her doubts evaporated. If it worked, it would be a triumph. As for Hannah, they were a team.

Her intention was strong; her mood, calmly assured. Yet she had to admit that all this confidence was somehow . . . not quite right.

The incessant clatter of voices made it seem as though she were adrift in a realm where everyone spoke their thoughts at once, interrupted by enormous, sonorous declarations from the gods: announcing, for example, the late arrival of the train from Frankfurt. How fanciful. But were her ears more sensitive? Were the lights suspended on decorative poles from the ceiling unnecessarily bright? What *was* her Talent rating?

"Excuse me, are you Miss Nora Copeland?"

Kim swallowed a chirp of surprise. "Oh. Why yes, I am."

Before her stood a stocky man in civilian clothes. "I am Luther," he said in English. The hand outstretched. She shook it.

"It has been inconvenient for you to be late." Said reasonably enough. She was five days late, to be exact.

"I've been sick. I couldn't even leave my hotel."

He narrowed his eyes, appraising her. She had reddened her nose and used ample powder. No lipstick. "I'm so glad you didn't give up on me."

"That remains to be seen." He looked her over as she did him.

He wore his hair shaved close on the sides of his head. White hair on top, grown longer. "You were told to be wearing a warm coat."

"I am wearing a coat." It was a long jacket. All that she and Hannah had been able to find in the rush to get her to the appointment.

"Carl Meed was supposed to tell you what to wear. Didn't your New Mexico contact give you instructions?"

"Meed? I don't know him. My contact was Ken Meyers. And yes, he told me to dress warmly. As you see, I have." Suddenly she had doubts about Nora Copeland. Who knew how far a committed fascist would go—even down to jeopardizing her own life—to resist divulging information? But Copeland didn't know which information was crucial. She could not guess that someone would try to replace her and how crucial certain information would be to her captors.

Luther snorted as though her knowing that it was Ken, not Carl, was some kind of trick that he was too clever to believe.

"I should leave you here. Our project does not favor irregularities. Or people who do not follow orders."

She didn't need to fake dismay. "I am so sorry, Herr Luther. Sir. I have done everything I thought was required. Perhaps I did not understand?"

Glancing at the tower clock in the hall, he made an impatient face and picked up her suitcase. He gestured her to accompany him past the booking desks.

She had passed. So far. Her confidence surged as she began to trust her cover. Kim had an alter ego that over the past few months she had learned to use. The sincere, rather clueless woman, eager to please. Her witless American role, as Owen Cherwell had first identified it when they had been hunting down the *Ice* conspiracy.

"Will we be traveling by train? I love trains. So much more dependable than ships. I mean, one can debark at any time. Not all cooped up." She looked around her in a show of amazement at the station.

"Oh, yes. Our trains go everywhere. They will need to when Berlin is the capital of the world."

"How thrilling!" He led her to a little eatery tucked behind the front portal of the station. She hoped she was not going to have to eat. Her stomach, all nerves, sent zinging waves across her middle.

He ordered two coffees, black, and one pastry.

"You do not appear ill to me, Miss Copeland. I am no doctor, but . . ." He shrugged amiably, as though catching her in a lie to her Nazi employers would be merely a faux pas. Now with a good view of him sitting opposite her, she noted his dark, intelligent eyes. She had hoped for someone brutish and slow. A flunky. But now: Luther.

She trotted out her story of the bad shellfish. A few embellishments, creating a drama of being on board a rolling ship *and* nauseated, the food on the room service trays never touched, the worry at having missed her appointment . . .

He smirked. "You did not foresee the poisoned seafood?"

She ignored this with a little frown of confusion. Nora Copeland could not guess that they had mistaken information about her *precognition* Talent. And this reference was a tad obscure to focus upon.

"I hope that my not speaking German won't be a difficulty," she said. "I've been studying, but haven't gotten far along."

"Don't give them any reason to reject you," Luther said, as though her not speaking German was a transgression she could avoid. It would be a long journey with this man who apparently enjoyed putting people in their place and making them squirm.

"I'll be on my best behavior."

He looked at her skeptically. "Your passport, then." He held out his open hand. She put Joel's handiwork in it.

After studying it for several minutes, he said, "The woman from the unpronounceable city."

She smiled. "It's not unpronounceable, it's just spelled badly."

His expression remained locked. No room for lightness. "Tell me about Albuquerque." Murdering the word. She did not correct him.

"Flat, but mountains ringing it. Hot and dry like every cowboy movie you've ever seen. Not a grand city like Berlin. Ruined by the remnants of native culture. A lot of cheap silver jewelry crafted by people who can't hold their liquor. You're lucky you don't have to put up with that."

"We have our own vermin."

She paused too long before saying, "Yes, we have those too."

He looked at her as though having Jews in America were her fault. The coffee having arrived, the conversation—the interview—lapsed, and he cut the pastry in half, shoving her portion toward her. German thrift.

At her expression—sincere repulsion this time—he laughed. "You would prefer a rare slice of veal?" He shook his head. "Never mind, you will see the joke, eventually."

"I'm afraid I can eat nothing right now." The echoing shouts from the Great Hall and the train shed had begun to exceedingly grate on her. Her senses, painfully vivid. She put her hand to her forehead, closing her eyes. This seemed to help.

"You do not feel well?"

She collected herself, her hands in her lap. "Better every

day." Worse by the hour. Unless it was her imagination. Hannah had said, *Do not talk yourself into something.*

Luther finished his pastry, then her portion. Wiping the crumbs from his mouth with a napkin, he checked his pocket watch. "We must be going, Fräulein."

Instead of heading for the train platforms, he led her outside to the taxi stand.

"I thought we were going by train."

He beckoned a taxi. "We are."

Twenty minutes later they were at the Lehrter Bahnhof. The great, vaulted transport palace. This had been her first real look at Berlin. That had been in October, seven weeks ago, a period that found her in Europe for the first time, pretending to be married to a charming man who betrayed her, being shot at by the Gestapo, making friends with a cynical journalist and a desperate wife of a *Nachkomme*, and meeting and coming under the spell of Hannah Linz, the woman who had no fear of death, who reveled in danger, free of nuance and the craving for love.

October seemed very far in the past.

Luther took her arm and pulled her directly through the arched entry to the train platform. A locomotive waited in its bay, venting gouts of steam as passengers boarded. Leipzig, Nuremburg, Stuttgart. He had already bought their tickets; the train was preparing to depart. Anyone following them who had not previously bought a ticket would miss this train. Luther was careful. He'd done this before.

Boarding the train she was very conscious of being on her own. She worked alone, or practically so. These last few days with Hannah had been a welcome comfort. But Kim did not have an Oberman Group; she had SIS, for what it was worth. There had been a time when she'd been thrilled to be part of it.

The club of spies. And was she in that club, truly? Perhaps always a marginal player; women made good informants but were not trusted as agents.

Well, now she had proven them right.

Hannah watched as the two of them boarded the train for Stuttgart. Kim had passed her first test with the Nazis. And if she had failed? Hannah had a Luger in her coat pocket, but unless inspiration struck, she would have had little chance of rescuing Kim had they arrested her.

She checked Kim's watch. It was a jeweled watch with a square face, too delicate for Hannah's taste, but it did keep good time. 5:10 PM. They would arrive at the nearest station, in Miesbach, by 2:00 AM. Here, the SS stored a car in a garage, and from there, it was twenty-five minutes to the Aerie.

Then Kim's second test: the intake center at the control post. It was a delicate matter to substitute the *spill* for *precognition* as Nora Copeland's Talent.

But when lying, it was best to be outrageous. To let them catch you in a big mistake, and then acknowledge it. Yes, a mistake. How clever of you to notice this. *You are right, I am not a precognition!* And then she is female, and looking so innocent. Not too pretty—the Nazis think female spies will be beautiful to snare officers—but then pretty enough, so the SS are disposed to help her, maybe a little. Add to that getting the sanitary pads past security, where they normally took all your possessions; Kim would pretend to be having her monthly so she could at least wear a pad in.

The third test: the Russian witch. The purification. Nothing must prevent Kim from fitting in with the others, being a part of the Christmas Day ceremony.

Kim would do very well. She had faced off with several *Nachkommen* already, so she would not lose her resolve. She had seen the worst.

There was nothing more Hannah could do for her. A pang of worry hit her squarely. She was used to taking on the most dangerous jobs herself and now it was Kim Tavistock out in front. If the mission fell apart, it would do so disastrously. Kim's life would be on her conscience for a very long time.

Her cigarette had burned down while she had watched the train leave the station. She ground it out in the ashtray by the wall. *You grind it out on the cement platform and they scold you. If you are a Jew, maybe they shoot you.*

Ja. And some Jews shoot back.

Buttoning her coat, she left the Lehrter Bahnhof and walked into the Berlin night, snowflakes falling here and there, catching the lamplight.

THE INTAKE CENTER, THE AERIE

THURSDAY, DECEMBER 17. The *Nachkommenschaft* had begun arriving at the intake center for the Christmas purification ceremony.

Dr. Kaltenbrunner put on his most reassuring demeanor in front of the patient seated opposite him. He leaned forward, clasping his hands on the desk, using the soothing, calm smile he had perfected as medical officer to what the Party called the Progeny.

This *Nachkomme* presented as characteristically slim. His wrists, heavily corded with muscle. Blond hair, what little there was, combed neatly over the enlarging dome of his head.

"And how are you sleeping, Herr Stuckart?"

This one was a civilian. He had been valuable in augmenting pro-Nazi demonstrations in Vienna. His 7.6 *transport* Talent, most useful. He had a finely tuned mastery of aim and could create panic in crowds. Rocks, small articles, sent hurtling a distance of five meters or more. Unfortunately, Josef Stuckart might be losing value.

"I do sleep. Very occasionally."

"How often do you sleep?"

"On Sundays." Josef Stuckart stared rudely at him, half amused. This was typical of the Progeny. An attempt at dominance, even here, in a physician's office. Perhaps Stuckart did not understand that he was facing a man whom Himmler trusted absolutely in evaluations of this sort.

He checked a box. *Once a week.*

"Your appetite?"

"Yes."

"You have a strong appetite?"

"It is difficult to find a good cook."

"Naturally. But your wife prepares adequate meals?"

"She died."

The doctor checked *Loss of appetite.*

Stuckart turned toward the window, frowning. The blinds were drawn, but little cracks between the slats let in vicious strips of light.

Kaltenbrunner got up and pulled the drapes closed. While he did so, he felt a frisson of anxiety, having his back to the *Nachkomme.* The reports of insubordination, lapses of judgment. He took his seat safely behind the desk again. In the upper right-hand drawer, his pistol.

"Your mood is . . . ?"

"My mood?"

"Yes. You are reasonably content? Troubled in any way?"

"An interesting question."

"I mean for it to be." He would not tolerate insolence.

"Let me see. This morning I woke in the hostel where I have

a room. My flatmate was playing the gramophone, which woke me. I rid him of the phonograph record. I flung it into the hillside snow bank where it buried itself. My roommate objected. For this, I beat him soundly. The proprietor knocked at the door, objecting to the noise, for Alfred was howling most annoyingly. I had stuck the phonograph needle in his eye. Then I demanded that the pension cook find me a suitable meal. When she offered bread and no apology, I caused her some consternation by wrapping her apron around her neck and squeezing, just a little. Eventually a meal was found, and my mood improved. Then the car came for me and, upon arriving here, I have had to endure your aimless and pompous questions. But I would say my *moods* are within range of what is normal. Wouldn't you?"

Another tick mark on the sheet. *Mood swings.*

When the form was completely filled out, Kaltenbrunner handed Stuckart an issuance card marked *Special Assignment.* It was unfortunate, but some individuals did not seem to tolerate repeated purifications, slipping into mental conditions that made them undependable, not useful to the Reich. Stuckart's record showed compliance with the ninety-one-day uplift intervals, but his constitution appeared unsuited to further enhancements.

As he opened the door for the patient, he observed a commotion in the waiting room. An SS captain strode up to Kaltenbrunner and clicked his heels. "Herr Doctor, Her Royal Majesty is outside."

"Outside?"

"Yes, she is just getting out of the motorcar."

"*Mein Gott,*" he hissed under his breath, and shoved past the officer toward the front door. "Why is she here, Captain von Lossberg? Why did no one inform me?" He straightened his smock coat, furious that he did not have time to change into a decent suit.

"We had no word that she would come down, Herr Doctor."

Kaltenbrunner burst out onto the icy, shoveled steps just as Madame Annakova—as he thought of her; he would not think of her as Her Royal Majesty—was handed out of the car by an attendant. Her son followed her out, that fool of a boy in a tsarist naval uniform, and there they stood, dressed in furs as though this was a Russian winter.

"Your Majesty." Kaltenbrunner turned to her son. "Your Highness. What a delightful surprise." His French was imperfect; he hoped he could understand hers.

"Oh, Dr. Kaltenbrunner, we were eager to see the arrivals," she said in French. "I hope it is not inconvenient." A light snow was falling and, settling into Annakova's dark hair, it looked fetchingly like jewels.

"Of course not! We are delighted. And the *Nachkommenschaft* will be honored by your visit." It was an alarming turn of events. The Progeny had not been sorted through yet. If any of them got out of hand in her presence, it would raise uncomfortable issues.

He led her into the intake center—a converted barracks—and instantly, those occupying it were on their feet. The SS officers, straight as sticks, saluting; the civilians bowing, the few female *Nachkommin* curtsying.

Annakova turned to Captain von Lossberg. "Captain, please ask them to be at ease."

"Stehen Sie bequem!" the captain ordered the group. The officers fell back into a marginally less stiff position.

Then she was moving among the Progeny, shaking gloved hands with each one. Fine so far, but any one of the unprocessed ones could conceivably slip into a stage-five event and create a scene. Someone would answer for allowing Annakova to leave the Aerie without at once calling the center. Though it was only a quarter mile down the road, they would at least have had a chance to clear the room of the most obvious candidates for Special Assignment.

"Lieutenant Lowenstahl," Annakova was saying to an SS officer, "I am happy to see you." She turned to her son. "Your Highness, the lieutenant is a distinguished cavalry officer."

Nikolai perked up at this. "I am happy to know you, sir. What horse do you ride?"

The officer managed to answer, recalling his French, as his eyes moistened with even more devotion than the purified ones normally displayed for Annakova. Kaltenbrunner heard the front door slam amid a commotion of new arrivals. The situation was disorganized in the extreme.

Nevertheless, down the line she went, remembering many by name, not skipping anyone. The woman would waste their whole morning.

He glanced meaningfully at Captain von Lossberg, managing to convey his anxiety that the Russian bitch have a smooth visit. The captain gestured for another officer to approach and quietly ordered him to bring the senior officers from their desks to control the room.

Annakova had made it to one end of the row of chairs, and before turning to move down the next row, she stopped and fixed Kaltenbrunner with what she no doubt thought of as a royal glare.

"Some of these do not look well, doctor. Why is this?"

Hiding his dismay, he responded. "Very occasionally there are adverse reactions, Your Majesty. With therapy we do try to reverse—"

"Yes, yes. But so many! I judge there are five or six in this room. So thin, doctor! They cannot be well."

The woman had no idea how fragile her creations were, how

much research had yet to be done on the purification procedure. Nevertheless Himmler would be furious at this lapse in security. "We have summoned a few individuals in advance, knowing that additional therapies may be needed. A few cases only! I hope it does not disturb Your Majesty. If we had known—"

"I wish a report on the condition of these men, doctor. See that it is done by tomorrow."

"Of course, Your Majesty."

She sailed on through the crowd, the boy at her side, as though this were some kind of royal soiree and not a military post. The hour dragged on. All eyes on the tsarina, with a fierce devotion in their eyes, such as should be reserved for the Führer alone.

Just as she had completed her tour of the room and was heading—at last!—to the door, Kaltenbrunner saw movement through the window. Someone was outside. He appeared naked from the waist up.

He called von Lossberg to his side, telling him to take charge of escorting Annakova and her son.

Making his way to his office, he withdrew his gun from the drawer and slipped out his private entrance into the snowy grounds. A guard noticed that he was armed and rushed up to him.

"There is a man out of uniform out here," the doctor said. "Apprehend him immediately. And make sure it is not in front of the building!"

The officer drew his weapon and, looking around, raced off to gather reinforcements.

It was a nightmare. Kaltenbrunner heard voices from the car park. The royal entourage leaving. The doctor began stalking around the building, slowly, pistol drawn, scanning the ragged line of alpine trees, brownish green against the snow.

A movement. From behind a scrub alpine tree, a man stepped

out. Kaltenbrunner was momentarily startled to see that he was completely naked.

Stuckart's skin was albino against the snow, the only color a bloodred smear across his mouth and chin. He held a squirrel by the tail, its throat cut.

"Too bright . . . ," Stuckart moaned. "The awful white. It hurts."

Kaltenbrunner approached him. "Of course it does. You should not have to endure it."

"The snow."

"Yes. We will make it stop. Would you like that?"

As her motorcar pulled away from the barracks, Irina thought that the visit had gone very well. Her Progeny were so happy to see her, and she them. And Kolya had comported himself superbly.

Some explanations were due from Dr. Kaltenbrunner, however. She would discuss this with Stefan when he returned from Berlin.

A sudden cracking sounded in the distance.

Kolya whipped around in his seat to look out the window. "*Maman*. Gunfire!"

She patted his knee. "The men shoot rabbits. Practicing their riflery, darling."

"But it was a pistol shot, *Maman*."

The car sped on toward the rock frontage of the Aerie. "Oh, Kolya, you and your guns!"

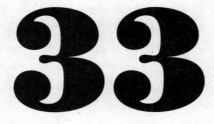

33

THE BRITISH EMBASSY, BERLIN

THURSDAY, DECEMBER 17. Alex Reed sat on a chair outside the offices of the British ambassador. He was being kept waiting and tried not to let that unnerve him. As second secretary for trade, of course, he didn't command an immediate hearing.

Elaine had gone missing. She had told Bibi and Albert that she was joining him in Bonn, but she had not shown up. Now he must inform Eric Phipps of this turn of events and do so to position himself firmly out of the way of censure. It was a sticky situation. He could not be sure how much Phipps knew, nor how much the Berlin station knew. Certainly they could not know that he had asked the Gestapo to watch the woman who was supposed to be his wife. The secret police would be discrete in this. But they owed no particular allegiance to him.

Christ God, he did not have it in him to be an operative of this sort. All he had wanted was deniability to his German contacts if she got herself caught working against German interests, as she seemed hell-bent on doing. Asking for his Gestapo contact to keep her under observation was a measure to distance himself from her if she got in trouble. Though at the outset it seemed a safe maneuver, he hoped he had not miscalculated.

The embassy first secretary approached, fetching him and leading him into Phipps's office.

Phipps sat at his broad, carved desk. Behind him a large rectangle defined an outline of the now-removed portrait of Edward VIII. Phipps waved Alex to a seat.

"I think I know what you've come to discuss, Alex," he said. Stocky, square-faced, revealing nothing in his face so far. "Your undercover wife has gone to ground."

"Sir? You put it like that?"

"Yes, I put it like that. The Berlin station received communication from her that she's off on her own. Apparently got a wild hare about a secret weapon and has broken ranks over it." He smoothed his mustache. "They wish to know if you can shed any light on this."

"I'm as surprised as everyone else. She said she wasn't interested in accompanying me to Bonn for my meeting with the economic group. Then on Sunday the staff telephoned me that she was on her way to join me after all. She did not inform me she was coming. And she did not arrive."

"Nothing that might point to her motives?"

"It's hard to say. She had been acting erratically. Late hours, that altercation with the security police in the Nollendorfplatz that you and I discussed. We had to assume it was part of her work for the intelligence service. I had no idea she wasn't under strict rein."

"How do you mean acting erratically?"

"She was keen on getting me to help a woman who wanted to leave Germany. A Jew who offered to trade information for expediting a visa. I told her that the embassy could not become involved in internal German affairs, but she seemed emotionally involved, wouldn't let it lie. I hoped that she had moved past the matter. Or was pursuing it through the station. In any case, she seemed to develop hostility toward our work here. She characterized it as bureaucratic. Turning a blind eye to Nazi excesses, that sort of thing. She struck me as headstrong, with poor operational judgment."

Phipps sighed. "I said nothing good could come of this. It's one thing to provide occasional cover for someone doing delicate work, but to place her in your household and have you introducing her around . . ." He shook his head. "It could place us in a bad light."

"I hope it hasn't gone that far, sir."

"Yes. Well." Phipps straightened his shoulders, looking to wrap it up. "I'll inform London and the Berlin station of our discussion. Anything else?"

"Sir, if I may speak personally?" Phipps nodded. "I wouldn't like any irregularities with Elaine to undermine my position in the bond repayment matter."

"Undermine?"

"Yes, sir. If there should be a taint associated with my name. It's not helpful when dealing with the Finance Ministry here. They need to know I'm on solid ground. Have firm backing."

"I thought you had it."

"In most regards, yes. But if my supposed wife becomes entangled in unsavory events?"

Phipps scowled. Unsavory events. He would want to steer

well clear of those. "We can only hope, whatever she's up to, that she doesn't get caught."

"Yes. It would help if there was a gesture of confidence from the Foreign Office." When Phipps did not respond, he plunged on. "If the secretary for trade is too ill to resume his duties, it might be time to look for someone who can step up to the post. I hope that my seniority would recommend me to that position."

A long stare that seemed to suck all the air out of the room. "I see." Phipps reached for a folder on his desk, but instead of opening it he folded his hands upon it. "As it happens, I was thinking exactly along those lines. You'd be a good fit, Alex. I'll put in a word for you with London."

The room, always gloomy from the deep well of the Hotel Adlon shading its windows, seemed to brighten. "Thank you, sir."

Phipps nodded. "Carry on, then. Try not to worry about this supposed wife of yours. You've been a good sport about it all, more than I would have been in your place. It won't go unnoticed."

Alex left, his mood greatly improved. He had been a good sport. And, looking ahead, he felt he would make an excellent first secretary for trade.

SIS HEADQUARTERS, LONDON

THURSDAY, DECEMBER 17. "He's expecting you," Olivia said.

Julian nodded at her where she stood behind her desk. In a nice brown plaid suit, hair gleaming, no strand out of place. The overhead lights made her look pale. He wondered how married life was suiting her. There was talk that her husband hated the cocktail circuit and was seldom seen at the usual watering holes.

She had only been married three months, so he supposed it was too early to hope she was miserable. He winced at the thought. He could not hope such a thing for the woman he loved. All right, not miserable, just not *very* happy. Perhaps *reasonably* happy. Good Christ.

She fixed him with a sympathetic look. "I'm sorry about Kim. Terribly sorry."

He started to say thank you, but the words didn't break free. He nodded to her, glad that she could say something personal to him after these weeks of strict formality.

"We don't have all the facts yet," he said. It sounded defensive. Damn, when she had been so kind.

"No. I just meant that it's a worry."

"Thank you," he managed to say without the slightest warmth. He wished he could have a do-over, but once you acted like an ass, there it was.

He pushed through the door where E was at the sideboard, pouring a drink. God, was it bad enough for whisky at two o'clock?

E handed him a glass, and they took their seats.

"Will you be off to Wrenfell for Christmas?" E asked. Whitehall was starting to shut down. Ostensibly His Majesty's Government was always on the job, but in reality, civil servants began trickling away from posts the weekend before the holiday.

"I expect so." He had picked up a few presents. A silver picture frame for Mrs. Babbage—even after all these years, he never called her Agnes—and sturdy leather gloves for Walter Babbage. For Kim, a fine tartan plaid neck scarf. She might have had use of it in Berlin where it was colder than usual. "A few days. I'll make the rounds of the Uxley yuletide festivities." Said with only a trace of irony, even though there were no parties in the offering, except general merriment at the Barley and Mow.

E gave a smile of appreciation. "Those Yorkshire parties one hears about."

"You're down to Litchfield?"

The smile lapsed. "Yes. Lydia has invited a houseful. You're invited, she wanted me to say. I warn you, she has a dreadful niece that she's hoping to pawn off on you."

"Thanks for the warning. Please thank Lydia and make my excuses, if you would."

They sipped their drinks while the real topic came fully into view.

E kicked it off. "Still no contact with Sparrow, Julian. Her handler says she may try to run her own show. Bit of a cock-up." He sighed. "Well. You read the report."

Julian kept his gaze steady. "Yes. She may yet be able to bring Vesta around. The threat to cut us off could be a part of Vesta's negotiating tactic."

"Are you picking up any mention of Monarch from our listening posts?" E asked. Julian had sent out queries.

"No. If it's an operation, it's not leaking out."

"But do you think Monarch could be a critical operation? A Russian princess turning German Talents into stronger weapons? And turned against Europe's defenses?" E glowered. "It's a far reach."

"Not if *catalyst* is a new Talent. That's exactly how it would be used."

E settled into a scowl, his habit when faced with things that he didn't want to be true. "Still. Sparrow has fallen for it. Obviously."

Kim could still turn up, Hannah Linz in tow, and no police incident or diplomatic stew at all. But Berlin station had said she'd spoken of trying to take out the Russian woman. How his daughter could possibly help with any scheme like that, he did not know, but it looked like she wanted a role. Thought she had one.

E had picked up his paperweight, turning it in his hand as though it were a crystal ball that could give him a glimpse into Kim's psyche. What she'd do next. He put it back on the desk, giving his best guess. "Looks like she's pulling out all the stops now to bring Vesta over to our side. I just hope she doesn't go too far."

Julian murmured, "The question is, what is too far?"

The two men gazed at each other, each one imagining a worse scenario. A rogue agent, a failed scheme, a Nazi propaganda coup, inflaming a notoriously erratic German chancellor. Those were the top issues, by no means exhaustive.

E said, "Too far? Letting a German partisan determine operational conduct." Before Julian could rebut, he plowed on. "Cutting off contact with her handler—"

"If she *has* cut off contact."

"Yes, if she continues this silence. Then there's the matter of assassinating a member of the Russian aristocracy in exile. On the word of a Jewish resistance fighter." The afterthought: "And getting caught." A pointed look at Julian. "*That* is going too far."

Julian countered. "Balancing against that, a potential threat to Europe foiled."

"You still give her the benefit of the doubt, then."

Feeling like the words would haunt him: "I do."

"So if Berlin station can find her, you advise they use reason with her, but let her proceed?"

"We can't judge the situation from six hundred miles away. But I would not encourage Berlin to treat her as hostile. She has proven her loyalty." He sipped his whisky. "And I do think it's been unfair of us to assume that her judgment is impaired by emotionality."

E had the grace to drop his gaze. They had been assuming that, and it did them no credit after Kim's emotional control had been tested by two recent threats to the realm. Finally he said, quietly, "That episode in Wales. You think she killed the Dutch assassin to prevent his death repeating that of her brother's?"

Good God, even E had thought of it.

"No, I think she killed him the same way any of us would have put down a horse with a broken leg. Simple mercy."

"Well. There's nothing we can do right now, not unless Berlin station finds her or she makes contact again."

Julian nodded. It was true. Neither Berlin nor London had the next move. "Meanwhile, we've got someone on Alex Reed?"

"Both he and Kim are on the report list, so he'll be watched. But it's damn hard to credit Alex Reed as working on the wrong side."

E didn't say it was hard to think the same of Kim. She wasn't Eton. She didn't know her role the way men of his class did. For starters, agents did not make political judgments. Of necessity, they played a role as a part of larger policies. But Berlin station had mishandled her, of that much Julian was sure. In the end, it wouldn't help her, the fact that the station had stumbled a bit. If things went south, she would be pegged as a rogue and quietly retired.

Unless she came in. Soon.

On his way out, Olivia stood up from the seat behind her desk. "I'll walk you out."

They threaded their way through the desks. In the hallway, they made it to the door to the outside landing before Olivia broke their silence. "I just wondered if you'd like someone to talk to."

He paused. A sympathetic conversation about Kim with Olivia was the last thing he wanted.

"I appreciate it," he said. "But . . ." It felt like hell to push her off. But friendship was not in the cards. Wounds and salt came to mind.

She produced a wobbly smile. "Yes, I understand. But if you change your mind."

"It looks like I'll be around here a good bit for the next few days. I'll give you the high sign if I'm about to cave in." Christ, sarcasm?

Her smile fled. "All right. Good luck, then, with all this." She turned, almost fleeing down the hallway.

He exited the suite, feeling confused by nearly everyone. His usual certainty pecked away at by boss, daughter, former lover. Or perhaps the usual *un*certainty was less bearable than it had been in the old days.

THE TRAIN TO MIESBACH

THURSDAY, DECEMBER 17. Kim slept in a dazed state, head against the back of the seat. Half heard, the rattling of the train punctuated by the screech of metal on metal as the train slowed for the stations. The thud of doors as passengers came and went. When not in a station, the stabbing lights went dim, for which she thanked God.

Luther sat next to her in second class, upright, stalwart, reading a book, while she leaned back, head lolling. Until now, she had not slept in twenty-four hours. She kept imagining standing in the line at the purification ceremony, her face dusted with the powder, fiends in front and in back of her. Inching closer to the tsarina. Irina Annakova—she imagined an imperious tsarina in a jewel-studded dress—pressing her face with her royal hands.

After Naumberg, Luther allowed her to make her way to the toilet by herself. It was funny. Where could she run off to? And besides, she had *wanted* to be here, she had asked to come. Still, Kim thought, sloppy tradecraft. The Nazis were not so deucedly clever as most people thought. Back to her seat and looking forward to oblivion. It would be seven hours to Miesbach.

It seemed it had been dark for many hours. The window was black, showing only her blurry reflection.

"You want to watch your step when we get there."

"Absolutely. Anything in particular I should be careful about?" Besides the *Nachkommenschaft* being a little mad, and her, a spy among them?

"Always use their titles when speaking to them. They like to hear that. Lieutenant, major, that sort of thing. You don't want to appear rude. Especially as a woman."

As though she would be rude to the SS. Or to the cadre of the *Nachkommen*. *Excuse me, Wilhelm, but you have blood on your chin.* She chuckled.

Luther snapped a look at her. "It is not a laughing matter. The doctor in charge, he can send you away if he does not like you. I bring them up the mountain, and sometimes . . ." He shrugged. "The Talents, they are wasted."

They sped into a tunnel, changing the timbre of the hurtling train.

He went on. "But I keep a record of my Talents. Yes, every one Kaltenbrunner sends home. It is a waste! If they ever ask me . . . I have a record." He cut a startled look at her. "It's no more than anyone would do. Go to sleep. You look fatigued."

He didn't like having told her about the doctor. Ah, a *spill?* Something to remember, if so. There is a doctor who sends people away. Well, it wouldn't be her. She closed her eyes.

She woke with a start when someone hefted a suitcase into a nearby overhead rack.

Luther handed her a sandwich wrapped in brown paper tied with a string bow. Foggy with sleep, she unwrapped the package and lifted one corner of the bread.

"Liverwurst," he said.

Normally a sandwich she would avoid, but she hadn't eaten for a long time. Needs must. She rolled the liverwurst into a tube and ate it like a pickle. The bread, set aside.

He was watching her.

A mistake on her part. She must give no indication she had been touched by a *catalyst*. She was supposed to be a natural 7. Not that rolling your liverwurst was a giveaway.

"I really can't eat yet. A sandwich is too much." Reminding him she'd had food poisoning.

He had withdrawn his attention, looking at two small photographs he carried in his billfold. She looked over, catching a glimpse of children. "Yours?"

"My sister's. This is Hans." Pointing to a serious-looking boy in knickers and formal shirt. "And Angela." The girl, older, in a school uniform, clasping her books to her chest.

"Very sweet," Kim said. Luther took a few moments to savor his nephew and niece. A man who loved children, carried their pictures. As long as they were Aryan, familiar, related. The children of some not admitted to the circle. How did a man who carried these pictures give his loyalty to the Nazi party? She would rather not have admired anything in him at all. But all of them had families, didn't they? All of them cared for aged parents, loved their nephews, were fond of, perhaps even in love with, their wives. And beat Jews in the public squares and made sure Hannah Linz could not attend law school.

"Do you have sisters? Brothers?" Luther asked. The train swayed into a curve, clacking past the dark fields, dotted here and there with the blurry lights of cottages seen through the rain-drenched window.

"No, sorry to say." Nora Copeland did not.

"Then you are missing out. The big family. You Americans are loners."

She had confirmed for him some impression of Americans as self-made people, striking out across the frontier, unmarried women with careers. Cowboys. Closing her eyes, she signaled the conversation was over.

Leaving her with the question of a brother. The reality of a brother, once upon a time. So few memories of those early days at Wrenfell. The ones she did have played over and over.

Standing in the drafty hallway outside the kitchen. There were no windows or even wall sconces between the drawing room double doors and the buttery, so one was always in darkness approaching the kitchen. She heard voices raised. Paused, listening. Robert and her mother.

"Just because everyone else is doing it," her mother said, slapping something down on the lead counter.

"It isn't that. Is that what you think?" Robert's voice.

"Patriotism, I suppose. For England, God and country. But it's the thing everyone believes, even the enemy."

They were fighting again about his wanting to sign up for the war. Father had said, "We'll hear no more about it, this is Robert's decision." But Mother had him alone in the kitchen, and she was going to make the most of it.

"You make it sound half-baked. Like it doesn't mean anything. It's not like that."

"Oh, Robert, so you keep saying. But what is it like?"

"It . . . It's just something . . ."

"For God's sake."

"It's just what you do. When the fighting starts, you have to choose."

Kim didn't think they ever reconciled the issue. He came home in uniform after his first course of training. When he left, his mother's eyes were dry and hard. Julian shook hands with him. Kim had never shaken hands with her father, so when he did so with Robert, she knew it was something important. Almost like they were equals, because Robert was in uniform and leaving.

It was all very complicated. Until it wasn't. Until it was over for Robert and no going back or arguing about things anymore.

She slept, the lights dim, like the hallway. Hearing voices murmuring in the kitchen. If she could just reach the kitchen door, they would all be there. Sometimes her mind acted like it didn't know what had happened and what didn't. Who was here, who was lost. Memory kept everyone. It would be unjust and cruel to let them slip away, so it must be best to remember, even if most days it didn't seem that way.

"Frankfurt," Luther said, speaking to Kim as though he knew she was just pretending to be asleep.

And later: "Nuremberg."

35

THE INTAKE CENTER, THE AERIE

FRIDAY, DECEMBER 18. "Nora Copeland?" The SS guard stood in front of her in the frigid hall. *"Folgen Sie mir."*

Next to her, Luther nodded for her to go.

She picked up her suitcase and the guard led her to a door that opened into a small room, not much warmer than the hall. An SS captain in a black uniform sat at a desk. He was young, with a round, unlined face and hair slicked back on top with close-cropped sides. Beside him, a piece of equipment that she recognized. A kind of dynograph. Her test, then.

He said something to her in German, but it went by too quickly to catch.

"Ich spreche nicht so gut Deutsch." I don't speak German well.

His expression, coldly flat. "You will learn," he said in English. His sober admonition struck her as amusing. It was not, of course. The urge to burst out laughing had become disquieting. Her passport lay on the desk, open to her photograph. The captain gestured for her to sit next to the dynograph.

She had not told Luther that her Talent was *spill*. She had not wanted to give him any reason to send her away. It was better to let it come out at the test.

The officer fastened leads to her head, carefully parting her hair to make contact with her skull.

The ink arm began to vibrate, tracing a pattern along the paper feed. She hoped it did not scream a damning message: *A spy, a spy.* But the dynograph could not read her thoughts, only record activity, activity that one trained on the machine could interpret as relating to one Talent or another.

"Breathe deeply," he ordered. After a few minutes he frowned. "You must relax, I cannot get a reading."

"Yes, I am trying." A little nervousness was to be expected, but she wished she were not terrified.

"Describe the drive up from Tolzried."

She described how the lights of the town disappeared behind them as they drove from the village into a forested area. Rain had become sleet as they ascended the steep, deserted road. The car swayed in the slush, fishtailing around a curve. Luther said they must keep up their speed, or they would lose traction. She was relieved when she saw the intake center. They had made it.

Her interviewer watched the needle swing back and forth. Then he asked mathematical questions, counting backward by sevens, simple multiplication. She knew that the imprint of every Talent suggested itself in stock graph tracings.

A dog barked outside. She had seen the Alsatians on leashes, sleek shepherds, ears high, eyes darting. She hated that the dogs had been trained to kill on command.

The captain handed her a booklet and pencil. "Begin to copy

what you see, but move quickly." The first pages were full of simple shapes. Owen Cherwell would be fascinated to see this booklet, part of the work-up for the precise German rating system of Talents. Triangle, hexagon, rhombus. She got as far as a parallelogram when the captain ordered her to stop.

He left her attached to the machine and went out. Now came the real test; whether she could convince them that the report of her supposed Talent had been a lapse, a mistake in transcription, or just carelessness on the part of her recruiter.

Soon the captain returned with a man in a white doctor's smock.

"This is Major Kaltenbrunner. We have a difficulty."

Ah. Kaltenbrunner, who Luther had mentioned. The major, tall and potbellied, ignored her, looking at the readout, pulling the long sheet quickly through his hands.

"You are not a *precognition* Talent," he said in excellent English, fixing her with an even stare, neither accusatory nor predatory, but in the crack between.

"*Precognition?* No, I have never had that ability. It is the *spill*, of course. They didn't tell you?"

Kaltenbrunner exchanged glances with the captain, who handed him a clipboard with a sheaf of forms.

As the doctor flipped through the sheets, he said, "You were to be a 7 for *precognition*, as rated at the Rawlings Institute."

"I am sorry, there must be some mistake."

"Obviously."

"I hope it will be all right."

"It is not all right. The *spill*"—he barely concealed his contempt—"is not of use to us." He handed the clipboard back to the captain, turning an annoyed glance at her. "The *spill* is only fit for spying."

The word sent a trickle of stomach acid down her insides.

"That is not to our purpose, even if you are an 8.6."

8.6? Kim felt weak. Hannah had taken her far past a 7.

"You have come a very long way for nothing."

Kaltenbrunner reached into his pocket and drew out a card. Handing it to her, she read the words stamped on it. *Special Assignment.*

"But Major Kaltenbrunner, I—"

"There is nothing more to say. Show the card to the intake officer in the lobby." He flicked a glance at the captain, who pulled the leads from her skull. "I suppose it was not, after all, your fault. You would not have lied. Unless it was to be more valuable?"

"Oh, I would never have lied. The dynograph does not lie, it would be foolish to claim something I'm not. Surely, doctor, I can be of some service?"

"I am afraid not. Back to Berlin with you. They may find a use for you. I cannot."

She wanted to grab him by the front of his smock and shake him, implore him. But he was already headed for the door. He turned, hand on the doorknob. "I am sorry, Fräulein Copeland." A look of pity? Such a long way she had come.

Kim looked down at the card. *Special Assignment.* Wherever she was sent next, this horrid little card said it all. She had failed.

"I must speak to Major Kaltenbrunner," Kim said in German.

She had been sitting in a side room for an hour. A little space heater was dutifully pumping out a trickle of warm air.

The guard outside the door said, *"Nein, nein."* He pushed her back inside.

"Major Kaltenbrunner, please!" she said with more urgency. He slammed the door shut.

Why, why hadn't she thought of what to do earlier when she'd had Kaltenbrunner's attention?

At the sound of a motorcar engine starting up, she looked out the window. A car drove past the window. Luther driving. She watched as he approached the intersection where the barrier arm barred the road. He turned down the road and headed away.

Leaving without her? Weren't they sending her back to Berlin?

She rushed to the door to implore the guard once more. The door opened and Kaltenbrunner stood there, frowning. A file was in his hand. Perhaps he was still considering the irregularity of her having the wrong Talent.

"You have been calling for me?"

"Yes, thank you! There is something you should be made aware of. I can be useful to you. I know something."

"Well. And what is this useful information?"

"Luther. He's not quite, well, regular. I don't know what it means, but . . ." She hesitated, pretending reluctance to get the man in trouble.

"Yes, go on."

"He *spilled* to me. Something that you may want to know."

"You criticize this man?"

"Maybe there is something to criticize."

"I have pressing duties, Fräulein." But he waited, frowning.

"Well, on the train—it was a very long train ride from Berlin." A twitch of annoyance in Kaltenbrunner's face. "And he said I was not to cause any trouble when we arrived because I would be sent home at the least infraction."

"As is the case."

"Yes, but he said that—please pardon me—but he said that you are too particular about regulations and have turned away several important Talents that you deemed unfit for service. And he has kept the names and details of each person he has brought you that you turned away in case your superiors ever require to know the situation more fully."

The doctor's face darkened. "Why would he do this?"

"I don't know. I thought it sounded disloyal. It was a *spill*, of course."

"I see." He stepped into the hallway. She heard him say, *"Bringen Sie mir Luther Bliel."* They would pick him up on the road. He might deny it, but if he did have documentation on Kaltenbrunner, they would find it.

When the doctor turned back to her, his face had softened.

She plunged on. "I am watchful for the Party, you see."

Kaltenbrunner held out a hand to her. "Miss Copeland. Give me your card."

The assignment card. She opened her handbag and found it, handing it over. He put it in his right smock pocket. From his left he took out another card. She accepted it, quickly scanning the stamped designation.

Intake approved. He smiled, as though they now understood each other, their little misunderstanding was past. Joy surged through her, as though a window had opened in an oxygen-starved room. She let herself smile, hoping it was not too triumphant.

"An 8.6 on the scale," he said, nodding. "You may have some use after all."

His German accent, with its staccato pronunciation, seemed amusing. A giggle started to come up, but she managed to suppress it.

"Thank you, doctor. You won't regret this. I will do everything I can for you." *And you will quite wish you had found me unfit.* She hoped her expression looked happy and not amused. How quickly she had passed from fear to mirth. There was nothing whatsoever to laugh about.

Kaltenbrunner signaled that she should pick up her suitcase, and then he escorted her down the hall to another room.

Leaving her in the hall, he went inside.

Her confidence surged. She had outwitted him, and her satisfaction at this became an acute pleasure. They couldn't touch her, they couldn't outthink her. But on the other hand, could they? She wondered if such confidence was the natural state of a high 8 on the scale. She doubted that it was, for surely she would have heard of such a thing. It might be Hannah's touch, the state of having been augmented.

Hannah hadn't said this was how it would feel. But Hannah hadn't experienced that state, having only been on the other end of the transaction.

Kaltenbrunner returned, no longer carrying her file. "Good day, Fräulein Copeland." He waved her through the door. "I hope that your arrival at the Aerie has no more bumps in the road."

She entered a windowless room. This one held yet another SS official. He sat behind a long table, and to one side stood another soldier. Ahead of her, facing the table was a man, a civilian, apparently going through his own intake process.

She waited by the door until beckoned forward. As she approached the table, she passed her fellow recruit, a short, squarely built man with a heavy accent, perhaps Polish or Czech. He left the room carrying a stack of things. Clothes, shoes.

The officer at the table, not as young as the last one, wore round wire-frame glasses and looked very much the clerk despite the uniform.

"Nora Copeland," he said. Her passport was now attached to a file, and he glanced at it. "American."

"Yes, that's right."

"You will put your suitcase on the table." His English was very formal. He glanced at her handbag.

She placed both the suitcase and handbag on the table, and the soldier began his search. After a time, he turned to the officer, nodding that they held nothing of concern. He left the sanitary towels in the bottom of the suitcase. As she and Hannah had guessed, handling such items was distasteful to the SS, particularly in front of other SS men.

The officer said, "We will take your suitcase now. You are assigned new clothes." He gestured at one of the bundles on the table.

"Yes, of course." She paused, a tasteful hesitation. "But I have need of the . . ." She glanced at the sanitary towels.

"You will have provisions for such needs once you are settled."

"But, well, it has been a long drive."

The officer, offended by the subject, swept a hand toward her suitcase. "You may use the toilet down the hall."

She took the nearly empty suitcase and left the room, finding the lavatory at one end of the barracks hall. Once inside a stall, she tore open one of the sanitary towels and, detaching a layer of gauze, spread it over her lap. Two of the napkins that held the tincture had been carefully sewn shut. She split open the stitches and tapped the powder onto the gauze fabric, then rolled it up and tucked it into a slit in another towel. She pushed this one into her underwear.

On her way out of the lavatory she threw the ruined towels into the garbage.

She tried to wipe the smirk off her face as she returned the suitcase to the intake officer. He narrowed his eyes at her. She had no right to smile.

Stop it, she told herself.

Her driver sped them up the road a short way to their destination. Her stack of supplies and clothes sat next to her. She now wore a shirt and slacks, sturdy black shoes, and a wool jacket. Her driver was a *Nachkomme*, or so she judged by the elongated skull beneath his peaked SS hat and the unnaturally long hands on the steering wheel.

He must have been augmented over a period of years, to have such decided markers for the . . . *disease*, she wanted to say.

The disease she had now contracted.

She was eager to meet her contact. So many things she needed to know about the Aerie. The back door. But at the moment, the main thing she wanted to know was, *When does the giggling stop?*

He parked next to several other black cars, one of them especially long and sleek, perhaps belonging to someone important. He motioned her out of the car.

She found herself standing in front of a massive cliff face rising five or six hundred feet. A knife-edged wind carried sleet sideways into her face. Soldiers dressed in the gray Waffen SS uniform and the SS black stood in knots, talking. The Aerie lay just above her. The Monarch's nest. A gun battery was just visible at the top.

All amusement fled.

She noted an officer emerging from a door carved into the

cliff. He carried a courier bag and hurried to a waiting car. When she passed through that door she would be inside the Aerie. It had been her goal, but the triumph she had felt moments before dimmed. She was walking into their redoubt.

Her driver, still not having spoken a word to her, ushered her through the door in the cliff.

In a brightly lit, chiseled stone hall, a lift. Flanked by two guards.

Her *Nachkomme* escort pulled the collapsing cage doors open, and securing them, punched the button to ascend. Standing next to her, he was taller than she, but not dramatically so. He took a moment to regard her. He kept his face professional, cool, but his nostrils flared.

Seeing this, she inhaled deeply to test her own sense of smell. Was that odor she detected that of his oiled hair?

They moved upward, accompanied by the lift's smoothly functioning hum.

THE AERIE

A FEW MOMENTS LATER. The cage rose into the open air. They were in a booth open on two sides. In front of them, a spacious courtyard flanked by a few buildings. The square was dominated by a massive lodge, its second-story windows hung with Christmas wreaths. Facing it on the opposite side of the yard, a snow-covered residence that must be Annakova's chalet.

Outside both buildings, guards with submachine guns.

Icy paths through the snow crisscrossed the square, showing the travel patterns of the Aerie's occupants. Her escort led her along one of these. Kim noted that the shelf on which this retreat had been built butted up against the sheer cliff of a mountainside. They were high in the German Alps, in a fortress location accessible only by lift, except for the secret way in and out that Hannah had spoken of. A back door. Somewhere. It certainly existed or otherwise, Hannah would not have been so sure. Clearly she was trying to reassure herself. And why? How wretched if she had been taken in, imagined a friendship formed under duress and she, committed to doing her part in the great struggle, had let herself . . . believe. This was not the time for doubt. It was only fear that brought such thoughts.

When they came to the edge of the plaza, the officer led the way up a sanded walkway into a barracks area dotted with fir trees. They passed a frozen pond with a shed on the bank.

Their destination, the nearest barracks. A few stairs led to the doorway, and they climbed these, entering a short hall with rooms on either side, doors closed. Farther on, a communal space was just visible: beds, storage trunks at their feet.

The officer opened one of the doors. Two women sat on bunks, with a third bunk empty. The door closed behind her.

One of the women, a thin, pinched-looking blonde wearing an alpine sweater, pointed at the remaining empty bed.

Kim placed her clothes parcel on it. Since it nestled next to the window, it was undoubtedly the coldest station. She sat on the precisely made bed and looked around her. Open shelves were already full of the others' supplies. A picture of Hitler in a cheap wooden frame hung over one bed.

"I'm Nora. Do either of you speak English?"

The blonde woman said, "I am Erika." She cocked her head at the other woman, stocky and dark-haired. "That is Hilde."

Hilde remained silent, reading a book.

"We will speak English if we must," Erika said, "though it would be better to speak German." She looked up at the picture of Hitler as though seeking his approval for the sentiment.

From the walls came a solid clunking sound followed by a brief gust of warmth from the floor vent. Kim shivered, pawing through her stack of clothes for a sweater. She found one along with a tan shirt, three pairs of knickers, large. Two pairs of wool socks. A brassiere shaped like a harness. A cream-colored night-dress incongruously patterned with bluebells.

On the sly, Kim assessed her roommates. Erika was in charge. She spoke first and had the picture of the Führer. The dark-haired one was nervous, afraid of the other woman, darting glances at her whenever Erika's back was turned.

It was crucial to know what Talents each of them had. Pray God it was not the *spill*; Kim was at high risk of divulging since her intention, her critical need, was to maintain her cover. So if one of them had the *spill*, she was at risk. Even if you were one yourself, you were no more able to fend it off. This, she had learned to her disadvantage with Erich von Ritter. Also a danger: *hyperempathy*. Kim was subject to bouts of alarm among Nazis, an emotion that would trigger suspicion. Perhaps worst of all: *precognition*.

"Where do you come from, Erika?" Kim asked. She smiled at the woman, but it was not returned.

After a long pause: "Düsseldorf."

Kim turned to Hilde, but the woman pretended she did not see.

"I'm from Albuquerque. I expect you haven't heard of it, but it's in the Southwestern United States. I'm not used to all this snow." Erika frowned. "Though it is exceptionally pretty, of course."

She mustn't lay it on too thick. She hoped that Hilde would be more amenable to conversation, perhaps when Erika was not around.

Her first priority was to make contact with Dietrich Adler, whom Oberman Group called Tannhäuser. There hadn't been time for Hannah to let him know that they had sent an operative. Adler was the one who knew the hidden escape route. She would need it if something went wrong. However, if all went according to plan, she would transmit the disabling drug to Irina Anna-kova at the ceremony and no one would be the wiser. Even if the woman knew something was amiss, she almost certainly could not guess what had happened.

Erika turned to her. "The lavatory is down the hall just before the great room. It is for women only, because this bar-racks is women's quarters. We are the only women in residence. The civilian men are in the barracks up the hill." Her tone and demeanor stiffened. "There will be no *fraternizing*," she said, as though Kim might be particularly susceptible. "Our seating for lunch is promptly at one thirty at the Festival Hall."

Kim was very hungry indeed. She suddenly craved a savory mutton stew or a brisket of beef. Rare would be lovely.

"What do they serve?" she asked.

"Potatoes."

Erika marched the two of them down to what they called Fes-tival Hall. This was the largest building in the Aerie, with the ground floor taken up by dining rooms, kitchen, and staff offices. Erika had made it clear they would be going together. Hilde, who had finally introduced herself, walked at their side.

Their barracks was on the hillside under the cloak of ever-greens, but ahead Kim noticed that the hall was covered with snow, brilliant in the sunshine. It struck Kim like a hammer between the eyes.

Erika glanced at her. "You are all right?"

"Oh yes, fine. I'm not used to the snow, is all."

"It is mountain altitude," Hilde said, trundling along, appar-ently happy to be out of the confines of the barracks. So she knew some English after all.

Shots came from the woods. Kim spun around to look.

"It is only target practice," Erika explained.

Before they resumed their walk, Kim saw a soldier patrolling in the woods, submachine gun at the ready.

"You are not used to being around guns," Erika said with conviction.

Kim longed to set her straight. "You are right. It gave me a start." As they entered the back door of the hall, she tried not to sigh in relief to be out of the molten daylight.

They filed down a hallway past a kitchen. In the wall, lunch servings were lined up on a counter. The three of them each took a bowl of soup and continued to a small dining area with long tables set up end to end. Farther down the hall was a great room where the SS *Nachkommenschaft* took their meals. Erika waved her to the end of one of the tables, pointing to where she should sit, but Kim pretended she had not seen the gesture and took a seat with her back to the window. She was next to the man she had seen in line at the intake center. Looking around, she saw five other men scattered at tables.

The one from the intake center smiled at her briefly and went back to his soup.

Potato soup, Kim discovered. She could not eat it. But she must. She spooned in mouthfuls. Bread and jam, also doubtful. She must not appear to have any symptoms of augmentation. They would expect that from her later, but not yet.

Three more souls joined the group, speaking German, presumably Talents. All civilians. They would be ones sent to infiltrate governments, judiciary, railroads, civil defense—all critical institutions requiring undermining and subversion to clear the way for the painless annexation—of what Hannah had claimed would be Poland, France, the Netherlands, Czechoslovakia. And

Russia. Or at least the rich Ukraine. A bit more than the osten-
sible *Lebensraum*, breathing room, that Hitler claimed was the
limit of his ambition.

On the other side of her, a white-haired man in a dark suit
took a seat. Down the table, Erika cast fretful glances at her. She
might have been directed to watch the occupants of the women's
barracks. Well, Erika would not be going into the toilet stalls
with her. Hannah's idea to smuggle the powder in sanitary prod-
ucts had been brilliant.

Only two of the men had the physical symptoms of the Progeny. Perhaps the others had not yet undergone a large number
of—or any—augmentations. She strained to hear the conversations in the room, curious about nationalities, the languages.

A server brought in a platter of cold sliced beef. The sight
was very welcome. The elderly man helped himself. Kim reached
for a share, taking a nice portion.

Even as busy eating as she was, she noted that one of the
Nachkommenschaft was wolfing down his food. It reminded her
that she must not.

The old man seated next to her turned in her direction. *"Es
ist gutes Rindfleisch."*

"Ich spreche nicht viel Deutsch." I don't speak German very well.

Speaking English with a heavy Russian or Slavic accent, he
said, "I think English, then.'"

She nodded. This might be the man Hannah had called
Evgeny, a friend of Annakova's.

He went on. "What I said to you: 'It is good beef.'"

"Very tasty," she agreed.

"Cook serves special when I am here." With a smug smile,
he fixed a look at his tablemates. *"Da,* she like it when I come
to table. Yesterday, goulash!" He went on. "You know goulash?"

"Yes. I am an American. I have heard of goulash." She smiled at him, and they made eye contact. "You speak German and English and I am guessing Russian as well, sir. Languages are a great skill."

"*Da!* And Czech. I do not get good English practice, though." His watery blue eyes strained to focus on her. Then he glanced at her plate and picked up a small roasted potato. Examining it, he tossed it back onto the platter. "Is cold. I do not like cold."

He frowned at his plate. "You will die," he murmured casually. Startled, she looked at him.

"Yes. Die."

She could not contain her look of dismay.

"I see picture." A sly smile. "Your death. You wish to know?"

"No." Instinctive. Of course no.

"*Da.* You want to know. This thing I see clearly."

What if he had *precognition?* "Don't tell me."

"I tell you, lady. Is important."

Rising from her chair, she pushed back from the table. "No. I said please don't."

Erika looked up, frowning.

What did he see? Her death here in the Aerie, out there on the plaza, shot in the head? A bad death in a Gestapo basement? In forty years, alone at Wrenfell? She had to get away. Because she most certainly did not want to know.

She fled the table, heading to the door. People looked up from their plates; Hilde rose from her bench.

The old man turned in his chair to shout at her. "Is blood in the snow! Blood staining on white shirt! A man with uniform. A gun. I see this!"

She hurried from the room, into the hallway.

He followed her, shouting, "Wait! Wait!"

Almost to the outer door, something made her turn to face him. The desperation in his voice. The pathetic state of an old man, mentally unstable, helpless. At her sudden calm, he approached her. She noted that he wore an old-fashioned suit with waistcoat and cravat. He walked by the pass-through where bowls of soup sat cooling.

Standing before her now, his voice was calm and soft. "I see city also. St. Petersburg, great city of Mother Russia. City I am born in. But Nazis, they kill her." He put a hand on her forearm, his grip solid, like a friend telling you something that you didn't want to hear but must for your own good.

He held up his hand, finger pointing to his temple. "Not just bullet to head. *Nyet.* Slow death. Mothers, fathers, babies, horses. And dogs—they are first to go! No food except crows and rats." His eyes filled with tears. "People eat body of own children."

Erika had come out of the dining room into the hallway but remained by the door.

"Bodies stiff in snow. Ground is frozen so no one buried, but in stacks." Tears slipped down his face. He struggled to speak. "How many die? A million. *Da!* A million. I see, I count bodies. And if you live, going insane from hungry, from sorrow."

He held up a finger as though making an academic point. "Who is killing city?" He looked behind at Erika, who stood watching from the doorway. He whispered to Kim. "German army."

"That is enough, Evgeny." Erika speaking up.

He turned to face her. "Oh. You say so?" He began walking toward her. Putting on a burst of speed, he rushed to the kitchen pass-through. Lunging at it, he swept the bowls off the counter. Crockery shattered on the floor, soup splattering the walls, himself, Erika.

People crowded out of the dining room, staring at the scene.

A woman shouted for help, as Evgeny rampaged through the shattered plates and bowls, kicking them and smearing potato soup as he went.

Two SS guards slammed into the hallway from outside and took hold of Evgeny, subduing him.

Kim caught her breath, stunned by the eruption of rage and despair.

As Evgeny was marched past her, he mumbled, "So many ways of dying. So many."

"I know," she found herself saying.

The light from the open door flooded her mind. The glare of snow blinded her for a moment. It wiped her clean of small things, leaving the larger truths, of suffering, insanity, death. And the simple thought: Only God remains. And He is a bright and indifferent light.

She followed the soldiers out onto the plaza. As they led the old man away, she heard him grumble, "I am needing lunch. My lunch."

They escorted him in the direction of a group of small cabins on a knoll across from the gun emplacement.

Feeling numb, Kim walked back up to the barracks. Erika hurried after her. "Wait, Nora."

Ignoring her, Kim increased her pace. Her heart pounded unnaturally, too fast, hammering at her breastbone.

Erika entered the room as Kim sat on her bed, head in her hands. "We all excuse ourselves from the meal table together," she intoned.

"Leave me alone."

Hilde rushed in, and Kim turned to the wall.

"He is crazy!" Hilde exclaimed. "Why do they keep him? Only because that ridiculous woman loves him."

"Be quiet!" Erika snapped.

Hilde looked disconcerted.

Oh, Hilde, Kim thought. *What a foolish thing to blurt.* Surely a *spill.*

Hilde murmured, "Her Highness has every right, of course."

Kim lay facedown on the bed, pulling the covers over her head, finding relief in the shadows. If people would just stop talking.

Leningrad, they call it now. What will they call it when it is dead? Blood on my shirt. The man in uniform who will kill me.

The purified ones: Sonja's husband. The patient at Treptow Sanatorium.

And me.

THE AERIE

SATURDAY, DECEMBER 19. Erika pushed a cup of hot tea at her.

"We have inspections on Saturdays. You wake up now." It was still dark outside.

Kim sat up, accepting the mug. *"Danke."* Erika had turned exceptionally nice. Under orders after Kim's scare from the old Russian?

She looked around the barracks: its sober, gray walls, the planked floor, the military bunks. Her barracks companions— or watchdogs. Despite her and Hannah's careful plan, she found herself daunted. The nest of the monarch bristled with menace.

Hilde was dressing, eyeing the two of them, maybe wondering about Erika serving tea.

After Evgeny Feodorovich's outburst yesterday she had spent the late afternoon in a Festival Hall training room with an instructor who briefed her on her *spill* assignment. It was to be at the British consulate in Paris, a *Nachkommenschaft* mission that would never be carried out. She pretended to be an earnest student, a little wide-eyed at the honor of her new role, eager to do her part. He had been a simple man to fool. Her confidence had swelled.

Erika made an impatient gesture. "You must make yourself ready."

A pair of long underwear had appeared on Kim's bunk, presumably another gift from Erika. Kim stripped off her nightgown and pulled on the welcome flannels.

She made for the door to get to the lavatory, but Erika barked, "Dress first!"

Kim grabbed her slacks and shirt, fumbling into them and then, as a statement of independence, left the room without putting her shoes on.

"Shoes!" Erika called after her.

The washroom smelled of mold and snow, the floor prickly with cold against her feet. She used the toilet, then cranked the pump to splash water on her face. If only there were a mirror. She needed to see her reflection, despite knowing that logically she should not be changing, not in that way of the Progeny, after just one session. Her hands looked normal. Only one purification. The only changes had been her appetite and a sense that she was not quite herself.

She remembered Duncan's words when they had first met in the Tiergarten. *Everyone has their limits.* She had wanted to ask about his two missing fingers. Had it happened under torture? Had he reached his limit then, and wanted her to know that there were some things that she was not expected to endure? She wondered how one knew when one had gone too far. Perhaps it was only after the fact that one might say, *I should have turned back*. She felt sure she would know her limits. But the thought nagged, that with the *catalysis*, her infusion of self-confidence was unreliable.

Limits. Perhaps an excuse for the timid.

Erika appeared in the doorway. "They are coming up the path! The inspection. Hurry."

As they rushed back to their room, she said, "Captain Adler expects us to be up early, but we let you sleep!"

Adler. Her contact. The SS officer. Kim heard the tread of boots on the steps outside. She and Erika charged into the room. Kim threw her bed together and kicked her nightgown under it. She jammed her feet into her shoes without socks.

Two SS entered the room.

Erika and Hilde moved to stand by the pillow on their beds. Kim followed suit, her shoelaces slapping on the floor as she walked.

One of the men, clearly the superior officer, scanned the quarters. Powerfully built, with a square, unlined face that looked like it had never known a smile. He noted the mug of tea that Kim had left on the floor.

"Ist das ihres?" he asked Kim.

"Yes, Captain. It's my tea." Flustered by the inspection, she forgot to speak German.

"You are the American." Speaking English now.

"Yes, Captain."

He swept his dark gaze over her, noting her shoelaces. "Tie your shoes, Fräulein."

As she did so, her pants hitched up, showing her to be sockless. She stood, expecting a reprimand, but the captain merely took off his hat and handed it to the soldier who accompanied him. He raked his hands through his hair. "You do not speak German. Strange that they find you valuable."

"Yes, Captain." Then the comment that she had planned to use: "But I love Germany. And Wagner is the best music. Especially *Tannhäuser*."

"Wagner," the captain said. "The Führer's favorite."

Walking farther into the room, he glanced at Erika's bunk and pointed to her bed. Kim noticed that the blanket was a little rumpled. *"Die Ecke ist nicht gerade!"*

Erika darted a glance in that direction, her cheeks coloring as she apologized in German.

By the captain's tone, it was a stinging reprimand. Erika stared at the floor, the blood rushing from her face. When the captain finished, he held out his hand in the direction of his adjutant, receiving his hat. "I will see you in my office, Fräulein," Adler said to Erika in English.

"Ja, Kapitän!"

He turned back to Kim. "You are all responsible for one another. You will immediately take her bedding down to the washing shed and clean it, remaking her bed properly."

Smoothing back his hair, he placed his hat on his head and gestured for Erika to precede him out the door.

Kim released a long, slow breath.

He had assigned a meeting place for Kim and gotten rid of Erika's snooping for a while. Neatly done.

As Adler left and his officer marched Erika out the door, Kim began stripping Erika's bed.

The washing shed's warmth fell over her, a blessed relief from the cold. Oversize wringer washers were tended by several women as large as their machines. In the back, clotheslines strung with sheets billowed under blowing fans.

One of the women frowned to see Kim. She pointed to a table where she should deposit the sheets.

As she did so, Adler came in. His dark, elegant uniform was a stark contrast with the laundry room.

"Räumen Sie die Kammer," he told the women.

They quickly dispersed, grabbing coats hanging near the door.

He turned to Kim. *"Sie werden bleiben, Fräulein."* She was to stay. Of course.

One of the women on her way out snuck a glance at Kim, perhaps thinking she knew the officer's intention now that Kim had been ordered to stay.

Adler cocked his head toward the clotheslines and led the way, ducking behind a wall of sheets.

Once they were hidden, he snapped, "Who are you?"

"Hannah sent me." The sheets billowed around them like ghosts.

"Who is this Hannah? Speak quickly, and be very clear."

"Hannah is with the Oberman Group. I'm with British intelligence, helping her."

He unsnapped his holster and drew his pistol, placing the barrel against her forehead. "You have made a very serious error. I know nothing of this."

She drew in a gasp of air. The barrel, pressed hard against her head. Bone and skin so fragile. The horror of the gun, its metal a promise of explosive death. She tried and failed to think of something to say. Only truth could help her now.

"I think . . . ," her voice wobbled. "I think you do know. You give information on foreigners coming to join Monarch."

"This is nonsense." He cocked the gun, pushing it hard enough that she took a step backward. He followed. The hot whirr of the fans, the air sucking and blowing against the white sheets. The unreal moment before the trigger was pulled.

"Please listen," she rasped. "I took the place of an American *precognition* Talent. They passed me through even though I'm a *spill* Talent, thinking it a clerical error."

"I received no advance warning of you."

"There wasn't time. Most of the Oberman Group was slaughtered in a raid last week."

He frowned. "Who survived?"

"I'm sorry, but Franz did not. I know he had been your friend."

Adler paused, absorbing this. The moment stretched on, a full minute, ten, she could not tell. Slowly, he holstered the gun.

She felt weak with relief. He was not going to shoot her. "Hannah is on her own. She said Tannhäuser would help me."

"This raid. Any of them captured?"

"One who has no knowledge of you. The others . . . dead."

He watched her, evaluating. "What is your plan?"

She paused for a calming breath. "I will disable the tsarina." The sheets bulged and flapped. Against this fluttering screen, Adler's dark uniform commanded her entire attention.

"One move and her guards will have you. You can never harm her. You think we would not have done it?"

You haven't done it because you didn't want to die.

"I have a way." She told him about the powder and its effects, watching the contempt and doubt her story brought to his face.

"She told me nothing about this drug."

"No, because you are not a Talent. You could not find a way to use it." She gave a brief and amended rendition of how the drug had been developed and what was known of its efficacy, while omitting any mention of Hannah's *catalyst* Talent. That critical piece was best left secret.

Distant gunfire caught Adler's attention for a moment. The gun range.

"But how . . ." He paused, raising his chin as the insight came to him. "You will transfer the powder during purification. When she touches you."

She nodded.

"It is enough? A few minutes touch with the powder?"

"We think so. But if not . . ." *At least we tried.* "What is the secret way out? I need to know. In case."

Adler shook his head. "I do not know."

"But Hannah said . . ." This was a setback. "You must know."

"I tried to discover it. Only a few people are privy to the information. I am not one of them."

Another thing Hannah had gotten wrong, she of the supreme self-assurance.

Adler went on. "But they will deploy you for the winter campaign, and you will leave at that time. So you will not need a back way."

"I *need* it," she said, putting venom in her voice. Always a back door, a backup plan.

"I will try again. I cannot promise. Come here with your linens tomorrow at dusk. The door will be open, the staff gone."

She nodded. "Thank you. Also, I need to know Erika's and Hilde's Talents."

"Erika? *Object reading.* For Hilde, it is *sounding.*"

Sounding. The ability to create a loud sound that instills fear. It was useful in a riot or a skirmish. Even a war. The ludicrous image came of Hilde on the battlefield. But at least neither woman had an ability that could blow her cover.

Adler said, "You are the one who brought on Evgeny's fit."

"Yes. His predictions, are they accurate?"

"Why ask this? Did he give you a vision?"

"Several of them. One of them was that the *Wehrmacht* will destroy St. Petersburg. A million people will die. Starve. Eating the family pets first, then their own dead children. Bodies stacked up in the snow like lumber."

Adler sneered. "He is mad, could you not tell? They will put him down presently. His execution is ordered."

So Irina Annakova's influence only went so far. She felt a pang for the old man.

Adler went on. "If you must contact me, tie a shoelace around the leg of your bed near the foot." He handed her a new set of shoelaces. So he had believed her from the start.

"Make sure that Erika does not see it. She is one who keeps track of you." He raised his chin. "You are reckless. Running on your emotions."

"So I've been told. If it were you, they'd call you brave."

A narrowing of his eyes. She imagined him shooting her now, blood dappling the white sheets. But instead he shook his head, turned, and walked away.

He stopped, looking back at her. "British intelligence sent a girl?" He shook his head and disappeared around the clothesline. She saw his boots underneath the sheets as he walked away.

"No men could be found who would risk it," she said, loud enough that he could hear.

He stopped. Stupid, stupid to goad him.

She saw his boots move on. Finally, the door closing.

38

SATURDAY, DECEMBER 19. Julian showed up five minutes early at E's summons. He shed his camel hair coat, sopping wet, into the arms of the valet and handed off his ineffectual umbrella. He'd had to wait rather long for a taxi and was the worse for it. Add to that not having slept the night before, pacing his flat. Where was Kim? Out on her own or picked up by the Gestapo?

E was waiting in the billiard room.

"Julian," his boss, his old friend, said. "Take a seat and warm up, for God's sake. Frightful weather."

A waiter brought whiskies, which Julian gratefully accepted. The meeting was likely related to Kim.

"You look ill-used, Julian. Getting along all right?"

"I'm waiting it out. All we can do."

"Yes." E stared at the fire for rather too long. "Four days now. I'm afraid she's flown the coop."

"Has there been corroborating evidence?"

"No. Just that message from Berlin station reporting on her phone call to her handler. We've had some communications from the embassy, though. Apparently she'd been expressing impatience with Alex Reed and the legation for dragging their heels on the Linz matter. Acting increasingly on edge, to the point that the cover of her marriage has been less convincing. The embassy is fed up with the arrangement."

Julian, annoyed, let himself shrug. The embassy had its own agenda.

"And so is the PM."

Julian straightened. "The PM?"

"Vansittart and I met with Baldwin this morning. If it blows up, we needed to prepare him. It was not a very satisfactory meeting."

Julian waited, apprehensive.

E sipped his whisky, frowning. Whatever had been said in the meeting, it was not a subject he looked forward to broaching. "They took the viewpoint—and it's not mine, you understand—that some of this is the result of the relationships involved."

"Relationships?"

"The PM doesn't like that you're running your own daughter. Come to that, they don't like that you report to me, bypassing the deputy director. They used the word nepotism, I'm sorry to say. Of course that's not it at all."

Julian braced himself for a bad turn of events.

E continued. "But they're right that the situation is mired by chain of command."

Setting his whisky down, Julian said, "She'll be handled by another case officer, then."

"If she comes in, if she can weather this, yes." E sighed and pursed his lips. Quite expressive for the head of SIS. "Look here, Julian. It's bad policy to have relatives working side by side, as it were. It does look like you stuck up for her, pushed her agenda. No matter the truth of it, you will always be accused of it."

"But *is* it true?" He just wanted to know if, in the Monarch affair, he'd failed to keep her at arms' length.

"No," E said. "I agreed with you. But that's another problem."

Julian began to see how all this would end. "You've let our friendship cloud your judgment, is that the conclusion?"

"Not in my view. But in the views that count."

They sat for a time then, neither one wanting to bring the conversation to its logical conclusion. Julian watched the sheets of rain pelting St. James Street. Washing away his world. His world, such as it was, always precarious, subject to the whims of Whitehall.

"Are they asking you to clean house?"

E frowned. "If her career is in the ditch, you can still survive."

It was a dismal hope that Kim would be moved out of her job. He could not hope for it. But that wasn't the only problem. E had become tainted with favoritism. Not a fatal mistake—His Majesty's public servants exercised favoritism as a right—but in this case it might have helped create a diplomatic incident. Never mind that it hadn't done anything of the sort. He could have recalled Kim weeks ago, and hadn't.

In hindsight, he could see how the problem had been stalking him. His clubby relationship with Richard Galbraith, upperclassman friend from Eton, now chief of SIS. A few early exploits solidifying his ability to pull off complex operations, making him the golden boy of the service. Access to privileges like reporting to E and running a member of his family as one of his field agents. All based on E's trust and indulgence. But brought into the open, it all looked too loose, too risky. Chain of command undermined. Agents' personal lives undercutting reliability. It was unsettling indeed to think that it might be true.

"Do you see a way forward?" Julian kept his face neutral. If they put him on a desk, he would leave. He wasn't an analyst or an up-and-coming recruit. Ten years in. Ten years.

"Best to let the Sparrow situation play itself out before we worry too much," E said. "But I wanted to give you the full picture."

The picture wasn't pretty. No matter what played out. "I'd like some time to think about this."

"Julian. We don't need to let this defeat us."

"I hope that's the case. Thank you." He rose, and they shook hands. The handshake solid, conveying decades of friendship, national perils, grievous losses, a few bright victories. Toasts to the King.

Watching the new generation rise up.

Julian found himself in the atrium, donning his wool coat, brushed dry, soon to take another drubbing from the London weather.

Unfurling his umbrella on the steps, he considered whether to get a cab home or walk to a pub.

A pub, then.

BERLIN

THAT AFTERNOON. Hannah squinted into the mirror, satisfied that she didn't recognize herself.

Her hair, chopped short. Eyebrows drawn heavily in, dark slashes over her shaded eyelids. Glasses that she had bought at a street market. The world was blurry seen through this pair, but not as bad as some. The trick in disguises was not so much looking different than you normally did, but in looking ordinary.

Putting the glasses in her pocket for now, she checked her shopping list. Sturdy boots and an alpine ski jacket. Heavy wool pants and socks. Ski gloves and hat. It would be a challenge to buy these things as well as a truck with the cash that Fivel had given her. She would have to shop carefully. The stashes of money in the Oberman Group hideouts would by now be in Nazi hands.

Of the Oberman Group, only she and Fivel were left of those willing to fight openly. After Franz, Micha, Leib, and presumably Zev died, the others had melted away. Maybe they were right to disappear. She remembered the terror: the sudden crash through the kitchen door, the guns flashing. Armed resistance was over, at least for their merry band of Jews in Berlin. Perhaps there were other groups. If there were, she wished them luck.

And now, getting to the Aerie. From Tolzried, she must go the long way around to the lake in the forest.

One more expense she must undertake: her ticket to Miesbach. Two way, for appearances, for her cover of a skiing holiday at a local lodge where skis could be rented.

She was prepared for the worst, that the English would not send a plane. Did they believe that she was a *catalyst?* Would they risk the possibility of losing a Talent like hers? It was impossible to know how they thought or what they thought.

If the British did not show up, then she and Kim must use the service road, a road that was sometimes used for ice fishing at the lake. But it must be a sturdy truck, and at the right price in Miesbach. If they escaped cleanly, they would be miles away before the SS could hope to catch them on the main highway. If something went wrong and they didn't have an hour or so head start, they would be captured. Then they must kill a few Nazis before killing themselves. She didn't know if Kim would be able to do it, but Hannah would make sure Kim was dead before she turned the gun on herself. There were worse ways to die. Such as how Zev had no doubt died under questioning.

So many dead. And worst of all, her father . . . and on the flickering screen the terrible face of the vulture, Lieutenant Becht, with the scar bisecting the right side of his face.

Staring at herself in the mirror, she saw a face with no reaction. The dead did not need her sympathy, only justice. She would not call it revenge, a word used when people wished to shame you for bringing down consequences on villains.

What she was doing was not wrong. What *was* wrong: the people of her country allowing criminals to head government and managing to feel righteous about it.

The top buttons of her coat were missing. A scarf looped around her neck closed the gap. She pulled a knit cap on, recounted and folded the last of the money into a sock, and stuffed it in her pocket.

Yesterday, after feeding the real Nora Copeland in the basement hideaway, she had told Fivel where to go to release the American. He would do so the day after Christmas. Hannah would have preferred eliminating her but she had promised Kim the woman would go free.

She wondered what Kim was doing at this moment. If she had passed the intake interview. If she had made contact with Tannhäuser. How she was handling that unnatural state of brightness that seemed to be the condition of those who accepted a *catalyst*'s touch. Whether she would be too unnerved by the strange land-scape of her own mind.

Kim would not lose her courage. The time for cowardice had been on the way to the train station to meet her Nazi con-tact. Before she met Luther, Kim could have bought a ticket to anywhere.

Not that this was the reason Hannah had followed them and watched them board the right train. But on the other hand, no sense going to the lake for nothing.

39

THE AERIE

SUNDAY, DECEMBER 20. It was her third day in the compound, and SS Lieutenant Voegler was going over the floor plan of the American embassy in Paris. Kim tried to pay attention, but her thoughts were on Captain Adler. She'd spent a sleepless night worrying about him. He was not happy to have her here. He was afraid.

"You are listening, Copeland?" Voegler, a thin man with a monocle, went back to the diagram of the embassy's first floor, where she would be placed as a receptionist. A spy.

A notebook at her side contained the backup, the legend, for yet another new identity that she would assume. It had been arranged that she would be rapidly promoted to offices where she would come into contact with high-level officials. She would have social interaction. Very social, if possible. They would *spill* intelligence to her. Kim learned that the US embassy had a Nazi mole, one who could arrange a job for her.

She was pretending to concentrate on this tutorial, but her mind was elsewhere. Evgeny said there would be blood, her blood. Adler had said the old man was senile. Why should she worry about an old White Russian whose mind was gone?

"Perhaps you did not sleep well last night?" Voegler's right eye, where he wore the monocle, looked larger than the left. She had an unsettling fancy that the eye with the monocle might discern more, might see past her deceptions. A bizarre notion; she carefully reined herself in.

"Please excuse me, Lieutenant. I am paying attention."

He collected his papers; his face reflected a thwarted efficiency. "Come back tomorrow. Memorize the notebook, *ja?*"

"*Ja*, Lieutenant. I will do a good job tomorrow." He dismissed her.

In the hallway, the commotion of the operational offices, the corridor full of uniforms. Two SS, watchful, left off a conversation and watched her as she passed. Businesslike, she kept her head down, clutching her notebook, striding for the door. She nodded at two men she had seen walking down from the men's barracks this morning. *No fraternizing.* The clatter of typewriters issued from offices. Beyond, in the great dining hall, there came a deep drone of many voices.

The *Nachkommen* taking luncheon.

Pushing through the doors into the officer's mess, she was hit by the strong smell of charred meat. Over one hundred men in uniform sat at tables. In their signature black they looked like crows settled over carrion. Despite herself, her mouth watered.

The *Nachkommen* talked among themselves, or some of them did. Not all these souls were beyond camaraderie; many were newly uplifted and did not yet have the characteristic distortions or social ineptitude. Here and there, faces turned to her, as though her steps were loud to their ears, her passing a bright spot of movement claiming instinctual attention.

There were more of them than she had thought. She quickly counted one table and multiplied: 136. And that was just the officer corp. Then there were the civilian Progeny. She couldn't judge those numbers, since they ate in shifts. And some might already be at posts, having been augmented too recently to bear it again.

She thought of the *Nachkommenschaft* spreading out into the target countries. Hannah had said it was Russia, France, Poland, Austria, Czechoslovakia, and Belgium. Not England? Kim had asked. Hitler did not believe England would honor its treaties; no need to subdue them, not yet. On the Continent, the *Nach-kommenschaft* would infiltrate all levels of government and the military, act as relentless assassins, enforce pro-Nazi ideas with physical and—Hannah had said—spiritual terror.

Looking at the assemblage of distorted beings ingesting their lunch, Kim knew how little it would take to instill that terror.

A man sitting close to the aisle looked up at her with sudden interest. His face, a profound oval created by the lengthening of his forehead and chin. Despite having all the features of a man, he did not appear quite human. He looked exactly like the ghoul from Treptow. But she knew it could not be that man. It came to her that eventually all the *Nachkommen* looked like the same person, distilled down to the rarified essence of powers beyond human.

She was glad to make it into the hallway off the civilian dining room. The droning behind her diminished. She found herself in need of a deep breath. Took it. She passed the small civilian dining room. Empty for now.

As Kim passed the kitchen, she noted that Erika was nowhere in sight. Erika might not expect her to be done so early, or at least was not lurking in wait for her. Wrapped sandwiches lay on the pass-through counter, and she took one, planning to eat it in her room rather than risk another encounter with Evgeny.

Outside, workers were clearing ice from the concrete path, breaking it up with the blunt ends of shovels and pushing it to the side. The day had clouded over, dulling the chill of yesterday. It was cold, but not frigid. She decided to have her sandwich by the frozen fire pond. Even as cold as it was, it could be pleasant if she ate fast.

Sitting on a log, she buttoned her heavy jacket to her chin and picked up the top slice of bread, taking a look, hoping for ham. Egg salad. She set the sandwich in its wrapper aside. Blessedly empty of thought, she sat in the middle of this high mountain Nazi outpost, gazing at the pond's ice lid. Yesterday's wind had scoured the surface to silvery blue. At the far end, a hut stood with pipes extending into the water underneath the ice. Finally she ate her sandwich, since there would be nothing more until five.

How satisfying it was that the operation had gone so well to this point! But that train of thought could be dangerous. She was learning to be on guard for that pronounced sense of infallibility that was likely a *Nachkommenschaft* mind-set. But now there was just one more thing she had to do and then she would go home and face the music. The displeasure of the Office.

For now, her thoughts turned to the purification ceremony. An hour beforehand she would slice open the sanitary pad and layer the powder on her face and hands. Then she would stand in line and submit to the tsarina. For another augmentation. The effects would fade in time. But while she was in this nest of

Nazis, she must temper her confidence. It could all spin out of control so easily.

Stuffing the wrapping paper in her coat pocket, she trudged through ankle-deep snow toward the path to the barracks.

As she began her walk up the hill, she heard a shout, and then laughter. A young boy was running from the woods on the path, waving a white paper and letting out whoops of joy. A man hurried after him. "Your Highness, walk please!"

The boy dashed down the path, and still thirty yards from Kim, he took a spectacular spill. His feet went flying out from beneath him, and as he fell, she heard the report of a gun and felt a bite in her shoulder. She sprawled backward in the snow, knocking her head against a rock.

She stared up at the sky, stunned. White sky. The sun, a yellow hole. The sound of voices far away. The snow, a nice cushion. She closed her eyes against the pain in her head, behind her eyes.

Boots came close, and someone knelt beside her.

"Is she dead?" In French.

"*Non.*" There was an SS officer bending over her. He said something in German to her.

"I am American." Oh, was she supposed to admit that? Her thoughts, slow and cold.

The SS officer opened up her jacket and pulled it back. He turned to someone and spoke in French about shooting people.

"I help you now to sit up. You can do so?"

"I . . . think."

With help, she managed to sit up. In front of her, a boy in a heavy pea coat topped by a Russian navy cap. He carried a target sheet full of holes. Her mind got traction, then. The tsarina's boy.

Where she had lain, a smear of blood on the snow.

The officer helped her to her feet. By now there were several other soldiers as well as Erika standing nearby. The boy—Nikolai, she remembered—was bundled off, and two soldiers helped her up the walkway to the barracks.

In her room. A commotion about the bullet having passed through her jacket and plowing through a little of the muscle in her shoulder. Erika had a bandage and ointment to apply, and gradually the room emptied. She was allowed to lie for a few minutes in peace and quiet.

Soon an SS officer came in and examined her wound. Then he held a finger in front of her eyes and asked her what her name was and when she was born. To her horror, she started to give them her real birthdate. She caught herself, mumbling in confusion. After removing her temporary bandage, the doctor reapplied another, and sent Hilde off for a glass of juice. The officer left, leaving her with the prediction that she would live but should be more careful around the gun range.

Ah, so the story was changing. Her fault. Tsars did not make mistakes.

When the juice arrived, she thought it tasted like vinegar. "Please, Hilde, you can have it."

Hilde said no, she couldn't think of having the juice, but when Kim insisted, she looked at Kim with newfound devotion. The drink was soon gone. Erika stood to one side pursing her lips, wondering if this was against the rules. She decided it could be let go, perhaps because the future king of Russia had almost killed her roommate.

Hilde shook her head in disgust. "Running with a gun," she whispered to Kim, her newfound friend.

But all Kim could think of was *this* is what Evgeny had seen. The one in uniform who would kill her. The boy in the naval cap. A slight turn of her body and he would have done so. She laughed to herself, a little ripple of sound in her chest. Evgeny had almost been right.

Hilde looked at her in perplexity. "You almost died!"

"I know." She looked up at Hilde. "I'm not giggling a lot, am I?"

The woman shook her head, throwing a confused look at Erika, who shrugged.

She was awakened from a nap by loud voices in the room. Out the window she saw that dusk was coming on.

An SS guard said that she had to come with him. Immediately.

"But it was not her fault!" Hilde said.

Her right arm hurt from shoulder to elbow. She got up and reached for her jacket. The guard saw that it had blood on it. He snapped his fingers at Hilde, who handed over her own jacket.

Then they were almost goose-stepping down the path, the guard holding her left arm firmly so she wouldn't fall. "Could we please go slower, Corporal?" she asked in German. You had to push back a little or, like Erika, they took you for prey.

"*Nein.*"

The clouds hung lower now, and the air smelled of woodsmoke from the officers' cabins on the other side of the compound. In the plaza, the lights had come on, downward-facing lamps, perhaps to make it harder to see from the air.

As they crossed the plaza, a roar came from near the Great Hall. The corporal stopped for a moment, looking at a sudden commotion.

Two men were fighting outside the front entrance of the hall. One man, with all the markings of a *Nachkomme*, charged forward, bodily lifting the other man. He hurled him against the porch railing. Then, with a snarl, he lunged forward, pouncing on the prostrate man. Other SS moved in to stop the fight.

The corporal hurried her onward, whispering in contempt, *"Verrückte!"*

Madmen. From the sanatorium she knew that the word *verrückt* meant insane. As they walked, he said, in English, "We have orders to respect them, but all we feel is disgust."

So the regular SS did not much care for the Progeny. She smirked. Very likely he had not meant to say so.

As they approached the booth that housed the lift, fear spiked through her. Were they sending her home?

But they passed the lift entrance. He brought her to the porch of the chateau. This was a surprise. Why here?

A guard at the door, submachine gun pointing down. Her stomach clenched. Annakova's quarters.

A plump servant answered the knock and led them inside. They were in a hallway of gleaming wood paneling. The smell of furniture polish and, as they passed the kitchen, of dog food. They entered a great room with a canted ceiling and tall windows giving out onto the leaden sky.

Seated by a fireplace, an elegant woman in a creamy rose dress. Irina Dimitrievna Annakova. Standing at her side, the boy who had shot her. The tsarevich. A small puppy played with a rubber toy on the fireplace hearth.

On the table in front of the divan, a pearl-handled revolver.

An SS lieutenant stood off to one side. He nodded to the corporal, who left the room.

Annakova lifted her hand a few inches and flexed her fingers, summoning Kim. She walked forward. Not knowing what else to do, she curtsied. "Your Highness."

The SS man said, "You should say 'Your Majesty.'"

"Your Majesty."

Annakova was a handsome woman, forty-five or fifty years

old. Or she was in her thirties and aging fast, as Hannah had said was the case with active *catalysts*. Her thick dark hair, pulled back in rolled braids. Precise curls at her forehead. A long satin gown, with a shawl neckline. A brown lace overcoat. As though it were still 1917.

"You are Nora Copeland," Annakova said in heavily accented English. "This is my son, His Imperial Highness Nikolai Ivanovich."

Turning to the boy, Kim curtsied again. "Your Highness."

He wore a dark uniform with epaulets. He nodded stiffly to her. There was an awkward silence that Kim knew not to break.

Nikolai said, in better English than his mother, "Miss Copeland, please accept my apology for my mistake in shooting and wounding you today. I am heartily sorry for it."

Kim took a deep breath. What did you say when a prince apologized to you? "I accept your gracious apology, Your Highness." She so hoped she was up to this new situation, since she had cracked her head solidly when she fell. She glanced at the little pearl-handled revolver. "It did not hurt very much."

Nikolai said, "What does it feel like to be shot?"

"Kolya!" whispered Annakova.

Kim asked, "May I answer, Your Majesty?"

Annakova paused, then nodded.

"At first, like a bee sting. When I fell, I hit my head on a rock. Now *that* really hurt."

Nikolai, who had been very serious up to now, let a tiny smile stab at his cheeks.

"And then later," Kim went on, "the wound did start to ache. Like your arm finally realizes what happened. But it isn't so bad."

"Thank you," Nikolai said. "That was very interesting."

Annakova flicked a glance at the officer, who moved forward, gesturing for Nikolai to precede him from the room.

"My gun, Your Majesty?" Nikolai said.

Annakova nodded to the officer, who retrieved the revolver from the table. He and the boy left, the puppy at their heels.

Kim curtsied and started to follow.

"Stay, Miss Copeland," Annakova said. She gestured to a chair next to the divan on which she sat.

Kim hesitated, wondering if she would now be faulted for being in the wrong place at the wrong time and getting the tsarevich in trouble.

When Kim had seated her herself, Annakova said fondly, "He is young. He still thinks these guns are . . . That they have . . . romance, is word?"

"Yes, Your Majesty."

It had grown fully dark outside. A small fire crackled in the fireplace.

"We have talk," the tsarina said. "You and I."

Oh, let's not, Kim fervently thought.

"I am curious to see that American comes to us. You come so far. Why?"

Kim had to dispose of her standard I-like-Hitler speech. She was talking to a Russian. What did the Russians believe? No, what did an *expatriate* Russian believe, and one moreover who wanted the vacant throne? It was too much to grasp. She cast about, conscious that she was taking too much time.

Finally she said, "I want to give myself to something larger than just me."

Annakova was attentive, encouraging her to go on.

A sudden thread occurred to her. "I see how the world goes. The masses become inflamed and pull things down. Then it is chaos." As Annakova was very well aware, in 1917 they had thrown Tsar Nicholas down a well in the woods.

"This word, ka-ous?"

"Excuse me, Your Majesty. Things in disarray. A mess."

"Ah. Anarchy, you mean. But your country, your United States, which side they are on? They think Stalin stands against Hitler? So they approve Reds?"

"They do not love the Bolsheviks."

"But you join with Germany. Is crime against your country? I am curious." She seemed to intuit that Kim was uncomfortable. "Is difficult question. You do not have to answer."

An elderly servant entered the room, her gray hair braided into a little bun. Annakova waved her away with noble contempt. A queen, Kim mused, knew many hand gestures.

"I forgot what you asked me, Your Majesty."

"Loyalty to country. A difficult decision, coming here?"

"I believe my country is not under correct leadership. And, also, we are not at war with Germany."

"This is interesting. My country, too, not under good leaders. I love my country with my life's blood. Is why I seek good allies."

The fire collapsed, breaking open coals that had been soft red, now flashing golden.

Annakova seemed momentarily lost in thought. "I give everything for country. What I give to my Progeny . . . it takes from me. It takes my days, my years. But all for Russia." She looked at Kim. "You see?"

"Yes, ma'am. Love of country is worth every sacrifice."

Annakova nodded, gazing at the fire. "I do not trust Hitler."

Realizing what she had said, the tsarina reacted with a startled twitch. Then she turned a blameful look on Kim.

"Oh, Your Majesty, forgive me. I cannot help these things." A *spill*. A horrid one, by Annakova's reaction.

The woman settled, staring hard at Kim, taking her measure. "I did not mean that."

"Perhaps, in fact, there is no one a ruler can trust."

Annakova raised her chin. "Yes, yes, that is right. More than you can understand." The fire burned low. "I am impressed by you, Miss Copeland." She paused. "I bring you under my wing. It can be now."

Kim blinked, not following.

Then, as Annakova gestured to the empty place on the divan, next to her, Kim began to realize what the tsarina had in mind.

But it couldn't happen. She did not have the powder. It was in the barracks.

"Sit by me," Annakova said. A knife carving the words on Kim's skin. "Come."

"I . . ." Kim cast about for some way out of this. "I am not . . . prepared, ma'am."

"And so? Is not necessary. Come."

Is not necessary? The chance, her only chance. Slipping by, second by second.

A small frown from the tsarina.

Kim swallowed. Then she rose and took her place by Annakova, feeling like she was dragging the world behind her. All their planning. All gone, gone.

"Do not be afraid. First times, they make anxious. But no need." The *catalyst* turned to her and cupped Kim's face with her hands. Then she pressed her palms gently into Kim's cheeks. Her skin where the powder should have been.

The Russian woman's perfume enveloped her. It was flowery sweet, nauseating.

"You are patriot," Annakova whispered.

The tsarina's hand lay against her cheek. With her other hand she grasped one of Kim's. Skin to skin, they could not have been closer together unless they had stripped. Annakova's power was by now flowing into her, the woman's voice preternaturally loud: "You will have great honors in our mission. I am sure for you."

Time passed. Kim was trapped like a mouse in a cat's paws, terrified at first, but then gradually giving herself up to something not entirely unpleasant. Heat entered her body from Annakova's hands. She felt herself lifted in a wave of excitement, a golden surge of confidence. She rode it with an exultation, a joy that shook off all thought, all nuance. Beyond sexual, it was the taste of something more important, more primal.

Power.

She was becoming a grander being, larger than before. She heard the wind caressing the porch outside, the thunder of the logs collapsing in the fire, the tsarina's heartbeat and her own.

Annakova's whisper came to her. "Never forget me."

"Never," Kim said, ashamed, joyful.

Annakova sat back, still holding Kim's hand. "Your eyes . . . ," Annakova said. "They are extraordinary."

"My eyes?"

Annakova looked at her wonderingly. "Yes. Eyes. I see a thing there." She nodded slowly. "You have gone far, my dear girl, so very far."

It was true. Untethered, Kim felt herself floating away from her old self, her old world.

Tears formed in the tsarina's eyes. "I think you have become so pure. Nora Copeland. You have already gone there."

"Gone where?"

"To the end."

A 10? She stared in terror at the tsarina. "It will kill me," Kim whispered.

"No." Annakova looked at her, very pleased. "Maybe only 9.8. It will be well. We shall be proud of you."

The old servant came in again. Annakova looked up, frowning. The spell was broken. She took her hands away from Kim, saying something in Russian, calling the woman Polina.

The ceremony was over. She was a 9 or a 10, Annakova said, or guessed. What difference, numbers? Her Talent burned in her, raging to work itself on others.

"You may go, Miss Copeland," Annakova said, watching her carefully, smiling indulgently as though to a child savoring a sweet.

Kim staggered to her feet.

"I see you on Christmas," Annakova said. "We are all together then."

Kim nodded.

Forgetting to curtsey, she moved to the front door. The corporal was waiting to accompany her back to the barracks. She felt a sneer curling at her lip and managed to control it. Striking off across the plaza, her escort finally gave up and let her go.

He had probably seen the like before.

You didn't get in the way of the newly purified.

40

LATER THAT DAY. Erika stood a few paces away from Kim, who sat on the stump near the pond. The only light a small fixture on the equipment shed, its pool of illumination adding nothing to the blackness of the early alpine night.

After trying to ignore her, Kim slowly turned to fix her with a gaze. "Go away, Erika."

"I do not like you to be alone."

If she ignored the woman long enough, perhaps she would leave. Kim felt power flush her skin. She didn't fear Erika or anything that she might do. Perhaps she did not fear anything. Annakova's words: *You have already gone there. To the end.*

"I am supposed to watch you," Erika said.

Ah. A nice little *spill*, but Adler had already told her that. She had the feeling that as soon as they were alone in the dormitory, Erika would be helplessly shedding secrets. Was her new *spill* rating as high as Annakova had said? 9.8? Or 10?

"You could do me a favor. Please tell cook that I will need some meat for dinner. Her Majesty will want me to have a steak."

Erika's face, incredulous. But then she figured out what had happened. It took her a moment to figure out who was in charge. "I will talk to cook."

"Yes, do." It wasn't Erika's fault that Kim had botched her mission, but she felt exceedingly snappish.

She thought of flicking her hand at the woman to dismiss her. Copying Annakova. She almost giggled.

Oh God, this was not good.

Of course it was not good. Her penetration of the Aerie, a failed operation. Now that she had undergone a private purification, Annakova would not need to include her in the Christmas Day ceremony. She must think of an alternate plan. She would be in Annakova's presence at the Festival Hall Christmas party, but what was she to do there, stab her with a dinner knife?

She was not an assassin. Last summer she had killed a man who had a string of child murders to atone for. But he had begged her to do it. His suffering. She still didn't know why she had pulled the trigger. Things that for most people were morally clear, for one in the intelligence service, it was . . . more complicated.

Erika had trudged off.

Stars poked through in the gaps between clouds. She did so love that it was dark. This was the shortest, darkest day of the year. The solstice. The *Nachkommenschaft*—of which she was now indisputably one—should have a celebration tonight. Something properly pagan. She imagined torches in the woods. People wearing antlers. Sex on a slab of rock.

It was said that Himmler favored pagan myths, so by rights today should have been the uplift celebration for the *Nachkommenschaft*. But reportedly Hitler found occult things ridiculous. They would use Christmas Day instead.

She had been thinking all along that the *Nachkommen* underwent their transformations out of fanatic loyalty to the Nazi cause. Most of them were SS, so surely that was part of it. But now she knew they also loved *catalysis*. As a Progeny, you were not in the world so much as creating the world. Events waited for your action, your manipulation. If they went awry, you exerted stronger measures. If these failed, you went back to Annakova and became stronger. Eventually you burned out, but by that time you were so far gone you didn't know what you had lost. Your mind. Your humanity.

A wave of nausea rolled through her. She leaned over and threw up.

When the spasm passed, she took a fistful of snow and cleaned her face, swallowing the melt. Her face now wet, she thought the water might freeze on her. She rubbed at her skin with her mitts, making it worse.

Someone handed her a handkerchief.

Evgeny. He stood before her, very pale, a long cape wrapped close around him, looking startlingly like a vampire. Gratefully, she rubbed the handkerchief against her face. It was a lovely piece of cloth, edged in lace. "Thank you," she said at last, handing it back to him.

"You are welcome."

She stood up, gesturing for him to take the only dry seat, the stump. He nodded at her, looking gratified. He sat, putting his hands on his knees, looking at the frozen pond.

"You saw my future."

"*Da*. You almost die." He smiled up at her. "But today, a reprieve!"

He looked happy to say so, and she appreciated it. "News travels fast."

"Is true. Everyone hear how the young tsarevich shoots you." He gazed at the ice, which glowed blue-gray where the wind had polished the surface.

"I also see a thing," he began.

Oh. Another vision. He was the only one she was really afraid of at the Aerie.

"You and I. Our destiny. Is together. Like skaters, holding hands and going round and round. And if one falls, so does second one." He looked up at her, smiling a little, as though to say, *And so it goes . . .*

"Evgeny Feodorovich. When you see these things, does it often turn out as you thought?" He did not answer. "And if it doesn't turn out, how do you ever know which visions are true?"

Evgeny closed his eyes, breathing deeply. Peaceful. She did not want to intrude on that. Such moments were hard to find in this place.

With that, she suddenly remembered: her meeting with Adler. She had forgotten it. She turned away, heading for the barracks.

Evgeny's voice came to her. "All are true. All."

She turned back. "But the bullet, was it just a reprieve for today? I will still die by the hand of a uniformed man with a gun?" It was a bad idea to pursue this, but she was in a reckless mood.

"I do not know. Maybe another girl named Nora dies instead. She is told by another Evgeny that a soldier is shooting you. I think the things I see, they are always true."

"Thank you for telling me. I think it's best to know."

He looked at her, finally, his face plainly visible in the moon-light, contorted in pain. "It is nightmare to know."

They looked at each other for a few crystalline, cold moments. "Goodnight, Evgeny Feodorovich."

She traipsed back through the snow toward the path. As she went, she thought she heard him say, *Goodnight, Kim.*

That was wrong. She did not really hear her true name. Did she? But she could not think about it; she must hurry to meet Captain Adler, if he would even be waiting for her in the wash-ing shed. Striding up to the barracks, she found the room empty. Hilde and Erika were at dinner. She quickly pulled the sheets off her bed and made her way down the path. The door to the washhouse was unlocked.

To her relief, Adler was waiting for her in the back by the hanging laundry. No fans ran, so they whispered.

"I was wounded today by a stray bullet from the tsarevich's gun."

He was smoking a cigarette and exhaled through the side of his mouth. "I heard this. And that Irina Annakova asked to see you."

"We had a nice chat. So nice that she decided to augment me on the spot."

He stared. "Augment? You were prepared for this?"

"No. It was unexpected. I didn't have the materials."

"Well." He drew on the cigarette, watching her. "It was not a good plan."

Convenient for him, that it had all come undone. "Maybe I'll come up with a better plan."

A smirk. "I am, do you say, all ears?"

He really shouldn't goad her. She might do something rash.

Rash seemed so appealing. "Did you find the Aerie's back door?"

"There is no back door."

"You said you would find it!"

His cigarette was down to a stub. He took his last puff, holding it as it smoldered. "I have tried, but it is closely guarded. Go home, Nora."

She laughed. "And miss Christmas with the *Nachkommenschaft?*"

He narrowed his eyes. Had she pushed him too far? He had been willing to destroy operation Monarch, but at the same time he was SS. He was not a garden-variety soldier, but a member of Hitler's elite corp.

"What exactly did your British handlers tell you to do?"

They told me to quit, the same as you did. "I'm to disrupt the operation to the extent possible."

"And put us all at risk." He ground out the cigarette under his heel, then picked up the butt and put it in his pocket. "You are out of control."

"If I can think of something, you'll be the first to know."

His face had developed a sheen of sweat. No doubt he was terrified of any new plan that, in her fragile state of mind, she might come up with. Perhaps he was thinking of Hitler's penchant for hanging traitorous officers with a wire noose.

"I will have you assigned to maid duty for the next week. Before you execute a plan, you will inform me. You will bring folded laundry to the senior officers' quarters and make the beds. There will be more than one maid, and I cannot be certain of your cabin assignments. Go to mine by mistake. Tie a string around one of the bed legs if I'm not there. I'll find you." He gestured to the linen shelves in back. "You had better get back to the barracks."

She was tired of him. She turned to go, but he took her arm. "You look half mad. Calm yourself, or you'll make a mistake." His hand tightened on her arm. "You understand?"

"Yes." She yanked her arm away and left him.

Outside the washhouse, she trudged through the snow, making a diagonal down the slope toward the Festival Hall. She looked up toward the pond, but Evgeny had disappeared.

It felt like she had not eaten for days.

Pray God Erika had talked to the cook.

THAT EVENING. "Please be at ease," Irina said to the gun crew in rudimentary German. "I am not here, *ja?*"

The officer in charge clicked his heels and gave a stiff nod. There were two of them manning a mortar mounted to command the road and the near slopes of the forested valley. Pulling her fur cloak more tightly around herself, she moved to the far end of the emplacement, looking out.

It was very cold. The soldiers wore bulky, belted coats and heavy gloves, but she could not pity them their night duty on this mountaintop. They had never seen a Russian winter. Irina had learned from a young age that the colder you believed yourself to be, the more biting the cold. One did not submit to it. She loosened her fingers on the closure of her cloak.

A rich vein of stars cut across the heavens. Below, the valley in its forest lay in impenetrable darkness. It was a vista that cleared her head, much needed after reading the report she had requested from Dr. Kaltenbrunner. At her inspection of the intake center, she had seen Progeny who were alarmingly thin, their skin so pale it seemed blood did not course through them. And of these four or five, two trembled exceedingly, with a vacant look in their eyes as though they no longer knew where they were. Who they were.

The report explained that the doctor's staff had specifically brought together the worst cases to give them the most thorough examinations in the hopes of discovering why some of them suffered more rapid deterioration than others. This was why there were so many individuals in poor condition at the time of her tour.

Some of the SS had been under her wing for well over a year. That they suffered such debilitation alarmed her, despite Kaltenbrunner's assurance that it was not typical. She did understand there was a price to pay for purification. They were altered, became more than human, for a time; then the gradual fade back to a normal. Ah, but some! What if some did not have the constitution for it, and these suffered, perhaps terribly, even to the point of madness?

She caught one of the soldiers staring at her. He quickly turned away when he saw her take notice. One could imagine what the Germans thought of her, those who were not in the elite circles. That she was a lesser being because of not being German, a Russian minor noble anointed by the Führer, a pretender to majesty. The Germans and their intolerable pride. Perhaps, once she was tsarina, she would banish them from the motherland. She had not decided about that.

Looking out over the bunker toward the road, she listened for the sound of a car, hoping for Stefan's return. He would know what to do about the doctor's report. But could her Nazi allies be counted upon to be truthful against their own interests? Even Stefan? What if the truth was that some individuals had not the capacity to accept augmentation of their Talents? Might the mind and body of some—God forbid, *most*—grow ill from the repeated interference that her touch represented? She could not know the truth of it, since until she had been taken in by her German hosts, she had scarcely touched another person of Talent.

How gullible she had been to accept Himmler's plan so easily. He had painted the picture of a cadre of powerful Talents who would precede the German forces in their sweep through Europe. The key role she would play. The reward she would have.

Of course, in her desperate state—those first weeks after she had been given succor by the Nazis—she could only think of her unalterable goal: the monarchy restored. Stalin toppled from his stolen throne. Herself, and then Nikolai supplanting him. It was to be a more generous reign than the old tsar's, with the people grateful to her, striving for the betterment of Mother Russia. She was not such a fool that she did not realize that Hitler meant to control her. At her birthday dinner Himmler had said that arms were not enough, that the people must be broken. She had not forgotten that. But Russia was vast. Once the German army left St. Petersburg, how could his long arm possibly control her?

She pulled her cloak tighter. It was late at night after a bad day. Kolya had slipped on the ice with a loaded gun and had almost shot himself. Irina had been stern with him, but inside, she felt nothing but relief that he had come away unscathed.

Without Kolya, she could not go on. She did not know how mothers survived the early death of sons, but she feared her own heart would never bear it.

Well. These thoughts must be banished for now. Kolya was well.

She looked out over the wall of the emplacement, hoping to see headlights coming up the hill. Soon she and Stefan would sit over mulled wine and she would lay bare her doubts. He must answer her honestly and without condescension. She would listen most carefully. She wondered if he had captured the woman who had maimed him. The Red Girl. She would have no trial, but would meet the fate she had earned. One did not grievously injure such a one as Erich Stefan von Ritter without ultimate punishment.

As she gazed out, the world remained in unrelieved blackness. No headlights. The soldiers stole looks at her now and then. They dared. She had an urge to make them pay for such presumption, but though they guarded her, she knew from the tsar's fate that allegiances could change. Guards lining up his family and shooting them in the little room. Their bodies, thrown in a well.

She nodded to the soldiers as she made her way back to the chalet.

41

THE AERIE

MONDAY, DECEMBER 21. Kim lay awake through the night until a gray dawn began to crank up the day. It wasn't good to be without sleep. Adler was right that in her present condition she was at risk of making mistakes.

But she was anxious to get on with the day now that she had a plan.

She slipped into her boots, grabbed a sweater from the foot of her bed, and went down to the lavatory. When she flipped the switch, a blast of light, like a nail in her eye. In the stall, she heard water dripping into the basin. They had left the water on a little so that the pipes would not freeze. Plunk, plunk. Was she to be tortured by sounds as well as light? But it didn't matter. She knew her way clear to disabling Annakova, and that left her light-headed with excitement.

She must get up to the cabins first thing, before Captain Adler went on duty.

It was Monday. Her shower privileges were Wednesdays and Saturdays. But she was sweating profusely and could no longer stand the odor, and now that she had the favor of the tsarina, she decided to have a Monday shower.

The water hit her like a sand blast, but its warmth renewed her. The huge cake of soap released a few suds and she rubbed herself nearly raw. On her shoulder, an enormous bruise around the wound, but it only hurt like a memory of pain, not the real thing.

Erika came in, standing at the doorway, a sweater over her floral pajamas. "So early awake. Are you well?"

Kim dried off with a stiff, grayish white towel. "I have maid duty today."

"I didn't know."

"I'll be back in time for breakfast." *You can pretend to control me then, Ja?*

In the bitter morning cold, Kim carried the folded linens up from the wash shed in a large canvas sack. She passed by the cabins she was assigned to, 1 though 10, and made her way to number 23, Captain Adler's.

He answered the door, ushering her quickly inside. He was dressed for the day except for his jacket. There were two windows in his one-room cabin, and he pulled the curtains shut on them before turning to her.

"Well?"

She placed the sack on his bunk. "You said they are going to execute Evgeny."

"It is past time to put him out of his misery."

"How will they do it?"

"They will say he goes to a nursing home, but he will not get so far." He glanced at the door, as though expecting discovery at any minute. "Why are you here?"

"I think we should tell Evgeny that he will be put down."

Adler stared at her.

"We have to tell him that he's been betrayed by his Nazi hosts. That he should tell Annakova about the fate of St. Petersburg, the vision that he blurted to me the first morning I was here. I think we can get Annakova to abandon Monarch. And leave here with me."

His next words, uttered slowly, as though he thought she might have trouble understanding English. "This will never happen."

"I think it will."

"You and Her Majesty just walk out of the Aerie?"

"No, we leave through the back door. I have a plane picking me up on Christmas Day."

"A plane." He shook his head. "Landing where?"

"A frozen lake in the woods."

"Perfect. An airplane engine draws immediate attention. Soldiers watch it come in for a landing and are waiting for it when it crashes."

He had lost faith. She'd have to bring him around to a better attitude. "Suppose the airplane skims over a shoulder of the deep valley and is only audible for a few minutes. In addition, the plane as it lands throttles back to dampen the sound. The soldiers are nearly a kilometer away and can't get there so fast. We're gone when they arrive."

Duncan, of course, would argue against sending a plane; she had walked out, pursued her own agenda, and he probably thought she deserved what she got. But London's calculation would weigh the risks of a plane against the acquisition of a *catalyst*. The plane would come. With Hannah on Britain's side, they could have a *catalyst* working for them instead of Hitler, adding to their arsenal a potential battlefield deployment of *darkening*, *transport, sounding* . . . So even if London had given up on her, the prospect of acquiring this weapon should be persuasive. And when they stepped off the plane in England, Kim would have brought them not just one *catalyst*, but deprived Germany of theirs, Annakova.

Adler snapped, "Where exactly is this lake?"

"In the valley about a half kilometer or a little more west of here. Hannah believes the exit from the escape tunnel is not far from the lake."

"I have told you. I do not know how to access the escape tunnel."

"Then who does?"

"There are three, but I can hardly ask them. The Aerie commandant, Irina Annakova, and a colonel who is her handler."

"All right, then. Irina Annakova will lead us to the secret way."

He shook his head, suppressing what might have been a snarl. "This will get us all killed. Evgeny will go wild. Then he will reveal I told him of the execution, or you did. It will be all over."

"I've seen him calm. He isn't always unstable. He would do anything to save St. Petersburg."

"Then perhaps he has already told Annakova!"

"Maybe he has. Maybe she didn't believe it. But now the Nazis have betrayed them, because they're going to execute Evgeny. She'll see she can't trust them. Plus, does Annakova realize what happens to the SS *Nachkommenschaft*, how they end up completely mad, strapped to their beds at Treptow?"

"How do you know about that?"

Met a guy in a straitjacket, came the thought. "Never mind. I just do. *Does* she know?"

"We have strict orders never to mention Treptow. She thinks that since the enhancements diminish over time, needing renewal, that the symptoms go away if a Talent is retired after a few years' service."

How excellent. Kim tucked that gem of intel away.

In the distance, sounds of gunfire seemed to presage Evgeny's death. The shooting range. Adler went to the window, parting the curtain to look outside. When he turned back to her, he had summoned a more patient tone. "You are losing control. I have seen it before, many times, with the *Nachkommenschaft,* of which you are now one. This plan, it is wild and will not work. Evgeny will not believe you."

"That's why you need to get the papers that prove it. You have records for everything. I'm sure it's in writing."

"Yes, papers that are in locked files! Papers that are in German—"

She struggled to contain her impatience. Didn't he see that this was their only chance to stop Annakova? "Evgeny knows German."

He took a deep breath. Paced away, turned back. "Why would Annakova give up her alliance with Hitler? He will deliver Russia to her."

"At the price of the ruin of St. Petersburg. Incendiary bombs. Starvation. Frozen bodies stacked like cord wood. Parents eating their children. Hell on a platter." She rushed on, trying to put her plan in the best light. "Annakova loves her country. Russia is her life, her purpose. It and Kolya are all she cares about. Not the throne, not the title. Didn't you people realize that? Did you think she was like you, living for power?"

A bad idea, to insult the man who could help her or kill her. *Stay calm. Must stay calm.*

"Annakova will think you mean to get her alone to kill her."

It was possible. So many ways for this plan to fail, and yet wasn't that true for any dangerous mission? A good plan now was better than a perfect one later. The *Nachkommenschaft* would be reinforced on Christmas Day and sent out the next. Christmas was four days away.

From a chair, Adler grabbed his jacket, buttoning it. "Your plan will end with both of us dead."

For a man who had helped the Oberman Group from the start, he was very eager not to get the job done. He was SS. Where was his courage? She kept her voice firm, confident. "Just get me a copy of the orders and I'll do everything. When you've delivered the orders, find a reason to leave. Say you have to go to Berlin. Then it all falls on me."

His face rigid, he looked at her as though considering whether *she* was the one needing to be put down.

"Think about it, Captain. This is what you've been trying to do since you first allied with the Oberman Group. The group is disbanded. But we can still do this."

Slowly, he shook his head. "I have to go."

She put a hand on his arm. It annoyed him, but he didn't shake her off. "I know you were close to Franz. You took a big risk for that friendship. Now he is dead, killed by the Nazis. Don't you want to finish this?"

"Why do you ask?" He pulled away from her and picked up his hat. "It doesn't matter."

She moved in front of him, blocking his way to the door. "It matters, Captain. It matters. The reasons we do what we do."

Adler returned her gaze. "I have reasons."

"What you've seen here," she guessed. "It must repulse you."

He spoke low. "My wife was Jewish. She died at a concentration camp. Dachau."

"I've heard of it. I'm sorry."

"They had forced us to divorce. We avoided it first, and then she insisted. Our hope was that it would satisfy them, but foolishly we kept seeing each other and in the end . . . they came for her. I could do nothing. So I told myself. But if, earlier, we had escaped together. . . ." He stared at her, shaking his head. "I did not mean to tell you such a thing. Of course, nothing private is safe from you now."

But his own SS had devised the plan for all these malformed Talents. "Your witch," she said slowly, "has transformed me, it's true." She felt a mean smile pull at her face. "Nothing personal, Captain."

He ran his hands through his hair, staring at the wall. Perhaps he saw something there: a memory, a reproach.

After a time, he murmured, "I will bring you the paper."

She remembered to breathe. At last, Adler was helping.

Looking at his hands gripping his SS hat, he said, "We must try to do something, or why else should we live?"

He had just said it all. The truth was often very simple.

"So," he went on, "you will try to leave on Christmas? Just before dawn?"

"Yes."

"And if the plane cannot get through?"

"Hannah and I have created a backup plan. You don't need to know what it is." He would understand that the less he knew about the details, the better in case he came under questioning.

"And you'll get out too?" she asked.

"I will have a packet of orders to deliver. An escape plan that I have long planned."

She was relieved. There was no room for him on the plane.

He went on. "So that I know your plan is going forward, Annakova must replenish the bird feeder in the chalet yard at noon on the twenty-fourth. When I am sure your plan is going forward, I will take a car."

"You'll leave on the twenty-fourth?"

"No, at dawn on Christmas, the same as you. To exploit the state of confusion that will happen when Annakova is discovered missing."

He put his hat on and took his gloves from the table. "If I am successful in taking the document, it will be behind the water tank in the women's toilet, the stall in the middle. A snap inspection."

"Thank you, Captain. Good luck." She noted the gun and holster on his belt. At least he had a quick way out if it all came apart. "Good luck to us both."

She left the cabin, her maid's sack over her shoulder.

A light snow had fallen during the night, silvering the trees and softening the outlines of the path. As she made her way back to her assigned cabins, a shape emerged from a stand of trees. Hilde.

"You are lost?" she asked. "Your rounds are with cabins one through ten, not up here."

Hilde had been watching her. How long had she been up here, noting the time spent in cabin 23?

"I got mixed up. I guess I saved another maid the trouble of that cabin."

Hilde joined her in the slog down to the lower cabins. "You were in there a long time. I would not like to think you were

going through the captain's things. I could make things difficult
for you."

Kim's thoughts sped through her options. It was as though
her mind fed off the stark snow and cold, transmuting her dismay into calculation. Hilde was looking for any advantage.

"I don't think you want to do that, Hilde." They stopped
outside cabin 12, and Kim rested her sack of linens in the snow
at her feet. "I don't want to make trouble for you, but Her
Majesty is well disposed toward me after the shooting accident. I'm sure she wouldn't want to hear a story that Captain
Adler has been taking comfort from one of her Progeny. She
would be disappointed in him. She really wouldn't thank you
for bringing it up."

Hilde's face crumpled into uncertainty. Then, slyly, "I don't
think Captain Adler was in his cabin."

Kim glanced up the path where Adler was just coming down
toward them. It was an acute pleasure to see Hilde follow her
gaze.

"You know, Hilde, I'd keep my mouth shut if I were you. If
you do, I won't complain about you. All right?" She conjured up
a friendly expression to mend things.

Hilde bit her lip. "I was just jealous. Erika thinks I have no
merit, that I am unworthy of purification. She has convinced
others. But if they do not give me an assignment, I think no one
goes home from here."

"I could speak in your favor. Would that help?"

Hilde nodded gratefully.

Kim picked up the linens and trudged over to cabin 10. The
spill from Hilde about Erika undermining her. Learning secrets
now was like grabbing a puppy from a box. Why had she ever
thought her Talent so difficult, so ambiguous? It seemed there

was nothing she couldn't accomplish, no obstacle that she could not manipulate in her favor.

Yet underneath the euphoria lay a coiling dread. She was edging toward madness. No, madness was too strong a word.

But what did you call it when you couldn't trust your own thoughts?

THAT AFTERNOON. In her sitting room, before a warm fire, Irina watched Stefan as he read the report. He was thorough and methodical, she was pleased to see.

At last he placed the report in his lap and gazed at her. "I can see why you are concerned."

"Can you, Stefan?" Her belly clenched, hearing this. She had expected him to . . . perhaps try to soothe her, even cover things up.

"Dr. Kaltenbrunner has not provided a satisfactory report," he said. "We need more details. Names and conditions specified, along with purification dates. I am disappointed in this." He tossed the report on the side table next to his chair.

"I saw them, so pitiful," she said. "Unnaturally thin, and some, so agitated! They could not tell me their pain. It was the language problem. We needed French, and not all had it, and then Dr. Kaltenbrunner was there, trying to hurry me along. And Kolya saw them too, and he asked me what was wrong with them. What can I tell him?"

"Well, he does not need to know these things. But we—we must investigate, and I shall, Your Majesty. I will go down to the intake center. Today."

She had not considered that this might involve Stefan confronting Kaltenbrunner. The doctor had Himmler's support, and Stefan, she had the feeling, did not. "Do not put yourself in jeopardy, Stefan. A talk with the man, but not an accusation. Himmler . . ."

"Pardon me, but *Reichsführer* Himmler would also want to know if there are difficulties. Do not concern yourself with that." He looked at her, his eyes soft, understanding her distress. "Please, Irinuska."

She wanted him to put his arm around her, wanted to rest her head on his shoulder. But they sat formally, opposite each other, in this public place, yes public, with officers coming and going and old Polina always hovering.

"You know," he went on, "we cannot have unstable individuals undertaking their assignments. If we do not have confidence in our *Nachkommen*, we cannot go forward. So you and I, you and the Führer, have the same goals in this regard. I believe that some individuals are not suited to taking your ministrations so far. But they are very few." His face sobered, and she saw the steel in him, the SS officer. "If this is not the case, I will discover it. This I promise you."

"Stefan." She paused, not wanting to say the next thing on her mind. She looked at her adjutant and friend. "You remember that Himmler said that the people must be broken. He is Hitler's servant, not mine."

"Himmler is a powerful man. However, not everyone agrees with his methods."

"But perhaps Hitler? Perhaps these are Hitler's ideas in any case?"

"The Führer longs for an ally in Russia. You are that ally, Your Majesty. Yes, lives will be lost. But we will not break the Russian people, because even were it attempted, it is impossible. Your people are too strong."

His words were a great comfort. She had dressed formally,

knowing that she would see him; she wore long silk gloves. Therefore she was able to invite him to sit next to her on the divan and did so with a small gesture.

He came to sit at her side and took her offered hand. "I would never have lasted here without you," she said.

"You would have. You are the tsarina. To you, much strength is given. Your rare ability, your rare blood."

Polina entered the salon from the hall, curtseying.

"Leave us," Irina said, thinking how the woman had an uncanny knack for coming in at the wrong times.

"I beg your indulgence," Stefan said. "I asked her to come in after a few minutes." He looked at Irina for permission, receiving her nod.

Stefan waved Polina in. She carried a package. Stefan glanced at the side table, and with that, Polina put the package down and left, smiling conspiratorially. Irina did not like to see it, as though the old woman had a secret in common with Stefan.

"I hope you will accept a small gift from me, Your Majesty. In honor of Christmas."

"Oh, Stefan, do not be so formal. We are alone, after all."

He smiled, heartbreakingly handsome. "Very well. We shall not be formal." He picked up the package, wrapped in fine white paper. "Irinuska, this is my small Christmas gift for you. I hope that you take some pleasure in it." He handed it to her.

She undid the ribbon that kept the heavy paper together. As the wrapping fell away, she found a small book. In Russian, the title read *Collected Short Stories of Anton Chekhov*.

"All your books are in French," he said, watching as she leafed through it. "The bookseller told me this is a first-edition printing."

It was a handsome gift, and she thanked him very sincerely.

Still, since he had decided to give her a gift, she wished it had been a more personal one. But why should he when . . .

"Also," he said, interrupting her thoughts, "as a token of my care for you, Irinuska." He drew out a folded paper from his pocket and handed it to her.

She drew off her gloves so that she could open the small packet. Removing a plain string that bound it together, she found a pendant, a perfect, yellow diamond on an elegant chain.

She gazed at the most beautiful diamond she had ever seen. One made wondrous by its giver. "It is beautiful, Stefan." Her hands shook as she passed it back to him.

Turning on the divan, she invited him to arrange it around her neck. As he worked the clasp, his hands touched her neck, fleetingly, startlingly.

She turned back to him, admiring his lean body, the planes of his face. She must always remember that he was a German officer. And yet, how difficult it was. And even those who were the famed SS, were they not men, men with hearts?

Stefan looked pleased that she wore his diamond, his expression proprietary as he regarded her. At that moment she would have done anything for him. Of course they could never be lovers. But they could be in love.

PART IV

FLOWERS IN THE WINDOW

42

THE AERIE

THAT EVENING. In the Festival Hall, Kim left her early-evening instruction session with Lieutenant Voegler. Outside the meeting room she took another look at the passport she had just been issued. The new identity, Janet Lowe. Her face, that of a stranger: thin, eyes black and lost. It was her imagination that her face looked too long. That could not be happening yet.

Through the windows in the crowded hall she saw that it was dark already. She didn't know what time it was, disconcerting since she had always worn a watch. Stark, tall figures strode purposively through the hallway carrying files and travel documents, bearing their inhuman purpose. An office door slammed, causing her to jump. Nerves flaring, she tried to soothe her teeming thoughts.

In a little over three days, the plane. She and Adler must recruit Evgeny to their plan, and after him, Irina Annakova. The

tsarina felt deeply for her Progeny, but deeper yet for her homeland. She would defect, Kim felt sure of it.

Yet in the back of her mind, an anchor dragged at her
thoughts. Would the tsarina have her arrested? Kim swept such
pessimism aside. It wouldn't unfold that way.

She walked through the busy corridor on the back side of
the Festival Hall, past offices with typists, officers on telephones,
couriers, stenographers. All still working, as they would into
the night.

Some of the office doors were open, and she heard a voice
speaking German, a voice she thought she knew. As she passed,
she looked in, noting a man seated with his back to the door,
talking to someone seated behind a desk. The man with his back
to her . . . he reminded her, even just seeing that much of him, of
Erich von Ritter.

Just a glimpse and she was past the office. What was wrong
with her? Hannah hadn't warned her how her imagination would
intrude so much; but after all, Hannah didn't know.

It was all she could do to keep her thoughts focused, to
remain practical. It was only the day before yesterday that she
had advanced up the rating system for the *spill*. All the way to a
high 9 or even a 10. Intoxicating one moment, alarming the next.

She couldn't tell if she was hungry despite the fact that she
had not eaten since yesterday. Her stomach felt warm as though
it were still trying to digest the normal and now unsuitable
food she had eaten before she and Annakova had sat together
on the divan. When the saboteur without her tincture became
the target.

She passed through the officer's mess with the strangely
lean men whispering to their fellow officers or perhaps just
muttering to themselves. Glances followed her. She stared back

at them. *I am one of you. I am not afraid.* As she moved on, a few of the creatures still watched her, she knew that they did, thought they did, imagined they did.

There was no one in the civilian dining room. No food on the pass-through. She found that she *was* hungry. All she wished for now was very rare red meat. An unnerving urge.

She went into the dining room and sat alone at a table. At length someone spotted her through the window in the kitchen door. One of the usual servers, an older woman. She came out. "The last seating was at six thirty," she said in German.

"I'm hungry now." Kim tried out a blank *Nachkommenschaft* stare, so effective unless you had to be rangy, tall, and insane.

The woman left, not promising anything.

Kim's thoughts went to Annakova. The woman knew the back way out . . . if there was one. The tsarina would never accept the extermination of St. Petersburg. She would be shocked to learn the ultimate fate of her Progeny. This was something Kim would attest to, and Annakova would listen because of the SS secret plan to put Evgeny down like a horse with a broken leg. With all these Nazi lies exposed, Evgeny and Annakova would turn against their German allies. They would all defect together. Their new lives, in England, new identities. The White Russians who had fled to England would treat them as royalty. The woman would not serve the Nazi beasts ever again.

The server came out with utensils and a cut of meat, warmed to a tantalizing fragrance.

Kim waited a beat as the server left, so as not to dive into her food. Then she cut off a large piece and stuffed the bleeding morsel into her mouth. It took her a long time to chew, but it was so delicious it made her ears ring.

Afterward she made her way up to the barracks under the

wan light of the plaza lamps. The air smelled of snow and pine sap. A distant report of a gun. She flinched, feeling it, remembering. The shooting range up the hill was lighted, extending the hours for practice.

Continuing past the pond, she imagined the lake in the woods. Imagined the drone of the plane London must send.

Then the anchor to her hopes dug in, hard. How difficult would it be to land?

She walked past the pond, the white surface like a sheet pulled flat. Four inches of snow. That did not present so much difficulty for a plane, if the lake in the valley was the same.

But fear descended on her all at once. She stopped on the shoveled path, pulling in frigid lungfuls of air.

Good Christ, it would be a disaster. Perhaps her letter did not reach her father. That would leave the decision about an airplane up to Duncan, or if he did ask for direction from London, he would certainly put things in the worst light. *Gone off the deep end, poor thing. Jews. Heroics. Feminine emotion.*

And then, how many could the plane hold? It would have to be a small plane to minimize its presence. Annakova would bring Nikolai and Evgeny. There was Hannah, as well. Five in all, plus the pilot. Well, one was a child.

She imagined the SS charging across the frozen lake. This vision turned into the *Nachkommen* walking slowly, intently, toward a stalled airplane. Too heavy to fly. Someone must stay behind. Who?

If that happened, they would flee down the service road. That assumed that the SS would be delayed in their pursuit at least twenty minutes, and perhaps longer, depending on when Annakova was found missing.

Tears formed along her lashes, cold as acid. Stark terror

brought them on, and the fear was oddly comforting. Here was her real self, the one who knew the danger for what it was: clear, imminent, lethal.

It was so good to have her normal thoughts back, even for a few moments. She savored this as she made her way up to the barracks.

TUESDAY, DECEMBER 22. Kim had awakened that morning hoping that Captain Adler had not been able to steal the execution order for Evgeny Feodorovich. That she would not have to go through with it. But an hour later, with Adler's surprise inspection, she knew it wasn't so. The papers would be behind the water tank.

The three women shared relieved glances that they had passed inspection without a reprimand. On each woman's bunk, a package of clothes they would need for their *Nachkommenschaft* roles.

Kim leaned against the wall as she sat on her bunk, trying to gather her courage for what was to come.

In a moment of absurdity, Hilde suggested that they have a fashion show, trying on the clothes they had been issued. She gave Erika an ingratiating smile. "Because what if they do not fit?" Erika rolled her eyes.

Hilde tore into her package, shaking out a skirt and sweater and a coat. "The shoes!" she cried, holding up a pair of high heels.

Erika opened her own package. A suit with an A-line skirt, nicer than Hilde's outfit.

"I'm going to the toilet," Kim said.

"But the fashion show," Hilde moaned.

"The toilet," Kim said, "not Austria." She used sarcasm so that Hilde would know she wasn't afraid of her. And she had no intention of trying on the dress and prancing about, or whatever Hilde had in mind.

In the lavatory she entered the middle stall, one of two that had a door. She felt behind the wall-hung water tank. Tape held something in the gap between the wall and the tank. As she began to peel the tape off, the outside door opened. Someone entered the stall next to hers. She looked under the partial wall, seeing a pair of high heels. Hilde.

"I had to go too," Hilde said, peeing.

Kim sat on the toilet, her face cold and sweating, hands in her lap like claws.

Hilde flushed the toilet. Kim heard her washing her hands, but then, no sound of the door closing. She was waiting for Kim to finish.

When Kim didn't come out, Hilde said, "You talked to them about me, then? You recommended me to the tsarina?"

"Yes. Now leave me in peace so I can finish."

"Because if you did not, I can still make trouble. I really can."

"Her Majesty and I have a special bond. One word from me, Hilde, and you're history."

"History?"

"Ruined."

"Oh. I only meant . . ." A long pause. "I should not have said that."

A little *spill*, showing Hilde's spite and delusions of importance. "No, you shouldn't have, and I'm annoyed."

"I am sorry, Nora. I really would like to see you in your new dress."

"What makes you think I got a dress?"

"We opened your package."

Kim bit her lip, trying to suppress a snide remark. "Is it nice?"

"I suppose it is, if you like green."

At last the sound of the door closing. Kim crouched down to look under the stall door. The room, empty. Springing up, she yanked at the tape behind the water tank, retrieving an envelope. She fumbled at the clasp and drew out the single sheet of paper. The name on the form: Evgeny Feodorovich Borisov. Some of the boxes checked. She couldn't translate the words, but Evgeny's German was better than hers.

She stuffed the envelope down her trousers, secured by her waistband.

When she entered the room, Erika was holding up a green print dress. "Someone has spent money on you," she said disapprovingly.

"The Third Reich?" Kim snapped.

Erika sneered. Her own outfit lay discarded on her bunk.

Hilde looked blamefully at Kim, presumably because of the green dress. Good God, at a time like this, they were going to have a catfight over clothes. But the mood for the fashion show had evaporated.

"Breakfast," Erika announced. She hauled on her jacket.

Pleading a bad stomach, Kim stayed behind. Once alone, she scanned the document again. One of the boxes: *Hinrichtung*. A typed *X*. She thought this might be the word for execution. A small number in pencil on the envelope: 4. Evgeny's cabin number?

She sat for a long time staring at the walls. The room, quiet; her thoughts, dark.

At last she put on her coat and boots and went down the hill to breakfast. As she neared the Festival Hall, she saw Captain Adler crossing the plaza on a path to intercept her. Perhaps he had been waiting for her. They stopped for a moment. No one else was nearby.

"I got the papers," she told him. "Hilde is going to make trouble for me." He could detain her. They only needed two more days where nothing went wrong.

"Go to cabin 4 now," Adler said. "He is there. I will keep Hilde busy." And strode past her.

Kim proceeded into the plaza, past the booth housing the lift, and up the other path to the private cabins.

A *Nachkomme* in SS black was coming down the walkway. As he drew closer he noticed her, watched her. She kept her eyes averted.

He stopped in front of her, saying something in German that, in her panic at being stopped, she could not quite catch.

"Please excuse me, Lieutenant, I do not speak German very well."

"What is business you have here?" he said very slowly in German. He bore a profound scar down his right cheek.

A rivulet of sweat ran down her side. "I had to make beds. I left my sack." She made a gesture as though carrying a heavy bag.

Gazing at her, expressionless, his nostrils flared. "You . . . are . . . ," he began in English. "Nervous. For a maid." He smiled, a terrible thing to see on the long, gaunt face. "Is this word? Nervous?"

She didn't know what to say, afraid she would confirm that she was nervous, afraid he would not understand her. Then, as the seconds ticked away, she managed to say: "I am not nervous, Lieutenant, sir."

He stared at her with distaste. Then he continued on his way, leaving her behind, feeling an acute relief. *Get ahold of yourself. This is only the beginning.*

At cabin 4, she saw that smoke trailed out of the chimney.

When she knocked, the door opened immediately. Evgeny. "I have been waiting for you," he said.

43

THE AERIE

A FEW MINUTES LATER. They sat in front of the fire drinking strong tea. Evgeny seemed anxious for company, asking if she would like bread and butter, more tea, and if she heard the owls.

Kim listened. Scrabbling sounds on the roof. Perhaps birds or squirrels. "Do *you* hear owls, Evgeny Feodorovich?"

Now and then his glance flicked to the envelope in her lap. "Owl tells me. I die soon."

Perhaps, as war loomed, he told everyone the same vision, and she wondered for how many it would be true.

Talking with the old man was difficult. She had not planned what to say, knowing she would have to follow what logic threads might appear.

"Evgeny," she began. "In your visions, you don't see Nikolai ruling Russia, do you."

He leaned forward in his chair, elbows on his knees, head in his hands. "My Irina. My Nikolai," he moaned.

"You told me a terrible thing happens to St. Petersburg. And also who brings this terror to the city."

Shaking his head, he whispered, "I cannot tell her what comes. Break her heart, she who is broken all life long."

And what *would* happen? Hitler takes over Russia? Another White Russian supplants the Bolsheviks? St. Petersburg in the frozen winter, stacking the bodies? But all that mattered was what Evgeny believed would occur.

"You must tell her." She leaned forward. "Evgeny, listen. She's too strong to break. And she has to leave this place, before she helps Hitler destroy your country."

He sat up, leaning back in his chair, gaining a semblance of dignity. "You and friend," he said. "Woman who is truly broken." He nodded. "*Da*. She bring you here for killing."

Referring to Hannah. What Evgeny knew and did not know was a chaotic tangle.

"But I won't kill the tsarina. I want to save her. And you. Evgeny, leave this place. Don't help Hitler. That's why I've come."

Then, with dignity, as though he already knew what it said, he held out his hand for the envelope. She slipped the paper out of its sleeve and handed it to him.

He glanced at it. It did not seem to trouble him. "I know these things. I see clearly."

"Her Majesty thinks they will send you to a rest home. But you wouldn't get that far. A soldier. A gunshot. It's not her wish."

A scrabbling sound on the roof. He pointed upward, smiling. "They try speaking. I listen. No one listen, but Evgeny Borisov."

"I listened to you about St. Petersburg. Now it is the tsarina's turn to listen. And when she understands, I'll take you both out of here."

"*Nyet.* Does not happen." He still held the German orders, his fingers trembling.

Don't tell me we fail. Don't tell me. It might not be so. "We must leave," she said, trying not to sound desperate, trying not to trigger any extreme reactions. "Will you tell her? Tell her the *Wehrmacht* will ravage the city where you were born?"

He looked past her shoulder, a blank expression. She was losing him. She plodded on. "You know the tsarina. What would break her are her own actions, her purifications on Christmas Day that would help to destroy her people."

He watched her for so long she thought they were done; he could not track what was expected of him. But at last he whispered, "*Da,* Nora Copeland, I tell her."

Yes, Evgeny, yes.

Something changed in his expression. "Maybe we go ourselves, down secret way, leave you here." His truculent expression cooled Kim's heart.

"I will help you find a home in England," she said soothingly. "We should go together. And when we do, it means that the tsarina will no longer help the Nazis. Her hands will be clean of this death you see in St. Petersburg."

He stood, smoothing his waistcoat, straightening his shoulders. He walked to the fireplace, bending down to throw the document in.

Kim leaped from her seat, rushing over to him. "No, Evgeny!" She snatched the paper from his hands. "You can't burn this!"

Evgeny stared at her, wild-eyed.

"Show it to Her Majesty. Show her. So she will see how the

Nazis are lying about everything, even about her good friend Evgeny Borisov."

He cocked his head, as though listening to something. "I hear big, long guns," he murmured. "Pound day and night. I see grandchildren asleep in snow. Too cold to bleed."

They stood for a long time as the fire burned, popping and hissing.

Kim folded the document and handed it back to him. Evgeny put it in an inside pocket of his jacket. "I go to her."

"When?"

"Tonight."

"Ask her to send for me. I'll tell her of England. I'll help you escape."

A look crossed his face, registering a new thought. "You do not believe Evgeny's visions."

"But I do. I have the gift of the *spill*. I can hear the truth. I don't see the future, but I see what's in the heart."

"Ah," he said. "The heart. Heart missing here." He looked around him, perhaps seeing the Aerie with its dark purpose. "Heart is Russian people."

Heart is what you have left when everything else is taken.

He put a hand on her arm, gripping it. Tears came to his eyes. "You not die by bullet."

"I know. Not this time. Nikolai missed. But everything you see, it is true somewhere."

"*Da.* Is truth."

Clasping her hand over his, she squeezed it and then pulled gently away.

They were talking about things beyond reason, beyond what they could ever know. Things that seemed true, seemed to be so, but just out of reach in a world tinged with power, faith, and magic.

"I'll wait in my room. Send for me, Evgeny Borisov."

She slipped out the door. The first lungful of frigid air hurt, but she pulled it deep to steady herself.

THAT EVENING. Polina left the polishing of the silver and went into the hall at the foot of the stairs. In the upstairs bedroom, the tsarina's voice, shrill, distressed. Evgeny Feodorovich was with her, his voice droning.

And so Evgeny Feodorovich comes again to disturb our peace, the poor, filthy thing who slurps his food and tried to kill himself over his mad visions.

He had come after dark looking sunken and exhausted. He would see Her Majesty. Alone. But he had been in her room for an hour, and now the tsarina was crying. Polina went up the stairs to see if she was needed.

Outside the tsarina's door, she stood, hesitating to knock. Then, deciding not to disturb, she leaned in to hear.

Irina sobbing, muffled but deep-throated. At last she quieted. "England? Do you say so, Evgeny?" His answer, indistinguishable. Then again, "What about my son."

His voice, a steady murmur. Hers, indistinct. They had moved, turned away. Polina could make out nothing.

The old man was unstable, and now he had upset the tsarina, as he always did, the old fool. Her Majesty indulged him intolerably, letting him summon her day or night, coming to her rooms to alarm and stir ancient memories. How he would go on and on about the days in hiding with the tsarina, as though they were the only ones who had suffered, who had starved, endured prison, lost everything. Polina shook her head and crept down the stairs. She thought of Tatiana Nazarova, her former mistress, Her Majesty's aunt, who had been driven from her grand home into the streets while the rabble took over, stripping furniture, shattering the porcelains, throwing the silks and velvets out the windows.

She shuddered. What good to remember the bad days? Now Her Majesty and Nikolai were safe, protected by the might of the Nazi government. And Evgeny Feodorovich, disrupting, complaining, predicting, as was his wont.

At last Evgeny came down the stairs and left, closing the door behind him.

Her mistress would need tea and soothing. A nice hot bath and her bathing salts. Polina finished the silver and placed the flatware in their felt sleeves.

When the tsarina did not summon her, she went up to knock on her door. Opening it, she found her sitting in a chair, staring at the remains of the coal fire in the grate.

"Go away," the tsarina murmured. When Polina hesitated, her mistress snapped a look at her, and she softly pulled the door shut.

Descending the stairs, she shook her head. What good did visions do, except to ruin one's sleep? At the bottom, she put her hand on the newel post, looking back up. The thought had been nagging at her: What could they possibly have been speaking of, when her mistress had said *England?*

WEDNESDAY, DECEMBER 23. 8:15 AM. Kim's book lay open in her lap. *Conversational German.* It was the only book she had, but she couldn't concentrate on it. It had been twenty-four hours since she'd talked to Evgeny.

Sounds of the outside door closing, and then Hilde and Erika came into the room, Hilde leaning against her roommate.

Erika helped Hilde to her bunk, where she lay down.

"What happened?" Kim asked.

"She is sick," Erika said without empathy. Hilde turned her back to them, curling up, facing the wall. "If it is influenza," Erika went on, "they should put her in another room."

Sick. Kim rose from her bunk and went over to Hilde. "Can I get you something? Water? Juice?"

Hilde moaned, turning over to look up at Kim. Her face, milk white, her eyes, unfocused.

She doubted it was the flu. Hilde might well have been poisoned—Adler making sure the woman could do no harm to their plan.

"If there's anything at all I can do," Kim said to her, putting her hand on Hilde's shoulder.

44

WEDNESDAY, DECEMBER 23. Outside the small pension, Hannah crossed the car park to the truck that, even though it was ten years old, had taken the last of her money. The yard's brown snow, packed down and mixed with mud, had frozen during the night after a brief melting at midday. The cold at this early-morning hour was bitter, reminding her of the challenge she would face, spending the night in the shack by the lake without a fire.

She started the truck, and the engine kicked over in a satisfying rumble. It had spent the night outside the warmth of a garage and still started. Satisfied, she switched the engine off and stood outside for a few minutes longer, looking up at the sky, gauging the weather. Clouds charged across the sky in the wind that tore off the Alps. Intermittently, the sun leaked through, shedding a gloaming light over the yard and distant fields.

Tomorrow she would drive to the lake, following a service road that the Oberman Group had long known about, one that was used by the hearty souls who went to the lake for ice fishing.

A few flakes of snow came down in slow motion, catching the sun. But no heavy clouds, so it was not likely to snow harder tomorrow. She hoped it would not, for the sake of their flight out on Christmas Day. She didn't relish fleeing down backroads in an old truck. The airplane was a better way, if the English sent one. If they could land. All they needed was a little luck.

A little luck, God. Would that be so much skin off your nose?

THE AERIE

WEDNESDAY, DECEMBER 23. Sitting in his wingback chair, a pot of tea on the table at his side, Evgeny watched as Kim paced.

He sat stiffly in his chair, dressed formally but his hair disordered, sticking out on one side. He poured himself tea, not offering any to her, but then seeming to lose interest in his own cup.

She paced the small perimeter of the cabin, her stomach knotted and churning. The clothes she'd worn since she arrived at the Aerie now bagged on her frame. It seemed her body fed on the unseen fuel of purpose and drive. In the past few days, she had taken two meals of venison, served steaming, but cool in the middle, easy enough to ingest, but afterward, nausea.

She wished Evgeny would speak to her, tell her more about Annakova's reaction to their meeting, but he was strangely subdued. He had only said that Kim should come midmorning, and that Annakova would join them. And if Annakova was willing to listen to her, that meant success was within reach.

"Do you know the time, Evgeny?"

He pulled out a watch on a chain, gazed at it, replaced it. "*Nyet.* Time, it lies."

She hated being without her Helbros. But how absurd. The least of her worries. Kim asked him again, "What did Her Majesty say?"

"She say she comes. Talk with you, but is secret." He picked up his tea, then put it down again, hand shaking. As nervous as she was.

The window curtains, though drawn tight, let in the light at the edges, little glaring flickers that stung her eyes. The day had begun to cloud over, but the snow made everything bright.

Someone at the door. Kim glanced at Evgeny, who gestured for her to answer it. She picked up her sack of Evgeny's sheets—her excuse for being there—and opened the door.

Irina Annakova stood on the porch in a hooded cape. Kim looked around for an SS escort, but the tsarina was alone.

Annakova entered and Kim closed the door behind her.

They faced off.

The tsarina let her hood fall. Her face, wan with creases between her eyes and down the side of her mouth, lines that Kim had not noticed in the more flattering firelight of Annakova's parlor. Three days ago, the day she became a 10.

As Kim put down the linens on the bed, Annakova went to Evgeny and they spoke in Russian. She moved to the back of his chair, placing a hand on the top, hovering over Evgeny like a dark angel. She looked at Kim. "And so?"

"I came to help you. You and the tsarevich. I have come all this way, Your Majesty."

"Come from where?"

"London. The British government." Now it was all out, the damning truth.

"Coming for purpose. What purpose?"

"To stop the *Nachkommenschaft.*"

"You mean destroying us." She did not remove her cape, did not sit. Kim felt she had only a minute or two to convince her.

"Your Majesty, the Nazis are not friends to Russia."

Annakova's mouth flattened in displeasure. "Everyone knows. No love between our countries. Except hating Bolsheviks."

"But to overcome them, the *Wehrmacht* will bring destruction on your people. As Evgeny Feodorovich foresees. As you must know will happen, because Stalin won't give up without a terrible fight. A million dead, so Evgeny says."

"You come to tell me this Nazi treachery. But they promise how Russian armies lay down arms. When they face . . . discipline . . . from German army. Is lies? You say so?"

"Yes, I say so. Because of orders for Evgeny to be shot. Which they have lied to you about."

Annakova went to the window at the front of the cabin, peering out. Evgeny watched her every movement as though waiting for something terrible to occur. And did he know, did he see, something terrible?

The tsarina turned back from the window and removed her cape, placing it on the extra chair.

Her gown was a rich ivory color, in a decades-old style, with high lace collar. From a pouch in her cape she pulled out a small pistol, pointing it at Kim. "Your name," she said. "Is not Nora Copeland. And not American? This also, a lie?"

"My mother is American. My father, English. I had to lie to come here."

"And you would like to kill me. Is why you came, after all."

Evgeny said something to her in Russian. She looked at him with a mixture of sadness and affection, seating herself in the chair across from him. She waved at Kim to stand in a place where she could see her clearly. "But I tire to talk of death."

"Your Majesty. Do you have to point the gun at me? I know what it feels like to be shot."

A tiny smile, conceding the point. She put the pistol on the table next to her.

"You tell me things," Annakova said. "Now I tell you. They do not dare to kill my Evgeny. I am tsarina."

"But Your Majesty, you saw the execution order."

"How you could get such papers that Evgeny shows me?"

"I've been working hard to uncover the Nazi lies. The orders were on file here in the SS offices. It was very dangerous to get them."

Annakova cast her glance around the cabin, as though searching for an alternate explanation, so that she did not have to believe that her and her son's future in Russia was a mirage.

"And more lies," Kim went on. "There is a hospital called Treptow. A Nazi prison for SS-*Nachkommenschaft* who have been purified too many times."

"You do not know this thing!"

"I was there. I do know. They tie them in beds by straps, behind locked doors. The Progeny beg to die."

Annakova became very still.

"I saw it. I would not believe what people told me, that the Progeny went mad at the end. That they must be caged like dangerous animals. So I went to see for myself, how those who are touched by you end."

"Strapped to beds?" Annakova's face went dark. She flicked

a glance at Evgeny, who raised his hand from his lap, allowing the point.

Annakova watched her for a second, thinking. "How many?"

"A dozen. Treptow Sanatorium is near Berlin. I got in to look."

"You are so good at this. Getting in," Annakova said, bitter.

"Yes. I saw them in their beds. And one broke free and ran mad, killing others. A horror. I escaped, my hair with blood in it."

Annakova looked at Evgeny, who nodded, though he did not seem to paying close attention. His gaze wandered here and there.

"But why in beds, strapped down?"

"Because the German doctors wish to see how they will die, for their records. They watch and write it all down in their charts. I know that they lie to you, because you would never do this to people pledged to your service. You would never allow it."

"I do not allow it," she whispered. The resolve seemed to flow out of her. She sank to the floor by Evgeny's chair, placing one hand on his knee. "I do not allow."

She looked up at Evgeny, who nodded gravely. "What I shall do? Tell me, Evgeny, tell me."

"You save St. Petersburg. Go to British. Go, Irinuska. Then I can die."

"Do not always speak of death! I beg of you." She buried her face in his thigh and wept.

His hand went to her head, patting her like a child. He cooed soft Russian words to her, stroking her head where her hair was pulled up in a braided bun.

He looked up at Kim. "She go with you. Make end of it, this long road."

As he sat there he looked like a royal himself. Serene and kingly. "And so, Nora Copeland, you say, you swear, that you protect Nikolai?"

"I swear it. I will protect him."

Annakova held on to Evgeny's knees like a daughter might cling to her father. A tableau of devotion and despair from the pretender to the throne who would never win back the royal court, whose son would never be tsar.

Evgeny sighed, putting a finger under Annakova's chin, lifting her face so that she would look at him, and he whispered, "*Dasvedanya,* Irinuska."

Removing a handkerchief from her long sleeve, she wiped her eyes and slowly got to her feet. "I am ready to do this thing." She gestured to Kim to bring her cape.

Evgeny watched as Kim helped Annakova into her wrap. He picked up his cup of tea that had languished on the side table and drank it down all at once. Then he poured another cup, and gulped it down as well. Gagging, he reached for the pot again.

Both Kim and Annakova turned to him. The thought occurred: Poison? Annakova cried out and rushed toward him. Kim got there first and lunging, swiped her hand at the teapot, sending it crashing to the floor.

Evgeny groaned as a spasm took hold of him. Head thrown back, he trembled violently, hands and legs shaking.

"Help him! Help him!" Annakova shouted at Kim.

Kim ran to the sink for water, filling a glass, and rushed back with it.

Evgeny vomited. The force of it bent him over, and he fell to the floor, gasping for air, his feet slapping against the floorboards as tremors shook him.

Annakova was on her knees at his side, holding his head, murmuring his name. His body arched backward, once, and again. The tsarina looked up at Kim, frantic. But they had not the slightest idea what to do. He could not take water. A foul trickle ran down his chin. Kim watched, helpless to save him.

Irina Annakova was moaning, saying his name and what sounded like endearments as she rocked at his side.

Kim thought Irina should run for a doctor but knew it would be too late as Evgeny shook on the floor, his eyes rolling up in his head.

The minutes passed as he slowly quieted. At last his body went slack. Kim reached down to check the pulse at his neck. He was gone.

Tears streamed down Annakova's face. "No one listen to old man. Old man having too much future."

Whatever future he had seen, he could not bear it. He could not bear any of them. And now he was dead.

Annakova sat at Evgeny's side for a long while. She held his hand, murmuring what sounded like a prayer in Russian.

Kim took the execution order and burned the paper in the fire grate.

At last Annakova rose and smoothed her gown. She raised her chin with a frightening royal poise. "Now you tell me, Nora Copeland, how we find airplane in forest."

THE WOODS NEAR A LAKE

WEDNESDAY, DECEMBER 23. In the silent forest Hannah was alone, heavily laden with a small woolen bed roll, two winter coats, sandwiches wrapped in waxed paper, a tin cup, and a small stove to melt snow for water. It was cold but her parka and hat with earflaps were enough to keep her warm.

Having left behind the truck at the end of the road, she had set out through the heavy trees toward the lake. The sky was high and clear, the snow on the ground only three or four inches thick. *A little luck.*

Tonight she would lie under her blanket and all the clothes she carried on her back. There might be blankets in the shack, but one of her contacts in the area had said no one had been ice fishing at the lake for a long time. Perhaps the mice had made tatters of the blankets. Or the SS had dismantled the hut.

Hannah did not relish spending the night outside if the shack was gone, but in truth, a cold hut would not be much better.

Her main worry was that she would sleep too late in the morning. Perhaps best not to sleep at all tonight. And Kim? She must carry out her part of the plan. How long would the plane wait if Kim did not come on time? Tomorrow's worry.

She emerged out of the trees and saw the lake before her. The hut still intact. The lake, flat, frozen, and ample for landing a plane. Hurrying now to be quickly out of view, she made her way to the hut.

THE AERIE

LATER THAT DAY. "Where did he get rat poison?" Commandant Bassman asked his assembled officers.

Captain Adler stood among the senior SS, his gut tight with anxiety. What had happened in Evgeny's cabin? The tsarina's story, as all had heard by now, was that she had paid a visit, had struggled with Evgeny Borisov as he threatened suicide, had watched in horror as he drank poison. But what really had gone on in Evgeny's cabin this morning? He wondered if Nora had been there before or during the poisoning episode. Annakova had likely met with her. The timing suggested the three of them discussed the execution order and, of course, the vision of St. Petersburg. Sometime during this discussion, Evgeny had swallowed poison. And what had happened to the execution document?

"The storeroom was not locked, Commandant," one of the officers responded.

At Bassman's glare, the officer said, "It is locked now."

"The tsarina's well-being is the priority of every one of you. We cannot have any mistakes that affect Her Majesty."

But they were going to kill Evgeny anyway. He had saved them the trouble. And now the tsarina was grieving instead of just regretting the need for his retirement rest at a home for the elderly.

"Commandant," Lieutenant Weiss said, "there is a document missing from Evgeny Borisov's file." At a nod from Bassman, Weiss said, "The paper authorizing his elimination."

Bassman's face darkened. Very softly he said. "Lieutenant Weiss, you will find out how it is that the paper is missing."

"Yes, Commandant!"

Bassman looked at the men grouped around him, searching the faces of his inner circle. His gaze settled on Adler, then moved on.

Adler thought that Bassman suspected that they had a traitor among them. Perhaps not someone in the room. But someone.

As the day darkened into late afternoon, Irina Dimitrievna Annakova sat by Evgeny's body and prayed. Here in a side room of the infirmary, he lay on a wooden table, his hands folded over his breast. There should be a priest, but she was all Evgeny Feodorovich had for prayers.

"Oh gracious Mother of God," she whispered, "have mercy on this soul, a sinner. Oh Mother of Christ, present my prayer to your Son, that He may for Your sake hear me and save my beloved Evgeny's soul and give him peace forever."

His body had been washed and dressed in his best clothes. On his collar, a discoloration where the maid, ironing his hastily laundered shirt, had scorched the linen.

How tattered their estate was! No time to buy suitable clothing in the rush to attain the Aerie where Hitler said they would be safe.

Safe. But they had never been safe. The British knew of Monarch. If she had not agreed to leave with the woman, likely this Nora Copeland would have killed her. So she and Nikolai had never been safe. And how safe would they be if they fled on Christmas? But what was she to do, stay and bring further sorrow on her Progeny?

There was no safety. Not even with Erich Stefan von Ritter. He did not know the truth of *catalyst* changes, that many of the Progeny—no matter the number, too many!—became ill beyond any possible healing. That they died, some of them, strapped to their beds for the tests of the Nazi doctors. Stefan did not know; she could not believe that he knew.

The Germans had lied and lied. Not Stefan, but his masters.

And yet. Hitler was her only chance to bring Kolya the throne. Back and forth, first horror, then resignation: people sometimes must suffer to bring a greater good. To defeat the Bolsheviks, who conducted their own slaughter of the Russian people.

And what if Evgeny had been wrong about what he saw? Sometimes he saw things . . . things that he said were true but might be avoided. Things that might even be true in a world that lived alongside their own.

Oh, Evgeny. Sometimes I think you saw things that you feared but that were not true.

What was she to do? Leave or stay? She had made her decision in Evgeny's cabin, but now. . . . She looked at her hands, and thought of the power in them. She was a *catalyst*. Had God given her this power for a reason? Was it to make her valuable to Hitler, so that he would make Kolya tsar? Or was it an evil power that she must resist? The thoughts circled round and round. She would go. She would stay.

And what of Stefan? This betrayal of him was almost beyond what she could bear.

She placed her hand on Evgeny's breast, remembering her duty to pray. "Give rest, Oh God, to the soul of Thy servant, and set him in Paradise. Give him rest, Oh Lord, and grant him forgiveness of his sins."

And mine, oh Lord. And mine.

45

THE AERIE

CHRISTMAS EVE, 7:00 PM. The gathering in the reception hall was like so many soirees Kim had been to, except the guests here were monsters.

At the notion, she chuckled with amusement. Take a little pressure off, and in her present condition terror became hilarity. It wasn't good, she knew. At Kim's side, Erika shot her an annoyed look. "Something is funny?"

"No, of course not. Shall we see what the canapes are?" She knew there were some, because she could smell them from across the room. The tantalizing fragrance of beef, unless it was venison. She struck out across the crowded hall, Erika at her side in a severe suited jacket and skirt, looking more like a prison warden than a Christmas party guest. How fine that Erika looked the part, since she *was* a warden. Hilde was in the infirmary recovering from her bout of indigestion, deflected for now from making trouble.

The great room occupied the entire Festival Hall's second floor, except for a few SS officer suites. Kim had seen the reception hall from the plaza, with its long bank of windows looking out on the Bavarian Alps, but she had never been in it. Despite its size, the room was crowded by what looked like the entire garrison. Annakova had not yet arrived, but word was that she would make an appearance despite the loss she had suffered.

An enormous Christmas tree dominated the far corner, liberally strewn with ornaments, lit candles in little holders and wrapped gifts beneath. Uniforms were on parade, brown of the *Wehrmacht*, the black of regular SS and *Nachkommenschaft* SS, and the civilians wearing, Kim supposed, their newly issued garb, as she did: her green dress with leather belt and black patent-leather high heels. She nodded to the few civilians she had met in the dining room, committed fascists looking starstruck among the elite SS, proud to be leaving soon for France, Poland, Czechoslovakia, Belgium, and wherever Hitler needed arms twisted and opinions firmly changed.

Despite Evgeny's terrible death yesterday, Kim was optimistic for her plan. Annakova had not turned her in, would escape with her. And Hannah would come to England. So many problems solved. The *Nachkommenschaft*, those lanky, pale experiments, would gradually recover. They would be able to eat corned beef cabbage again.

It would have been funny, but the thought of cabbage turned her stomach.

Bringing home two *catalyst* Talents would be a stunning success, lovely to think of. There were no limits to what a spy could do in the right place at the right time. She would make sure to press home the point with Duncan, he of the timid cautions.

Not that she was entirely calm. In addition to *Wehrmacht* soldiers, the room was full of Hitler's elite units, both regular SS and those who wore the vulture insignia. Were it not for the experience of the Berlin soirees among uniformed Nazis, she thought this gathering might have completely unnerved her.

In the back of her mind, a warning curled. *You* should *be afraid. Stay on guard.*

Some of the *Nachkommen* stood along the wall, a phalanx of thin men in black, as though lining up together would excuse them from socializing. Others mixed freely, some even laughing, their expressions wolfish. Tomorrow the purification ceremony would make them . . . more. More of what they already were.

She had not yet seen Captain Adler. They had not spoken since yesterday morning when he alerted her that Evgeny was in his cabin. Even had she seen him here now, and as harmless as it might seem for the two of them to exchange a quick few words, she did not plan to approach him, and hoped he would not attempt to communicate.

Everyone waited for the tsarina. Erika and Kim had practiced on the way down from the barracks how to greet her with appropriate solemnity, given her loss. For example, one could not say Merry Christmas. Erika decided on "Your Majesty" with a deep curtsy. And for Kim, "An honor to see you again."

They looked over the canape table with its cheeses, liver pate on quarter-cut black bread, deviled eggs, cake wedges and, for special constitutions, tiny raw slices of venison on crackers. Waiters groomed the table, removing crackers that had been left behind as the Progeny picked the toppings off.

"Disgusting," Erika huffed. "They have no manners."

"Manners?" Kim flicked crumbs from the bodice of her dress. "I hope you're not criticizing, Erika." She turned what she hoped was a predatory look on her. "We *Nachkommenschaft* do the best we can. Under the circumstances."

Erika refused to be impressed by Kim's standing. She expected to be purified tomorrow after Christmas dinner, and so Kim was merely a little ahead of her. "Do not forget that I found us lipstick."

"So you did. You deserve a medal just for that."

"Over there," Erika said, nudging her. "The Commandant, Colonel Bassman."

A gray-haired, barrel-chested officer stood by the Christmas tree in the company of several officers.

"And who is the man with the scar?" Kim asked.

Erika turned to look at an SS officer standing by the window drinking something red. He was a *Nachkomme* by the tall dome of his forehead and long chin. The one she had met yesterday near the cabins.

But Erika didn't know him. She excused herself to reapply her lipstick. Kim realized she didn't feel comfortable being near the officer with the scar since he'd seen her approach Evgeny's cabin yesterday morning. She made her way to the table with the champagne.

A stir rippled through the crowd. Voices in the corridor outside, and people turned in the direction of the tall double doors.

Over the heads of the assembled soldiers and administrative staff, Kim saw movement in the hallway; the tsarina approaching, stopping to greet some who were in the foyer. Kim supposed she would wear gloves since she would be shaking hands with people.

Kim glimpsed the sparkle of jewels, a white gown. Heels clicked and men in uniform bowed. Senior officers stepped forward to greet the tsarina.

And then Kim saw the entire entourage.

The room shifted. Her champagne flute tilted and cold splashes slopped onto her dress.

Annakova had come into full view on the arm of Erich von Ritter.

Kim slammed the flute down on the linen tablecloth, breaking the glass stem, spilling the contents. Lurching away from the table, she looked for a way to hide. She was in the direct path of the tsarina and her escort.

Thoughts flew at her, trying to land. Erich von Ritter was dead. Dead at Rievaulx Abbey on the North York Moors. He would recognize her. But he was dead. She must get away. They were blocking the door. A *Nachkomme* near her jerked his attention her way. The broken glass. Her hand, bleeding.

The *Nachkomme* approached her, nostrils flaring. What, he would lick her hand? He was offering her a paper napkin. She took it, saying in English, *thank you*, pressing the napkin into the palm of her hand, making a fist to keep it there. How could she move into a corner of the room and avoid the advancing couple? The man on her arm—he was limping. That could not be von Ritter.

But in another moment Annakova was standing before her. Now that the tsarina was an arm's length away, Kim knew her situation was real, even if it was impossible. Annakova was still on Erich von Ritter's arm.

"Sir Stefan," the tsarina said, "here is American who took bullet from my son and is so brave. Nora Copeland." She nodded at the man at her side. "This is Sir Stefan."

Kim stood speechless. Small, bleeding, dressed in green. Words stuck in her throat. The room continued tipping as lights from the chandeliers splattered into her eyes like shards of ice.

"Come now, you must greet us," Annakova said. Her face, a pale mask with a welcoming smile pasted on.

"Your Majesty," Kim whispered. She looked up at von Ritter. "Sir Stefan."

His face bore a surreal calm as he gazed at her. Not a flicker of recognition. Perhaps her bangs, her short hair? The green dress. He didn't know her.

But he did, of course.

"Nora Copeland, is it?" A faint expression began to make its way across his face. Amusement. Yes, of all things, amusement. Her life, over, and Erich von Ritter, as always, finding reason to be delighted by what the world held up for him. As now, standing before him, Kim Tavistock, the erstwhile Yorkshire spy who had once foiled all his plans. And did so with enough grace that, at the end, he had let her go.

It would not be the case this time. He had her. And two hundred SS to back him up.

Somehow the awful moment passed. The tsarina and von Ritter moved on, leaving her stunned and unable to think.

Run. She must run. But where could she go that she would not be immediately apprehended?

Then von Ritter was standing in front of her again, having come to join her at the champagne table. He took her by the arm and led her away. To her surprise, it was not in the direction of the foyer, but to one of the divans strategically placed around the room.

"Please sit down, Miss Copeland. I should not like for you to fall to the floor as appears likely."

She sat while he remained standing. Perhaps she should say thank you, to keep things pleasant for just a few more moments, but her words fled. Caught. She was caught by the only Nazi in Germany who knew who she was. Would he be kind? Could she somehow—but how?—avoid an interrogation? Why did she think he would be kind?

"Rievaulx," came her hoarse whisper.

He looked down at her. "Survived. As you see."

"The limp."

"Not from Rievaulx." A few beats of dreadful, static terror during which her thoughts evaporated.

He murmured, "Go out into the vestibule and wait for me." A small, ironic smile. "You are over your surprise, I think. Yes?"

"I don't know."

"Collect yourself. Then go." He turned and walked away, threading through the crowd, no doubt confident she would follow his order. As she would. He joined Annakova, who turned to look in her direction. Annakova did not know who she was; von Ritter did not know her plan. A faint thread of hope began to replace shock and alarm.

But had she completely lost her mind? There was absolutely no hope.

She waited in the foyer outside the hall doors, fading down the corridor a bit when Erika emerged from the lavatory. Her mood swung from panic to hope and back again. Here was von Ritter's revenge for the thwarted invasion of England: now he would stop her assault on Monarch, exposing her as a mole, spy, saboteur.

But since von Ritter had not immediately arrested her, he might be her only hope to survive. What did he want from her? Names, contacts, places. He was *Sicherheitsdienst*, German intelligence. Kim's thoughts fell into a dark and tarry place. This was the disaster that Adler had predicted. That Duncan had predicted.

Finally von Ritter emerged from the reception hall in the

company of Annakova. Another officer escorted the tsarina away and von Ritter approached Kim. He led her down a corridor, and at the end of it he opened a door and took her in, switching on a light.

It was a small but finely furnished room with a desk, bed, and wardrobe. Outside the window, snowflakes drifted down, sparkling in the plaza lights. In the curve of the window, a small, padded seat.

Von Ritter motioned her to a chair at the table. She sat, looking up at him.

"You are my undoing, Kim."

Why did he put it like that? *She* was undone. Baldly stated, she had infiltrated the headquarters of a highly secret military operation at a stronghold in the Alps to subvert a German military mission. There was no finessing it.

"It's war, Herr von Ritter. Or shall I call you Erich?" He had suggested the familiarity when they thought they would die at Rievaulx.

He paused, his amusement now gone from his face. "You choose. In your time remaining, you may choose."

Time remaining. The way he threatened: offhand, terrifying. Drawing up an extra chair, he sat before her, this impossibly handsome man, this charming spy who had given himself to a corrupt and degraded ideology.

He watched her with no hint of pity, just watched, not yet making any demands. How would she answer him, how could she protect Captain Adler and Irina Annakova? Whatever was coming, she desperately wanted to postpone it. She mustered a steady voice. "What happened at Rievaulx? I heard a gunshot."

"I took aim at the nearest British soldier. And he at me, but in my wounded state, I missed. After that . . . they tell me I passed out. If it had been Germany, one such as myself would have been summarily shot. But when I awoke, I was on a small fishing boat headed for Germany. It seems your country did not like to admit how they failed to protect their shores. In any case, all the German soldiers were returned home by one route or another." He shrugged. "It disturbed me to have missed that soldier and at close range."

The Office might have told her he had been repatriated. So many things they might have done better. "Why are you called Sir Stefan?"

"It is a name Her Majesty prefers. Stephen is my middle name, which she pronounces in the Russian way. She petitioned the Führer to allow her to bestow a title as a reward for my care of her."

He went to the dresser by his bed and removed a small box from a drawer. Inside it, medicinal supplies. At the small sink in the corner, he wetted a cloth and joined her at the table with the cloth and a length of gauze. When she opened her hand, von Ritter cleaned the cut and wrapped the gauze around her hand.

As he worked, he said, "So then, the British government knows of our operation."

"We'd been tracking it for months." She knew how interrogations went. Start with small questions, get the words flowing, moving to the larger things that the subject hoped to withhold.

He gestured for her to hold the bandage in place while he cut tape. "We knew there were disclosures, but we did not realize how badly we were compromised." When he finished the taping, he looked at her critically. "You have grown thin, Kim. Purification does not suit you."

"As you know, it suits no one. You know how they end."

"Ah. So you were the one. You left your small camera at

the sanatorium." A broad smile. "I will have to kill you quickly, before you bring down the Third Reich."

She snorted a laugh. It *was* funny.

He put the first aid box away and sat down on the window seat. "Someone revealed the Monarch operation to you. Even before you became a 10, you were a strong *spill.* I would like to know who told you."

"Rikard Nagel. An SS captain." Now the lies began, and she brought to bear all her determination to keep track of them.

"So. Göring's man. And then you killed him."

"I don't do that."

"Your people, then. And he also gave up the Aerie?" She shrugged, letting him draw that conclusion.

"And so you knew about Irina Annakova."

"Yes."

He looked out the window for a time, although there was nothing to see but his own reflection and a few bright, spinning flakes of snow. "Do you hunger for blood yet?" His voice, bitter. "Perhaps a small cup to last until your next meal?"

"If you find it so repulsive, what about all these people here, all the gaunt men, all the broken minds?"

"They are soldiers, ready to sacrifice. But you, Kim . . . you always went beyond what anyone could expect of you." He was very near. His power, both physical and psychological.

"Really?" Sarcasm leaped out. "More than a mere girl could do?"

His dark eyes hardened. "More than a person can do." He spread his hands, looking around him, as though encompassing her failed mission in the Nazi stronghold.

"What of your master race, then?"

He looked away. A pause lengthened. "I wish that you could

have been spared." His tone changed. More businesslike. "What was your assignment here?"

"To kill her."

Turning, he raised an eyebrow. "How did you hope to do this?"

"Poison." He must not know about, or have, the drug. Britain would soon have its own *catalyst*. "And then there was never a way to deliver it. So I used it on my roommate, Hilde, who dislikes me. She watched me too closely."

"The one in the infirmary." An appraising gaze. "You have become more ruthless. I think you do not trust our chancellor." A slow, easy smile. She tried to join in and failed.

Noises in the hall. A man's voice nearby. Von Ritter looked to the door, but the voices faded.

He turned back to her. "I have a question. Answer it truthfully and I may let you go."

Let her go? Her breath went shallow. A little spike of hope surged up inside her, ripping as it went.

"How did you pass the test at the intake post? Since you had been a 6, and it does not meet requirements."

Oh, not good, that question. It was obvious how she passed the test. A *catalyst* had brought her higher. But clearly it could not have been Annakova, not before Kim arrived at the intake center.

She paused, mind racing in place.

"Kim. Your country. They have a *catalyst* as well. Am I right?"

"Yes."

"And the name?" He spoke softly, deceptively gentle. "You will tell me the name and also where they are."

She had never seen him in uniform, that severe black, with leather and piping. A look to inspire fear. It was working. "Where does this end, Erich?" She sat up straight, so as not to be cowed or not to look like it. "You promise to let me live, but I must give up all my secrets, and then you kill me anyway?"

His reaction to that, undecipherable.

She wanted to say, Can it be quick? But couldn't bring herself to say it.

His face revealed nothing as he watched her.

New lies came to mind. Her brain was kicking back into gear. "Since this man, our *catalyst*, is safely in England now, what good is it to know his name? A name that was not his real name in any case, when he *catalyzed* me."

Von Ritter remained silent. Letting her talk, now that the time had come.

In the quiet of the room she began to speak, softly, without any purpose except to delay further questioning. "My first day here I sat next to an old man at dinner. Evgeny Borisov. It was in the civilian dining room. He told me that he saw my death. It would be at the hands of someone in uniform. It was like a terrible burden that he carried, to know such things, and by telling me, I think he hoped that his load would grow lighter. I didn't want to know, but I couldn't stop him. And when Nikolai, in his naval uniform . . . when his stray bullet found me, I thought it was the death the old man saw. But now I think I know who he saw. You."

"I do not like to think so."

She wanted to be brave. It was important, now that she had come so far, keeping her mind under steady control, navigating the Aerie. Almost succeeding. "It's all right. I knew it could happen this way."

He rose. "Come here, Kim."

She stood, and he reached out his hand to take hers. He pulled her gently toward him. "I will do what I must," he said, looking at her with what looked like regret. "Honor demands it, despite what I might want." She allowed him to bring her into his arms. She pressed her face into his uniform jacket, the buttons gouging her cheek. How bizarre it was to have feelings for one's executioner. At the last, she supposed, one would do anything for a little comfort.

His voice, soft in her ears. "I have not forgotten you, my Valkyrie." He released her, pushing a strand of hair back from her face. "Perhaps you thought of me once or twice."

Of course she had. When she looked back on the past half year, she had to admit how often Erich von Ritter had come to mind: the memories of the confusion and the fear he had inspired. The pull he had exerted on her. Allure mixed with aversion.

"Yes. I thought of you. Many times."

Voices in the hall.

He took her gently by the shoulders. "We cannot be gone longer. I want you to go back to the reception, Kim. Everything is normal. Tomorrow, after the purification ceremony, your assignment is to be sent to—" He made an inquiring look.

"Paris."

"But you will of course not go to your assignment. You will go home and tell your handlers of our location. It will do no good. I will find evidence that a spy was among us, and we will take the tsarina elsewhere for her safety. A place that even you would never find."

She listened to this recitation with astonishment. "You're . . . letting me go?"

"Oh, not yet. Tomorrow, Kim." He fixed her with that firm, black gaze so effective in eliciting terror and attraction. "Tomorrow, when we are finished. You will remain in this room tonight, since you are hard to trust."

A reprieve. Against all odds, a reprieve. But locked in this room would not suit, not at all.

"If I don't go back to the barracks tonight, Erika will report me missing. She's at the reception right now probably wondering where I am. You can't tell her to keep it quiet. It would draw attention to you. If she were questioned."

He narrowed his eyes. "I see. Very well then. Perhaps it does no harm if you spend the night in the barracks. You are watched there. The woman, Erika. Do not give me cause to be the one Evgeny foretold."

The one. The soldier who kills her. No, Erich. I will be on a plane to England soon. A profound relief rushed through her. The barracks. Not under lock and key.

"So, then. You must go back before your barracks mates become concerned about your absence." He led her to the door.

When he prepared to open it, she stopped and put her hand on his arm. "It will be dangerous for you to let me go, won't it?"

He shrugged, straightening his jacket. An ironic, devastating smile. "It is, shall we say, a professional courtesy. One spy to another." He opened the door, checking the corridor, then nodded to her.

Out in the hallway, she made her way to the party, overwhelmed, almost giddy. An image came to mind of looking down on herself as she walked toward the Great Hall. Here was a slim figure in green, walking lightly, amazed by the world and that she had more hours in it.

Now she had to tread so very carefully, but the plan, her plan, was back in play. Von Ritter was back from the dead. And so was her mission.

† † †

7:41 PM. Captain Adler crossed the plaza, carrying a humbly wrapped package with a bright bow. A Christmas gift.

Earlier, he had returned from the intake center, having created an excuse to deliver documents. When he had arrived back at the bottom of the Aerie's cliff, he had pulled the motorcar into the car park and disconnected the ignition.

Now, as he entered the Festival Hall, he noted that Annakova was leaving early. She would need her sleep for the rigors of what was coming. The purifications tomorrow. As she passed him with her escort, she didn't make eye contact; she didn't know that he had contributed to the escape plot, nor that it was for him that she had been instructed to put out seeds on the bird feeder near the shed in the chalet garden. As he had seen her do at noon.

So far, it was working. Nora Copeland's desperate plan had gone undetected. The peace of the Aerie would not last long, he knew. He would make sure of that.

8:02 PM. "Kolya." Irina closed Kolya's bedroom door behind her. "I must speak to you."

He stood up from where he had been playing with the dog. "Yes, *Maman.*"

"It is very important that you listen to me." He grew solemn and waited. "You must not ask any questions, darling, but you will obey me in everything."

His voice was brave, but his face betrayed his anxiety. "Yes, *Maman,* I will."

Irina looked at him, with his soft brown eyes and her chest ached, down to her very heart. Heartache was not just a phrase to describe a mood, but a physical pain. This escape was fraught with danger. How could she lead her son into such peril? Look-

ing at him, she almost lost her nerve. But enough of this prevar-
ication! The Germans did not love them and would doubtless
betray them in the end. So she must betray the Germans first.

She began speaking very softly, conscious that Polina might
be nearby, even listening, the old crone. "We will be going down
into the valley, into the woods tonight."

Excitement flashed across his face. Another jagged cut at
her heart.

She pushed on. There was, she explained, a secret way down
to the forest, and they must take it before a very bad thing happened. He must trust her and be the brave young man she knew
him to be.

He must pack a small knapsack with extra trousers and
socks. This he would place under his bed. But Polina must not
know of their plans, nor anyone else.

His eyes, wide with alarm. "A bad thing happens otherwise,
Maman?"

"A very bad thing, my darling. So we both must be very
brave. There will be one more person who will go with us. The
American woman, Nora Copeland."

She put her finger to her lips. No questions.

"But what about my puppy?"

"I will ask Sir Stefan to bring the puppy afterward." A lie. A
necessary one, for they could not bring Lev.

When she had finished telling him what would happen,
and how he must be prepared, she opened her arms for an
embrace. She pressed him to her, and Kolya, being eleven, was
still able to cling to her unashamedly. When they drew apart
he resumed his poise. Oh, he would have made such a tsar!

"You will pretend to sleep tonight, sweet one. Or sleep, if
you can, and I will wake you when it is still dark, and we will go."

"Will I wear pajamas?"

"Yes, going to sleep, and when Polina tucks you in. But also under your bed, warm clothes to put on quickly. Your heaviest jacket."

At the door she turned to him. "Do not be afraid, Kolya. We must be brave and serve our country. It is expected of us, for we are not like other people. We have royal blood and can do very hard things."

"Yes, *Maman.*"

She looked at her precious son. It had all been for him. Her life was still all for him, even if he would not rule Russia.

Once back in her room, she pulverized a dozen of her sleeping pills, using a large, smooth-cut emerald ring that her aunt, Grand Duchess Tatiana Nazarova, had given her on her seventeenth birthday. When the tablets were ground to a fine powder, she swept it into a carefully folded piece of paper.

Then she began sewing the few jewels preserved from the old days into the lining of her riding skirt. She left Stefan's yellow-gold diamond pendant on the dresser.

46

CHRISTMAS EVE, 8:10 PM. In the bar, Julian was well into his third drink, waiting for a little numbness to arrive. The whisky was having no affect whatever. Just as well, he thought, since he wouldn't be sleeping tonight.

Women in fine dresses made their entrances, conscious of their stagey moment, embracing waiting friends. They were escorted by men in cashmere coats and opera scarfs, snow dusting their shoulders. From across the hall, the strains of "God Rest Ye Merry Gentlemen" from the string quartet. *Ohhh, tidings of comfort and joy . . .*

E had graciously offered to share his Christmas Eve in London. He wouldn't be going down to Litchfield, as Lydia was visiting her mother in hospital, giving him a chance for yuletide with his mistress, Ida Mae. Would Julian come for a drink? He almost accepted, but then Olivia caught his eye on her way out of E's office, raising her chin. *Come by my desk.* He must have looked worse than he'd thought, because after his meeting with E she offered to join him for a drink at Claridges.

Everyone was offering him a little company on Christmas Eve, knowing he was staying in London until Kim came home. They were all careful, even Julian was, to say "when" and "until."

But she was in a Nazi stronghold in Bavaria. . . .

Olivia appeared at the lounge door, looking for him and then spotting him at his table near the window, the one he had been anchoring since six thirty. He stood, taking her coat and seating her, trying to appreciate her gesture of meeting him. But seeing a former lover on Christmas Eve wasn't likely to bring comfort and joy. Although he *was* grateful; or he should be. Perhaps another whisky.

"It's a madhouse out there," Olivia said as she got settled. Wearing a soft suit that emphasized her waistline, she had come straight from the office. Working late on Christmas Eve. And now she would be even later getting home to Guy, so he steeled himself for the brief, obligatory drink.

When her gin fizz arrived, he raised his glass to wish her a Merry Christmas, but she beat him to it, saying, "To our brave Kim."

Very decent of her. "Kim," he repeated.

She stared at her drink.

A mistake to meet? "How are you, Olivia?"

A wry smile. "Oh, good. You know; the same as always." She turned toward the hall, noting the Christmas music. "What *does* 'Adeste Fideles' mean?"

"I certainly didn't take a first in Latin, but I believe it's *all you faithful.*" He watched her for a moment, seeing dark pools around her eyes, unless it was the dim lights of the bar throwing shadows. "Olivia. You're not all right, are you?"

She sipped her drink. "You have so much on your mind."

"Then take my mind off it. If I can help, or even if not, I'll listen."

A pause. "I've left Guy."

He absorbed this, letting it filter into his fogged brain as he tried to figure out how to express what he was feeling without giving offense. No, he wouldn't express what he was feeling. Relief. Shame. Joy.

"Olivia," he said, finally ending the long silence. "How awful for you. Life is so bloody unfair."

"I suppose it is. I'm not really sure if I expected fair, just a little luck." A lovely smile, fleeting but stellar.

"What happened with Guy?"

"Oh, I can't blame him. We were both miserable. We had made our decision too fast, and nothing between us worked." She made a small, helpless smile. "He hated that I couldn't share my work life with him. It felt like withholding secrets. As, in fact, it was."

She took a deep breath. "I'd feel better not talking about it right now. I just wanted to tell you." After a moment she asked, "How are you doing?"

He knew she was referring to Kim and how the Office had decided it was too dangerous to send a plane to pick her up.

"I'm so sorry, Julian. About the plane."

"The weather," he said, needing to say something sensible, but unable, unwilling to pour out his worries in a bar in Mayfair.

"Right up until the last," she murmured. "Right up until the last moment, they might have approved it. I'm just so sorry."

"The German Alps in the snow." He shook his head. "No, we can't send a plane."

She put her hand on his. A light touch, and withdrawn.

"Santa Claus Is Comin' to Town" drifting into the lounge. He nodded at the waiter to bring another round.

THE AERIE

CHRISTMAS EVE, 9:50 PM. Polina set a cup of hot chocolate on her side table and sat on the edge of her bed, pulling her hair onto her breast to plait it into a long braid. How terrible the last two days had been! Irina, frantic with grief, but insisting to go to the Christmas Eve gathering. Poor Evgeny Borisov, dead by his own hands, God rest his soul. He had been a sour, mad old man, but to die like that! And poor Nikolai, crying himself to sleep. And all this among the German barbarians here on this cold mountaintop.

What had the tsarina and old Evgeny fought about two nights ago that he would take such a terrible step?

She shoved her feet into her slippers and went to check on Nikolai as was her custom before bed. Turning on the hallway light—always a miracle, these electric lights—she padded past the tsarina's room, noting a light still under the door. The poor thing, never a good sleeper, now less than ever.

Pushing open Nikolai's door, left ajar for Lev, she crossed the room to his window, pulling the blinds against the stark light of the full moon, appearing now and again through scudding clouds. Moving to the bed to pull up the covers that the tsarevich had tossed off, she stumbled over something, nearly falling.

In the dim light of the room she saw a belt protruding from under the bed. She bent down and tugged on it, finding that it was a strap attached to something. Drawing it out, she saw a knapsack.

By the feel, it appeared to be stuffed with clothes. Slipping her hand inside the flap, she took hold of a book and pulled it out. She could not read the English, but did not need to. It was that dreadful tract by the American writer, Edgar Poe. What on earth Nikolai would want with a knapsack, she did not know, but tomorrow was soon enough to suggest to His Highness that he not leave out things for people to trip on.

As she left, Lev jumped off Nikolai's bed and followed her out.

In the hallway, the tsarina in her dressing gown was waiting for her.

"Polina, my stomach is upset. Perhaps your special peppermint tea?"

"Yes of course, Your Majesty."

A cup of tea that could not have been asked for earlier? When the tsarina went back to her room, Polina allowed herself an exasperated sigh and went downstairs to the kitchen.

As always, when one wished a teakettle to boil, it took twice as long. And now here was the puppy, looking up at her, as though he would be fed at this time of night!

Then up the stairs, and getting Irina settled in bed, and finally her own bed, soft and waiting after such a long day. Christmas Eve, observed only with prayers, except for the small package from Her Majesty, containing the lovely lace handkerchief. A keepsake, for Polina would never wipe her face with a present from the tsarina.

She sipped at her hot chocolate, but it had gone cooler than she liked and seemed too bitter. Her little night table just had room for a lamp and her bible. She placed the cup on the floor, telling herself not to be so clumsy as to kick it over in the morning. No hot chocolate for old Polina tonight, but she was tired, and tomorrow would be busy with a special breakfast for her charges.

† † †

11:37 PM. Kim lay awake listening to Erika snore. Every few minutes she sat up in bed, pressing her face against the window to see if it had begun snowing again, but it had not. More luck. Snow had been a constant worry.

Each time she sat up she pressed her hand against the window to soothe where she had cut it on the champagne flute.

She must not sleep tonight. Annakova would send for her, but when, Kim didn't know. If only she had her Helbros! It would have been a small comfort, and in some way would have anchored her. Hannah had it. She hoped Hannah would remember to bring it tomorrow.

Down the hill at his Festival Hall quarters, von Ritter would be retiring soon. He thought she was under control in her barracks room, watched over by Erika. There was no reason he would be outside now, watching her barracks from the tree line. But if he thought she had the ability to further her plans, he would never have let her spend the night in the relative freedom of the bunkhouse.

Sleep, Erich, sleep. And by breakfast, when people would expect to see me, I will be gone. Having not said goodbye. I am sorry.

She didn't let herself think about all that could go wrong. Hadn't the worst already happened, and it had not been able to touch her? Von Ritter recognizing her at the party. Von Ritter, returning from the dead, the only one who could identify her as SIS. And still, her plans survived. She survived.

The sky was clear, the plane would come. And if it didn't, there would be a car and the forest service road. Hannah had said. By the time the SS found their tracks in the snow outside the tunnel, Kim's group would have a good head start.

The thought came round again: *Erich von Ritter was alive.*

He had not turned her over to the SS. Strange miracles. He had every cause to hate her, but he did not. She thought he loved her, at least a little. But more so, his country. He would do what honor demanded.

As she lay in bed, the moon, that great cold eye, passed through the trees and shone on her bunk. Reaching up, she pressed her palm against the frosted window again. For comfort. To keep from falling asleep.

But lying back down, and despite everything, despite her agitation, she dozed.

A thunderous noise. A pounding on the door. Kim shot up to sitting position, momentarily terrified.

Someone stood in the doorway, the light of the corridor throwing a soldier's form into harsh relief. He barked an order. Erika scrambled from her bed. Outside, it was still full dark.

The soldier said Kim was to come immediately; the tsarina wished to speak with her.

Kim quickly dressed as the soldier waited in the hall.

"Why does she call for you?" Erika asked. "What have you done?"

"She likes to hear stories of America."

"America. Why?"

"Erika, go back to sleep. I'll see you tomorrow."

"But are you in trouble?" Erika's nightmare: to be in trouble with the SS. Of course, that was everyone's nightmare.

"No, don't worry. The tsarina has trouble sleeping, that's all."

Down the hill they went, she and her escort. The snow lay on the compound in an opal sheath, burnished in the bluish, fey light of the moon. At this moment, when her fear might have overtaken her completely—thoughts of the SS waiting for her— she felt nothing but a preternatural calm. Now it would be what it would be. She had done everything that she could, everything that honor demanded, everything that Robert would have done if he had been on a mission and knew the sacrifice required to carry it through.

At the chalet, Annakova answered the door. She dismissed the soldier but beckoned to the one who stood nearest her on the plaza, the one who watched over the chalet.

In halting German she explained that Nora Copeland would sleep on the divan and keep her company tonight because she could not sleep.

The guard nodded a bow. *"Jawohll, Eure Majestät."*

Annakova closed the door. They regarded each other solemnly.

"And so we begin," Annakova said.

"Where is the maid?" Kim asked.

"Upstairs. She sleeps very well tonight with powders in her drink."

Kim looked down the hallway leading to the living room. At her right, the kitchen, and on the left the staircase leading to the upper floor. "Where is the hidden way out, then?"

Annakova led her into the kitchen, where a window looked out toward the garden and the gun emplacement beyond. She pointed to the shed in the midst of the garden.

"When they build lift shaft, they make twice as wide as needful. Then they split shaft. Make two, by building big wall between, of brick and then plaster it over. But only a few know the second one, and that it goes belowground in tunnel to forest."

"Another lift? They will hear the gears."

"No, is stairs. No one hear."

Kim looked out on the small garden, the shed a mere thirty

yards from the bunker where the big guns were trained on the road, manned day and night by soldiers.

Annakova murmured, "Today, I ordered my walkways cleared. It is for safety of His Highness, against falling. They do not see our footsteps leading there."

Kim smiled. "Well done."

Annakova flicked a look at her for dropping the honorific. But her tsarina days were over.

From the porch of his cabin, Captain Adler had watched Nora Copeland escorted to the chalet. He took a last draw on his cigarette and flicked it into the snow.

47

THE AERIE

DECEMBER 25, 4:05 AM. The three of them stood in the dark downstairs hallway of the chalet, out of sight of the stairway.

Annakova supplied a coat for Kim, lined in fur with a hood. Kim sweated in the bulk of it as they waited to set their escape in motion.

"*Maman,*" Nikolai whispered to his mother. Then he remembered to speak English, since she had said they must speak it in front of Nora Copeland. "I did not say goodbye to Lev. I could not find him."

Annakova snapped a look at the stairs, then knelt down in front of him. "Yes, Kolya, is hard. He may be in Polina's room, but we must not wake her." She lifted his knapsack and helped him into it. "So heavy! I did tell you, bring only what is necessary. You have sweater? Extra socks?"

"Yes, *Maman.*"

Their pockets were stuffed with food in case of need. In Kim's jacket, a flashlight provided by Annakova.

It was time.

"I go first?" Annakova asked, confirming what they had discussed, or perhaps putting it off for just another moment. Kim nodded.

"Nikolai, you wait with Nora; when she say it safe to go, you make your way. Very silent."

The boy seemed remarkably calm. Perhaps he would have made a good tsar, Kim thought. A better one than his namesake.

Kim entered the kitchen with its garden door, noting the broom that Annakova had placed against the counter. She peered out the window. The bunker was on higher ground than the chalet and the garden. It made it difficult to see the soldiers and which way they were facing.

Annakova looked to Nikolai and nodded at him. Then she was out the door, moving toward the toolshed. She went slowly, as they had discussed, stepping carefully. Kim saw the shed door opening and closing.

Then Nikolai's turn. As she opened the door for him, his knapsack swiped against the counter, sending a plate crashing to the floor.

He looked up in alarm.

"It's all right. Follow your mother." She pushed him toward the door, opening it softly. "Go." Then he was a gray shadow on the narrow walkway. No alarms from the lookouts.

Kim looked behind her, toward the hall and the stairs. Was Polina awake, or would the sleeping pills make sure that she was not? She couldn't wait any longer. Taking the broom, she slipped out the door, closing it carefully.

The world was cold silver. The sky, a tarnished gray, the

garden in slumbering white, recently dusted by snow. Every
three steps Kim turned and brushed the frosted sidewalk to hide
their footprints. Her face was rigidly cold, but the rest of her
body was bathed in a suffocating warmth. She worked carefully
but fast, her breath catching in her chest unless she commanded
herself to breathe. Her mind, in control of all things, leaving
nothing to chance. Sweep, breathe, sweep. Checking the bunker
for silhouettes—seeing none—she turned into the last, short
stretch to the toolshed. Sweep, breathe, sweep.

Then inside.

Annakova and Nikolai were just lifting the trapdoor lid.
Straw and rags were affixed to the top to disguise the lid outlines when it was shut. Kim moved forward to help them.

4:10 AM. A loud cracking sound had awakened Polina. She
sat up, trying to come fully wake. There was no help for it, she
must go look. She threw off the covers and slid her feet into her
slippers.

She padded to the head of the stairs, ready to shout for the
guards if, incredibly, there was an intruder. But it was probably
Lev getting into mischief. She listened. Nothing further.

Hurrying back to her room to turn on a light, she found the
puppy lying on the floor. It had vomited and lay breathing heavily. The dog, sick all over her carpet!

But then, it could not have been Lev who made the crashing
sound.

She returned to the hallway and knocked lightly on the door
to the tsarina's room. No answer. Opening the door, she found
the bedclothes cast off and her mistress not there. Perhaps she
had gotten up and gone to the kitchen. Polina bustled off to help
her if she was making tea. It was unlikely that she would do

so, but it was the middle of the night and she might not have wanted her old servant disturbed.

Proceeding to the tsarevich's room in order to make sure all was well, she pushed open the door. By the wan light of the moon through the window, she saw that his bed was empty as well. But why would the young master be up? She glanced down to the bed skirt. A terrible surmise began to form in her mind. But no. What a foolish old woman she was! Clearly, neither mother nor son could sleep, and now, the tsarina in the kitchen, fumbling the tea things.

Still, she reached under the bed, slapping the floor as far as she could reach. Then on her hands and knees, bending over, not an easy thing to do. She could see nothing. Heavens, to be so stiff! She struggled to her feet and turned on the bedside lamp. Then down to look again, and no easier this time. She peered under the bed.

The knapsack was gone.

Polina's heart beat so hard she thought she might be having an attack. Holding on to the side of the bed, she lifted herself to her feet and rushed to the stairs, slapping on the hall light as she went. She clambered down the stairs. All in darkness. The great room down the corridor lay in deep shadows.

She turned on the light switch by the kitchen door. A shattered plate lay on the floor. What was happening? It could not be that her mistress had left so suddenly, for what reason would she have left with Nikolai and not summoned Polina to help?

Her hand went to the counter to steady herself. Irina Dimitrievna Annakova had not wanted Polina's help. Because she had poisoned her chocolate. And now the dog had come into her room during the night . . . Hurrying into the great room she turned on all the lights. No one was there.

Mother of God in heaven, they were running from the

Germans. No, that was madness; no one could leave the Aerie
without permission, not even the tsarina.

Her heart thudded as she turned to and fro. At the windows,
she looked out to the veranda. Surely they would be outside,
they would be standing there. But they were not. Polina remembered the night Evgeny had come, and the tsarina was crying,
and she had heard "England" and "my son."

They were running away. A new thought came stabbing at
her. If they were defecting, Polina would be blamed. It was not
believable that they could have fled without the tsarina's attendant taking note. Colonel von Ritter would have her shot. He
had told her to take care of the tsarina, or he would see her suffer
for it. He was, like all the SS, a man without pity. He would bring
her into the yard and make an end of her.

She rushed to the front door, throwing it open. "Guard!" she
shouted in Russian, and then in French. Two guards came rushing down from the plaza. "Colonel von Ritter," she cried. "Tell
him to come immediately!" She did not speak German. "Colonel
von Ritter," she repeated. One guard raced off in the direction
of the Festival Hall, and the other shoved past her and entered
the chalet.

4:20 AM. The shaft smelled of mud and bird droppings. By
the light of the flashlight Kim held, the three of them made their
way down the tight spiral of metal stairs. This was the back
door of the Aerie, paralleling the lift shaft, but leading into the
woods. Through small, deep apertures in the outer wall, bands
of moonlight striped the staircase.

"Kolya, be very careful," Annakova said, turning around to
watch him as he followed her. Kim, at the rear, shined the beam on
their path. At the bottom was the tunnel leading into the woods.

"Be careful, but hurry," Kim said. "When we left, we had an accident. Something crashed to the floor."

"And so? Polina is well asleep tonight."

A strange noise stopped them.

Shadows flicked on the stairs. Looking up at an aperture in the wall, Kim saw a small owl perched, its shadow black against the moonlight-soaked sky. Flapping its wings, it hooted, a forlorn sound. They continued their descent. How strange, for all Evgeny's talk of owls, she had not seen one in the forested stronghold, only here.

As they made their way down the stairs, Nikolai between Kim and Annakova, he turned his head just enough so that Kim could hear him. "Your name is not Nora, is it? If you are a spy, then you have another name."

"Perhaps I do."

"What is your name? And you can call me Nikolai, now that I am not tsarevich anymore." So he knew. Annakova had told him the harsh truth.

"Kolya!" hissed Annakova, as though she still could not accept it.

They might be halfway down. Kim listened with her whole concentration for any sounds from above. Had the maid awakened despite the sleeping pills? It had been a very loud crash. She tried to quicken her steps, but Annakova led the way more slowly.

The owl hooted, turning its face to watch their progress down the steep turns.

Nikolai was waiting for her to answer, and at last she did. "My name is Kim."

Annakova stopped, forcing them all to do the same. "What did you say?"

They could not pause for conversation. Her tone urgent, Kim hissed, "Don't stop. We have to hurry."

Annakova didn't move. "What do you say is your true name?"

"Kim."

"Is a woman's name? Kim?"

"It must be, because it's mine. Now we have to hurry!"

"Where is your home?"

"Uxley."

"Is in England?"

"Yes, in Yorkshire." She was so anxious for them to be moving she almost put a hand to Nikolai's shoulder, to force him to step downward.

Annakova said something to her son in Russian. He sidled by his mother as she flattened herself against the wall, allowing him to pass. When he had disappeared around the curve, the tsarina withdrew a pistol from her coat pocket and aimed it at Kim.

"You lie to me. This escape, a lie."

Kim's chest clutched up in panic.

"You and Stefan. You arrange this."

Shock froze Kim where she stood. "Sir Stefan knows nothing about this."

"You two do not discuss me?" Annakova's voice wavered with emotion. "You two, being lovers?"

What was this madness? It felt more than wrong; it felt like a looming disaster. "We aren't lovers. What are you saying?"

"I say you ruin me. You destroy Nikolai, and all his future. You come here, are in Aerie, because Stefan brings you. So to have a scheme, taking away the throne, taking Russia from me."

"But why would he do this? He obeys Hitler, who needs you. I am with the British!"

"I do not believe. Whatever your country, you come here to

be with him. I leave here, trusting you. And now you take my Stefan."

"Your Majesty, you must know. No one takes Erich Stefan von Ritter. He's for the Nazi cause only."

"Another lie." She cocked the gun. "I am miserable fool." The dark shadow of an owl swept down from the wall and over their heads.

Kim snapped off the flashlight.

But it was not dark. By the moonlight leaking through the slits in the wall, Annakova pointed the pistol at Kim's chest.

The roar of a gun, and Annakova fell backward, crashing headfirst down the steps.

Nikolai's plaintive cry came from far below. *"Maman!"* Kim heard him scrambling up the stairs. Annakova lay slumped and unmoving against the wall.

In terror, Kim turned to see who was coming down the stairs. A man in uniform. Von Ritter.

Annakova lay crumpled and still. Kim looked at him in stunned dismay.

He grabbed her arm and pushed her against the wall, cocking the gun and pressing it to her temple. "Where are you to meet your people? Tell me quickly."

Her chest had constricted so tight she could hardly breathe. She had not imagined dying in a dark shaft, a stony mausoleum. It was over, over.

"Tell me," he hissed. "Or I will kill the child."

She whispered, "At the lake."

"And leaving how?"

"By plane." No hope to protect Hannah. Her only thought: to obey von Ritter so that Nikolai might live. They might kill him anyway, but she wouldn't help them do it.

Keeping a harsh grip on her arm, von Ritter forced her down the stairs, stepping over Annakova's body.

"You killed her," Kim said, bewildered, dumbfounded.

He shrugged. "She was a traitor."

After another turn, Nikolai met them.

"Sir Stefan! Where is my mother?"

"She is dead, as she deserved. You will do as I say, or I will shoot you, too. Move. Quickly!"

Nikolai obeyed. Kim heard sobs, but subdued, as the boy stumbled on down the stairs.

"The Aerie is waking up. They will be coming," von Ritter said.

At the bottom of the staircase, Kim saw the opening to a tunnel, completely black.

"Give me the flashlight," von Ritter said. Kim did so. He switched it on.

He pushed them into a near run down the tunnel, keeping his gun at Kim's neck, Nikolai driven before them. As they rushed, she noted how von Ritter limped, so pronounced, the faster they went.

Von Ritter said, "Tell me the name of the *catalyst*. I know that he is not in England. I believed I had time to persuade you to the truth, but now you force things."

The tunnel, deep-earth dark, was barely wide enough for two people to walk side by side. Von Ritter was close behind her, the gun nudging her neck.

He went on. "We have intelligence intercepts that the British tried to extract a German national. A *catalyst*, yes? Since I know details, I will also know if you are telling the truth. Now you will tell me the name and location of this person, or I will shoot the boy."

He would, she had little doubt.

"I think you do not wish me to kill the boy. You of the tender heart. But I have no such heart."

Yes. His heart: dark through and through, using kindness and brutality to have his way.

The tunnel became an emblem of her mission, pressing on and on in darkness, leading to failure and the silence of the deep earth. "Hannah Linz," she whispered. "She's waiting for me at the lake."

His voice betrayed surprise. "Hannah Linz?"

Nikolai stumbled and fell. Von Ritter yanked him up and pushed him forward.

"Let me help him," Kim hissed. She took Nikolai by the arm and they went forward together.

"Erich," she said as they rushed on. "What will happen to us?"

"Monarch has failed. You turned Annakova, and she has paid the price. There is no reason for you to die too. When I have what I want, you are no further threat."

No reason for you to die. He was letting her go. Hope rushed back to fill the space that had moments before been filled with despair. "Are you going to escape too? Leave here with us?"

His voice from close behind. "Of course I am not. What time does the plane come?"

"By 7:30."

"You cannot wait that long. Soldiers are twenty minutes behind us, perhaps less. What was your backup plan? You had one?"

"There is a service road to the lake. A truck."

"They will be waiting for you at the bottom of the road."

"Not if we move fast enough." They rushed on.

Beams supported the walls and ceiling. Their boots splashed through small pools of water, some with a scrim of ice.

Von Ritter pushed them onward. "I cannot let you have Linz. You will deliver her to me, and if you do, you and the boy may leave. If you can forgive yourself for this bargain, you may go with him. If not, the SS awaits. And they will take everything from you. Your information, your pride, your life."

So this was the final ordeal: she would be forced to betray Hannah.

Letting go of Nikolai's arm, she stopped. Turning to von Ritter she said, "Erich, please. I beg you."

Von Ritter pushed her against the wall, the flashlight pressing cruelly against her neck. "Please what?" he hissed. "You cannot beg me for more. You have nothing to offer. You are a lowly spy who consorts with terrorist Jews, and who pays back my mercy with many lies."

Her voice was a thin rasp. "Please do not take Hannah."

His laugh was short but full of mirth. "Oh, I will take her." Yanking his arm away from her throat, he pushed the two of them on.

4:40 AM. Every light was on in the compound. Juergen Becht watched as the SS formed into their units in the plaza. Some units had rushed to the lift. No one knew the threat, only that it was imminent. Soldiers swarmed around the chalet.

His mind darkened with fury. If anything had happened to Her Majesty . . .

Commandant Bassman and his lieutenants appeared from the Hall and strode past the milling soldiers and through the plaza, disappearing into the chalet. After a few minutes, Bassman appeared again, this time in the small yard between the chalet and the bunker. He went to the toolshed. Soon he was back in the yard, but a unit of SS began disappearing into the garden shed.

So. Another way out. There had always been rumors.

Then the plaza went dark. Every light in the large square between the Festival Hall and the chalet was extinguished. Several SS ran into the hall, and there, too, lights began to disappear. They wished to thwart an attack by air. Surely no one would dare make an air strike against Germany, but they took no chances.

The moon that had flooded the night sky was just setting behind the mountain, leaving the Aerie in true darkness.

Becht saw with disgust that there was a queue of soldiers waiting for the lift. That no one had thought of that! If the threat came from outside the Aerie, there was no way to bring a force of superior numbers to bear, not quickly.

And speed might be of the essence.

48

4:45 AM. The tunnel ended in a metal door. Von Ritter pulled away the heavy bar that kept it barricaded. When he shoved open the door, a dull glow flooded over them. In the predawn, patchy snow reflected a gray light, poking soft fingers of pain into Kim's eyes.

The three of them emerged from the tunnel door. Kim pointed down the hillside. "We follow the ridgeline down the valley."

Von Ritter told her to carry the flashlight and gestured them on. There was only the crunch of their footfalls through the snow and the sweep of the wind, high and intermittent in the trees.

Nikolai went forward, stunned and silent, a small, hunched child carrying his little knapsack with the extra socks that his mother had told him to pack. Irina Annakova, dead on the stairs of the shaft. She had finally seen the error of siding with the Nazis, but Kim had no pity for her, only for Nikolai. And for Hannah.

She knew that the lake was nestled below in a broad valley lying west of a prominent ridge. Hannah and she had studied the topographical map with great care, but here in the darkness, all they could do was make their way down the steep hillside. It was hard going amid thick underbrush camouflaged by pockets of snow. Von Ritter half dragged Nikolai along, as the boy struggled to make his way.

The world was only trees and black, frozen ground. Nothing was familiar. On their left was a ridge; all ridges here led to the lake.

In the east, the mountains began to show a ragged profile. Although the moon had set, leaving them in the shadowy forest precincts, a false dawn now pushed up against the night.

So close to the ridge, she couldn't see the Aerie. They tramped onward, weaving their way to avoid humps of snow that hid fallen logs and boulders. It was slow going, their tracks obvious to any who followed them. The wind scoured over the tops of the trees, sending down light cascades of snow. Already they were wet, especially von Ritter, who wore only his uniform.

He spotted the lake first, pointing in silence. A broad oval in the valley bottom, its surface unblemished. She and Hannah couldn't wait for dawn and the airplane. The SS would arrive momentarily.

As they descended the last slope to the lake, Nikolai lost his footing and fell, sliding a few yards on his backside. He got to his hands and knees, but would go no farther.

Kim hurried to his side. "Nikolai, get up."

"I can't."

"You can. You must."

He stood, gazing at the lake. Kim saw that there was a hut by the lake's edge. A light flashed from it. Hannah.

Kim started down, but Nikolai sat on the ground. "I can't walk any more. Besides, there is no airplane."

"It doesn't matter! There is a forest road and a motorcar."

Von Ritter watched them. His gun had been in his holster, but now he drew it out. "Move." He gestured for Kim to continue.

At last she managed to pull Nikolai to his feet, and they went the last hundred yards to the lakeside. They paused for a moment, as Kim waited for von Ritter to say how they would proceed. Hannah must come out. But when capture was unavoidable, Hannah would kill herself. The thought, dark and chilling.

Two lone fir trees stood sentinel nearby. Von Ritter led them there, taking refuge behind the larger one. Nikolai sat in the snow, his head between his knees, his knapsack a lump near his feet, a picture of despair.

"Tell Hannah Linz to come out," von Ritter said.

"And you will let me take Nikolai?"

"I have no need to lie to you. Take your motorcar, if it is there."

"And if it isn't?"

"Then you are lost anyway. And so am I. Leave quickly. I will say I got here too late to prevent you. But if we are all here when they arrive . . ." He shrugged.

Hannah came out of the hut. She flashed the light, thinking Kim still had not seen her.

An ear-ringing crack of a gun. Kim spun around to see who had come upon them. No one on the slope.

But von Ritter braced a hand against the tree and sank to his knees.

Then she focused on Nikolai. He stood there, a pearl-handled revolver in his hand.

Von Ritter was wounded. He slid down the tree into a sitting position.

Nikolai's voice was soft but clear. "He killed the tsarina. He killed my mother."

Kim went to von Ritter's side, unable to see how critical his wound was. But she knew already that it was bad, because her senses were filled with the smell of warm, coppery blood.

He rested his head against the tree trunk, his gun still in his grip. Kneeling by his side, she saw blood seeping out from von Ritter's jacket closure.

He looked at Kim, trying to speak. Finally he managed, "Kim. Take . . . my gun."

She took it, placing it in her lap. His eyes went to slits.

His voice, very soft. "Use the gun. If they find you, you will die slowly. It does not hurt if you . . . aim well." His blood pumped hard, and his eyes closed. Dying. He was dying.

"Take it," von Ritter repeated, unable to feel that she had already done so.

"I have it, Erich," she whispered. "I will use it if they come."

She heard Hannah nearby, saying something to Nikolai.

Bending close to von Ritter so that he could hear, Kim said, "Another time, a different country, we wouldn't have been against each other."

A small smile. "Another time, Kim. Perhaps you will . . . follow me."

"Yes, Erich." Her thoughts had gone slow and dark. "Perhaps I will."

He closed his eyes. His head fell forward. Gone. Erich von Ritter was dead.

Hannah came over to them. "I know that one," she said, shrugging. "He was SS."

Kim stood, leaning against the rough bark of the tree to anchor herself. "They are coming," she said softly. "Our escape went badly. They know we ran." The brutal night was about to turn into the brutal day.

"And what of Annakova?"

Kim cut a glance at Nikolai and shook her head.

Hannah nodded and pointed away. "Let's go." Her head jerked up as she saw something on the hillside.

"They're here."

On the slope, a line of soldiers in black, snaking down the steep face of the ridge. The *Nachkommenschaft*.

Swearing under her breath, Hannah said, "We can't get to the truck! The road is on the other side of the lake. They'll see us and open fire."

Hannah grabbed Nikolai by the arm and the three of them began to run into the woods, away from the hut and the lake.

Kim thrust von Ritter's gun in her pocket as she ran. "But where can we go?"

"I don't know," Hannah said. "Find a place with some cover. Fight them. For a while."

Their alternate plan of the service road now abandoned.

Dawn came on relentlessly. They would be easy to spot now, but with no gunfire, perhaps they hadn't yet been seen.

"They will see our footsteps in the snow," Kim said.

"I made tracks all over the lakeside. It will confuse them for a little."

Once they were deep in the woods, they stopped to catch their breath. Around them, the sharp smells of pine sap and needles.

Nikolai sat on a fallen log, looking lost.

Hannah drew Kim aside. "When they come, do we let them have him?" Alive, Hannah meant.

"Yes." Maybe they would try to make him tsar. She doubted it, but there was still that chance. The odds were always bad, trying to imagine what Hitler would do.

Hannah placed her hand on Kim's arm. "It is over. I am sorry."

"Oh, Hannah." Kim took in a deep breath of cleansing cold air. "But we did it. We stopped them."

"I know. I am proud of this, very proud. But I am sorry that it ends this way."

Kim was facing the slope up to the tunnel. Just visible between the trees, the *Nachkommen* working their way down, carrying automatic weapons that at this distance looked like black sticks.

Yes, it was over. No other plan. Over because they were only two women and an eleven-year-old boy vastly outnumbered by trained German soldiers. The summary did not sound promising.

And yet.

They were armed. No matter what happened, they were not without a fighting chance. Kim had been preoccupied for the last hour with the threat of von Ritter killing her, killing the boy, but now . . .

From someplace deep inside, the strength of her Talent surged through her. Flooding her mind, a conviction: she could not die here, would not die this way. It might be an unnatural rapture, a false sense of mastery, but there was, she felt, one more chance.

Kim gazed steadily at Hannah. "We're not giving up. We have to keep moving."

Hannah snorted. "Move where?"

"The road. The main road. Tannhäuser is coming with a car." At dawn, he'd said; still two hours away. But now that the Aerie was alerted, he might be leaving early.

"You are not thinking straight. The SS are everywhere and watching the road especially!" She grabbed Kim by the shoulders. "How far did Annakova take you? 8? 9?"

A short laugh escaped Kim's lips. "A 10, Annakova guessed." She saw Hannah's incredulous look. "The road, Hannah." She pointed east, where the valley sloped up to the main road.

Kim rushed over to Nikolai and pulled him to his feet.

A boom in the distance.

"What was that?" Hannah asked.

"I don't know," Kim said. It sounded as though it came from the Aerie.

She set out with Nikolai, hoping Hannah would follow. At last she did, bringing up the rear, but turning to gauge when the soldiers would overtake them.

5:05 AM. Adler finally made it down in the lift with four other soldiers. The moment they exited the lift carriage, one of the soldiers pushed the button to return it to the top.

Bassman had ordered Adler to collect four or five others and reinforce the new control point that they were setting up outside of Tolzried.

They rushed into the car park, with Adler making sure he was in the lead. Soldiers had formed a barricade butted up against the cliff, MG-34s trained on the road and surrounding forest. He made for the last motorcar left, the one that he had disabled so that at least one would be left. As Lieutenant Hoff tried to start the engine, it did not turn over.

Sitting in the front seat with the driver, Adler leaned in

close to the dashboard, pretending to make a discovery. He pointed to the loose wires, and Hoff spent several frantic moments connecting them to the ignition. When the connection took hold, they roared away from the Aerie. At the intake center control point, they stopped as a guard looked into the car. He waved them on.

The road with its walls of trees was still dark. When they had gone far enough that no sounds would draw undue attention, he called for his driver to stop the car near an overgrown forest service road.

"Light!" he barked. "Up there. Someone with a flashlight."

"One of ours, Captain?"

"No. Pull off the road farther." The side road was impassable, but it afforded a parking place, and one that had a chance of not being spotted from the road. Cutting a look at Adler, Lieutenant Hoff pulled the car to a stop.

"Silence," Adler ordered the men. He got out, gently clicking the door shut, and the others followed suit. "Fan out." He pointed to right and left, and the group split up, Adler with a corporal.

After two or three minutes, the others were out of sight.

"There, at the top of the hill. You see?" Adler pointed. As the corporal peered into the darkness, Adler shot him in the back of the head.

"Over here!" he called to the others to get them running toward him, into his trap.

When he had finished them off, he would walk toward the lake, hoping to find Nora Copeland. But if not, he would return to the car and drive down the mountain and effect his escape, alone.

† † †

5:10 AM. Black forms stalked the forest. Submachine guns strapped around their necks, they slowly paced through the woods, appearing now and again in the near distance, then disappearing behind rocks or the black pines.

The trees afforded Kim and her companions cover, and they moved from tree to tree, with Kim leading the way, choosing a path east, toward the main road.

Hannah had spent the night making tracks around the hut and in various directions into the trees, so, until daylight made clear it was a ruse, the *Nachkommen* and the other SS among them were thinly spaced.

Kim pressed her body close to a fir tree, its sap sharp in her nostrils. She held von Ritter's gun. *Perhaps you will follow me.* The moments they had spent by the lake had been expensive. While von Ritter lay dying, she had stayed, and that might have made the difference now, with the *Nachkommen* moving through the woods.

She wouldn't have left him dying alone in the trees. Even though he had forced her to give up Hannah's location, that terrible betrayal, she would not have abandoned him. More fool, she. But he had tried to give her a chance to leave. She believed he would have done so because he had let her go once before, at Rievaulx. He had been sitting against one of the fallen stones of the abbey and said they would die together. Then, impossibly, he decided to let her go. He stayed behind with his gun. The shot rang out . . .

A dozen feet away, a *Nachkomme* stepped out from behind a tree. His long face, turning, turning.

He smelled her.

She pointed her gun up, to keep her profile small, protected by the tree.

The fiend came into view, head down, following her tracks in the snow. Closer to the lake, there had been tracks everywhere, but here, it could only be his quarry.

From the direction of the road, the sound of a gunshot.

The *Nachkomme*'s head came up, alert. Turning in her direction, he spotted her.

He shouted a command in German.

Kim stepped out. She still held her gun, pointing it in the air, as though surrendering, but ready to bring it down to take her shot. Then she saw Hannah behind him.

Kim dropped her weapon to the ground, playing for time.

Hannah stepped forward and plunged a knife into his back. He fell forward, sprawling. Like a fiend herself, Hannah jumped on his body, yanking the knife out and using it on his throat to finish the job.

Kim grabbed her gun from the snow. She saw that Nikolai stood to one side, lowering his pearl-handled revolver, which he had apparently been pointing at the man.

Hannah stripped the submachine gun off the *Nachkomme* and pulled the sling over her head.

"Hurry!" Hannah said, and they rushed up a ridge, Nikolai in tow, leaving tracks more clearly than ever in the snow that had drifted deeper here.

They clambered up the slope. "I thought you took Nikolai's gun," Kim said.

"Why? He is a good shot."

They topped the ridge. An SS officer crouched behind a massive rock. "Nora," he said. He came out.

Hannah took aim, but Kim pushed her hand down. "It's Tannhäuser." Pocketing her weapon, Kim walked toward him.

"I have a car," Adler said. He glanced at Hannah and Nikolai. "The trunk. It only has room for two."

Kim turned to Hannah. "You go with him." England had more need of her, a *catalyst*, than they had of a spy who didn't follow orders.

Hannah shook her head. "I am going back."

"Back?" Kim asked. Back to a valley filled with *Nachkommen*?

"Remember that I told you that a Nazi murdered my father?" Numbly, Kim nodded. "He is down there in the forest."

"Hannah, don't do this. I won't let you."

A smile, half affectionate, half ironic. "As you have seen, I tend to be disobedient."

Kim wondered if she could bear losing this friend. Lamely, desperately, she threw out, "Your father wouldn't have wanted revenge."

"But my father is dead. Now it is about what *I* want."

A noise from behind her. Kim saw that Adler had taken a step toward Nikolai.

"They want the boy for their Russian plans," Adler said, "now that his mother is dead. We cannot allow that."

Kim rushed over to Nikolai, pulling him in back of her. "They can't have him."

"No? Well, there is only one way to be sure." He fingered his gun.

"Captain," she said. "He goes to England."

They faced off. Adler hissed, "You do not know what you are doing."

"He's coming with me."

Adler shook his head in frustration, holstering his gun.

When Kim turned back to Hannah, she was already striding down the side of the ridge. Without looking back, Hannah lifted her hand in farewell.

49

THE VALLEY BELOW THE AERIE

5:20 AM. At the top of a low, scrub-covered hillside, Kim and Adler watched the road. A towering cloud of black smoke had risen high above the Aerie, although they couldn't see the compound from there. The wind had sheared off the smoke into an anvil-shaped cloud, black against the pewter sky.

"I left them a Christmas present," Adler said. "Strong enough to take out the front of the Festival Hall. Perhaps it helps." He went on. "I have a safe place in the village. We will change cars there."

"There will be soldiers everywhere."

"No more so than here." He yanked open the trunk of the car and gestured for her to get in. He would brook no more opposition. "I have had months to think it through. A change of clothes, and we take a mountain road into Switzerland. They have not had time to set up checkpoints everywhere yet. Get in."

She looked at Nikolai. He nodded, eyes trusting, exhausted.
They crawled into the empty trunk.

"No talking," Adler said. "Not even a whisper." The lid
slammed over them.

Then they were on the road, moving very fast. Nestled in
her arms, Nikolai, his knapsack underneath his head for a pillow.
Her heart, already scraped and bruised, ached anew for Hannah.
Had she really seen the *Nachkomme* who had killed her father?

Or had she just wanted to make room in the trunk?

She remembered asking Hannah how all this striving would
end, and she had answered, *When they kill me.* Then Evgeny's
words came to her, how he had said Hannah was the one who
was truly broken. Perhaps only the broken ones could carry out
the darkest missions, those in which no one would survive.

They swayed as the car rounded a curve. Kim hugged Nikolai tighter to keep him from rolling into the metal sides of the
trunk.

5:25 AM. Hannah made her way down the hill, into the patch
of forest where the *Nachkommen* were methodically hunting.

She had seen Juergen Becht just before the other *Nachkomme*
called Kim out and Hannah had used her knife on him. Becht's
was a face she could not forget; the long scar splitting his right
cheek from eye to chin. His face, impressed on her memory, not
from those confused minutes in her home's parlor, but from the
terrible screen, the flickering light of the cinema. He was a man
needing death. She would give it to him.

The forest was strangely silent. She walked carefully, placing her feet tentatively before giving them her full weight. Her
senses on alert, the submachine gun held at the ready, she swiveled from side to side, watching for the slightest movement.

The predawn twilight grew stronger, a wan light finally making it to the forest floor. Her eyes watered as she strained to see any movements, hardly daring to blink.

She saw no one. Perhaps, with the explosion at the Aerie, the soldiers had been ordered back. But what would they be protecting? The Russian witch was dead, her son fled from the compound.

Using the larger trees as cover, she moved onward.

Then she saw him. He had been crouching down looking at something in the snow, and she caught his movement as he stood up. A short burst from her weapon sent him flying. Rushing up to finish him off, she saw there was no need. His face was half torn off. The good half.

Blood speckled the snow.

She backed away, watching for the *Nachkommen* who would have heard the machine gun burst. The forest was eerily silent after the burst of gunfire.

Where were they?

Slipping quickly through the trees, she put distance between herself and those who were sure to come.

If they did come . . . Well. She had an extra clip for the machine gun. Because she knew there could be many black forms converging. Let them come. She would lead them on a merry chase.

From tree to tree. Dances with demons.

5:41 AM. In the trunk, Kim sensed that the car was slowing down. Her throat was sticky and tight, preventing her from swallowing. She stroked the hair on Nikolai's head, calming him. He was shaking so hard he might draw attention. Voices, speaking German. She couldn't make out what they were saying.

Nikolai's hand found hers and they held on to each other.

Then, to her immeasurable joy, the car got underway again.

Switzerland. They were going to Switzerland. With just a little more luck. But in case luck ran out, she was armed. *Hannah*, she thought, *you could have been the one to leave. I promised to bring you home.*

Terror had driven lesser feelings out of reach. Thoughts came unraveled and reformed—memories of the last hours.

Erich von Ritter. Her enemy, who had helped her escape at a terrible price for himself. His entrance into the Great Hall with Irina Annakova on his arm. The embrace in his quarters. Under the tree, blood welling through his jacket. *Kim, you are my undoing*, he had said. And so it was. Underneath it all, the thought that Erich von Ritter had loved her, perhaps even past honor.

The car made a turn. Then another. She heard Adler shut the driver's-side door. She heard the trunk latch release, and the lid came up. Fresh, frigid air.

They were in a small barn.

Adler helped her and Nikolai out. "There is a control point at the bottom of the forest road. More soldiers are arriving to set up other checkpoints. We must leave here before the highway is blocked."

He opened a box on a shelf and began removing civilian clothes. "I have to change. You can use the toilet through the door over there."

Kim pulled a sandwich out of her pocket and gave half of it to Nikolai. He sat on the floor of the barn and looked doubtfully at it, but soon was hungrily eating.

The door led into a small farmhouse, dusty from lack of use. She found the toilet and cleaned herself up.

Coming back into the barn, she found Adler dressed in a wool cap, stout boots, and a loose wool jacket over baggy trousers. He looked like a different person without the powerful, emblematic SS uniform. She handed him her half of the sandwich.

He pulled the meat out of the sandwich and gave it to her, keeping the bread.

Within another minute they were in an old pickup, its cargo area loaded with a chest of drawers and a cardboard-sided suitcase for show.

The sound of the motor coming to life was a great, rumbling, thrilling sound.

When Kim opened the barn door, he drove the pickup out. Closing the door on the Mercedes, she hopped in next to him, Nikolai between them. They drove down the deserted street, their thin cover agreed upon, that they were a German family up before dawn to make a trip to Zurich.

In the middle of the village, a commotion. Two trucks had collided, and men were crowded around them, voices raised, flashlights slashing the air.

"This is trouble," Adler said under his breath. The accident was on the main roadway north and south that went through the village. They were blocked.

Adler began to back up, intending to find a new route, but a car had come up behind them. They had to move forward. Closer to the scene, they saw that one of the trucks with an open bed and high sides had spilled an enormous load of potatoes onto the roadway. Several soldiers were directing villagers to shovel it clear.

"It will take an hour!" Kim whispered.

"They are concentrating on the lake, but soon they will complete a more thorough cordon. We cannot wait an hour."

"Nikolai and I are getting out," Kim said.

"Do not be a fool. Where would you go?"

"Back to the farmhouse."

"Everywhere will be searched. Just wait and see."

"I'm not—"

She fell silent, focusing on the largest truck, the one that had lost the siding from its flatbed. Through the windshield she saw flowers. Flowers in a vase secured on the dashboard.

Under the shouted orders of the soldiers, the workers continued to shovel, throwing the potatoes into the ditch. A man stood beside the truck, shaking his head as he watched his cargo being thrown away. She saw him gesturing with one of the soldiers, pleading the case of his ruined delivery.

"I know that man," Kim said.

"Then pull up your hood."

"No. I need to get his attention. He's come for me." She looked at Adler, her heart thudding heavily. "For us."

"Who could be coming for us?"

"Duncan."

"Who?"

Kim felt a smile cut across her face. "The British government."

In another minute Adler pulled down his cap very far on his head and stepped out of the car. He approached the truck driver and they spoke briefly, the driver shaking his head and spreading his arms at the mess on the road.

Kim had told Adler to say, "I'll trade you a Sparrow for a few potatoes."

The car behind them that had been blocking their way backed up on the road just enough to allow Adler to do so as well. At the first widening of the road, both cars turned around. As he had been hastily instructed, Adler followed this car down several winding streets until they approached a hay truck parked in an empty lot.

Someone opened the door on Kim's side of the pickup, and a sandy-haired young man looked in at her. "Good day to you," he said. "Just hop out and we'll get you in the hay wagon."

Kim and Nikolai crawled out of the car. She resisted an urge to throw her arms around the fellow. "You know they'll search a hay truck," she said.

"Not this one, they won't." He grinned and gestured her toward the back of the flatbed. "We're north of the truck accident. We'll be on our way before the mess is cleared away."

In what was starting to reveal itself as a smoothly choreographed sequence of actions, another man appeared to take charge of Adler's pickup, driving it off.

"How did you know when to have the truck accident?" It was two hours earlier than Kim had said they'd be escaping.

"We had several accidents planned. When we heard the explosion, we set one of them in motion." He lifted up a flap of tarp, revealing rolls of tightly baled hay. Pulling the false front from one bale, he uncovered a gaping hole.

"There are three of us," Kim said, instantly worried.

"Yes, ma'am. I can count." He lifted Nikolai up and urged him inside. Adler went next.

The young man said, "We thought there'd be another woman."

"There was." Kim looked in the direction of the Aerie and the forest-clad lower slopes. "There *is* another woman."

"Where is she?"

Kim stared into the distance, trying to conjure scenarios where Hannah might live.

"You have to leave now, ma'am."

Turning back to him, she said, "Call me Sparrow."

She was SIS, and even if it was just for a little while longer, she wanted her code name.

"Sparrow. Right you are," he said.

"And watch for the other woman."

Adler was waiting, crouching in the passageway. He extended a hand to help her up. She took it, and then the false front of the bale slammed shut.

Kim and Nikolai slept on blankets smelling of horses and dust. After a time, sunshine found cracks in the hay bales, stabbing at her eyes, forcing her to keep them shut. Now and then she saw Dietrich Adler seated on a bale, smoking a cigarette. Once she thought it was von Ritter, until she remembered it could not be.

At some point they were herded out of the wagon and rushed across a field to a waiting airplane.

On board, seated next to Kim, Nikolai said, "I have never been in an airplane."

"Neither have I."

The plane taxied, and in a long glide eventually managed to take to the air.

Nikolai leaned in to her, to speak above the roar of the plane. "They don't have to call me Your Highness anymore, do they?" His tone was flat, just checking out the new protocols.

"That's true. Is it all right with you, Nikolai?"

"Yes. It would have been very dangerous to be tsar."

Kim took his hand, and he gripped it tightly as they watched the fields grow small beneath them.

† † †

Duncan had deployed his assets throughout the village and in blinds along the road. The Nazis were still looking for a woman with short black hair who might be accompanied by a young boy, but Duncan and his men were watching for a woman in a brown parka.

In the empty house the Office had taken over in the village, one of his men brought in a woman wearing a gray plaid coat and a blue scarf. Not the garb they had been expecting, but she had apparently found different clothes and had convinced Duncan's man of who she was.

"So you are Hannah," Duncan said, thinking about how much trouble she had caused and how poorly he had handled things.

She pulled off the headscarf, revealing bright red hair. "Yes. And I hope you have a good plan for getting out of here."

Duncan gazed at this small, pale woman who looked half-starved and had a faint blood smear on her forehead.

"We do indeed."

50

FRIDAY, JANUARY 8, 1937. Kim sat at a long table in the center of a windowless conference room. By a lamp on the table, she saw that she was facing four men. She didn't recognize any them—not that in the clandestine services she would—and they had not been introduced.

Along the wall, out of the lamplight, several chairs. One of them was occupied, the person's face in shadow. She suspected it was the chief himself, the man called E.

It was the third time she had relayed the sequence of events and her actions in Germany. Once had been to Julian, alone in a hospital room where she had rested for two days and undergone tests. The second time was to a two-man team that recorded her narration in an all-day session.

This time she had the feeling she was relating everything again for the man who sat in the shadows. She had been perfectly candid except for a few details of the meeting in the Festival Hall with Erich von Ritter. The embrace. That wouldn't have gone over, not at all, and she wasn't sure how to explain it.

Another question came at her. "Isn't it possible that Alex Reed was told of your being at the Wittenberge train station because they were fishing for intel on you, and knew Reed socially?"

The questions all came from the one with the thick glasses.

Kim knew they were eager to absolve Alex Reed of jeopardizing her cover. He was in line to be first secretary for trade, and the "niece in London" incident was awkward. The story they preferred was that Alex had been the innocent recipient of news from Gestapo acquaintances derived from a routine check at a train station; news that Alex's wife had mentioned a niece in London.

Doggedly, Kim answered the leading question. "Alex told me that a man I saw him talking to was with the German Automotive Association, but I discovered a business card revealing that he was Gestapo. Alex spent some time with this agent on a porch at the Belgian embassy Christmas party. Why would he lie about the man's identity if he was merely a social contact?"

Her interrogator consulted his file. Kim had the impression that he wasn't really listening but rather going through a formality of an interview. Who were the others? The deputy chief of SIS? Representatives from the Foreign Office?

"How would you characterize your relationship with Alex Reed before you began to suspect his involvement with the Gestapo?"

"He distrusted my role and made clear his concern that I would sour his political relationships with Nazi officials if my undercover mission was breached. We didn't trust each other after Hannah Linz appealed to me for extraction. I began to feel that the house on the Tiergartenstrasse wasn't safe."

"And you also didn't trust your handler at the Berlin station."

"I had doubts. More importantly, Hannah Linz didn't trust him. She assumed the intelligence service wouldn't back her. By the time you approved extraction, she had lost faith in British involvement. She revealed details of the Monarch operation to me and said she would work only with me. I had a few hours to decide whether to walk away or exploit this opportunity to infiltrate the Aerie. I saw that I didn't have much support." *From any of you*, she wanted to add, and didn't. Even before she had taken the mission into her own hands, the Berlin station hadn't backed her, and London had stepped up too late to make a difference with Hannah.

Although it was true that on Christmas Day they had infiltrated the village and brought a hay truck.

Her interrogator moved on. "What do you think would have happened if Hannah Linz hadn't been able to bring you to a level 7 to allow you access into the Aerie?"

"They would have sent me home."

"Or eliminated you."

She shrugged. Death was a possibility in some missions. These men knew that.

"Therefore, without proof of any kind you went to the Aerie, trusting her story of *catalysis*. Risking your life."

You're welcome, you pompous, self-justifying bastard.

He added for good measure: "Risking a diplomatic incident of the highest order."

"Where would we be now if I had turned her away? The Nazis would still have Irina Annakova, and her *Nachkommenschaft* would be undermining and spreading chaos among our closest allies."

"They are no doubt already at their posts."

"But they can't be sustained. Without Irina Annakova, their powers will fade. I attempted to bring her out, but she died during the escape. And now you have Hannah Linz." They had told her that much. Kim imagined Owen Cherwell's delight in having an entirely new Talent to calibrate at Monkton Hall.

"Is Hannah undergoing testing?" She did wonder how you tested for *catalysis*, other than submitting another Talent to the infecting touch, and then watching them become unbearably confident and unable to eat biscuits.

"We won't be discussing that."

"But you admit she's a valuable asset?" She didn't expect they would discuss that, either. Surely the men in this room couldn't still be thinking that Hannah Linz was just a Jewish agitator misled by conspiracy theories. She had played a central role in disabling Monarch.

As her questioners began to close their files, she brought forward her final piece of intel. "The house the embassy found for Alex Reed and me in Berlin was very likely a Jewish home that had been hastily confiscated by the German authorities. A man and wife and an infant lived there. They left all their possessions behind." Hopelessly, she added, "I thought you might want to look into that. How embassy staff are taking advantage of"—she let sarcasm creep in—"*the Jewish problem.*"

Silence greeted this. The man in glasses put his pen in his shirt pocket.

From the shadows along the wall came a voice. "How are your symptoms from the *catalyst* treatments you underwent?"

It was the first time an official other than a doctor had asked her this. "I feel like I've drunk too much coffee. I'm experiencing a high degree of irritation at the reception I've received here. At the same time, I don't trust my own perceptions, at least not my logical thoughts. To the extent that they *are* logical. I still crave rare meat."

Shuffling around the table. They hated that part.

Now that she had been given permission to describe the results of her nearly disastrous augmentations, she had a little more to say. "People tell me things. More than ever. Things that are very hard to ignore and apparently ruinous to act upon, even in the clear interest of His Majesty's Government."

She looked over at the shadow. "Also, I have trouble eating." And sleeping. Awful, dark dreams of the *Nachkommenschaft.* "I'd like to go home. Until . . . I'm feeling normal again."

Her interrogator with the glasses said, "When do you think that will be?"

"In ten weeks." But whether her symptoms and her ability would subside gradually or steeply at the end, she didn't know.

"Will I be able to see Hannah?"

"I'm afraid not." The man in glasses again.

"What about Captain Adler?"

"He is being resettled here. With our gratitude."

She was glad they were grateful for *something*.

"And Annakova's son, Nikolai?"

"He'll be placed with a Russian family here. It's best if you have no further contact."

The voice from the shadows spoke softly. "What is your interest in the boy?"

"I made a promise to protect him."

The shadow voice again. "A promise about a Russian child you hardly knew."

Her anger lay just behind her teeth. If she opened her mouth, she'd be saying things no one wanted to hear. What the hell. "Yes, I hardly knew him. But Evgeny Borisov helped me convince Irina Annakova to turn. A man whose *precognition* ability caused him immeasurable pain, and who loved the boy and his mother. Before he swallowed rat poison, he wanted to know that someone would look out for the child."

After a long, uncomfortable pause, the interrogator pulled the file together and closed it. "I think we are done, here." He fixed her with pitying look. "You have several important and bravely executed missions to your credit. For those, we owe you a debt of gratitude."

Sturmweg on the North York Moors; *Nachteule* in Wales. Probably he didn't mean Monarch in the Bavarian Alps.

The voice in the shadows said, "I agree, we've heard enough." He paused, and the men at the table put down their pens and turned to him.

"I think you've earned a rest, Sparrow."

"Thank you for listening to me." She gathered her purse and gloves. "I didn't actually think you would."

"When you've recovered, I'd like to see you back here."

Kim stared in the direction of the man at the sidelines whose features she couldn't see.

The interrogator flattened his mouth, probably restraining a comment that would love to get out.

Had E just confirmed that she still had her job? She sat quietly, trying to absorb this, but his words kept bouncing off her heart. The bullet wound in her shoulder ached. She thought of Erich von Ritter dying as he sat against the tree. Her emotions were awash in things that were over and done with but that lived on.

"You don't have to answer now. When you trust your

judgment again, you can decide if you'd like to stay."

"I'll just be a 6 for the *spill*," she reminded him.

"Quite enough, Sparrow. Quite enough."

ON THE WAY TO WRENFELL HOUSE

SATURDAY, JANUARY 9. Kim was pleasantly surprised that Julian had arranged a car hire for the trip home instead of going by train. But for once neither of them was in a hurry. Their food was packed. Someone at the Office had put together lunches for both of them, assuring that Kim would have nourishment of the sort she needed.

Julian had decided to retire, saying it was a young man's game. Another factor: some of the higher-ups had taken notice of his privileged position with E, and he didn't care for how he was being second-guessed. "It's time anyway, Kim," he assured her. In the face of what seemed a remarkable cheerfulness on his part, she set aside her immediate reaction of distress. Her father was sixty-three; not old, but the service took its toll. She felt there was more to come on this topic. And with a long stint together at Wrenfell, there would be plenty of time.

Still, it was the changing of the guard for the Tavistock household, and she felt it acutely. How impossible this would have seemed a year ago. So many ways that was true. As Julian drove, she looked over at him with a great welling in her heart.

Before they had set out, he had given her an envelope. Inside, her watch. No note. Of course they wouldn't have let Hannah include a note. Kim put on the watch, rubbing her forefinger against the crystal, thinking of Hannah saying goodbye and wishing it could be in person. Kim's diamond ring from her cover marriage was no doubt by now the property of His Majesty's Government.

They drove north. For the first two hours, Kim had told him a more detailed story of Berlin, Hannah Linz, and the Aerie. He didn't interrupt except for the occasional "Mmm," his understated way of reacting to the most outrageous things. A few times he reached down to put a gentle pressure on her hand.

"I hope you won't treat me like an invalid," she said, but put a smile with it.

"Not at all."

"And especially not a demented invalid."

"Of course"

"But if I do seem—off-kilter—at any point, you *will* tell me?"

He shot an ironic look at her. "Three months, maximum. Then no excuses."

"Agreed."

"I don't suppose you met Hannah Linz," she said, probing for any lingering connections to that extraordinary woman.

"No. I wish I could have done."

Ironically, the service had made the assumption that she was letting her heart lead her in relation to Hannah. Yet when the mission was over, one was presumed to have no feelings in the matter. There was a time for heart and a time to refrain, she knew this. But sometimes caring, intuition, and judgment were braided together, each informing the other. Even her male counterparts must know this at some level, though they would never say so.

As they continued their trip north she heard a startling piece of news. News lightly delivered, so as to remove its sting: Alice Ward and James Hathaway had been married on Christmas Eve.

Kim remembered how last summer Alice had told James

of her *trauma view* Talent, and his reaction that it was against scripture. The very reason she had never told him before. She and Kim had been sitting on a hotel porch in Wales after stopping the youth serial killer. Alice had told her that she had finally decided James could love her for what she was or leave her. How heartening that he had finally made the right decision. Perhaps he saw that it was a spiritual decision as well, not to cast off people who were a bit different.

Julian watched her carefully to see how much it hurt that she hadn't attended the wedding of her closest friend. But Kim knew which things deserved mourning and which didn't. "I'm so glad," she finally said. "And I suppose once they decided, they had to move quickly, or one or the other of them would have gotten cold feet." She cut a look at him. "Did you go?"

"Yes. And the whole village turned out. She wanted me to tell you that she can hardly wait to see you."

A small shadow fell over Kim. Actually, missing the wedding did hurt. But just a little, once she remembered how long Alice had been waiting for a proposal.

They pulled into Uxley, passing All Saints, Alice's knittery, then past the park memorial with Robert's name carved in it. They swung around the curve in the road where the animal shelter had been, the one that had gotten rid of unwanted cats and puppies, but not in the way they had planned. It all seemed new, or if not new, then perceived through new eyes. The rich normalcy of Uxley and the places that anchored it. For all its imperfections, today it seemed impossibly tender and kind.

Julian pulled the car off onto the verge and killed the motor.

"Something else has been . . . I mean, I've been trying to tell you. But we've had so much to talk about, Kim."

"My God, what it is?" He was not usually at a loss for words.

"You're not ill, are you?" A diagnosis, a grim hospital report. She desperately hoped not.

"No, no, nothing like that. It's about Olivia."

"Who?"

"Olivia. The woman I'm going to marry. After she gets a divorce."

Kim stared at him, feeling a smile warm her face. "The woman you're going to marry?"

He told her a little about Olivia, how she worked for the Office, and now that he no longer did, that they had decided they needed to be together.

"She's at the house, waiting to meet you." They drove on. The late-afternoon sun should have been queued for a cheerful appearance, if the weather was going to match the joy in the car, but instead it began to pelt down rain.

When they pulled into the yard at Wrenfell, Julian went around to her side of the car, shaking out his umbrella, but Kim saw Mrs. Babbage and Walter and Rose on the porch and ran up to them through the rain. A woman stood with them, a lovely smile on her face.

Shadow came racing from inside the house, pushing open the door that had been left ajar and shouldered past people to get to Kim first. She knelt on the steps and hugged him.

Then someone put a sweater over her shoulders, and the welcoming party moved indoors where there was tea and sherry and the delirious fragrance of a roast in the oven. Kim dearly hoped her portion would be rare. But in the scheme of things, she thought she would take it as it came.